A TASTE OF HEAVEN

They stood on the darkly shadowed deck, wrapped in each other's arms. Alex was trembling, her hands on Winn's shoulders, and she could feel the power of him.

He bent his head, his gaze fixed on her lips, and whispered her name. "Alex . . ."

It was heaven, that first kiss. Winn's mouth moved over hers, the kiss deepening.

"You're beautiful," he whispered.

Alex melted into him. "I love you, Winn," she breathed against his lips.

Then his mouth took hers in a fiery kiss . . .

Books by Bobbi Smith

DREAM WARRIOR

PIRATE'S PROMISE

TEXAS SPLENDOR

CAPTURE MY HEART

DESERT HEART

THE GUNFIGHTER

CAPTIVE PRIDE

THE VIKING

ARIZONA CARESS

ISLAND FIRE

HEAVEN

Published by Kensington Publishing Corporation

HEAVEN

BOBBI SMITH

ZEBRA BOOKS
KENSINGTON PUBLISHING CORP.
http://www.kensingtonbooks.com

ZEBRA BOOKS are published by

Kensington Publishing Corp.
119 West 40th Street
New York, NY 10018

Copyright © 1994 by Bobbi Smith

All Kensington titles, imprints, and distributed lines are available at special quantity discounts for bulk purchases for sales promotion, premiums, fund-raising, educational, or institutional use.

Special book excerpts or customized printings can also be created to fit specific needs. For details, write or phone the office of the Kensington Special Sales Manager: Attn. Special Sales Department. Kensington Publishing Corp.., 119 West 40th Street, New York, NY 10018. Phone: 1-800-221-2647.

Zebra and the Z logo Reg. U.S. Pat. & TM Off.

ISBN-13: 978-1-4201-2237-4
ISBN-10: 1-4201-2237-1

First Printing: May 1994

10 9 8 7 6 5 4 3 2

Printed in the United States of America

This book is dedicated to Charles Brennan, Kevin Horrigan and Paul Grundhauser of the Mighty 'Mox,' KMOX Radio, St. Louis. They are three true heroes who would look great on the cover of any romance!

Also, to Lulu and Joe Bagatti.

A note of thanks to Walter Whited, Lynn Selinger, Cathy Perrine and Bob Comotto for all their help with research.

Prologue

The city of Thebes in Ancient Egypt

Princess Analika could barely contain her excitement. The day of her marriage to Prince Kamil had finally arrived! Her anticipation had grown so great during the past week that each day had seemed an eternity. But soon their separation would be over. Kamil would arrive at her family's palace, and once he had presented her with his gift, the Crown of Desire, they would be joined forever, man and wife.

The golden crown with its heart-shaped ruby had been in Kamil's family for many generations. Its beauty was legendary throughout the land. As was tradition, it was given to the bride of the first-born son, on their wedding day. Analika knew it was a tremendous honor to be entrusted with it, and she planned to do all she could to prove to Kamil that she was worthy of that honor.

At the thought of her handsome prince—of his dark hair, dark eyes and lean, powerful build—Analika's eyes shone with an inner glow and a flush of eagerness stained her cheeks. She could hardly wait to be in his arms again, feeling his lips upon hers. Kamil was her soul mate, her love. Many women had vied for his attentions, but he had chosen her. She loved him more than life itself, and she knew theirs was a love that would last for all time.

Analika picked up her mirror and studied her reflection. Kamil would be arriving soon, and she wanted to make sure she looked her best. Before her maid had left, she'd anointed her hair with sweet-smelling oil, and made sure her thick, black tresses were tamed and shining. Her eyes had been lined with kohl, and her lips painted red. The sheer, white linen gown she wore was straight in style, fastened at one shoulder by a single jeweled strap. The gown caressed her slender body revealing enough to tantalize, yet demure enough to proclaim her virtue. Analika wanted Kamil to be proud of her. She wanted to be perfect for him and to spend the rest of her days pleasing him.

Prince Kamil stood at the front of his fifty-foot barge as it made its way down the Nile toward his beloved Analika. Soon, he would be with her. Soon, he would present her with the Crown of Desire and make her his bride.

Kamil smiled at the thought. He loved Analika with all his heart and soul. This day was going to be the happiest of his life. He had waited a long time to choose a bride, and he had done so with great care, knowing that many of the women who sought his favor were merely after the coveted crown. Analika, however, was not like the others. She cared for him, not the riches he would bring her. It was her purity of heart and gentleness of spirit that had won his devotion, and he knew he would love her forever.

The barge slowed slightly as it followed a bend in the river, and it was in that moment, as the boat drifted close to shore, that disaster struck. The screams of the attackers broke the peace of the morning as a barrage of arrows rained down upon the boat.

Kamil called out a warning to the men in his guard, rallying them to his side, but it came too late to save many onboard. Several of the oarsmen were killed and many others wounded by the ambush. Kamil knew that without the oarsmen's strength, the barge was helpless before the current. They drifted toward the bank where the attackers waited. He could see the viciousness in their faces, and as the barge ran aground Kamil drew his sword . . .

Analika had never known time could pass so slowly. She'd expected Kamil to arrive an hour before, yet there had been no sign of him, and no word. She had just left her room to seek out her parents when horrified cries and shrieks of terror echoed through the heart of the house.

Analika raced down the hallway toward the main hall, when she reached the entranceway she stopped, frozen in place by the gruesome scene before her. Two strangers had entered, carrying a grievously wounded man.

As if in a distance, she heard her mother saying,

"Take him into our bedchamber and send for Analika immediately!"

In that instant, she recognized the battered, bloodied man as her love, and a cry of desperation erupted from her. "NO!!"

She ran after the men, following them into her parents' room. The moment they'd laid Kamil upon her parents' bed, she was beside him, dropping to her knees and clasping his bloody hand in hers.

"Kamil!" She sobbed his name as she stared down at him, seeing the savage, mortal wounds he'd suffered. "My love!"

This couldn't be happening! This was her wedding day! Kamil was coming to marry her. They were going to be happy for the rest of their lives. They were going to have children and live to be old and wise . . .

There was a flurry of feverish activity as her mother and father, Nafissa and Ahmed, and all the household servants raced to deal with the emergency, but Analika was oblivious to their presence. It was as if she were suspended in time and space. She clung to Kamil's hand, trying to will him her strength, to force him to live, yet knowing that his life's blood was flowing from him.

"Kamil!" she cried in frantic desperation, needing to hear his voice, needing to know that he was still alive, wanting to believe that he would be all right, that there was hope.

Kamil heard her cry and dragged himself up from the depths of the torturous black sea of pain that engulfed him. Analika was by his side. He had to get back to her. He had to see her again, just one more time. "Analika . . ." He said her name in a hoarse, ragged whisper.

"Oh, my love! Thank the gods you're alive!!" Her tears flowed freely as she clutched his hand to her breasts, unmindful of his blood upon her.

The prince opened his eyes slowly, and he gazed up one last time at the woman he adored. Despite her weeping, she looked more beautiful than ever to him. "My love . . . I . . ." The words were in his heart, but it was a life-draining battle to say them. Excruciating pain wracked his body, and it took all his strength to draw another breath.

Analika saw his distress. She wanted to help him, but there was nothing she could do. He was dying, and she couldn't stop it! "I love you . . . I will love you forever."

"Analika . . . I love you with all my heart. Our souls are one. Though our bodies may die, we will never be parted . . ."

"Don't say that!"

"Analika," he spoke more strongly as he gathered the last of his strength. "My love, be my wife before I die . . . Take my gift and seal our love."

Ignoring the pain that wracked him, he lifted the blood-stained crown he'd held clutched in his other hand. He had defended it with his life, and he would now give it to his bride.

Analika stared at the crown, and hysteria welled up within her. Kamil couldn't be dying! He couldn't! "No . . . No . . . Not this way . . ."

"This is my wedding gift for you . . ." he whispered. With a superhuman force of will, knowing it was the last thing he would ever do for her, he offered her the crown.

She met his pain-fevered gaze and saw his own desperation and need. Her heart swelled with love and agony. She wanted to flee, to deny the truth, to turn back time and be happy again. But reality forbade it. Kamil was here, offering her his life. She could do no less than be a woman worthy of him . . . of his love.

"I love you, my prince," she whispered as she took the bloodied crown from his hands.

With infinite care, she bent to him, her lips meeting his in a kiss of wonder. For a second, they were whole and vital and one. They had no cares. Life was perfect. They loved. But there could be no denying the inevitable. Analika felt the moment of his passing just as surely as if it had been her own.

"Kamil! I don't want to live without you!" A guttural, soul-wrenching scream of torment erupted from her, and she collapsed upon him. His blood, still warm with life, stained her clothes, her flesh, her hair, but she didn't care. Kamil was gone . . . lost to her forever. Their future destroyed.

Moments before, the day had promised laughter and love, and now, all happiness and light had been devoured by Ammit, the monster of the dead. There would be no joy, only sadness and misery. The prince had been murdered, struck down by thieves who'd coveted the Crown of Desire.

Analika clung to Kamil until Ahmed went to her

and gently tried to pull her away. Wild-eyed and crazed with grief, Analika tore away from him and fell back to her knees beside her prince. She would not be separated from Kamil again! With infinite tenderness, she touched his hair, then his cheek. She leaned closer to him and kissed him softly one final time, whispering, "We will be together, my love."

She rose and stared down at the crown she held. Kamil's blood covered her hand and dripped from the crown. The revulsion she felt for the bloody treasure showed clearly in her expression. "This crown, cold to the touch and without heart or soul, was the price of my love's life? They murdered my prince for this?!" Her cries were demented as she lifted it up for all to see.

All in the room gasped as they saw the blood-stained golden crown for the first time.

Analika had been so eager to wear it. But no more. The Crown of Desire was no longer a symbol of Kamil's love. Now, it symbolized his death.

"I curse this crown and the men who would kill to possess it!" Analika's voice turned hard, and her eyes burned with a madness born of loss. She lifted the reviled object even higher. Light glinted off the ruby, and it shone blood-red as she spoke. "I curse all who seek it in greed! May Kamil's blood mark them and may they suffer the torment of the damned! Only those whose love is pure may possess the crown in peace!"

Analika's gaze fell to her father and the ceremonial jeweled dagger he wore in honor of her marriage. Suddenly beyond reason, beyond caring, she reached out and snatched the knife from his belt. Without pause, she plunged the dagger deep into her own breast. The pain was terrible, but she didn't stop. No physical pain could be worse than living without Kamil. She had to join her beloved.

Cries of horror erupted around her, but she didn't hear them. Her parents reacted quickly, trying to get to her, wanting to pull the knife from her body, but Analika turned away and slumped down beside Kamil, still clutching the crown.

"I am coming with you, my husband . . . my love," she whispered, caressing his cheek.

As Analika's life's blood mixed with Kamil's, their fates were sealed; they were together . . . in heaven.

One

London, 1830

The tall, dark-haired man stood at the window of his study anxiously surveying the deserted, night-shrouded street below. A steady rain had been falling all day, and it continued, cold and miserable, into the night. A sudden, vicious gust of wind splattered rain against the window pane, blurring Lawrence Anthony's vision. He turned away in frustration.

Glancing at the mantel clock, Lawrence noted the time; nearly nine. His meeting with Dwyer had been scheduled for eight. *Where was the man? Had something gone wrong?*

The last thought brought an inward grimace. Tonight he would achieve the goal he'd set for himself ten years before, when he'd first heard the legend of the Crown of Desire. Tonight he would actually have the crown in his possession. He smiled at the prospect. *Now, if only Dwyer would show up . . . .*

Forcing himself to be patient, Lawrence went to sit at his desk and review his notes on the crown one more time. A passionate lover of Ancient Egyptian history, he'd learned of the relic and its curse while on a trip to Cairo all those years before. Having always found a great challenge in solving the unsolvable, he'd begun investigating the intriguing tale of the dead royal lovers. There had been times during the past decade when he'd almost believed the legend was just that—a story with no basis. Even so, he'd never given up, and now his obsessive need to discover the truth had given him the answer he'd long sought. The Crown of Desire did exist, and tonight he'd long sought. The Crown of Desire did exist, and tonight it would be his.

Lawrence knew many of his fellow countrymen didn't share his interest or devotion to things of the past. He'd been called a rich eccentric by some and an art collector extraordinaire by others, but it didn't matter. What was important to him was finding and preserving the rare and beautiful artifacts that had been lost beneath the sands of time, and he didn't trust governments or museums to do an adequate job of it. And the Crown of Desire was the rarest and most beautiful of all.

Lawrence felt no fear as he reread the legend of the beautiful princess and her curse on anyone who sought the crown in greed. He didn't covet the crown for its value, though if the stories were true, it was worth a fortune. No, he sought the crown for the love of its history.

Lawrence got up and returned to the window to take up his watch once more. This time, he saw a man slowly making his way down the street, his cloak wrapped tightly around him to protect against the wind and rain. Lawrence waited and watched, hoping this was Dwyer and that his quest for the crown was finally at an end.

Outside on the street, the eerie moaning of the wind rent the silence of the dank night and sent a shiver through Dwyer as he hurried through the fog. The sound of his footsteps echoed hollowly as he completed this last leg of his journey.

The rain was unrelenting, and he realized that he'd forgotten just how ugly the weather could be in London at this time of year. For one perverse moment, he almost missed the burning sun and dry heat of the land he'd just fled, but he quickly pushed the thought aside. He was never going back to that wretched life. The prize he carried, hidden in the folds of his cloak, guaranteed it.

At the thought of the treasure in his possession, the man quickened his pace. He was almost at the home of the collector now, and he was eager to turn the prize over to him . . . especially after what had happened to Bailey and Green, his bosses on the dig. *The curse.* Dwyer shivered again, but this time it wasn't from the cold, it was from the memory of how the two men had died . . . so suddenly, so horribly, so mysteriously . . .

Dwyer reached Anthony's house and hurried up the walk to the door. As soon as he turned the crown over to the collector, he'd have enough money to buy himself anything he wanted. The idea brought him great pleasure, for he loved money. His fear of the curse faded as he patted the ebony case he carried so close to his body. Soon he was going to be very rich. He smiled, then knocked on the door and waited.

A somber silver-haired butler opened the door to his summons. "May I help you?"

"I'm Jerod Dwyer. I have an appointment with Mr. Anthony," he stated.

"Mr. Anthony is expecting you. Please come in." The servant held the door wide for him to enter. "May I take your cloak?"

"No." Dwyer responded sharply. He wanted to keep the prize hidden until he was face-to-face with the man who was buying it.

If the servant thought his behavior odd, he betrayed no trace of it. "Then, please, follow me."

Dwyer glanced around at the expensive furnishings as he followed the butler from the cavernous, marble-floored foyer down a long, wide hall toward the study. He was pleased that the transaction was finally to take place. Anthony obviously had the money he needed, and he had the treasure Anthony so desperately desired. It would be a simple exchange with each of them coming away satisfied.

The butler stopped before a closed door and knocked.

"Sir, Mr. Dwyer has arrived."

"Show him in, please, Martin."

Without pause, the servant opened the door and motioned to Dwyer to enter. Dwyer moved into the room where a studious-looking man came forward to greet him.

"Mr. Dwyer? I'm Lawrence Anthony." Relief and excitement commingled within Lawrence as he faced Dwyer, but he managed to project an image of outward calm as he offered him his hand.

"A pleasure, sir," Dwyer responded, and he meant it as he shook Anthony's hand. It was indeed a pleasure to be at his journey's end. All that was left was to get his money and leave. The past few months had been hellish, but they were over now. His future lay before him, bright and shining and rich.

"You have the crown?" Lawrence kept his tone businesslike as he got straight to the point. He'd followed so many false leads in his quest that he could tolerate no further delay. He had to see it. He had to know.

"Right here." Dwyer drew the chest from within the folds of his cloak and stepped forward to place it on the desktop.

"Would you open it for me, please?" Lawrence asked quietly as he moved to stand behind the desk. His anticipation was so great that he was surprised to find that his voice was steady.

Dwyer produced a key, unlocked the chest, then turned it toward the other man and lifted the lid. He watched the collector cautiously, and he smiled in triumph when he saw the other man's expression turn rapt.

"May I touch it?" Lawrence's voice was hushed for he was mesmerized by the beauty of the relic before him.

Dwyer pushed the chest across the desktop closer to him.

With shaking hands, Lawrence reached for the crown.

"It's every bit as magnificent as the legend says," he said, lifting the cherished object and holding it up to study the huge, heart-shaped ruby that adorned it.

"It certainly is," Dwyer fought down his own greedy impatience. He didn't want to stand there and watch this man ogle the crown. He wanted to get his money and go!

"I find it difficult to believe that something so beautiful could be tainted with such a cruel curse."

"Ah, the curse . . . just part of the legend as far as I'm concerned. I've had no problems. I think perhaps the curse was invented to discourage looters," Dwyer said evasively, hoping Anthony would believe him. He did not mention what had happened to Bailey and Green.

"Perhaps you're right. It's amazing to find the crown in such perfect condition." Lawrence reverently placed it back in the satin-lined chest.

Dwyer nodded. "We were very fortunate. It seems that after the crown was sealed in the tomb, about 1200 B.C., it went untouched until I discovered the burial site this past spring."

He neglected to mention that he hadn't really been the one to discover it, that he'd only been a laborer who'd stolen it after the deaths of the two men he'd worked for, and that he'd fled the country with it before anyone could catch him.

"Many seek the crown," Lawrence reflected thoughtfully as he turned his gaze on Dwyer. "Why did you offer it to me?"

"I'd heard you were a discreet and discriminating man."

"Discretion has always been very important to me," he told Dwyer as he opened his desk drawer and took out a heavy leather pouch. "You needn't worry that any word of our meeting will pass beyond this room."

"I appreciate that."

The collector tossed him the pouch. "You'll find a generous bonus in there, along with the agreed-upon fee."

Dwyer smiled wolfishly as he weighed the value of the pouch in his hand. "If there's ever anything else I can do for you, sir, you just let me know."

"I certainly will." Anthony gently closed the lid on the chest and then escorted the man from the room. "Thank you for coming."

"Thank *you*," Dwyer replied in earnest as he departed.

Dwyer was thrilled as he started back toward his hotel. Ever since he'd smuggled the crown from Egypt, he'd been cautious about his activities. Now, though, the weight of that worry was gone. He could relax and enjoy himself.

Dwyer thought briefly again of the curse—it had promised death to those who coveted the crown for greedy purposes. He quickly dismissed it as nonsense, a part of the legend meant to scare fortune-hunters. He had his money and he was still alive. There was no curse.

Dwyer didn't understand why Anthony or anyone would spend his life searching for long-lost treasures and then, when he found them, keep them only for their history and not for their monetary value. He knew that if it had been up to him, he would have plucked the ruby out of its setting and sold the gem for the fortune it was worth; then he would have melted down the gold and sold that, too. The reward the collector had offered, however, had made it worth his while not to, but he still didn't understand the person that would merely want to simply possess such a potential fortune.

Never one to ponder anything too deeply, Dwyer shrugged off any other thoughts about it. He'd been very well paid for his efforts. What Anthony now did with the crown was Anthony's business.

Dwyer's excitement was so great that he no longer felt the cold and rain as he made his way back to his hotel. His life was going to be perfect. He reached his hotel and went straight to his room, wanting just to sit and count his money and dream of how he was going to spend it. From this moment on, he would never have to take orders from anyone again! He was rich!

He entered the dark hotel room and locked the door behind him. He moved to the bedside table and struck a match to light the lamp.

The blow came out of nowhere, crashing down on his skull. The power was such that he collapsed on the floor. Just as the match he'd struck flickered and went out, so did his life end.

No words were spoken as another set of hands worked to light the lamp. The glow that lit the room revealed two darkly clad men who'd been hiding there, awaiting his return. One of the assailants dropped down beside Dwyer to search his pockets. He found the pouch and snatched it up. He glanced at his silent companion, smiled, and nodded. The light was then extinguished, and they unlocked the door and crept from the room and off into the night . . . unknown and unseen.

As soon as Dwyer had gone, Lawrence hurried back to his study. He instructed the servants that he was not to be disturbed and then went to open the chest again and gaze down at his treasure. Lying on the bed of white satin, the crown glowed vibrant gold in the lamplight, and the huge ruby seemed blood-red. He stared, marveling at its perfection. The prize was as magnificent as the legend had claimed. It had been worth his years of searching, and certainly worth the reward he'd paid.

"You need have no fear, Princess Analika," he spoke softly to her through the ages. "I will cherish your crown and guard it with my life. No one shall take it from the haven of my protection. It shall remain in my safekeeping as a tribute to your undying love."

He reverently touched the crown once more, then closed the case. Taking it with him, he went to the fireplace and turned one of the carved lion heads that decorated the mantel. When he did, a heavy dark oak panel at the side of the fireplace slid open to reveal a hidden passageway.

Lawrence quickly stepped inside and lit one of the lamps there before sealing the panel behind him. Taking the lamp with him, he followed the dark, winding corridor. He made his way through the bowels of the mansion to a small chamber at the hall's end. Besides himself, only his sons and Henry knew of the room's existence. He did not allow them inside often, but he knew he would have to share the glory of the crown with them. After opening the triple-locked door, he entered the small, windowless room beyond.

The light from the lamp he carried turned the darkness of the chamber into day, for the walls were lined with mirrors. Lawrence glanced around and noted with satisfaction that nothing had been disturbed. This was his private gallery, an almost sacred place where his most prized possessions were kept. He smiled in appreciation at the treasures he had displayed on fluted, alabaster pedestals. Until now, the bejeweled, golden armbands from Cleopatra's reign and a chalice from the time of Christ had been his most treasured possessions, but now that would all change. Now, he had the Crown of Desire.

An empty pedestal stood just before him in the very center of the room. This particular black marble pillar was plain in comparison to the other columns, but he'd specifically ordered it that way to enhance the crown's glory by its very simplicity. Placing the lamp on a table nearby, he opened the coffer and took out the crown once more.

Excitement trembled through him as he placed the crown upon the pedestal. He would keep the royal relic safely hidden away from those who sought it in greed and lust. It would remain here forever—the center of his collection.

Lawrence's eyes misted with unshed tears as he thought of his beautiful wife, Caroline, dead now some two years. She'd been as intrigued by the legend as he had been, and he would always regret that she hadn't lived to see the crown here. He did, however, have their two sons, Philip and Robert, and he was determined to teach them to appreciate the relic for the beauty of its history and not the wealth it represented in gold and jewel.

Drawing up a chair, he sat down before the pedestal to enjoy the wonder of his newest acquisition. He knew he would continue in his quest to locate lost artifacts, but nothing would ever mean more to him than this.

Many hours passed before he finally left the room, and when he did go, it was to find his sons. This was their legacy, their future. He wanted to see their expressions as they gazed upon the crown for the very first time.

The boys were asleep, but Lawrence didn't care. This was too important to him. He woke Philip and Robert. Sleepy-eyed and mumbling their complaints, they followed their father through the house's in- ner maze to the hidden room. When Lawrence stopped be- fore the door, both boys looked up at him expectantly.

"What I'm about to show you is a treasure that has been my life's goal. I just acquired it tonight, and I wanted to share it with you."

"What is it, Father?" Robert, the younger of the two boys, asked as he rubbed his eyes.

"I now possess the Crown of Desire."

"You found it?" The two were amazed. They'd heard him speak of it often, but had always thought it was just a legend.

"Yes, and now I want you to see it." With that, he unlocked the door and led them inside.

Eight-year-old Philip followed his father into the room first. As soon as he saw the crown, he stopped and stared, open-mouthed. Nothing that his father had ever said about it equaled its true beauty. The gold was smooth and polished to a high gleam, and the heart-shaped ruby shone as if it had its own inner life.

"It's beautiful . . ." Philip said quietly. Unable to help himself, he moved forward as if beckoned by some greater power. He reached out to touch the prize, expecting the metal to be cool to his fingers. To his surprise, it felt warm, almost hot, and he drew back immediately as if burned. Robert, ever the cautious one, saw his reaction and decided just to look on from a distance.

"Yes, the crown is beautiful," Lawrence agreed. "I'll keep it here, locked safely in this room. You must both give me your word that you won't speak of this to anyone. Henry will be the only other person who'll know about it. Do I have your promises?"

"Yes, sir," they replied dutifully.

They gazed at the crown for a moment more, and then Lawrence ushered them from the room. As he started out the door, Philip paused for just a second to glance back at the crown. Open hunger shone in his eyes. One day that golden prize would be his.

London, 1855

Philip sat at the desk in his father's study drinking his father's finest brandy. Robert sat opposite him, doing the same. They had grown into a study in contrasts, these two. Philip was fair; Robert was dark. Philip was tall and thin; Robert was short and tended to fat. Where Philip was shrewd, calculating and quick to act, Robert was slower and more methodical. Given the choice, they would have avoided each other. Philip thought his brother a dullard, while Robert despised Philip's sharp tongue and vicious wit. One common bond held them together, though, and that was their love of their father's money.

"I'm glad our father enjoys the finer things in life," Philip told Robert as he leaned back in the chair and, with casualness of the supremely confident, propped his elegantly booted feet up on the desktop. It didn't worry him in the least that he might scar the fine woodgrain. "But sometimes his obsessions leave me cold."

"Like the crown?" Robert asked wryly.

"Exactly. What earthly good is the Crown of Desire locked away in that private collection of his? Nobody knows it's there but Henry and us, and we've only been allowed in to see it three times in all these years."

"The crown is his most prized possession."

"As well it should be. It's worth a fortune. He should sell the damned thing."

"I'm sure Father thinks we're rich enough." He took a drink of his brandy, wearying of his brother's greed. No matter how much they had, Philip never thought it was enough.

As usual, Robert annoyed him, and Philip turned a contemptuous eye upon him. "You can never be rich enough." A look of greed was mirrored in his eyes as he imagined having the crown for his very own. "Sometimes I think about hiring someone to steal it, but I know Father would somehow find out I was behind the theft. After all, there are only three of us who know about it, and we're sworn to secrecy. Still, whenever I think about the size of that ruby . . ."

"You might as well relax, dear brother," Robert cut him off. "As long as there's a breath left in his body, father's not going to part with it."

"True enough, but the day he dies . . ." He raised his snifter in salute as he considered his inheritance.

"Yes, yes, the treasure will fall to us. But let me remind you that Father's in perfectly good health."

Philip paused, his devious mind racing. After a moment, he smiled thinly. "Pity."

Unbeknownst to them, Lawrence stood in the hall just beyond the door. He'd been on his way to the study to work for a while, unaware that his sons had returned. Usually they stayed out through the night. Now, having overheard their conversation, he was both stricken and angry. For years, Lawrence had tried to instill a sense of values in Philip and Robert, but the only value they were concerned with was the money lining their pockets. He'd often sensed that there was no deep moral fiber in either one of them, and it seemed now his impressions were true. They were both completely amoral.

Without letting them know of his presence, Lawrence went back upstairs to his bedroom. His mood was dark and pensive as he thought of their hunger for the crown. Over and over his memory replayed their words as they reflected how much they were looking forward to his death, and he was filled with a deep, abiding pain.

A soul-weary sigh wracked Lawrence as he realized that he had to do something to change his sons' hearts before it was too late. Certainly, he wasn't going to live forever, and he had to make them understand the importance of the crown. If he didn't, he knew that one day they would destroy all that he'd worked a lifetime to create.

Lawrence paced his room, trying to think of a way to impress upon his errant offspring the truth of riches—that wealth did not bring happiness and that God had not created man merely to enjoy the physical pleasures of this world. Each person had been put on Earth to accomplish some good.

Judging from what he'd just overheard, Lawrence realized that that thought might prove quite novel to his sons. He could not remember the last time he'd seen them extend an act of kindness to anyone, so caught up were they in their own decadent desires.

A glimmer of an idea came to him. As lazy and self-centered as Philip and Robert were, Lawrence knew he had to redouble his efforts to teach them that true happiness came from giving to and helping others.

Retiring for the night, Lawrence lay in his bed planning the trip he was about to take. He smiled as he considered it. He could be ready to leave the following day, but he decided to wait until his sons had departed for their weekend at a friend's country estate before going. He didn't want any questions asked about his destination.

The delay in leaving didn't bother him too much. All that mattered, ultimately, was changing his sons' hearts. They were his flesh and blood, and, in spite of their vices, he loved them. If it took drastic action on his part to force them to become the men he wanted them to be, he would do it.

Philip and Robert returned from their weekend to discover that their father had gone on an extended trip overseas. They were a bit surprised by his departure, but not concerned. He often went off in search of treasures, so this sudden venture was nothing unusual for him.

Lawrence returned five months later, satisfied with what he'd accomplished. He greeted his sons with warmth and a secret sense of hope.

Philip and Robert were somewhat surprised that he'd brought back only three nondescript leather-bound books that were neither old nor valuable. But they shrugged it off as just another of his idiosyncrasies and continued their debauched lifestyles.

In the ancient ruins near Thebes.

It was dawn. The sky to the east was emblazoned red and gold promising yet another day of unrelenting heat. Alexandra Parker wasn't thinking about the heat, though, as she rose and quickly dressed in her usual long-sleeved white blouse and khaki split skirt. She was too excited about what they'd discovered the night before to be worried by something so unimportant as the weather. Late last night, they'd found a clue that proved the Crown of Desire really did exist and that it had been buried somewhere nearby. This morning, they would return to the site and continue their dig. They'd been searching for the crown for years, and today just might be the day they were actually going to find it.

Eagerness filled Alex. She was anxious to get back to work, so she sat down on the edge of her cot and picked up her boots, pausing only long enough to check carefully for any desert creatures that might have taken refuge in them during the night. It wasn't unusual to find a scorpion hiding there, and she had to be careful. This was no time for accidents. She had too much to do! After pulling on the boots, she stood and smoothed out her skirt, appreciating the freedom of movement it gave her. Her clothes might not be fashionable, but style didn't matter when she was in the middle of the Sahara Desert working on an archaeological dig with her father. When you're climbing through the ancient ruins and digging for treasures buried beneath centuries of sifting sand, your clothing had to be comfortable and practical.

Before leaving her tent, Alex stopped at her small washstand to freshen up. She washed quickly, then ran a brush through her tumble of short curls. Checking her reflection in a small hand mirror, she smiled. It had been a revolutionary move on her part to cut her hair so short, but living a few weeks in this climate had convinced her that waist-length hair was too difficult to deal with. Her father had been upset for a while, but once he'd understood the necessity of it, he'd said no more. Certainly, she'd never regretted it. She didn't have a lot of time for a morning toilette.

Alex had begun to work with her father several years earlier when his eyesight had started to fail. Now, at twenty-one, she traveled with him everywhere, sketching and cataloging his finds whenever he was on a dig and accompanying him to the various museums and universities to research. She loved Egyptian history as much as he did, and she shared his passion for locating the missing treasures of the past. They'd been digging at this site near Thebes for almost a month now, and she hoped that today would be the day they'd find the elusive, supposedly cursed, crown.

She grabbed up the hat that she wore outdoors to protect her from the fierce sun and left the tent to find her father. To her surprise, he was already up and waiting for her.

"Good morning, Papa," she greeted him as she went to kiss his cheek.

"Good morning, sweetheart. I thought for sure you'd sleep a little later this morning." Enoch Parker smiled at his daughter. Though his sight was bad and getting progressively worse every year, right now he could still see Alex's smiling face and that made him a happy man.

"I'm too excited," she admitted, giving him a hug.

"I've got a feeling that we're very close to finding it, and I hope it's not just my imagination running away with me."

"After all these years of searching, it would be the high point of my career to actually lay my hands upon the crown."

"Let's get started."

Enoch's smile broadened at her enthusiasm. "What about breakfast?"

"We can eat anytime. I want to find the crown!"

Alex led the way through the ruins of the partially collapsed ancient structures.

Enoch gave a rueful shake of his head as he followed her confident lead. Alex was his pride and joy. Sometimes she reminded him so much of himself he was amazed. Her determination, forthrightness, and intelligence were all wonderful characteristics, but they were not exactly the attributes men looked for when choosing a wife.

Certainly, Alex was a lovely girl. Tall and slender, with her red-gold hair and dark, enchanting eyes, she was prettier than many a young woman, and yet he worried about her. At twenty-one, she was well past the age when a woman should marry and have children, and now that she'd cut off her hair. . . Well, he worried.

Enoch wondered what kind of life he was giving her, taking her with him as he did. She would never meet a suitable mate in the middle of the desert. But even as he considered leaving Alex behind, he knew he wouldn't. He didn't want to travel without her. She was perfect as his assistant. Alex always anticipated his needs before he knew he had them, and he doubted he'd be anywhere near as successful without her. Her keen intellect, clever wit, and undying thirst for knowledge made her invaluable to him. As much as he fretted over her future, he was glad she chose to stay with him. He wouldn't have known what to do without her any more.

They reached the site of their excavations and began to search again. The fellahin, peasant workers hired to work with them on the dig, soon joined them, and they labored long into the morning. Near ten they were forced to stop, for the blazing sun became too intense for them to continue. They rested until mid-afternoon, then started again. Alex was hot and tired, but she wasn't ready to quit. They were close and she knew it. She was determined to explore every inch of the area until the entrance to the tomb was found and the crown located.

It was near dusk when they found the tomb but to their horror and disappointment, the entranceway had already been breached. With the workers crowding around them, Alex held the lamp up high so her father could see as he entered the dark burial chamber. Finding the crown had been one of his dreams, and she wanted him to be the first one into the tomb of the prince and princess.

"Alex . . ." Enoch said in an agonized voice. "It's as we feared. The looters . . ."

Alex followed him inside the dusty room and stared around in horror. The chamber had been ransacked, the mummies stripped of their gold and jewels, their bones strewn about in sacrilege. "It's been desecrated."

"And the crown's been taken . . ." Resignedly, he spoke the terrible truth.

"Father, look!" Alex was holding the lamp near the wall so she could study the hieroglyphics written there.

Enoch came to her side and peered at the writings.

"It's just as we've always believed!" Enoch said, a note of awe in his tone. "These writings confirm everything! It's all here! The story of the prince's terrible death and the princess's curse."

"Look at this, Papa."

Her voice was soft yet urgent and drew his attention. He turned to find her standing before the doorway they'd just entered. "The inscription over the entrance reads 'Let only those who possess true love pass this way in peace.'" A shiver skittered down her spine as she spoke the words out loud.

"It was true . . . all true."

They remained in the chamber late into the night, making detailed drawings of the remains. It was after midnight when they emerged.

"If looters stole the crown and brought it out, why didn't we hear of it?"

"It could have been stolen centuries ago. There's no way of knowing."

They stood among the ruins in silence, breathing in the fresh night air. The knowledge that the crown had been stolen and probably destroyed filled both father and daughter with a great sadness.

"I don't know how we'll ever find it now," Alex said

with great weariness. Her disappointment ran deep. She'd felt so sure of finding the crown, and now there was nothing more she could do. They would finish working in the tomb, trying to salvage what could be saved, and then they would journey back to their home in Boston, empty-handed. Their dream of returning with the crown had been shattered.

"There's one important lesson you have yet to learn," Enoch told her as they walked slowly through the night toward their tents. A full silver moon above lit their way.

"What's that, Papa?" She turned to face him in the moonlight, her expression serious as she tried to deal with her disappointment over their defeat.

"Never give up your dreams."

Two

London, 1857

Henry, Lawrence's personal valet for over thirty years, had just started down the main hall toward the foyer when he heard the sound of angry voices coming from Mr. Anthony's study. He stopped where he was, uncertain whether to continue on his way or turn a tactful retreat. He hadn't intended to listen to the argument, but he couldn't help hearing the loud voices.

"We're your sons! Your flesh and blood! What do you mean you're going to cut us off?" Philip's outraged words could be heard clearly in the hall.

"You heard me, Philip. You, too, Robert." Lawrence's voice was strained. "You've spent every pound I've given you and then some. I refuse to play the indulgent fool any longer. You know what amount I allow you each month, and from this day on, you both are to find a way to live within your means or suffer the consequences!"

"What consequences?" Robert asked.

"I'll cut you both off. And don't think this an idle threat."

"How can you treat us this way?"

"Treat you what way? Try to make you responsible for your actions like most men? I'd say that's a father's job, wouldn't you?"

"You'll be sorry for this," Philip declared.

"I'm already sorry. I'm sorry you two behave so irresponsibly. I'm sorry you haven't learned that there is more to life than drinking and gaming."

"Some day, you'll regret this," Philip said. "Let's go, Robert. There's no point in staying. This man who calls himself our father is determined to humiliate us."

Henry took an instinctive step backward as he heard them crossing the study to the door. Though he was prepared for their appearance in the hall, he still jumped when they burst through the door and stormed out. Henry knew it would be best to remain silent until they'd left the house. As the two men departed, they slammed the front door in testimony to their fury. Henry had long known that things were not good between father and sons, but he still wondered what had happened tonight to touch off such rage in Mr. Philip and Mr. Robert. He approached the study cautiously.

He stopped in the doorway to look in. Mr. Anthony was standing at the window behind his desk, gazing out. His face was pale, his lips were tinged with blue, and his hands were unsteady as he held the curtain back. The look in his eyes was of immense sadness and pain. Henry could tell he was deeply shaken by the encounter that had just taken place and he felt a real concern for his employer and friend of so many years.

"Are you all right, sir?" he softly inquired.

Lawrence was lost in thought and didn't respond for a moment. For all the years he'd possessed the crown, Lawrence had thought himself safe from the curse. It occurred to him now, heartsick as he was, that he had not been safe from its fury after all. The curse had indeed fallen upon him, but it had come to him not through death or danger, but through his own sons. For years, Philip and Robert had made his life a living hell. This latest quarrel merely reinforced once more the futility of his hope that they would one day come to be men he could love and respect. Drawing a painful breath, Lawrence slowly turned to look at the man who was his friend as well as his servant. "Some days, Henry, I wonder."

"Is there anything I can do, sir?"

Lawrence paused in silent reflection. He trusted Henry with his very life, which is much more than he could say about his sons. Finally, he said, "Come in and close the door."

Henry did as he was told while Lawrence went to stand behind the desk.

"There is something you can do for me." His heart and soul were more weary than he could say. "A favor . . ."

"Yes, sir." Their gazes met, and the valet could see the agony in the other man's soul.

"If anything should happen to me . . ."

Henry's face mirrored the shock he felt at his statement.

"I'm not a young man any more, and we both know

my health is not the best. If I should die, there's something extremely important I need you to do."

"You only have to name it, sir."

Lawrence sat at the desk and opened its biggest drawer. "There's a secret compartment in this drawer. You and I are the only two who know about it."

He slid the false back out to reveal a compartment that was just big enough to hold the three books inside it.

"If anything happens to me, I want you to see that these books are delivered to the people whose names are on them. Will you do that for me?"

"Of course."

Lawrence's troubled expression eased a bit. "Your faithfulness will not go unrewarded, my old friend."

"I do not require a reward for helping you, sir." Henry's reply was stiff, his honor offended.

The older man managed a sad smile. "If my sons possessed one tenth of your devotion and kindness, I would not be doing this . . . But I fear . . ."

"Fear what, sir?"

"Nothing . . . nothing . . . If the time comes when you have to deliver these books, you may not be so glad you've given me your word."

"I'll deliver them as you've instructed."

Lawrence nodded, knowing Henry would do exactly as he promised. "Just remember, my sons are not to get their hands on these." His voice hardened as he spoke.

"Yes, sir."

Knowing he was dismissed, the valet left and closed

the door behind him. His thoughts were troubled as he returned to his duties.

When Henry had gone, Lawrence sat down at the desk and took out some paper. He wrote three letters, put one in each book, then quickly wrapped the tomes. That done, he carefully inscribed the names of the three people who, he knew, treasured the Crown of Desire as much as he did.

Book #1, he addressed to Professor Enoch Parker, a man whose love and appreciation of Egyptian history and legend was as strong as his own. The second, he addressed to Matthew McKittrick. Though he'd never met McKittrick, they'd carried on extensive correspondence about the crown for the past six years. Lawrence had discovered him to be not only brilliant, but daring as well. Though the man made his living as a bookseller in the city of Boston, he'd also made several treks to Egypt trying to prove the legend and find the treasure. His feelings for the Crown of Desire were as intense and personal as Lawrence's own, and he knew McKittrick could be trusted with the second book. The last and most important book he addressed to Edward Bradford. Though Edward had joined the priesthood as a young man, he'd still always remained Lawrence's best friend and confidante. There was no one Lawrence trusted more. His work done, he returned the books to their hiding place and shut the drawer.

Lawrence sat quietly reflecting on the ugly fight he'd just had with his sons. For many years he'd held out hope that his sons could be redeemed—that there was some good in them—but today's confrontation had dealt the final blow to his hope. He felt nothing for them now. So foreign were their ways to him that he had trouble believing they had sprung from his and Caroline's great love. As soon as he could contact his barrister, he would change his will. It was over. He no longer had any sons.

The mood in the smoke-filled game room at Merryfield, the Fulhams' country estate, was one of hushed anticipation. The gambling had begun after the late meal at seven o'clock, and now, as it neared four in the morning, only three players remained—Justin Davies, Charles Fulham and Winn Bradford. All were peers of the realm, wealthy men, and shrewd gamblers. The crowd of onlookers pressed in close, eager to see which man would triumph.

"Isn't he wonderful?" Lucy Cardwell whispered to Amelia Bernard, her gaze fixed on the darkly handsome Winn. She'd been watching him all night and was determined to have him in her bed by dawn.

"Lucy, control yourself, for heaven's sake. You're a married woman!" Amelia said.

"Frederick doesn't care what I do as long as I'm discreet." She dismissed her friend's admonishment without a further thought.

Amelia knew there was no reasoning with Lucy when she set her mind on having something or someone. She was as headstrong as she was beautiful and spoiled, her blonde good looks having gotten her whatever she wanted in life.

Amelia had to admit Lucy did have good taste in men, though. Tall, lean, and muscular with black hair, a mustache, and arresting green eyes, Winn Bradford was the best-looking man there—next to her own husband, John, of course. Amelia quickly amended her wayward thoughts. Were she not madly in love with John, she might have tried for Winn herself. He was, after all, rich, titled and available.

"Damn you, Bradford!" Justin Davies swore as he stared at the cards Winn had just spread out before him. He slammed his own hand down in defeat, not even bothering to show them. "You have all the luck!"

"Luck or skill, Justin, old boy?" Charles Fulham chided with good humor, conceding his own defeat by tossing down his own cards.

"I knew Winn wouldn't lose!" Lucy whispered excitedly to Amelia. She slipped from the room unnoticed as the others moved in closer to congratulate Winn.

"Well done, Bradford." The onlookers murmured their approval.

Several of the men clapped him on the back, impressed by his daring. They'd been wise enough to stay out of the game for they knew they were no match for him. He played with abandon, knowing he could afford to lose and not caring if he did. When a man entered a card game with that attitude he was a dangerous opponent.

Winn smiled slightly in acknowledgment of their praise as he raked in his winnings. It had been a lucrative night for him, yet he felt no thrill of victory, no sense of accomplishment. All he felt was tired. He'd won the card game, just as he'd won on any number of other occasions.

"Shall we go outside for a while? Get a breath of fresh air?" Charles, his host, suggested as the others wandered off to pursue new and varied entertainments.

"If you don't mind, I think I'll call it a night."

"Not at all, Winn. I'll see you in the morning."

Winn excused himself and left the gaming room. He made his way up the curved staircase to the bedroom that was his for the week's stay. Charles was known for his opulent parties here at Merryfield, and this one was proving to be no exception. The estate was a fifty-four room 'country house' with ornate furnishings, plush carpets, and an army of servants to cater to the guests' every want.

In the past, Winn had always enjoyed the time he spent here, but somehow, now, it was all beginning to seem rather pointless. He had more money than he could spend in a lifetime, yet he constantly gambled for high stakes, and generally won. There were many who envied him his luck at cards, but sometimes he wondered if winning was a blessing or a curse. If you could have anything and everything you wanted, what was there left to desire? The women at these affairs were not known for their virtue. Many, married or not, were eager to share his bed. For a while, he'd found the hot couplings arousing, but lately they seemed more sordid than erotic.

As Winn reached the top of the stairs, he saw Barry Richmond knock softly once on Alicia Somerset's bedroom door at the far end of the hall and then slip quickly inside. Winn could only assume that Alicia's husband, George, was safely occupied elsewhere for her to be so brazen in her dalliance.

Winn entered his own bedroom and found that the servants had already been there and had anticipated his needs. A lamp was glowing softly on the night-stand, and on the dresser a bottle of whiskey and a crystal tumbler had been set out for him. The bed looked to have been turned down and the canopy cur-tains around it had been partially drawn. He went to the dresser and poured himself a half-tumbler of whis-key. After taking a deep drink, he unbuttoned his shirt.

Winn was tired, exhausted in fact, and he looked forward to getting some sleep. Setting the glass aside, he moved toward the bed. It was then, just as he started to strip off his shirt, that he saw Lucy. She was lying in a seductive pose, a sheet pulled up just far enough to cover her breasts.

"Good evening, Winn," she said in a husky voice. Her gaze went over him, and she gloried in the sight of his naked chest. Raw hunger shone in her eyes. She considered herself a connoisseur of men, and Winn was the most gorgeous man she'd ever seen. She longed to touch him, to strip the rest of his clothes from him, to caress his hard-muscled flesh and run her fingers through the crisp mat of black hair that covered his chest.

"It's been a long night, Lucy. It's late and I'm tired," he said as he pulled his shirt back on and began to button it. "I plan to have one last drink and then go to bed."

"That's just what I was hoping you'd want to do," she purred, a slow, inviting smile curving her lips.

"I want to go to bed alone, Lucy."

Not about to be denied, she rose up on her knees, letting the sheet drop away, displaying for him all of her womanly secrets. "You don't really mean that . . ." She leaned forward and reached out to stop him from rebuttoning his shirt. She wanted his chest bare; she wanted to be able to look at him.

The sight of her naked, ample curves left Winn curiously unmoved, and he took an evasive step backward. "Oh, but I do. Besides, now that the card game's over, won't your husband be looking for you?"

"Oh, Frederick doesn't mind." She was slightly irritated that Winn wasn't more receptive, but far from discouraged. She wanted him, and she meant to have him.

"Well, I do," Winn said. "I'm in no mood . . ."

"But I could change your mood." There was heated promise in her words. "I could make you feel much better."

Winn saw that Lucy wasn't going to take no for an answer, and his patience quickly wore thin. He moved toward her, and Lucy, thinking he had changed his mind, lifted her arms to embrace him. When he grasped her wrists, she relaxed against him, believing he'd finally succumbed to her charms. To her shock, he dragged her from the bed and all but hauled her over to the opposite side of it where she'd left her clothes. He then scooped up her gown and handed it to her.

"Good night, Lucy." He released her and stood back to watch her dress.

Lucy could tell by his cold-eyed expression that he'd meant every word, so she quickly donned her dress and left the room. She felt no shame as she went, only disappointment.

Winn waited until she'd gone, then locked the door after her. He picked up his whiskey glass and drained it in one swallow. He glanced up and caught sight of his own reflection in the dresser mirror. Staring at his image, he wondered why his life suddenly seemed so empty. Not too long ago, the drinking, whores, married women, and card games had been enough, but now his life seemed an exercise in futility. Nothing he did mattered. He'd accomplished nothing of note in his twenty-eight years. Since gaining control of his inheritance after his parents' deaths ten years before, he'd spent his time and money indulging his every wish, in spite of his Uncle Edward's admonishments that wild, unprincipled living would not bring him happiness.

The thought of his uncle, a priest, momentarily shamed him, and he wondered what he would have thought had he seen him tonight. As he pondered it, Winn smiled. Perhaps, for once, his uncle might have approved of his actions. He had, after all, sent Lucy on her way.

Feeling jaded and world-weary. Winn took one look at the bed where Lucy had lain and knew he did not want to sleep there. He rang for a servant, and then, rather than wait, began to pack. He was determined to return to London right away. He wanted to go home.

Lawrence faced Enoch Parker across the table in the hotel dining room and smiled. Since they'd last met, his friend's hair had gone completely silver, and he'd added a few pounds to his already portly stature. The changes suited him for they made him seem even more the studious professor. "It's good to see you again. I was surprised by your invitation. I didn't know you were back in London."

"I've been doing research at the university for several weeks now and this is the first time I've allowed myself any diversion," the bespectacled scholar explained. "I'll be going home next week, and I wanted to see you before I left."

"Well I'm very glad you contacted me. I always enjoy our visits," Lawrence told him, and in truth, this was the first pleasant moment he'd had since his confrontation with Philip and Robert. It seemed the stress of disinheriting them had affected his health, and though he'd been taking his medicine as the doctor had instructed, lately he'd begun to have serious chest pains. None of that mattered to him right now, however, for he was with his friend and he was going to pretend that all was right with the world, if only for a little while.

"The food here may not be as exotic as the dinner

we shared in Cairo, but your company is every bit as delightful."

"Thank you. I enjoy our talks, too, but where's Alex? Still up in your rooms?" Lawrence knew Enoch rarely traveled without his only child, his daughter Alex, who served as his assistant. Alex's thirst for knowledge was as great as theirs, and Lawrence always enjoyed matching wits with her.

"My sister was unwell, so Alex stayed home to help her. If it hadn't been for Alex, I would have missed this opportunity at the university. Thank God for children."

Lawrence wasn't so sure he agreed with Enoch's opinion of children. "Is her condition serious?"

"It wasn't life-threatening. I wouldn't have left if it had been. I received a letter from them last week, and she's much better now."

"I'm glad. It's difficult when someone you care about is sick." He remembered how devastated he'd been when his wife died. It had taken him years to adjust to life without her. For just one sad moment, Lawrence wondered if anyone would grieve when he died. Then the direction of his thoughts annoyed him, and he quickly changed the topic. "Did you learn anything new and exciting while you were working?"

"A few things from the time of Ptolemy I, but, alas, my friend, nothing about the crown. I'm beginning to fear that it will never be found—at least, not in my lifetime." Frustration darkened his expression, for proving the existence of the Crown of Desire was one of his lifelong goals. "Have you heard anything?"

"Nothing new," Lawrence replied without lying. He

saw the disappointment in Enoch's eyes and began to wonder if perhaps the time had come to tell him everything. This man was his friend, one of the few people he trusted in the world. He suddenly had doubts about the provisions he'd put in the will.

The waiter arrived then with their meals, and the conversation lulled while they ate. Lawrence was glad, for it gave him a quiet moment to consider telling Enoch the truth. He knew his friend would be stunned, but he hoped Enoch would understand that his motive for these years of silence had been pure. He'd kept the secret to keep the crown safe.

Lawrence made his decision, and as they finished dinner and ordered brandies, he spoke, "You know, we've been friends for many years now."

"Indeed, we have."

"Well, Enoch, I have a confession to make," he began.

"A confession?" Enoch frowned, perplexed. Lawrence was an upstanding man, and Enoch couldn't imagine what he had to 'confess.'

"You may be angry when you hear what I have to say, but I hope you'll try to understand why I did what I did . . ."

"I don't understand."

"Enoch." He paused to draw a deep breath, then met his friend's puzzled regard squarely. "I have the crown."

"You what?" Enoch was stunned. "But how? When did you get it?"

"I've had it for some time . . ."

"Why didn't you write and tell me? Why didn't you let me know? You know how I feel about the crown!

This is wonderful! Tell me everything! How did you find it! When did you first hear about it?"

"Enoch," Lawrence said quietly. "I've had the crown for over twenty years."

The professor surged to his feet, jarring his chair backward and drawing looks from the others in the dining room. His face reddened and his eyes flashed with the fury of betrayal. "You mean all the time I've been searching for it, you've had it and never said a word? How could you?"

"Let me explain . . ."

"You say you're my friend and yet you didn't trust me enough to tell me?!"

"Please, Enoch, sit down, and let me explain."

His anger did not abate, but he did sit back down.

"Gentlemen?" the waiter spoke cautiously as he approached the table. He could see that the two gentlemen were arguing, and hoped to distract them. "I have your brandies." He set the snifters before them.

"Thank you." Lawrence's tone was dismissive, so the waiter quickly moved off.

"I'm not so sure I care to drink with you right now," Enoch ground out as he leaned forward in furious frustration. "You call yourself my friend and yet you keep this from me . . . You all but lied to me, and not just for a few months, but for twenty years!"

Lawrence had feared this reaction and thought better of pursuing the topic further. "Perhaps you're right. Perhaps this isn't the time for us to share a drink and discuss this." He stood, aware of the attention they were drawing from the other diners. "Thank you for dinner." With quiet dignity, he strode from the room.

For a moment, Enoch remained where he was. His thoughts were confused as he tried to sort out just what he was feeling. Betrayal, anger, and hurt competed with excitement. After a moment, excitement won. While it did hurt that Lawrence had had the crown all along and had kept it from him, there was no denying that he was still desperate to see it. Throwing enough money on the table to pay the bill, Enoch surged to his feet and ran after Lawrence.

The diners looked on with open interest as Enoch, looking very angry, rushed out. A murmur of gossip threaded through the room.

"Lawrence! Wait!" Enoch called as he emerged from the hotel and saw him about to climb into a hired carriage.

Lawrence stopped and turned to join him.

"I'm sorry," Enoch said with true feeling. "I was wrong to react as I did, but I was so shocked by the news . . ."

"Would you like to come back to the house with me? I think it would be better to speak of this in private."

"Thank you. You know what an obsession this has been for me. I want to know everything."

They climbed into the cab together, and a short time later they were settled in Lawrence's study. They'd forsaken brandy for tumblers of whiskey. The house was deserted and Lawrence was glad. The last thing he felt like doing was dealing with Philip or Robert tonight.

"You've really had the crown all this time?" the professor asked, his anger now replaced by anticipation. He had a multitude of questions and was desperate to have them all answered.

"It was found twenty-seven years ago, and I've had it in my keeping ever since."

"And you told no one . . ."

"You know what a furor the discovery would have caused if it had become public. Other than myself, only my sons and valet have seen the crown, and then only on very rare occasions."

"Why did you decide to tell me now, after all this time?"

"Things in my life have changed . . ." Lawrence paused as sadness filled him. "My sons . . . Well, suffice it to say that I've disinherited them."

"I'm sorry, Lawrence. I had no idea."

"I'm past being sorry. I thought I could redeem them. God knows I tried, but I realized a short time ago that it was hopeless. As far as I'm concerned, I have no children."

As close as he was to Alex, the idea was anathema to Enoch, but he said nothing. He could see the pain in his friend's eyes and knew there was nothing he could say or do to help the situation.

"Which is why I decided tonight to tell you the truth about the crown."

"Is the crown here? In the house? May I see it?"

He could no longer deny his excitement.

"The way things now stand, no one will see the crown again until after I'm dead."

"What are you talking about?"

He quickly explained his motivation in hiding the treasure to keep it safe, and how afterward he'd written the three books. "I originally intended the books to go to Philip and Robert upon my death. I'd thought working to find it would make them better men, but I know now it's useless. They're beyond redemption. So I've designated that, upon my death, the books are to be given to the three people who love the crown as much as I do. One is to go to you, another to Matthew McKittrick, a young man I correspond with in Boston, and the last to my closest friend, Father Edward Bradford."

"But Lawrence, why hinge finding the crown on your death? That's morbid. We're your friends. You know yourself that I haven't been searching for it all these years because of its value. I've wanted to find the crown because of its historical significance."

Lawrence realized he had a point. He'd written the books to thwart his sons in what he knew would be their quick attempt to sell all of his valuable possessions. They held nothing of value but money. Thinking of his sons and their greed brought on chest pain, and he fought against it. "Perhaps you're right . . ."

Enoch could see how pale his friend had become.

"Are you feeling all right?"

"I suppose I'm a little tired, that's all." Lawrence tried to shrug off his concern, but the weight pressing on his chest would not ease.

"We've waited this long, another day isn't going to matter. Shall we talk tomorrow?"

"Tomorrow will be fine. Let's meet in the evening, shall we? Say, seven o'clock?"

"I'll be here." Enoch stood to go, but there was one question that he could not wait to ask. "Tell me this before I go—is the crown as beautiful as the legend claims?"

"More so," he confided, his eyes shining as he remembered the first time he'd seen the Crown of Desire.

"I'll see you tomorrow night."

Lawrence saw him out, then went straight upstairs to his bedroom. He was feeling terrible, and he desperately hoped his medicine would help.

As was his custom, Henry had placed the bottle and a spoon on the nightstand. Lawrence sat down on the bed, poured himself a double dose, and swallowed with a grimace. He wondered why the medicine seemed to taste more bitter than usual tonight, but he dismissed it as his imagination or perhaps an aftertaste from the liquor. He told himself that maybe if it tasted worse it would work better and ease the terrible tightness in his chest.

Lawrence barely had time to undress and put on his nightshirt when the vicious, searing pain struck and his hands began to shake uncontrollably. He clasped them together, trying to still them, but there was no stopping the violent tremors. He stared down at his hands in amazement. He'd known his heart was bad, but he'd never thought a really serious attack would feel like this . . .

He lifted his gaze to the medicine bottle then, and suddenly his expression changed . . . hardened. *Philip . . . Robert . . . Would they have? Could they have?*

The agony that suddenly screamed through every fiber of his being was his answer. *Poison . . .*

Lawrence could feel his throat constricting and suddenly he was struggling to breathe. He began to tremble uncontrollably and knew he needed help. Desperate to summon Henry, he frantically tried to reach the bellpull, but his legs would no longer support him and he fell to his knees. The silken cord was his lifeline, but even as his hand groped for it, a convulsion wracked his body and he collapsed on the floor. Lawrence tried to cry for help, but his pain was so great that it strangled him.

Darkness closed in on him. As Lawrence succumbed to the potent poison, his last thoughts were of the crown and how right he'd been about his sons. The only peace he knew as he surrendered to death's dominion was that he was glad he'd changed his will. He'd seen to it that they would never get their hands on the Crown of Desire. All their plotting and murder had been for nothing . . .

Three

Henry knocked on Mr. Anthony's bedroom door early the next morning. When there was no immediate response, he knocked a second time, then opened the door just enough so he could look in. He was prepared to find Mr. Anthony asleep, and then quietly leave him to rest a little longer, but instead, on looking in he found his beloved employer sprawled on the floor.

"Mr. Anthony!" His cry was hoarse with fear as he rushed to his aid. Henry grasped his hand, but it was cold to the touch, telling him all he needed to know.

Since the day Lawrence had instructed him about the disposition of the books, Henry, had suspected that his health was not good, but he'd had no idea that he was deathly ill. He rang for help, then drew a blanket over the lifeless form. Penny, one of the maids, was nearby and she was the first to respond to his call. He quickly ordered her to send for the doctor. Martin appeared only moments later.

"What is it?" the butler demanded, horrified. "What happened to Mr. Anthony?"

"He's dead, Martin." Henry's gaze was filled with sorrow as he looked up at the other servant. "I'm not sure how it happened. I've already sent Penny for the doctor."

"Dear Lord . . ." Martin was stricken.

"Is either Mr. Philip or Mr. Robert here?"

"I haven't seen either of them this morning, and their beds were not slept in."

Henry nodded. "Someone must go find them."

"I'll see to it, though there's no telling where they might be. When the physician arrives, I'll bring him right up."

Henry remained by his employer's side until the doctor came. After telling him everything he knew, the valet took one last look at the man he'd served for so long, then left the room. He made it a point to speak to no one as he hurried to the study and locked himself in. This was one time when he could not risk being interrupted.

With Philip and Robert still not back, Henry had time and opportunity to carry out Mr. Anthony's last wish. Opening the drawer with the secret compartment, he removed the hidden book to find the books and an envelope addressed to him. He opened the envelope and was surprised to find that it contained a substantial amount of money and a letter.

My Dear Henry,

If you are reading this letter, then you know I am dead and you have the books in your possession. If at all possible, it is important that the books be delivered personally. Enclosed find enough money to pay for your passage to America. Any money you have left over is yours to keep. Beware of Philip and Robert. They are not to be trusted in any way. I wish you Godspeed on your journey, and I thank you for your years of dedicated service.

With greatest affection and appreciation,

Lawrence Anthony

Henry again sensed the urgency of the request and knew he had to act immediately. Taking the books, he replaced the false back to the drawer so that the compartment would remain a secret. Without telling anyone, Henry slipped from the house and rushed off to deliver the book marked for Father Edward Bradford.

Winn spoke quietly to Arthur, his butler, at the bedroom door, then returned to his vigil at his Uncle Edward's bedside. He sat beside the bed, gazing at his uncle who slept now in fitful agony and wondering how his own life could have changed so completely in such a short time. Just after he'd returned from Merryfield a week ago, he'd received an urgent message that Edward had taken seriously ill. Winn had gone to the seminary and brought him to his London home where they would be closer to the best doctors, and he would be able to personally care for him. For all their differences, Winn adored him. It had been pure hell for him to learn from the physicians that his uncle's illness had no cure; he was dying.

Edward Bradford had once been robust, healthy and

tireless, and he'd gone about doing God's work with great energy and joy. Now, Winn realized as he kept watch over him, he'd become a wasted shell of a man. The vicious disease had progressed rapidly during the last few days and had robbed him of all but his dignity and his faith.

Winn was not one for prayer, but he bowed his head now in supplication and fervently pleaded with God to spare his uncle's life. He hadn't realized that he'd spoken out loud until his uncle called to him.

"Winston . . ." Edward managed weakly, having come awake to hear the dear boy trying to convince God to let him live longer. Had he more strength, he would have chuckled at Winn's daring. He'd tried the same tack himself early on, but he'd learned through the years that God did not make deals.

"Yes, Uncle Edward?" Winn leaned forward and took the older man's hand. It felt cold and frail in his, and again the undeniable realization that his uncle truly was dying struck Winn's heart a savage blow.

"You're a good boy . . ." Edward's voice was a whisper. He loved his brother's son as if he were his own. They'd grown very close since Winn had been orphaned and forced, at eighteen, to confront the finality of death and assume the responsibilities of an adult. Edward knew it had been hard for him, and though he hadn't approved of Winn's reckless rebellion with his fast living during the last few years, he'd understood it.

"You think so?" He was surprised by his words.

"A little wild, but good." Edward fought for a breath

as he turned his still powerful gaze on his nephew. He searched Winn's strong, handsome features for some sign of weakness, but found none, and that pleased him. Undisciplined though he might be, he knew Winn would be all right once he came to realize what was really important in life.

While Winn returned his regard with outward calm, inwardly he was unnerved. When he was younger and his uncle had looked at him this way, Winn had always believed he was looking into the very depths of his soul. Winn knew the darkness that lurked there, and he wondered what his uncle was seeing.

"I'm proud of you, Winston." Edward's words were strong and heartfelt.

Winn was caught off-guard by the praise, and his surprise sounded in his voice. "You are?"

"I am." Edward nodded slightly. A sudden wracking fit of coughing tortured him, and he fought to catch his breath. When the agony finally passed, he was much weaker, but even so, he tightened his grip on Winn's hand. "You know, I've counseled you many times in the past." Edward smiled faintly, thinking of all the discussions they'd had over the last few years.

"Yes, sir." In spite of his sorrow, Winn returned his smile. There was no forgetting how his uncle had often advised him to change his life and how he'd always managed to find some way to ignore him.

"Well, this time I want you to listen to me and remember every word. What I'm about to tell you is more important than anything I've ever said in the past."

Winn saw the fervent glow in his eyes. "I will."

"Good." He paused to draw a strangled breath. "Winston, when you finally realize that all your worldly ways aren't making you happy, then know there's one thing left that will."

"What?"

"Love, Winston. Love is the answer. Selfless, giving love. Reach for it. Embrace it with your heart and soul. Love will be your strength. It will sustain you when all else in the world fails you. If you remember nothing else, remember that . . ."

Edward went limp as he finished speaking, the power and urgency of his message having drained him of energy. He closed his eyes.

Winn stared down at him, seeing the grayness of his coloring and the pain-ravaged grimness of his features.

"I'll remember. I promise," he pledged.

Henry knocked on the door to the palatial home of Lord Winston Bradford. His trip to the address on the book for Father Bradford had been a wasted effort, for he'd discovered upon arriving that the priest had taken ill and had gone to stay with his nephew. He'd met Father Bradford many times at the Anthony home and hoped his condition wasn't serious.

"Yes?" A uniformed servant opened the door.

"Is Father Bradford here?"

"Yes, he is."

"May I speak with him, please?"

"I'm sorry, but he is indisposed at the moment. Is there something I can do for you?"

"This package is for him. Would you see that he gets it, please?" He held out the book to the servant.

"Of course. Would you care to leave any message?"

"Tell him Lawrence Anthony passed away this morning, and that the package is a gift from him."

"I shall deliver the message, sir."

"Thank you."

Henry sighed in relief as he left the house. One safely delivered, and now only two to go. He took out the next book. This one was addressed to Professor Parker at his home in Boston, but Henry knew the professor was in London, for Mr. Anthony had dined with him the night before. He did not relish being the one to tell the professor that Mr. Anthony was dead, but he knew it was important to give him the book as soon as possible. He made his way across town to the hotel and went inside to the front desk.

"I need Professor Parker's room number, please," he told the hotel clerk.

The clerk gave him a startled look. "He's in 304, but if you wait a minute, you'll see him coming down."

"Oh? Is there someone else here to see him?" Henry wanted to be as discreet as possible.

"So to speak. The authorities are here. I think they've come to arrest him."

"The Professor?" Henry could only stare at the man. "For what?"

"The man he dined with in the hotel dining room last night was found dead this morning—poisoned!

They were seen arguing and then the professor chased him from the dining room. Witnesses saw everything."

Henry was taken aback by this news. *Mr. Anthony—poisoned?* He mumbled something to the clerk, then moved numbly away from the desk. It had been difficult enough dealing with his employer's death when he'd thought he'd died from natural causes, but to hear that he'd been murdered sickened him.

No matter the malicious words of the clerk, Henry was certain that the professor was innocent. The idea that they'd had a fight that turned deadly was ridiculous. They'd been friends. There were only two people who wanted Mr. Anthony dead, and he knew exactly who they were.

A commotion on the main stairway drew everyone's attention. Henry saw the authorities appear with Enoch Parker in tow.

"But I don't know what you're talking about . . ." Enoch was saying as he was led away. "I just saw Lawrence last night and he was fine . . ."

Henry could see the horrified look on the professor's face, and he clutched the two remaining books more tightly to him. There seemed to be some terrible, devious plot at work here, but he didn't know how to thwart it. Right then, he knew the most important thing he could do was his duty to Mr. Anthony—to see the books delivered.

Henry waited until the excitement over the professor's arrest had quieted down, then left the hotel. As he went outside, he glanced around at the crowd that had gathered to watch the professor being taken away.

It was then that he saw Philip and Robert, standing across the street.

Henry's blood ran cold at the sight of them, for their expressions were not those of two loving sons relieved that their father's murderer had been caught. Their expressions were of smug triumph and victory.

Henry knew a moment of panic. He did not want them to see him, especially not while he had the books in his possession. He didn't want to explain why he was at the hotel. He turned to retreat into the hotel just as the two brothers happened to look up and see him. Across the distance, their gazes met and locked. Henry looked away first and disappeared inside. Philip said something to Robert and went after him.

Henry rushed across the lobby and out another door. His thoughts were racing as he tried to distance himself from the pursuing Philip. He was beginning to understand now what Mr. Anthony had meant when he'd warned him that he might regret giving him his word that he would deliver the books.

Glancing back over his shoulder, Henry saw that Philip had followed him from the building, but had not yet seen him. Henry darted into an alleyway, and, undaunted by the stench of rotting garbage, he hid behind some crates and waited. Only then did he realize his hands were shaking and a cold sweat had broken out on his brow. After a moment, he saw Philip pass by. Not convinced that the other man was gone, he continued to hide, and a short time later he saw Philip retrace his steps in the direction of the hotel. Still not daring to reveal himself, Henry stayed where he was another minute, then quietly emerged to look around.

Relief washed over him as he found that he'd eluded Philip, but he didn't relax his guard. His nerves stretched taut as he debated what to do and where to go. The most important thing was to get the books into the hands of the right people. He had to talk to the professor in jail and find out what had really happened, but he knew he wouldn't be able to get in to see him until the next day.

Frustrated, Henry started back to the Anthony home. According to what Mr. Anthony had told him, neither Philip nor Robert knew about the books. Still, Henry didn't want to take any chances. He hoped they hadn't returned home, so he would have time to hide the books before they did.

"I couldn't find him," Philip told Robert as he rejoined him in front of the hotel.

"It's not really important, but I do find it curious that he was here in the first place and seemed to be avoiding us."

"We'll ask him about it later. Right now, all I want to do is get over to father's lawyer's office and arrange for the official reading of the will," Philip said. "Tomorrow as soon as he's buried sounds good to me."

"Do you suppose Dell will have any objection?"

"Who cares? He's in our employ now, not father's. He'll read the will when we tell him to."

The two brothers were feeling quite invincible. It had been a successful 24 hours. Everything had gone exactly as planned. They still couldn't believe their luck in discovering that the professor was in town and had made a date to dine with their father. The fact that a friend of theirs had been in the dining room when the two had had a heated argument and told them about it had only been an extra bonus. It had been a simple matter then to put their plan into action, and now all was done. Now, because of their brilliance, their father was dead, the professor had been arrested for his murder, and they were going to be very rich men.

A few months before, Philip had stolen a copy of their father's will and had shared it with his brother. They'd been furious when they'd discovered what he'd done with the crown. It annoyed them to no end that they'd have to waste time tracking the damned thing down, using the books of clues he'd written, but that was just like him. Even from the grave he planned to torment them. The delay in claiming what they believed to be rightfully theirs hadn't stifled their enthusiasm. They had merely bided their time. Now, glad he was dead they would go about finding the crown and then they'd be able to get on with enjoying their lives.

Philip thought of Penny, the maid who loved him so slavishly, and knew he would have to give her a special 'thank you' for slipping into their father's room early that morning and switching medicine bottles. She'd already returned the one he'd filled with poison to him and replaced it with the correct bottle. Philip planned to make her a very happy woman just as soon as all the fuss died down and they had some time alone. Sometimes things did go as one planned. Sometimes life could be wonderful.

"You realize, after our visit with Dell, we have to go home and play the dutiful, mourning sons," Philip pointed out with distaste.

"Do you suppose he's heard yet?"

"If not, we'll have the pleasure of telling him." His smile turned cold. He despised his father's attorney and couldn't wait for their business association with him to be through.

Henry was up at dawn the next day. A terrible sense of urgency filled him. Philip and Robert, in their rush to bury their father and be done with their responsibilities, had set the funeral for noon that very day, and the reading of the will for seven that evening. He had to get to the jail and speak to the professor right away, for he wanted the books out of his possession before the reading. He'd been lucky the night before. When the two had returned to the house they had obviously been drinking heavily. He doubted their state was the result of grief; it seemed more like celebration. They had questioned him briefly about his presence at the hotel, and he'd been relieved when they accepted his answer that he'd been there to see a friend who worked at the place.

Now, as he slipped from the house before anyone else had risen, he took the books which he'd hidden under his mattress for the night and some of the money

Mr. Anthony had left him. It was common knowledge that access could be gained to the prison by bribing the guards, and he wanted to be prepared. A little later, after parting with a substantial amount of his money, Henry waited in the center yard for the guard to bring the professor to him.

"Henry? Thank God!" Enoch spoke his name in surprise and relief as he followed the guard from the dark, dank, miserable building.

"Professor Parker . . ."

They clasped hands, and Enoch thought perhaps that things would finally change for the better. He hoped desperately that the valet had some kind of news that would help to set him free. One day in the filthy prison had been enough to last him a lifetime.

"This is all so terrible. They think I murdered Lawrence! Have you heard anything? Anything at all?" the professor asked. His hopes were high as he awaited his reply.

"Nothing. I wish I did have some good news for you, but I don't."

"Damn!"

"I do believe you are innocent, sir," he offered.

"Thank you." The older man gave him a heartfelt look. "I'm not sure why I've been arrested, other than the fact that Lawrence and I argued over dinner. He told me some very startling news, and I was shocked and angry, but we never came to blows. In fact, we went back to his house and talked for several hours afterward. When I left him, he was fine. I don't know what could have happened."

"I don't know what happened either, but I do know that Philip and Robert have arranged for Mr. Anthony's funeral to be today at noon."

"So soon?" Enoch stared at him in amazement.

"Then everything Lawrence confided in me was true."

"Everything?"

"He told me that he'd disinherited them. . . . He felt he had no sons, no family."

Henry had suspected as much after the night he'd confided in him about the books. "They don't know it yet, and they won't until tonight when they have the reading of the will. Did Mr. Anthony tell you about this?" He drew the wrapped book out of his coat pocket and handed it to him.

"The book . . ." He took it from Henry and held it as if it were the most precious of relics. He wanted to rip the package open and devour every word, but he didn't. When he looked up at Henry and there were tears in his eyes, what he did next was the most difficult thing he'd ever done in his life. He handed it back to Henry. "I can't keep it."

"But Mr. Anthony insisted I deliver it to you."

"The book is too important to be put at risk, Henry. I dare not keep it here. God only knows what might happen to it, and we can't risk letting it fall into his sons' hands. We just can't."

"What shall I do with it, sir?"

"Send it on to my address in Boston. It will be safe there. Alex will know what to do with it."

"You're sure?"

"We have no choice," he answered solemnly.

"I'll do it."

"Thank you, Henry. You're a true friend, to Lawrence and to me." For a moment, he'd been able to forget his own dire straits as he'd thought about the crown and the book, but now reality returned. He would have to return to the hell of the prison.

"Professor Parker, I'll do everything I can to help you. I know you didn't poison Mr. Anthony."

"You seem to be the only one who believes in me."

"Time's up!" the guard announced coming back to claim his prisoner.

"Henry, you're my only hope."

The guard led him away.

Henry watched the good man go back inside, and he vowed to try to find some way to prove his innocence. He understood the professor's very real concern about the books, and so when he went to post his book to his daughter in Boston, he also mailed the one to Matthew McKittrick. He felt tremendously relieved once they were out of his possession, for he didn't trust Philip or Robert at all. It was not going to be a pleasant evening once they had heard the terms of the will. He knew they would be furious when they found out that they'd been disinherited, and he was not looking forward to the repercussions.

Threatening clouds hung low and dark over the city and thunder rumbled ominously in the distance as the minister spoke at the graveside. Philip stood with his brother next to the casket, taking care to look suitably sorrowful and wishing fervently that the man of the cloth would hurry and finish his damned prayers. He wanted to get this over with before it rained. It was bad enough that they were going to have to receive visitors at the house for the rest of the day and listen to declarations of respect and love for their dead father. He'd despised his father and his parsimonious ways, and as soon as he got his hands on his share of his inheritance, he was going to show London how to live!

"Amen."

The minister's last word broke through Philip's annoyed musings and brought him back to the present. Irritating as it was, he had to follow custom or possibly arouse suspicions about his motives, and that wouldn't do. He'd already surprised a lot of people by rushing the burial and reading of the will, but that didn't matter. He and Robert had been telling everyone that they were so grief-stricken that they wanted to be done with it as quickly as they could. Most believed them. Some did not.

Meanwhile as the coffin of his dear friend was being lowered into the grave, the solemn muted prayers of the priest filled the bedroom where Edward lay near death. Edward's mind wandered, his breathing became more and more labored, and rampant fever burned away the last of his vitality.

"Winston . . ."

"Yes, sir." Winn had been up all night, keeping his vigil, praying for a miracle, and the sound of his uncle's voice jarred him from his exhaustion. He reached out to touch his arm, to let him know he was there, and he could feel the heat of his illness even through his bedclothes.

"You've been like a son to me, Winn." Edward gazed at him for the last time. "Don't waste your life on useless pursuits. Use your strength and knowledge to do what's right."

"How will I know?" he asked, confused.

"God will show you, if you ask him."

Winn was tempted to argue, for he'd been pleading for God to heal his uncle for days now, and God hadn't listened. His torment must have shown on his face, for Edward spoke again, but more weakly this time.

"Winn, I'm not afraid to die."

His words, so bluntly spoken, jarred him. Somehow, it seemed wrong to speak of dying.

"If I truly believe all that I've preached through the years, and I do, then this day will be a celebration for me. Love is my legacy to you, Winston. Remember . . ." The old man's eyes drifted shut.

"I love you, Uncle Edward . . ."

Winn was never certain his uncle heard him for in that moment the old man's agony was taken from him and he found final peace with God.

Father Michaels understood, and he concluded his prayers and blessings. That done, he quietly made his way from the room, leaving Winn alone with his uncle.

It was a long time later when Winn finally emerged from the bedroom, his face haggard, his broad shoulders slumped in defeat. The vigil had ended, and death had won. Weariness weighed upon his soul. He looked up at the servants who'd heard of Father Edward's passing from Father Michaels and had gathered in the hall to comfort Lord Bradford.

"It's over . . ." His voice was tight and hoarse with grief and pain.

"We're sorry, sir." Arthur took it upon himself to speak for the entire staff. Father Edward had been a frequent visitor to the house and was loved by all.

Winn gave them a grateful look. "So am I. He was a good man. I'll miss him."

"We all will, sir," Arthur said. "Is there anything we can do for you?" He wanted to ease his employer's burden, if he could. Winn and his uncle had been very close, and the butler knew this was as painful for him as his parents' deaths had been all those years ago. One never became accustomed to death, though one did eventually manage to deal with it and accept it.

"No. I'm just going to speak with Father Michaels and then I'm going to rest for a while."

"If you need anything at all, just call for us. Father Michaels is waiting for you in the parlor."

"Thank you, Arthur."

Winn went downstairs and spoke with the priest at length, making the necessary arrangements for the funeral. When everything was completed, he saw the priest from the house and then retired to his own bedroom.

Winn was amazed anew by Arthur's insight and abilities. A hot bath and a tray of food awaited him. He bathed quickly, too tired to enjoy it. Then he got ready for bed. He ran a hand over his face in an exhausted gesture and was surprised by the roughness of his beard. A quick glance in the mirror over the wash-stand confirmed the dark shadow of more than three days' growth. He rubbed his jaw idly as he contemplated shaving, then thought better of the idea and went to lie down. As tired as he was, there was no telling how accurately he would be able to wield a razor. The bed's softness was a welcoming embrace, and he gave a low groan as he stretched out upon it and rested a forearm over his eyes. Emotional and physical exhaustion claimed him, and he slept.

Philip and Robert were excited as they returned to the house after the burial. Everything was working out perfectly. By 7:30 that evening, they were going to be rich. They sat alone in the study and passed the balance of the afternoon drinking and trying to estimate how long it would take them to find the hidden crown once the lawyer gave them the books that night. The thought of having to pack up and go chasing after the damned thing angered them both, but they knew the prize was worth the inconvenience. When at last the hour neared, they freshened up so they would be ready for Thomas Dell when he arrived for the reading of the will.

Dell reached the house promptly at seven. He summoned Henry and Martin into the study, along with both Philip and Robert. He knew the next few minutes were going to be traumatic, but he was prepared. He thought the two sons despicable, and he realized now that Lawrence had been right about changing his will.

"If everyone is ready, I'll begin," Thomas announced

as he sat down at Lawrence's desk to read the document. He let his critical regard sweep over the four men who were seated before him.

Though Philip and Robert were taking great care to appear somber and serious, Thomas could see the mocking gleam of victory in their eyes. He knew they were immensely satisfied with themselves, and he found he was actually looking forward to disclosing the terms of the will.

"I, Lawrence Anthony, being of sound mind and body as of this day, 18 March, 1857, the year of our Lord 1857, do hereby leave the sum of 1000 pounds to each of my faithful servants, Henry and Martin. They have served me well through the years, and I thank them. The balance of my estate . . ." Dell paused for effect before continuing, for he wanted both Philip and Robert to feel the full brunt of their father's disgust with them. "I leave to the Church . . ."

"What!!" Philip and Robert both went pale.

The lawyer continued to read, "Through the years, the good works of my closest friend, Edward Bradford, have shown me the importance of love, kindness, and faith. It is with great pleasure that I leave absolutely nothing to the two men who, only now in my death, take pleasure in claiming me as their father. Their behavior has proven more painful than I can ever say, and I have decided that from this day, 18 March 1857 forth, I have no blood-related family."

"You can't be serious," Philip stated with dead calm.

"This has to be some kind of joke Father's playing on us," Robert insisted.

"This is no joke. I am completely serious. This will was signed by Lawrence Anthony and dated 18 March 1857. There is also a requirement here that you vacate the family home within five days of your father's death. He did provide a complete inventory of the estate, so there is a record of all of his possessions." He finished reading and looked up.

"It can't be valid!"

"Oh, but I assure you, it is," Thomas told him. "Your father had predicted that you would react just this way, so he took extra care to make sure this document was ironclad."

"We'll challenge it!"

"You'll be wasting your time." Thomas removed his glasses as he leaned back in his chair.

The two brothers' faces were mottled red with rage as they stood up.

"Get out of our house!" they snarled.

The lawyer stared at them, feeling as pleased as he could under the sad circumstances. "You may remain here three more days, after which time I shall return and see that all your father's property is turned over to the Church."

Four

It was near midnight, and Philip and Robert were in a savage mood. After the lawyer had gone, they'd ordered the servants to their quarters and then made a thorough search of the house. Their efforts to find the books had turned up nothing, though, and they stood in the middle of their father's bedroom, the room itself in a shambles from their search, feeling frustrated and furious.

"What do we do now?" Robert demanded.

"We're going to talk to Henry," Philip snarled. "You know how close he and Father were. If anyone knows what happened to those books, he does."

They shared in a knowing look and quickly made their way to Henry's room. They were glad now that the valet's room was apart from the other servants' for they wanted privacy while they talked to him. They didn't bother to knock, but barged right in.

"Hello, Henry," Philip greeted the startled servant. Henry had been unable to sleep and had been sitting on his bed contemplating what to do next when they burst into his room. He jumped up nervously and though he stood calmly before them, he was, in truth, more than a little afraid.

"We need to talk to you. We have a problem that we think you might be able to help us with," Robert broached the subject carefully.

"Oh?"

"We know how close you and Father were."

"I respected and admired your father," he said cautiously, not trusting them. He was extremely thankful that he'd followed the professor's advice and mailed the books that morning.

"Father had several books in his library that were very important to us, and they seem to be missing. We were wondering if he told you where he put them?"

"All of his books were kept in the study," Henry replied, avoiding their question.

"Now, Henry, we're not talking about his regular library. These books were special. I'm sure Father would have kept them some place safe. He wouldn't have left them just sitting out on the shelf."

"I'm sure I don't know what you're talking about, but it doesn't really matter."

"Why is that?" Philip wondered at his answer.

"According to Mr. Dell, an inventory of all household possessions has been taken and all of your father's things are to be given to charity."

His words were the spark that ignited the frayed temper of the already-maddened Philip. Reminded once again of how his plan had failed, his fury exploded into a mindless rage. The will be damned! He was Lawrence Anthony's oldest son! He intended to gain his rightful inheritance—one way or another! He snatched up the fireplace poker and struck the valet savagely in the head.

Henry hadn't seen the blow coming, and it caught him totally unawares, knocking him to his knees, stunned.

Beyond reason, Philip continued to strike the servant with bone-breaking fury.

"Stop . . ." Henry cried frantically trying to escape. But Philip was relentless and remorseless. He'd always hated Henry and the way he'd always stood with his father, looking so confident and superior. The more he thought about his father, the angrier he became.

When at last, Henry slipped into unconsciousness, his last words were, "The professor warned me . . ."

Philip didn't stop. He swung again and again, pretending all the while that he was hitting his father. His blows rained down harder and faster, until a steely hand finally gripped his arm in mid-swing.

"Philip! Enough!"

Robert's icy voice cut through the red haze of his emotions, and Philip stared down at the servant's bloodied body.

Robert bent to check Henry. When he looked up at his brother, his expression was cold and filled with loathing. "You fool! You've killed him. Now we're never going to find out what happened to the books!"

A shudder ran through Philip as he dropped the poker. "It doesn't matter."

"What do you mean it doesn't matter? He was the only one who could have led us to them."

"Didn't you hear what he said? He said 'The professor warned me . . .' When has he had time to talk to the professor? Either Henry was at the hotel that night to see Parker or he's been to the jail since the professor was arrested."

Robert's eyes narrowed as he considered the possibilities. "I'm glad it's late. We'll be able to cover this up without too much trouble. If anyone asks, we'll just tell them that once Henry got his money from the will, he left. Then first thing in the morning, we'll make a visit to the professor."

"Why wait for morning?" Philip refused to be put off. He wanted answers, and he wanted them now. "The sooner we find out what's happened to the books, the sooner we'll get our money. Besides, I've already spoken to the guards. We won't have any trouble getting in to see him."

Several hours later in the early hours of the morning, the two brothers were face-to-face with the professor in a small windowless room. The guards had been glad to see Philip again for they'd met with him before and knew he was more than generous when it came to enlisting their help.

Enoch had been momentarily thrilled when the guards had come for him. Though the letter he'd written to Alex at home couldn't possibly have reached her yet, perhaps the letters he'd written to his friends at the university and the British Museum had brought the help he'd so desperately sought. He'd believed, as the guards led him out of his cell, that he was going to be released. He'd thought the whole ugly misunderstanding had been cleared up and he would be exonerated of all the charges. Now, standing before the two Anthony brothers, his spirits plummeted. Shock and horror filled him as he realized that they had come to question him about their father, not to free him.

"Where are the books?" Philip demanded without preamble as he cornered the exhausted professor in the small room.

"I've never seen any books," Enoch answered quickly, terror filling his heart as he looked from Philip to Robert. Their expressions were so cold, their manner so deadly, that he grew even more certain that they were the ones responsible for Lawrence's death and his own imprisonment.

"Don't lie to us, professor. We know better. We know you stole them from our father just before you killed him. Now, where are they? What did you do with them?"

"I don't know what you're talking about! I didn't steal anything from your father! He was my friend. I would never have harmed him in any way!"

"Denials . . . denials . . . Look, professor, we know Henry's been to see you," Robert announced with a cool, knowing air.

Enoch paled at the news. "I still have no idea what you're talking about."

"Come, come, now, professor," Robert followed up in a scolding tone. "Playing ignorant doesn't become you."

"If you think Henry's going to help you in some

way, think again. Henry won't be helping you or anyone else anymore."

A look of panic flickered across Enoch's expression. "What are you talking about? What's happened to Henry?"

"Why, nothing that I know of," Philip replied looking completely innocent. "What about you, Robert? Do you know of anything happening to Henry?"

"No. All I know is that he got what was coming to him in the will, and he left. So if you were looking to him for help, you're going to be disappointed."

"I have other friends who'll help me! I didn't have anything to do with your father's death and I intend to prove it."

"Oh," Philip said smoothly as he drew a packet of letters from his pocket. "You mean like Dr. Knowlen at the university? Or Professor Greene at the museum? Or maybe even your daughter?"

Enoch lunged at him, trying to snatch back his letters, but Philip eluded him easily.

"All we want from you is a little cooperation, Professor. That's all. You tell us where the books are, and we'll see what we can do about getting you out of here."

Enoch felt trapped and frightened. His letters had been intercepted and stolen, and without Henry's help, he was as good as convicted and hung. "I've never laid eyes on them," he denied again.

"You can keep denying it all you want, but we know you know about them, and we're going to find them.

Why don't you just tell us now, and save all of us a lot of trouble."

"I know what kind of men you are, and I wouldn't help you if it meant saving my life!"

"It might very well come to that," Robert said coldly.

"Well, Robert, since the good professor doesn't want to talk to us about the books, maybe his lovely daughter Alexandra will."

"Alex doesn't know anything about this!" Enoch panicked at the thought of Alex dealing with these two.

"She's not even along with me on this trip."

"I guess we'll just have to travel to Boston and see what she knows, won't we? I wonder what she'll think when we tell her that you're a murderer?"

"You wouldn't!"

"Wouldn't we? That is, unless you'd like to tell us now what happened to those books?"

"I have nothing to tell you!" Enoch came back at them, infuriated by their cold-blooded daring. "You're murderers! First you killed your father and now you're trying to blame it on me!"

"You're going to have difficulty proving that," Philip countered smoothly.

"You won't get away with it!"

"Oh, really? It appears we already have. Let's face it, everyone saw you arguing with Father in the restaurant and then they saw you chase him outside."

"Just because we argued, doesn't mean I murdered him!"

"You're certainly a much more likely suspect than we are," he pointed out. "Especially since we had nothing to gain by his death. No, I think the court is going to believe you poisoned Father, and I think you'll pay the price for it—unless you choose to help us now, and then we could bring our considerable influence to bear on your behalf."

Enoch knew they were right. He had no power, no influence. He was without friends. He'd been unjustly accused and imprisoned, and no one cared. He was helpless before them. The only thing sustaining him was his sense of what was right, and he held on to the belief that some day the truth would be revealed. "I may not be able to prove my innocence, but the day is going to come when the two of you will be known for what you are, and then you'll pay for what you've done. There is a justice greater than man's."

Philip laughed. "Ah, but you'll be encountering man's justice far sooner. Good night, Professor."

Philip and Robert knocked on the door to signal the guard. He let them out, then took the professor back to his cell. Neither Philip nor Robert spoke again until they were in their carriage heading back to the house.

"What do you think?" Robert asked.

"I'm not sure. It's obvious that he doesn't have the books with him, but he did seem worried about us visiting his daughter."

"Perhaps we should plan a trip to Boston."

"Perhaps." Philip's mind was racing as he tried to put himself in his father's place. "If Father didn't give the books to the professor, then who did he give them to?"

"There was only one other man Father would have
trusted with the treasure, and that's Edward Bradford."

"Of course," Philip replied. Since their father had
left the bulk of his estate to the Church, it only followed that he would have given the books to the priest.

"We'll go see him first thing in the morning."

Dressed in black, Winn stood solemnly in the parlor.
He'd managed to get some rest, but it had been fitful
and haunted, and as he greeted the visitors who'd come
to pay their respects, he was still exhausted. The conversation was muted around him as his uncle's friends
spoke quietly of their sorrow at losing him. Winn
missed Uncle Edward already, and his heart felt heavy
with loss.

The funeral mass was set for the next morning, and
Winn both dreaded and looked forward to it. While
the funeral would mean an end to the agonizing ordeal,
it would also be the final parting for them. As he
thought about saying his last good-bye to his uncle,
Winn realized that there was no painless way to do it.
The death of a loved one always meant pain. No matter
how you tried, there could be no avoiding it.

"Good evening," he said as two men who looked
vaguely familiar entered the parlor and moved directly
toward him.

"Good evening, Lord Bradford," Robert replied.
"I'm Robert Anthony, and this is my brother, Philip.
We were very sorry to learn of your uncle's death."

"Thank you." He remembered them now that they'd

introduced themselves. His uncle had been a close friend of their father, but he knew these two were not well thought of around town. Their decadent ways were well known, and made his own escapades seem tame by comparison. "Is your father here?"

"You hadn't heard? We buried him yesterday."

Real surprise showed on Winn's face. "No, I hadn't heard. You have my deepest sympathy."

"Thank you."

"Lord Bradford, we were wondering if we might speak to you alone for a moment?"

Winn saw Arthur admitting more visitors, and declined. "This is not a good time."

"It's a serious business matter that has to do with our father and your uncle," Philip put in.

Winn sensed an urgency in the men, but something in their manner annoyed him.

"We have a lot in common, you know," Philip added a little slyly, hoping to encourage a mutual regard. After all, he had heard of Lord Bradford's reputation with the ladies and at the card tables.

However, his remark had the opposite effect on Winn, for it brought him up short. Winn suddenly found himself wondering if he really was like these two—unprincipled, cold, and ruthless. He hoped not. He certainly would not be so crass as to intrude and try to discuss business with the relative of a recently deceased man. Still, the fact that they thought of him that way left a bitter taste in his mouth. He frowned. "This is hardly the time to discuss such things, gentlemen."

"We wouldn't disturb you now, if it weren't important." Philip would not be put off. He was already irritated that they'd wasted half a day tracking down the priest only to discover that he'd died. Winn would be amenable to their needs and check his uncle's things right away so they could get the books and go. After all, how difficult could it be to find a few books written by their father among the priest's possessions? Didn't priests take a vow of poverty? Surely, Father Bradford didn't have so many personal belongings that it would take Lord Bradford a long time to find them.

"Perhaps we could meet later in the week?" Winn was still trying to maintain a courteous demeanor, but their persistence wasn't making it easy.

"This shouldn't take long," Robert added. "If we could just step into your study for a moment?"

Winn's jaw tightened as he fought to control his temper. "This is not a time to speak of business, *gentlemen*. If you'll excuse me?"

He started to walk away to greet each other, newly arriving guests, but Philip stepped before him, blocking his way. He pressed him once more.

"Lord Bradford, we've been led to believe that your uncle had some of our father's books in his possession. If you could possibly return them to us, we'd be greatly appreciative."

Winn stiffened at their ill-mannered crudeness. His gaze was condemning as he regarded them. "When the time is appropriate, I will consider your request. This is not the time. Good day, gentlemen." His dismissal was curt and undeniable.

The two brothers left, frustrated from pursuing their prize. They had only one more day before they were to be evicted from their home. Since their funds were limited now, time was of the essence. Their survival depended on finding those books.

The following morning, the funeral mass was held. It was a glorious celebration. The church was filled to overflowing with people who'd loved his uncle, and Winn felt better knowing that he'd touched so many lives, so deeply.

During the service, Winn had happened to catch sight of the Anthony brothers in attendance. Their presence irritated, and he hoped to avoid them after the ceremony. When the mass had ended and he went outside to enter his carriage, he saw the pair again, climbing into their own vehicle to join in the procession.

The funeral cortège had over thirty mourning-coaches in it, and with the hearse in the lead, it wound its way through the city streets to the cemetery where the priest was to be interred.

Winn's mood was somber as he said his final good-bye to his uncle. He felt desolate and very alone as memories of his uncle's love and support threatened the tenuous hold he had on his composure. He'd been young and innocent in the ways of the world when his parents died, but Uncle Edward had been there to guide him through those difficult, formative years to manhood. Winn would never forget him—or his advice.

The graveside ceremony was short, and Winn was

relieved. It would be good to be done with this last painful ritual of separation. The others who'd traveled to the cemetery came up to him and offered their final condolences before moving off. He remained there alone, standing quietly over the grave.

"Lord Bradford . . . ," Philip and Robert had waited until all the others had gone before they'd approached him. They were determined to get their answer.

Winn recognized the voice immediately and looked up at the two of them.

"Since it seems your business here is finished, we were wondering if we could have that talk with you now?"

"Business?" Winn turned on them, his eyes hardening at their intrusion on his grief. He'd had little respect for them after their visit to the house the day before, and now he was jarred by their cold-blooded indifference to his situation. "I'm afraid this is more than just business to me, gentlemen. I loved my uncle, and I am in mourning for him."

"But as we've told you before, this is very important, and it won't take much of your time," Philip persisted.

"My uncle was very important to me," he ground out, thinking the two men were little better than vultures. "If I happen to run across the items you're looking for, I'll let you know. I suggest you wait until you hear from me. Good day, gentlemen."

With all the dignity of a man of his rank and privilege, he turned his back and walked away to climb into his waiting carriage.

Philip and Robert stared after him, cursing beneath their breath. This damned arrogant nobleman was going to ruin everything. They had only one day left—one day to find the books that would secure their future.

"We're supposed to wait until we hear from him?" Robert sputtered angrily.

"We'll give him twenty-four hours, and then we'll take action."

"What kind of action?"

"You'll see," he promised.

Winn sat at his desk, holding the letter and book that Arthur had just given him. Apparently, they'd been delivered while his uncle lay dying, and Arthur had just remembered them now that the confusion of the funeral was past. Curious to see what it was the brothers were so eager to get their hands on, Winn opened the letter first and began to read.

My dearest Edward,

It is with great sorrow and heaviness of heart that I am writing this letter to you. I have decided on this day to disinherit Philip and Robert. I had long hoped that I could change them—make them contented with what they had and appreciate life for what it really is, and not for the money that they think so important. Unfortunately, I have failed. They are greedy, shallow men, who, I'm certain, will come to no good. It shames me that they bear my name.

You will only receive this letter after my death. I have instructed Henry to deliver it, and this book, upon my passing. Let me say that your friendship has been a balm to my soul, and your faith has been a light for me in the darkness of my life.

There is one treasure in my collection that has meant more to me than all the others. It is the Crown of Desire, an ancient Egyptian relic that was supposedly cursed by the last princess to possess it. Those who claim it in greed are also said to be cursed. Only those whose love is pure can possess it without danger. That is why I have chosen you, my dear Edward, to lead the search to find the crown, which I've hidden away. Many would steal it, if its location were known. I hid it several years ago with the intention of making true men of my sons in the hunt for it. They are, however, far beyond any hope of redemption, and so I have left the books with the clues in them to the three people I know who would own the crown for the right reasons. All of you must work together to find the prize. The books are numbered and clues in each must be followed in order.

It is essential that you lead the hunt. Your faith has marked you as a man to be trusted. Without you, the others will not be able to achieve their goals. There are three books. One has been sent to you; one to my friend Professor Enoch Parker in Boston; another to Matthew McKittrick, also of Boston. I have enclosed their addresses below:

Go to Enoch first. He is a scholar of the first order who works with an assistant named Alex. I'm sure they will be thrilled to hear from you. They have been hunting for the crown for many years, as has Matt McKittrick. He, too, will be glad to work with you. They will know about you, but I have not told them about each other.

Know that I have chosen you for your faith, your eternal optimism, and your unshakable, undying love. You are a leader, Edward, and I'm sure the others will follow you without question. I trust you, my friend, with my greatest treasure. Find the crown and use it for good works. It is a beautiful relic that deserves a prominent place in the annals of history.

Please beware of my sons. Since I have disowned them, it would not be safe for you to trust them. I have often felt that the crown's curse was played upon me through them, for they have brought me nothing but heartache and misery all these years.

Thank you for your friendship and love, Edward. I hope the Crown of Desire brings you the peace and joy I've never experienced.

With warmest affection, your friend,
Lawrence

Winn stared at the letter for a long moment, studying the names and addresses enclosed, then picked up the book. He opened it and read the baffling inscription within.

Rising from his desk, he paced the study as he tried to decide what to do. He remembered what Philip Anthony had said to him—*We have a lot in common . . .* He shuddered at the thought that he was like the Anthony brothers.

Suddenly, Winn knew what he must do. Lawrence Anthony had been counting on his uncle's help. Now, Winn could do no less than fulfill his request. He would prove to himself that he was not like the brothers. He would assume his uncle's role and lead the quest to find the crown.

Winn went upstairs into his uncle's room and sorted through his personal belongings until he found what he needed. That done, he rang for Arthur and began to pack. He would leave right away.

Five

Alex sat on the sofa in the parlor of her Boston home, staring down at the letter she'd just received. Her hands were trembling and her expression was strained.

"What's wrong, Alexandra?" Felicia Parker asked, seeing the change in her niece. A moment before, they'd been having a lively, animated discussion, and now, after reading a letter she'd just received, she'd become very quiet, almost tense. "Is it bad news from your father?"

Alex glanced quickly at her aunt. Seeing how frail the elderly woman still looked after her lengthy illness, she hurried to set her fears to rest. "No, Aunt Felicia, it's nothing like that."

"Thank heaven. What is it then?"

"Do you remember Papa and I mentioning a gentleman named Lawrence Anthony?" At her aunt's nod of recognition, she continued. "It seems he's died."

"I'm sorry. You cared for him, didn't you?" She could see the shadow of pain in her niece's dark eyes.

"Very much. So did Papa." It was difficult for Alex to think that Lawrence was dead, for he'd always seemed so vital and full of life. "If you'll excuse me, Aunt Felicia, I think I'll go up to my room for a while."

"Of course, dear. Unpleasant news is always such a shock."

Alex made her escape. When she reached her room, she locked the door behind her. It hadn't been the news of Lawrence's death that had sent her in search of privacy. It had been what was contained in the rest of his letter. Sitting on the edge of her bed, Alex reread the letter. She wanted to make sure she hadn't misunderstood.

Excitement and resentment warred within her as she finished reading. *The crown!* Lawrence had had it all these years, and he'd never told them! While they'd been digging in the ruins at Thebes, hoping to find some trace, some clue to its location, the crown had already been in Lawrence's collection.

Though Alex's anger flared, it was quickly tempered. While it was frustrating to know that their years of searching had been in vain, what really mattered was that Lawrence had left a clue to the crown's location. She realized it was perfectly in character for him to have hidden the crown, for he'd always considered solving the riddles of the ancients the greatest of accomplishments. Alex was certain he'd laid out quite a challenge for them, and she could hardly wait to begin the hunt.

She wondered how soon the priest, this Father Bradford, would arrive. Tomorrow wouldn't be soon enough as far as she was concerned. The only trouble was, her father hadn't yet returned from his research trip to

London. She knew she would have to wait until he got back, but as soon as he did, in another two weeks or so, they could be ready to leave.

Alex thought of the priest Lawrence had described in his letter. Father Bradford sounded like a wonderful man, a true man of God. Lawrence had written that they'd been friends for many years, so she was sure he was someone who could be trusted to lead the search.

Glancing down at the letter again, Alex scanned the part about Philip and Robert once more. She'd met Lawrence's sons only one time in London, and her impression of them hadn't been good. There was something disreputable about the pair, though she'd been hard put to say just what it was. Obviously, her instincts had been right since Lawrence had disinherited them. She hoped she would never have to worry about the collector's warning not to trust either of them. If she never saw Philip or Robert again, she'd be happy.

Rising from her bed, Alex locked the letter safely away in her desk. As frustrating as it was, there was nothing more for her to do but wait. She had no doubt that every minute was going to seem like an eternity as she awaited the priest's arrival and her father's return.

"Thank you, Mr. McKittrick. I knew you'd be able to help me." The elderly, elegant Mrs. Carver smiled brightly at the handsome, young bookseller. She'd been desperate for a copy of a rare book, and, as usual, Mr. McKittrick had found it for her.

"It was my pleasure," Matt assured her as he handed her the book. He enjoyed helping his customers find what they wanted. But while he liked owning the bookstore, it was not his first love. The bookstore just provided him with the base he needed to do what he really loved—finding real lost treasures.

"I'll see you next week, that is, if you're going to be here," she remarked with a smile. Matthew McKittrick was a charming, intelligent man, and she looked forward to her visits to his shop. "You are going to be in town, aren't you?"

"I should be," he assured her, knowing of nothing at that particular moment that might call him away. Things had been very quiet lately. Of course, all that could change with one urgent message. He never knew from day-to-day what might come up, and that was the part of treasure-hunting that he really loved.

"Good. I miss you when you leave unexpectedly." She had been patronizing his store regularly since he'd opened it seven years ago, and she knew it wasn't unusual for him to disappear for several weeks at a time without explanation. Whenever she asked him about his trips, he told her he was searching for more books for the store.

"Enjoy your book." Matt was still smiling as he watched her go.

Peace and quiet surrounded Matt, and he was almost glad for the reprieve. Business had been steady all day. He glanced at the clock on the wall and was surprised to find it was almost closing time. Matt was never in a hurry to close the store, though, so he settled in behind the counter to catch up on his paperwork. He was engrossed in reading the day's mail when he heard the door open. Wanting to finish the letter before he looked up, Matt continued to read.

Valerie Stewart Chancellor paused just inside the doorway. A physical ache grew within her as she stared at the man who held her heart. She'd never stopped loving him. It had been weeks since she'd last seen him, and Valerie couldn't believe that she'd stayed away that long. Matt looked more handsome than ever. Her hungry gaze caressed the hard line of his jaw and the broad width of his shoulders. His dark blond hair was sun-streaked now and cut to just above his collar. She remembered well the texture of that hair and how she loved to run her hands through it.

Valerie jerked her thoughts away from memories of the passion-filled nights they'd spent together. Matt haunted her dreams by night and her every waking thought by day. She loved him, and for what seemed like the thousandth time she cursed her own weakness in giving in to her parents' desires.

Valerie's parents had disapproved of Matt and his mysterious, almost nomadic lifestyle, and they'd pressured her to marry someone suitable, someone acceptable, someone who would fit in with their social circle. Loving money and the comforts wealth could bring, she'd given in to their wishes. Today, though, as she stared at Matt, she knew she'd been wrong, terribly wrong. She hoped it wasn't too late. "Hello, Matt."

At the sound of that voice, so well remembered, Matt felt pain mixed with a desperate hope. He looked up sharply and his breath caught as he saw her standing before him. Valerie was as beautiful as ever, and try as he might to deny them, searing old memories besieged him—memories of her smiles and laughter, memories of her lips upon his, memories of her lying naked beneath him, her slender soft body melded to his as she matched him in both passion and desire, memories of her vows of love and devotion only to him, and finally memories of her marriage to another man, a man her parents had chosen. Matt had thought Valerie was everything he'd ever wanted in a woman. He'd thought he loved her. She stood before him now

. . . another man's wife.

"Valerie . . ." Matt spoke her name as he came to his feet, and he was surprised by the casualness of his voice. He'd feared that his tone would betray him.

"I had to see you, Matt." She stepped further inside and closed the door behind her. It was a move designed to create a feeling of intimacy between them. It was a move she hoped he'd welcome.

"I don't understand why. I think we've already said all that needed to be spoken." He tensed as he watched her move toward him.

"I couldn't let things end this way. I had to tell you what you mean to me. I was so foolish to listen to my parents. I love you. You're the only man I want, Matt."

"Valerie, you're only going to make things worse." At that moment Matt was glad the counter was a barrier between them; he wanted her so badly that he wouldn't have trusted himself not to sweep her in his arms and make love to her right there in the store.

"How can things get any worse, Matt? You're the man I love . . ." she told him, tears shining in her eyes.

"You should have thought about that before." He tried to sound hard and indifferent, but it wasn't easy. Just seeing her again set his body on fire. He longed to strip away her clothes right now and bury himself deep within the heat of her body. He wanted to hear her cry out her love for him as he made her his own. But the knowledge of her marriage to another man held him immobile. Never again would he touch her or kiss her. Matt fought the most difficult battle of his life as he denied his desire and forced himself to remain where he was.

"But Matt . . . please, listen to me. You don't understand . . ."

"I understand, Valerie."

"Do you understand that I love you, and only you?"

"You love me as long as it's on your terms," he replied. "You love me as long as there's no sacrifice involved."

"Matt . . ."

"No, Valerie, it's too late. You're another man's wife now." He hardened his heart to her even more.

"I made a terrible mistake when I accepted John's proposal. Don't turn away from me now. Not now. Not when I need you so badly."

"What are you offering me? A sordid night in a room on some back street? Sneaky liaisons when your husband and parents aren't looking? When you left me, you left me with only my honor, and that's the one thing I'm not going to lose. Not even for you, Valerie."

"What we had was special. Don't you understand that I've regretted marrying John every minute since?"

"You got what you wanted, Valerie—a husband who pleases your father. John has money and a brilliant future. He'll always be in town. Whenever your father speaks, he'll jump to attention and obey his every command. I wish the two of you all the best. I'm sorry you're not happy. You'll have a lot of years to think about what might have been."

"Matt, please!" she begged, desperate to make him understand. "Without you, my life is empty. I love you, Matt. We can still be together! Don't be so stubborn!"

"It's too late, Valerie."

"It can't be! Listen to me . . ."

"No, you listen to me." He spoke with finality. "You pledged yourself before God to another man. John's a good man. He deserves more from you. I won't cheat both of us just to satisfy your desires. I wish I didn't love you, but I won't damn myself to the hell of being your illicit lover."

She went pale at his harsh words.

"John's the perfect husband for you. He'll always be at your side. He's successful and rich . . ."

"You know he doesn't mean anything to me!"

"He may not mean anything to you, but he pleases your parents, and that, my dear, matters to you." Matt remembered how her father had come to him at the store and tried to force him to give up his dreams and come to work for him. Matt had refused. He needed to live his life his own way. He needed to be his own man. He couldn't give it all up—not even for Valerie.

"I should have defied my father! It doesn't matter to me that you'll never make a lot of money. It doesn't matter to me that you take those long trips looking for treasures that may or may not exist. I shouldn't have listened to my family! I should have . . ."

"It's over, and it has to stay that way." He cut her off. "You're a married woman now."

"That doesn't stop me from thinking about you, and wanting you, and remembering . . . What we shared was so wonderful . . ." She brazenly approached him, coming around the counter and touching his arm.

"Valerie, you'd better leave." Matt's hands clenched into fists at his sides as he ordered her from his life.

"I know, but Matt, kiss me just one last time . . . please . . ." She tried to loop her arms about his neck and pull him down to her. Her lips were but a breath apart from his. He was tempted, so very tempted, but his honor held fast.

"No," he said, taking her by her upper arm and pushing her away from him, breaking the intimate contact. He steered her to the door. "Good bye, Valerie."

She looked up at him, her desire for him shining in her eyes. "You really mean it . . . You don't want me?"

"Go home to your husband." He opened the door and all but pushed her out.

"I'll always love you, Matt."

The words were in his heart, but he couldn't say them. He wouldn't say them. Though he had nothing else, he still had his honor. She was another man's wife. "Good bye, Valerie."

Matt closed the door, drew the shade, and slid home

the bolt, locking her forever out of his life. He remained standing there, staring at the door, long after she'd gone. Bitterness filled him. He had loved her. He had given his heart to her. He would never be so foolish again.

Finally, Matt turned back to the desk. He felt drained, empty, as he sat down and returned to reading his mail. He was merely going through the motions as he unconsciously ripped open a small package, pulled out the letter within and began to read.

As he read the missive, the pain of Valerie's visit was tempered. The letter was from Lawrence Anthony, and it was about the Crown of Desire. Matt was saddened to learn that the older man was dead, but the news that he'd had the crown and was giving him a chance to join in the hunt to find it thrilled him beyond his wildest dreams. All he had to do was wait until he heard from a priest named Father Bradford. Evidently, Lawrence had trusted this priest implicitly, and because of that, Matt knew he would trust him, too.

The crown. . . . Matt picked up the book written in Lawrence's own hand and studied it, but the odd lines of free verse made little sense to him. He realized that he'd have to bide his time and wait for the good Father to arrive. He hoped it would be soon. He'd been searching for the crown for years and now could hardly wait to begin.

Later, as Matt locked the book and letter away, Valerie slipped back into his thoughts. In that moment, he knew he'd done the right thing by refusing her father's wishes. No matter how hard he might have tried to please her family, he would never have been able to deny his love of adventure and his need to travel the world in search of missing treasures. He didn't love money, and he had no great desire for power. He loved unlocking the secrets of the past and revealing them to future generations. As centered on wealth as Valerie's family were, they would never have understood his need to follow his dream. And that's just what he was going to do.

"I'm looking for Professor Parker," Winn announced to the servant who answered the door at the address Lawrence had provided.

"I'm sorry, Father, but I'm afraid he's not in," Mary, the maid, told him.

"Is his assistant, Alex, here? I'd like to speak with him, if I may?" He noticed the servant's puzzled expression, but paid little attention. The trip to Boston had been long and tedious, and Winn wasn't about to be put off. He'd checked into a hotel as soon as they'd made port and then had immediately set out to locate the professor.

"Alex? Of course, just a minute." The maid scurried away.

"Miss Alex?" she said as she found her mistress in the kitchen talking with the cook about plans for dinner.

"Yes, Mary, what is it?"

"There's a man . . . er, priest, here to see you."

"There is? Did you show him in?" Her pulse quickened. He was here!

"No, ma'am. He's . . ." Mary had not expected her reaction.

"Well, why not?"

"I didn't know . . ."

Alex didn't wait to hear her excuse. Instead, she raced for the front hall, her heart pounding. As she'd suspected, Mary had left the priest waiting on the porch. Alex smoothed her hair into place and straightened her skirts before going out to greet him. No doubt Father Bradford would be an elderly gentleman of about the same age as Lawrence, and she wanted to look her best for him.

"Hello," she said as she opened the door and stepped out.

Winn heard the door open, turned, and found himself staring at the loveliest woman he'd ever seen. On any other woman the short cut of her red-gold tresses would have been outrageous, but on her the style was perfect, emphasizing the beauty of her dark eyes, the delicacy of her features and her high cheekbones. Her creamy complexion was flawless and her slender curves enticing. She was stunning, and it took Winn a minute to gather his wits enough to speak. When he finally did, he was struggling to control his reaction to her. "Yes, hello. I'm sorry to bother you this way. I'd told the servant that I needed to speak with Professor Parker's assistant, Alex."

"I'm Alex," she managed, completely taken aback by this young, handsome priest. She'd thought he would be in his fifties, that he'd look like Lawrence. Instead, he was tall and fantastically good-looking. His hair was black, his eyes green and sparkling with good humor. His features were chiseled and as perfect as a man's dared to be, and his jaw was firm and determined revealing the strength of his character. Her gaze dropped to the collar he wore, a gentle, abiding reminder of his calling, and she swallowed, feeling suddenly ashamed of her wayward thoughts about how handsome he was. He was a priest.

"You're Alex . . ." Winn was shocked. Good Lord! When he'd planned to undertake this trek in his uncle's place, he'd had no idea the Alex mentioned in the letter was a woman.

"Yes, I'm Alexandra Parker, the professor's daughter."

"I'm Father Bradford," he replied. "Lawrence Anthony sent me."

"Father, it is so good to meet you. I'm so glad you're here." Alex graced him with a delighted smile as she tried to ignore how handsome he was. She held out her hand to him in welcome, and she couldn't suppress a shiver when he took it in his firm, warm grip.

"It's nice to meet you, too," Winn took her hand, and the power of his reaction to that simple touch unsettled him. Rationally, he told himself that he was only feeling this way because he'd been without a woman for so long. It had been a long five weeks since his uncle's funeral. He told himself that he would have reacted that way to any woman's touch right then. Still, he released her hand quickly.

Alex invited him inside. "Please, come in so that we can talk. Lawrence's letter arrived last week, and I was hoping I would hear from you soon."

"Thank you." He followed her into the small, comfortable, well-kept house and down the hall into the parlor. Floor-to-ceiling bookcases filled with leather-bound volumes lined the walls of the room. "Impressive collection," he remarked as he paused to read the titles. The majority were historical reference works.

"Father and I love to read. History is our driving passion," Alex told him. "Please, sit down. Would you care for any refreshments?"

"No thank you. I really just needed to meet with the professor. Do you know how soon he'll be back? It's important that I speak with him personally, right away."

"My father's been in London doing research, but he's due to return the end of next week."

"I see. Well, I'll come back then. It will be better if I deal directly with him."

Alex bristled at his dismissive attitude. "Father Bradford, I handle all of my father's correspondence," she said with great dignity and more than a little force. "I'm aware of all his business as I travel with him on most of his trips. I know all about the crown. In fact, Father and I have been looking for it for years."

"It's important we begin the search as soon as possible," Winn explained.

"I agree, and I'm sure my father would, too. The Crown of Desire means too much to him. Can you handle the delay? It wouldn't be right to make the search without him."

"Of course. According to what Lawrence wrote, it's essential that we make the trip together." Winn didn't even consider going without the professor. Though Alex might be very competent, the last thing he wanted to do while playing the priest was travel across the country with a beautiful woman.

"Good. As soon as Papa returns, I'll let you know. I'm sure we can be ready to leave right away."

Winn told her his room number at his hotel. "I'll be waiting to hear from you."

"Father Bradford, my papa's going to be more excited about the possibility of finally finding the crown than I am. I'm looking forward to making the trip."

Winn knew he had to discourage her right then and there from any idea she might have that she was going to accompany them. "I'm afraid your traveling with us will present a problem, Miss Parker. There will be myself, your father, and one other man making the trip, and the traveling conditions may be rather difficult at times."

His arrogant assumption that she was some simpering miss who needed to be pampered set her nerves on edge, and she felt it necessary to make it clear to him right away that her father trusted her completely and accepted her as his equal. She squared her shoulders and her dark eyes flashed as she told him, "You needn't worry about me, Father. I've been working with my father on his archeological digs for quite some time now. I'm used to the hardships. I won't present any problems for you."

Frustrated with her response, but not quite sure how to convince her to stay behind, he decided to let it pass until the professor returned. He stood to go. "In that case, please let me know as soon as you hear from him, and, if there's anything I can do for you in the meantime just send word."

"I will."

She showed him from the house and watched him walk down the path to the street. As her gaze lingered on his tall, dark-clad figure, she thought he moved with exceptional grace and that, unfashionable though his coat might be, it certainly fit his broad, powerful shoulders to perfection.

Philip and Robert checked the address on the note they carried with the address on the house.

"This is it," Robert announced.

"Good. I thought we'd never get here." Philip was relieved that they'd finally reached their destination. The long journey from London had nearly driven him to distraction, and he was glad that they would finally be able to take some action now.

"Neither did I. I just wonder if Bradford's already been here."

"I imagine we're going to find out right now."

"I didn't think I'd ever say this, but your idea to break into Bradford's house was brilliant. We would never have known for sure about the connection between them if we hadn't found that note on his desk."

"It was providential that he left the good professor's address as the place to contact him, should his servants need him for anything."

"And since we have the professor right where we

want him, I think the crown will be ours in very short order."

They shared a satisfied look as they started up the walk to the door. Philip knocked.

"We'd like to speak with Alex, please," Philip told the maid in a cordial tone.

"One moment, I'll find her for you." Mary hurried off to get Alex.

Alex couldn't imagine who'd come to see her, and she hurried out to see who it was. "Philip? Robert?" At the sight of them, she stared aghast. She was horrified that they'd come to her home. They had changed little since she'd met them in London. They still looked jaded and dangerous, and she faced them uneasily.

"Good afternoon, Alex," they greeted her.

"It's been a long time. What brings you to Boston?" She hesitated to invite them inside, remembering Lawrence's words of warning in his letter.

"Business, actually. We were wondering if we might speak to you in private. It won't take long."

"Come in. Have a seat in the parlor."

When they'd settled in, she broached again their reason for coming. "You said you were here on business. What does that have to do with me?"

"Oh, we think you know the answer to that, Alex," Philip said smoothly.

Robert was in no mood to play games. They'd been traveling endlessly, and he was tired. "We're here about the books, Alex. We know you have at least one, and we want it back."

"Books? What books?" She tried to pretend she didn't know what they were talking about.

"This is no time for games," Philip's tone was harsh, angry, and threatening.

"I don't know what you're talking about."

"Perhaps you would prefer that we talk to your father. Where is he, by the way?"

"He's been in London, but is on his way home right now. He's due to return next week."

"I don't think so." Philip's statement was cold as was his calculating smile.

"What do you mean?" She glanced at him, her eyes narrowing in suspicion as the first inkling of real fear stirred in her breast.

"I mean I don't think your father will be back any time soon."

"I don't understand."

"Right now, he's in jail in London," Philip continued. "He was arrested for our father's murder. All the evidence points to him, and he's going to stay locked up until we get what's rightfully ours."

"I don't believe you!"

Robert took the packet of her father's letters from his coat pocket and handed them to her. "Perhaps these will help to explain."

"Read the letters."

She did, and her terror grew. Each letter had been written to one of his close associates begging for help in freeing him from jail. None had been delivered. There was even one written to her.

"Alex, we know you have the books. All we want

is the crown. Father had no right to hide it as he did. It's ours. We're going to make sure we get what's coming to us. Now, you can cooperate or your father's going to pay the price for our father's murder."

Alex saw the true nature of their souls. Her mind raced as she tried to figure a way out of this. Drawing on all the courage she had, she challenged them. "I'll go to London and tell them the truth!"

Philip and Robert both chuckled evilly. "Feel free, my dear, but no one will believe you. You'll just be wasting precious time. The men who gave us those letters are the same ones who hold the key to your father's fate. They aren't going to do anything until they hear from us."

Her moment of valor failed as she realized there was no escape from their treachery. She was trapped.

"What do you want me to do?"

"We want the books."

"There's no way I can get them all."

"Why not?"

"Other people are involved. There's Father Bradford and . . ."

"Father Bradford?" The brothers shared a look.

"Yes, and another man I haven't yet met. I don't even know his name. You're welcome to my book right now if it will free my father from jail, but it won't do you any good by itself. According to Father Bradford, the three books must be used together or the clues won't make sense."

"How soon were you planning to start the search?"

"When I spoke with him the day before yesterday, he was going to wait until my father returned."

"All right. If you want to see your father alive again, contact this Father Bradford right away and tell him you've changed your mind. Tell him that you've heard from your father and that he's going to be delayed in London. Tell him that you've reconsidered and don't want to wait for him to return. Tell him you want to leave immediately."

"And then what?"

"Go find the crown. We'll find ways to keep in touch with you. Just know that we'll be watching you every minute, and we'll know exactly what you're doing." The threat in his words was blatant and heartless.

Alex glared at him as she answered, "I'll remember."

"Good. Very good. Father always said you were bright. I can see now that he was right."

"Remember, Alex, your father's life depends on how well you see this through. Don't let anyone else know we're involved. Once you find the crown and get it to us, we'll see that your father is freed."

"Don't think we're not serious. I'd hate to see your father hang for murder. Wouldn't you?"

"Don't worry," she told them tersely. "I'll get the crown for you."

Alex watched them as they left. She was terrified, but she was also angry. They were the most vile men she'd ever met, and while they did have power over her, if she could find a way to outsmart them without endangering her father, she would do it.

Satisfied that they'd made their point and were on

their way to great riches, Philip and Robert headed back to the hotel where they'd taken a room.

"Alex said a Father Bradford was the one she'd already spoken with, isn't that right?" Robert broached the subject that puzzled him.

"Yes," Philip answered. "Surprising, isn't it, since the real Father Bradford is dead?"

"Perhaps our friend Winn Bradford is trying to claim the crown for himself."

"We're going to have to make sure that doesn't happen. The arrogant bastard . . ."

"After the way he treated us, I'm going to be glad to bring the high and mighty Winn Bradford down."

Six

Winn was surprised to find that the address he'd been given for Matthew McKittrick was a bookstore. He entered the small shop to find it seemingly deserted of people but crammed with books. Books were everywhere, stacked in what looked to be random piles and stuffed in bookcases that ran floor-to-ceiling from one end of the store to the other. The shop was a book-lover's dream.

Glancing at some of the various titles, Winn realized the owner had eclectic tastes. Subjects ran from light fiction to heavy historical reference works. He paged through a few as he waited close by the front desk for someone to come, but when no one appeared right away, he knew he had to do something.

"Is anyone here?" Winn finally called out.

"Be with you in just a minute. I'm in the back putting some books away," came the muffled reply from somewhere in the rear of the store.

Winn wandered down an aisle and paused before a large collection of books on Ancient Egypt. Intrigued, he picked up one that looked particularly interesting.

He was lost in thought, studying the volume when a man spoke from behind him.

"May I help you?" Matt asked as he approached him. He'd just finished shelving the books and had returned to the front to see who'd come in. When he saw the tall man in black standing with his back to him halfway down one aisle, he went to speak to him.

"Hello, I'm looking for Matthew McKittrick. I understand he owns this store," Winn answered, putting the book back and then turning toward him.

"I'm Matt McKittrick, Father. Is there something I can do for you?" His tone was curious. He knew, according to Lawrence's letter, that he was to be contacted by a priest named Father Bradford, but there was no guarantee that this was the man.

Winn eyed McKittrick cautiously, wondering when the surprises connected with the crown would end. First, he'd thought Alex was a man, and now, this. . . . When Winn had pictured a bookseller, he'd imagined someone old and bespectacled. He'd been wrong again. Matt McKittrick looked to be about his own age. He was tall, broad-shouldered and seemed to be quite fit. He looked equal to any challenge they might encounter on the trek to come.

"I'm Father Bradford. Lawrence Anthony gave me your name . . ."

"Of course!" Matt shook his hand in welcome as he smiled. "Lawrence's letter arrived a few days ago. I was wondering how soon I'd hear from you."

"Then you know why I'm here."

"Yes, and I'm ready to leave as soon as you say the

word. I've been looking for the crown ever since I first heard the legend years ago. Finding it will be the most exciting thing I've ever done. I'm honored that Lawrence trusted me and believed in my true motive for wanting it."

"Lawrence was a good judge of character," Winn agreed.

"So how soon do we start? All I have to do is lock up the store and I'm ready to go."

"There is one other person involved. Are you familiar with Professor Parker?"

"I've heard his name mentioned in academic circles, but we've never met. From what I understand, he found the tomb where the crown had originally been buried, only to discover that it had been looted. It must have been a very frustrating dig for him."

"I'm sure it was. The professor is the other member of our party, but he's in London right now and isn't due back for another week or so. As soon as he returns, I'll contact you and we can be on our way."

"I'll be waiting to hear from you. Would you like to see the information I've gathered on the crown? There isn't a lot available, but I've tried to get my hands on everything I could."

"I'd like that. Actually, I know very little about the treasure."

"Give me a minute to close the store, and we'll go upstairs to my rooms."

As soon as Matt had locked the door, he led Winn up a narrow staircase in the back to the three rooms he called home when he was in Boston. His furnishings were genteel yet shabby. It was obvious that he was a man completely unconcerned with creature comforts or impressing people. The rooms were serviceable, but unremarkable. Only his art collection stood out. He had a variety of statues and paintings dating from the biblical times to the present. All were of excellent taste and value, and Winn recognized more than a few as very important works. Matt waved Winn toward a threadbare sofa.

"Have a seat. I'll be right back."

Winn sat down and a moment later, Matt returned with all the information he had on the crown. He sat beside Winn and spread a map out on the table before them.

"This is a map of the Valley of the Kings and the surrounding area near Thebes. From what I've learned reading all the reports on excavations there, the crown should have been recovered by the professor and his assistant Alex several years ago, for they located the actual tomb of the prince and princess. Do you know the crown's history?"

"No. I don't. Lawrence and I were close friends, but we seldom spoke of his collection."

Matt proceeded to tell him about the crown and its curse. "It looks like the curse might have been just part of the legend. From what Lawrence wrote in his letter, he'd had the crown for some time and nothing tragic happened to him."

"Perhaps his sons were his tragedy," Winn remarked. "Did he mention them in your letter?"

"Yes, he did. I've never met them, though. Are they as bad as he implied?"

"They're worse," he answered flatly, hoping the pair had crawled away into the night never to be seen or heard from again, but doubting he would be that lucky. He'd seen the greed in their eyes and knew they wouldn't give up so easily.

"That's too bad."

"They believe the crown should be theirs, and I don't think they're willing to give it up without a fight. I left London right away for I didn't want to give them the chance to follow me."

"Good idea. It's going to be hard enough finding the crown without batting them, too."

"I just wish we could get underway. It's frustrating to sit here and wait."

"I understand."

"Tell me, Matt, is the crown really as valuable as Lawrence estimated?" Winn asked.

"Probably more so. Lawrence never thought of things in terms of money. He always thought of them in terms of historical value. The crown is worth a fortune in both."

"Lawrence was a very special man."

"Exceptional, and I'm sure he's set quite a task for us. As fascinated as he was by the riddles of the ancients, I'm certain finding the crown won't be easy. I'm not sure what the other books say, but mine makes little sense. I've tried working out clues from it, but nothing particularly stood out."

"Once we have all three together, I'm sure we'll be

able to decipher at least the first clue. I've spoken with the professor's daughter, Alexandra, and it was obvious that they are just as enthused about going on this hunt as we are."

"They?"

"Evidently Alex accompanies the professor on all his excavations."

"Do you think it's wise to bring a woman along, Father?" Matt wondered.

"I suggested to her that it might not be comfortable traveling with us, but she argued that she'd been on digs in the Sahara and this could hardly be that difficult. I'm proposing that we wait for her father to return and then discuss it with him."

"So we aren't leaving right away?"

"With any luck at all, we might be able to start by the end of next week."

Matt's expression grew intense as he realized that he might really find the crown this time. "It's not soon enough for me, but then again, tomorrow wouldn't be soon enough as far as I'm concerned."

"Is this a rendering of the crown?" Winn picked up a watercolor painting from among Matt's other papers. It was of a golden crown with a large heart-shaped ruby in the center of the front.

"Yes. I painted that myself after I saw a picture of it on a wall in the ruins near Thebes."

"It's beautiful."

"I know. I hope Lawrence isn't sending us on a wild goose chase. I hope this is the real thing."

"I can't imagine that Lawrence would be less than

serious where a treasure from his personal collection is concerned."

"You're right. Let's just hope the professor comes back early."

"Yes, let's," Winn thought of Philip and Robert and wondered where they were and what they were doing.

Winn breakfasted in the hotel dining room and then returned to his own room to read the paper and bide his time. Being generally a man of action, it tested his patience sorely to sit alone and cool his heels this way as he awaited the professor's return. His mood was not the greatest as he stripped off his priestly garb and donned some of his own clothes. While he had to play the clergyman in public, in the privacy of his room, he was free to be himself. He had to admit that it felt good to be just Winn Bradford for a few minutes. Settling in comfortably in a chair at the window, Winn began to go through the Boston newspaper.

He'd been reading for quite a while when a knock sounded at his door. The interruption surprised him. He hadn't expected to hear from anyone this soon. He was glad for the diversion, though, and quickly opened the door. Winn was startled to find Alex standing before him, looking more lovely than he remembered in a dark green gown that set off her hair color to a fiery splendor. "Miss Parker?"

"Hello, Father Bradford." Alex almost stumbled over her words as she stared up at him. She'd thought him attractive before, but now, seeing him dressed in regular clothes, she found him utterly magnificent. The fine, white linen shirt he wore fit his broad shoulders perfectly. Partially unbuttoned at the collar, the shirt was open low enough to reveal the strong, tanned column of his throat, and Alex had to force herself to look up and meet his eyes. His expression was reserved, yet interested, and she was glad he was unaware of her dilemma. "I was wondering if I could speak to you for a moment?"

"Of course . . ." Winn started to ask her into his room, then he stopped, perplexed. As much as he would have liked to have this beautiful young woman behind closed doors, he knew he couldn't do it, not and maintain his dignity. "Give me a minute, and we'll go downstairs to the lobby. It would be better for us to talk there."

"Thank you." She was grateful that he had time for her.

Winn closed the door and quickly began to change back into Father Bradford. Two months before he would have swept her into his arms and, ultimately, into his bed. Now, he was going to escort her to a very public lobby so they could converse without anyone suspecting their motives. Winn smiled wryly at his own predicament, and he hoped his uncle was happy. His collar in place, Winn donned his dark coat, then got his key. He emerged from the room, looking very much the priest, the noble rakehell in his heart successfully restrained by the rein of his promise of good intentions.

"Ready?" he asked as he found her waiting for him.

"Yes," Alex answered, relieved that he looked once more the man of authority, and not the man who set her pulse racing. She knew it was wrong to feel that way about him, and she was glad that he was once more distanced from her in his clerical garb.

Winn locked the door behind him, then escorted her down the hall toward the main staircase. The subtle, yet deliciously feminine scent of her perfume came to him as he walked by her side, stirring his long-denied male instincts. His baser urges prodded him to reach out and touch her. He told himself "NO." His instincts argued that he should play the gentleman and take her arm or at the very least put a guiding, possessive hand at her waist. He held himself back.

By pure force of will, Winn directed himself to concentrate on the real reason for her visit. She wasn't there to see Lord Winston Bradford. She was there to see *Father* Bradford, and no doubt her visit was about the crown. Still, he couldn't help but admire the graceful way she moved. He was glad when they reached the lobby. They sat in two chairs in a quiet corner away from the main desk.

"Is something wrong, Miss Parker?"

"Please, call me Alex, Father."

"All right, Alex. It will be my pleasure. But tell me what brought you here? Is your father back already?"

"No, and that's why I had to come to see you. I received a letter from him today," she began, struggling to appear calm. She had always made it a point to speak the truth. Honesty was a way of life for her, and lying to the priest right now was one of the most difficult things she'd ever had to do. The only thing that gave her the will to follow through was knowing that her father's life hung in the balance. She had to be convincing in her story. She had to make Father Bradford believe she was telling the truth.

"Good news, I hope?"

"I wish it were. The trouble is, he's been delayed and won't be back for at least another month."

Winn frowned. "I see."

"Father Bradford," she began again, bolstering herself with the knowledge that at least a part of what she was saying was true. "I know my father wouldn't want to risk something happening to the crown while we were waiting on him. So, if you have no objection, I think we should go ahead on the trip without my father. I can be ready to leave tomorrow." Alex looked Winn in the eye as she spoke.

"I appreciate your enthusiasm, but I'm not sure going without your father is a good idea. Perhaps it would be better to wait for him."

"There's no need," she insisted, struggling to hide her desperation. "I have the book, and I'm certainly as well-versed in the crown's history as my father."

"I have no doubt that you're very accomplished in your studies. I'm more concerned with the propriety of the situation. You would be a single, young woman traveling with two men who are not related to you. It might not serve you well to undertake such an adventure."

"Father Bradford, I hardly think my reputation will suffer from being in your company, and, as far as the other man traveling with us goes, you can act as my chaperone. Lawrence did say you were completely trustworthy and the best, most honorable man he'd ever known. Was he wrong?" she challenged. She felt her chance to save her father was slipping away, and she had to do something to convince him to take her along.

"No, no, of course not. I was just thinking of the awkwardness of the arrangements and of the risk to your reputation. We have no idea where Lawrence's clues might lead us, and it might prove difficult." Winn tried to sound pleasant, but he thought he'd never met a more exasperating female. Then again, he'd never dealt with a woman in his present 'occupation' before either. He reminded himself that he could not think of Alex as a beautiful, desirable woman, that he was going to have to deal with her completely on an intellectual level. Having never denied himself anything, he wondered if his uncle was watching him now from above and getting a laugh out of his dilemma. He didn't doubt it, knowing his uncle's sense of humor and how he'd always been after Winn to change his ways.

"You may be right, but I'm not afraid of hardship, especially not when the prize is so valuable. We must think of the crown."

Alex waited for him to say something. When he didn't speak right away and his expression remained strained, she reached out and put her hand on his arm to reassure him.

"This means a lot to me, and to my father. I promise I won't get in your way or cause you any trouble. I just want to find the crown as quickly as possible."

She lifted her gaze to his, wanting him to see in her eyes the earnestness of her plea. There was no deception in her words this time.

The touch of her hand on his arm added fuel to the heat that was already burning within Winn, and as her gaze met his, he felt as if time were standing still. Without conscious thought, he covered her hand with his. It felt small, delicate and soft. "I understand, and I'm sure Matt feels the same way you do."

"Then you have no objection if I go?" She positively glowed with excitement as she drew away from him.

"No. It's all right." Winn had a hundred objections, but he was so entranced by her smile that he voiced none of them.

"We should leave right away. There's no need to delay any longer."

He thought of Philip and Robert again, remembering Lawrence's strong warning against the pair. The sooner they left Boston, the better it would be for everyone concerned. "The other man making the trip is Matthew McKittrick. Lawrence gave him the other book. He'll be searching for the crown with us."

"I've never met him. Would you like to bring Mr. McKittrick to my house tonight so that we can discuss exactly what we're going to do?"

"That would be good."

"Shall we say 7:00 P.M.?"

"We'll be there."

* * *

They gathered at the Parker house that evening, and Winn quickly made the introductions.

"Alexandra Parker, this is Matt McKittrick. Matt, this is Miss Parker."

"Please, both of you call me Alex," she told them with a smile as she extended her hand to Matt. "There's no reason for us to be so formal."

Matt smiled as he took her hand in a warm grip. "And I'm Matt. What should we call you, Father? We're going to be in pretty close company for the next month or so."

Something in Matt's familiar tone as he spoke to Alex irritated Winn. "Winston's my first name, but my friends call me Winn," he answered a little tersely, wondering how soon Matt was going to let go of Alex's hand. He was relieved when he finally did.

Alex looked at Winn as she moved away from Matt. "Winn . . . what an unusual name." As she said it, she thought how very well it suited him. He was a strong, intelligent man, and she doubted he lost very often.

"It's a family name." He tried not to think about how wonderful his name sounded when she said it. He forced his attention to the reason for their being here. "Shall we take a look at the books? If we're leaving tomorrow, we'd better find out where we're going."

"This is my book— #1," Alex handed it to him. Winn opened it and began to read out loud. "'Travel west to where wide rivers flow, two joining to become as one.' "

"Since we have no idea where Lawrence hid the

crown, it could apply to just about any city west of Boston," Alex broke in.

" 'So two hearts should join together—one in name and purpose—till all is done.

Seek first the man from France to lead, don't be afraid to follow your dreams.

Be not fooled by appearances. Sometimes, all is not what it seems.

Let not your desire rule your soul, instead be ruled by the faith

That a good act done with a gentle heart is a treasure that will open heaven's gate.' "

He finished reading and glanced up at the other two. "What do you think?"

"Let's take look at a map," Matt said as he unrolled the one he'd brought along with him on Alex's dining-room table.

"First, we're looking for rivers, then for anything French," Alex remarked, poring over the map, shoulder-to-shoulder with Matt and Winn.

"There's the Ohio, the Mississippi, the Missouri, and God knows how many others," Matt remarked, tracing the course of each waterway.

"What about 'the good man from France'?" Alex wondered aloud as her gaze traced the length of the Mississippi. Then she saw it. "It's St. Louis! Look, the Missouri River joins the Mississippi just north of the city. That has to be it!"

"What's the fastest way there?" Winn asked.

"The train. Depending on connections, we should

be able to make the trip in a little over a week," Matt answered.

"I'll get the tickets first thing in the morning."

They shared a satisfied look as they contemplated the journey they were about to begin.

"It's hard to believe we're really going to find the crown." Matt's eyes were shining with eagerness.

"I know. Father and I have been looking for it for years, and now . . ." Alex was instantly sorry she'd brought up her father. She hadn't wanted to think about his being in jail and the danger he faced or about the Anthony brothers and their horrible blackmail. She felt a sting of guilt as she wondered if Father Winn and Matt would ever forgive her for what she would ultimately have to do.

Winn mistook the touch of sadness in her words as regret that her father wasn't traveling with them. "If you'd rather wait for your father to accompany us, we can," Winn offered one last time.

"No. I don't want to wait. There's no telling how soon he'll be back, and we've delayed far too long already. Let's find the crown."

"All right, Father Winn. Since you're in charge of this expedition, what do you plan to do with the crown when we find it? Did Lawrence leave any instructions about what he wanted done?" They couldn't cut it up in three equal pieces, and Matt certainly didn't want to sell it.

"Of everyone he knew, Lawrence trusted the three of us the most. I'm sure he believed that we'd make the right decision when the time came."

"I want the crown preserved, somewhere safe. Preferably a museum of some repute that will give it the honor it's due," Matt said. "It's been lost for so long. Its glory needs to be seen by the public."

"What about you, Alex?" Winn asked.

"I think the crown is one of the most beautiful treasures ever created by man, and I think it should be cherished as such. There are so many stories of tragedy surrounding it. I just hope that after we find it, there will be no more sorrow attached to it. Only joy and happiness."

"Father? What's your interest in the crown? Why are you here?"

"I'm here because Lawrence had great faith in me. He believed I would do what was right. When the time comes, I hope I will." Winn didn't doubt that he'd do the right thing about the treasure. The promise of money wasn't what had drawn him on this trek—keeping the crown from the Anthonys was. His biggest concern right now was resisting the temptation Alex would be during the long days and nights of intimate travel ahead. There was no telling where this search would lead them, and he hoped he had enough fortitude to play his role with honor. He was doing this for his uncle. He would not shame him.

"We'll honor Lawrence's memory when we discover the crown. I'm sure he'd be pleased to know that he chose well when he picked us to follow his clues," Matt said.

"Yes, we can honor him with the crown . . ." Alex replied a little distractedly, harboring her terrible secret, haunted by the knowledge that she was going to betray Father Winn and Matt. She knew the crown was cursed, and she wondered, now, if she'd somehow been already touched by its evil.

"I'll contact both of you in the morning just as soon as I find out about the train schedules," Winn told them as they prepared to call it a night.

"I'll be waiting to hear from you," Alex said as she walked them to the door.

They said their good nights, and Winn and Matt left the house. She watched until they were out of sight, then turned back inside, and closed the door.

Alone at last, Alex fixed herself a cup of hot tea and sat in the parlor to drink it. Her mood swung between elation and despair as the thought of Philip and Robert and their threat. Philip had said they'd be in touch with her, but if she was leaving with Winn and Matt tomorrow for St. Louis, she wondered how she could get word to them of their destination.

Alex didn't have long to wonder. After finishing her tea, she went upstairs to bed. As she let herself into her bedroom, a low, hushed man's voice came to her out of the darkness, frightening her nearly out of her wits.

"So, you met with Bradford tonight, did you?"

"What are you doing here?!" she gasped, her hand going to her throat as she fought down the terror.

"I told you we'd be watching you."

"I should scream for help!"

"You want to see your father alive again, don't you?" Philip stepped forward out of the shadows. He was smiling and confident as he crossed the room toward her. Ever since he and Robert had dared to break into Bradford's house, he'd become more and more bold in his thinking and planning. He was in complete control of the situation, and of her, and he reveled in the power.

"You . . . You're vile . . ," she seethed, wishing she were a man, wishing she had the power to wipe the smug expression from his face. She hated this man and his brother, and some day she would see that they got what was coming to them. For now, though, she was forced to do as he bid. The reality of it left her frustrated and furious.

"Has anyone ever told you that you're beautiful when you're angry?" Philip taunted. He lifted one hand to caress her cheek.

Alex wasn't about to suffer his filthy hands upon her, and she slapped his hands away. "Don't touch me! Don't ever touch me!"

Philip chuckled. "I wouldn't dream of ruining our perfect working relationship, my dear. But should you ever change your mind, I'll be more than willing to oblige."

"It'll never happen."

"We'll see," he murmured with a smile. "Now, what are your plans? It's important you let me know what you're doing. I wouldn't want us to become separated. Why, something might just happen to your precious father in prison if we didn't know where you were, and we wouldn't want that to happen, would we?"

"You don't have to worry, Philip," she said tightly.

"I have every intention of saving my father from you."

"Then tell me what this meeting was about tonight. I want to know everything." His voice was cold.

She quickly related everything she could remember. "According to the first book of clues, Father Bradford, Matt McKittrick, and I have to go to St. Louis. I don't know what's there or why. I suppose we'll find out once we arrive."

"St. Louis, eh?" He frowned. "Well done, my dear. Robert and I will be keeping track. Don't think you can elude us."

"Don't worry. I'm not going to endanger my father's life."

He started to leave the way he'd come, through her bedroom window, then he turned back to say one last thing. "Remember, Alex, Bradford and McKittrick can't help you. Only Robert and I can save your father. We'll be keeping an eye on you. You'll never know when we're near. So be very careful for we'll know your every move."

Alex said nothing more, but waited until he'd climbed from the window. When he was out of her room, she quickly slammed the window shut and locked it. She was shuddering uncontrollably as she drew the drapes. Unable in her bedroom to quell the feeling that Philip was still nearby, watching her, haunting her with the power he held over her, she fled the room and spent the night, sleeping fitfully on the sofa in her father's study.

Seven

Winn sat on the hard wooden bench in the train station and tried to ignore the heat, the smell, and the crowd. They'd been traveling for four days, and he was seriously wondering about the state of his sanity when he'd convinced himself to take this trek. He ached all over from being jarred by the less than comfortable train cars, his collar was tight, and he longed for a hot bath, clean, normal clothes, a bottle of brandy, a willing woman, and the peace and quiet of his London townhouse.

Reflecting back, Winn knew he'd decided to search for the crown because he'd believe it was what his uncle would have done. But with each passing mile, he was discovering more and more that he was nothing like his uncle. Edward Bradford had been a kind, considerate man. Winn was finding that he fell far short of his uncle's genuine goodness, no matter what his uncle had told him on his death bed. His Uncle Edward might have believed him to be a good man, but Winn was beginning to have serious doubts.

It had all started that first day on the train. People saw his collar and came up to him. They introduced themselves and then would immediately begin pouring out their hearts to him. Winn had been taken aback by all the attention he'd received. It wasn't that he didn't want to listen or help. He'd consoled and sympathized when he could, but mostly, he'd just sat and listened. Winn wondered how priests were trained to deal with this outpouring of emotion. He wondered, too, if the many blessings he'd bestowed upon the other travelers really counted. Deep in his heart he hoped they did. The people seemed so desperate to believe that he could somehow help them just by uttering a few words over them, that he wanted to believe he did carry some weight with God, however small.

"Father?"

A woman's voice dragged him from his thoughts, and Winn glanced up to see a cherubic white-haired lady standing before him.

"Yes, ma'am?" He started to rise.

"No, don't get up. I just wanted you to have these cookies," she said, pressing a small box into his hands.

"You're looking a little tired, Father, so maybe they'll help."

"Why, thank you, Mrs. . . .?"

"Wilson, Father. Margaret Wilson." She was beaming as he opened the box.

"I'm Father Bradford. Bless you, Mrs. Wilson. These cookies are just what I need." They did look delicious.

"Oh, good. My train's about ready to leave, so I have to go, Father."

"You have a safe trip."

"Thanks, Father Bradford. You, too." She was smiling as she moved off to catch her train. She thought him the handsomest priest she'd ever met, and her heart was light as she hurried away.

"You're a very nice man," Alex said, giving him a soft smile. She'd been sitting quietly beside him for quite a while and had been watching him with those who came to speak to him.

"Thank you," was all he answered, but he wondered what she'd think of him if she knew what a fraud he was. "Here, have a cookie." He held out the box to her.

"Does this happen to you all the time? People coming up to you and imposing on you this way?" she asked as she took one and bit into it. "Ummm, this is good."

"I don't think of it as imposing," he answered, taking a bite of a cookie of his own, though in truth he felt terribly uncomfortable and awkward giving blessings in public. He wondered if there was a course in blessings that priests were required to take when they were in the seminary. "If I can help one person, if I can change one heart, if I can brighten someone's day just a little, then it will have been worth it." He surprised himself by actually believing what he'd said.

A gentle glow shone in Alex's dark eyes. "You're very special, you know. There aren't many men like you."

Winn gazed at her, entranced. She was lovely, and he had the greatest urge to take her in his arms. Her mouth was soft and infinitely kissable, and he wondered how she would taste . . . sweet, delicious. . . . He amended his earlier wish for brandy and a willing woman. He still wanted his fine brandy, but it wasn't just any woman he wanted right then, it was Alex . . .

He quickly ate the rest of his cookie and looked away. He wondered what she'd think if she knew his thoughts. "I'm really no different from most men."

"Oh, yes, you are. You're a gentleman above all else, and then to have dedicated your life to God and the church . . . That sets you apart. You're a man to be admired."

He ached under her praise, knowing she would soon change her opinion of him if she knew the truth. Still, he told himself quickly that he wasn't really all that bad, for his motives were pure. He wasn't carrying off this deception for his own personal gain. He was doing it because it was what his uncle would have done. According to Lawrence's letter, his uncle's faith would serve them well on the hunt. It was necessary for him to travel as a priest. He would do it, no matter how difficult it became. Hadn't his uncle told him he needed more discipline in his life? Well, it didn't get much more disciplined than this.

Alex's nearness coupled with the suddenly suffocating heat of the station soon closed in on him. Winn knew it could be hours before their train finally showed up. It had been due in at ten that morning, and here it was already three in the afternoon. The station master had told them there was trouble up the line, and though they understood the necessity of the delay, it didn't make the wait any easier. They wanted to get to St. Louis.

"I think I'll go outside for a while," Winn told Alex and Matt.

"We'll stay in here, just in case there's any word," Matt said. He'd been reading as they'd waited for news of their connection, but even as he'd concentrated on his book, it had been impossible not to notice all the people who'd approached Father Winn to speak with him about their personal troubles. He wondered what would make a man like Bradford take up the collar. He guessed the calling had to have been strong and unwavering, and he admired him for his dedication. He doubted that he could handle it.

Giving the cookies to Alex and Matt, Winn left the station and wandered away from the tracks. He saw a bench a short distance off facing away from the station beneath a shade tree, and he headed toward it, wanting to relax and enjoy the fresh breeze.

"Father?"

Winn almost groaned out loud. All he'd wanted were a few minutes alone . . . a few minutes of peace . . . just a little time to himself. "Yes?"

He looked around to see a young boy of maybe eleven looking up at him with a very serious expression. The youth obviously hadn't bathed or combed his hair in quite some time, and his clothes were ill-kempt and shabby.

"I was wonderin' . . . Could I talk to you for a minute? In private like?"

Winn could tell it had taken a major effort for the

boy to come up to him. "Well . . ." He was hoping to put him off, but when he saw the flicker of suspicion and doubt in the boy's eyes, he couldn't refuse him. "What do you say we go sit on that bench over there? It looks nice and cool."

"Sure, Father."

He led the boy to a bench.

The boy started talking the minute they'd sat down. "My name's Bobby, Father, and I want to tell you up front that I ain't Catholic."

"I see," Winn was perplexed. If the child wasn't Catholic, why did he want to talk to him? "What can I do for you?"

"Well, Father . . ."

"Father Bradford," he corrected himself and then went on in a combination of nervousness and bravado. "Is it true that if I did somethin' real bad, you could forgive me for it?"

"My name's Bradford."

Winn stared at the child, wondering why someone his age would be worrying about doing bad things. He was little more than a baby. "Well, it depends," he hedged, wracking his brain, trying to remember everything he'd been taught about confession in school. It had been a very long time since he'd been in a confessional.

"On what?" Bobby's eyes narrowed as he studied the man he thought was close to God.

"On whether the person is truly sorry for the things he's done."

"Oh, I'm sorry all right. But Father, I just needed

to know that you could forgive stuff . . . Big stuff, like even murder."

Murder? Winn turned a piercing gaze on him. "Yes, even murder can be forgiven, if one is truly sorry for his actions and repents."

Bobby had been holding his breath while he'd waited for his answer, and he let it out audibly when he replied. "Father, even if I ain't Catholic, will your forgivin' work on me?"

"Forgiveness comes from God, not from me. I'm only his instrument here on Earth."

Bobby's gaze was intense as it met Winn's, and Winn felt as if the child could almost see into his soul. "Father, I did some bad things . . ."

"Do you want to talk about them?"

"Well, I ain't really sorry for some of what I done. My old man, he used to beat me. He'd get all liquored up and come home and beat up on me and my ma."

"I'm sorry."

"Yeah, so am I. But Father, I shouldn't have done it, but I ran away. I couldn't take it no more, so I hopped a train and here I am."

"How long have you been gone?" Winn saw the despair and loneliness the boy had been trying so hard to hide.

"Almost a month, and I been doin' all right. I'm eating pretty regular, and all, but you know . . .". He lifted pain-filled eyes to the priest. "I didn't tell my ma good-bye. I just snuck off in the middle of the night. I miss her, Father. I miss her bad. I worry about her, and I know she's worrying about me, and I don't want her to worry no more."

Winn heard the agony in his voice and understood his struggle. "You're on the verge of manhood, you know. You've proven yourself intelligent and resourceful by handling yourself so well around here. Can you read?"

"I went to school for a little while, but I ain't too good at it. I had to stop going and earn some money to help my ma. I got two little brothers and a sister."

"Here's what I want you to do." The boy had suffered more abuse in his few years than Winn had known in his life. He thought of the boy's poor mother trapped in a marriage to a drunken, vicious man, and he wondered how he could help them.

The boy listened raptly as the priest spoke.

"I want you to go home to your mother. There is no one in the world who loves you more than she does. Things won't be easy, but at least you'll be together. Find the parish nearest your home, and tell the priest there that I sent you to him. Tell him your problem and ask for help. Have him talk to your father."

Bobby looked frightened. "What if it only makes him mad?"

"Does your mother have any relatives?"

"I got an uncle who owns a farm."

"Tell your mother to contact your uncle and take you and your brothers and sister and go live with him. If your father refuses to get better, you have to get away from him."

Bobby brightened considerably at the thought. He

knew how miserable his mother was, and he'd been hoping for some way to escape from his father. "Can you forgive me, Father, for running away and leaving my ma all alone?" he asked.

Winn touched the boy's shoulder, then his head. "Your sins are forgiven, Bobby. Go and sin no more. You'll be the man of the house now. Remember to be kind." He pronounced the blessing over him solemnly and with great feeling. "Come with me."

"Where we going?"

"We're going to buy you a ticket home. There'll be no more hitching rides on trains for you. I want to make sure you get home to your mother safely."

Bobby gazed up at him with wide, worshipful eyes. This man had worked a miracle. He was sending him home to his mother, and he was paying his way. "I'll send you the money for the ticket when I get it."

"No," Winn stopped and turned to look down at him. "I'm not worried about the money."

"But I don't like owing people, Father."

"Then the way I want you to pay me back is to go home and succeed. I want you to work hard and take care of your mother and your sister and brothers. I want you to study hard and learn how to read. Then, when you are making some money of your own and feel that you want to pay me back, I want you to take that sum and use it to do good. Pass along the goodness to others, and it will multiply."

Bobby blinked as he stared up at him. He saw the earnestness in Winn's eyes and believed every word he said. "I'll do it, Father. I'll make you proud of me."

"Good boy, Bobby." Winn clamped a hand on his shoulder as they went to the ticket window. "Where's home, Bobby?"

"Pittsburgh."

"I want a ticket to Pittsburgh, please. And how soon will the boy be able to leave?"

The agent told him within the hour, and he bought the ticket and handed it to the boy, then gave him a few dollars to help him on the trip. "Remember what you promised."

"I won't forget, Father. Thanks!"

Then in a totally unexpected move, Bobby threw his arms around Winn and hugged him tight. He'd been afraid to approach the priest in the beginning, but now he knew it was the smartest thing he'd ever done in his life. He knew what he was going to do. As soon as he gathered up his things from where he'd stashed them, he was going home to his ma. He'd missed her and could hardly wait to see her again.

"You're welcome, Bobby. Good luck, and Bobby?"

"Yes, sir?"

"Pray. Always pray. When things look bad, rely on God to get you through."

"God was the one who told me to talk to you. He's pretty smart huh?"

"He's very smart."

"I gotta go get my stuff. Will I see you again before I go?"

"If our train doesn't come, you will."

"I'll hurry."

They parted company then, and Winn watched the boy hurry away.

"You're wonderful." Alex's voice cut through Winn's thoughts as he waved to the boy.

Winn flushed at her praise. "How long have you been listening?"

"Long enough. He sounds like a good boy."

"He is, and with any luck at all, he'll make it. It's not going to be easy, but I think he's smart enough and determined enough to do it."

"With you praying for him, how can he lose? Matt thought we should get something to eat, so I came to get you. There's a small restaurant just down the street."

As Alex walked by Winn's side to where Matt was waiting for them, she thought of how safe and secure she felt in his presence. There was something about him, a deep, abiding strength, that inspired trust and confidence. She wondered why the men she met never made her feel this way. She smiled at Matt. He was a handsome man, too, and brilliant, but there was something special about Father Winn that touched her heart.

"So you're going to join us?" Matt asked Winn as they walked up.

"Yes, let's get something to eat. At the rate we're going, we could be here for quite some time."

Winn watched in helpless frustration as Matt took Alex's arm and guided her ahead of him toward the restaurant a short walk away. He struggled to keep his expression calm as he watched the gentle sway of her hips and listened to the sound of her laughter in response to something clever that Matt had said.

Winn wanted to be the one walking beside Alex, making small talk with her. He resented the fact that Matt could do it so easily, while he had to hold himself at bay. As he began to wallow in his resentment, he thought of his uncle. What he really wanted to do was find the crown for his uncle's sake and see it properly handled. As soon as that was done, he could go back to his old life with his old friends and the gambling and the drinking.

It surprised him that the thought of his old life now held no appeal. It wasn't women and drink he wanted, it was Alex. He stifled a sigh of exasperation and told himself he was just feeling this way because he'd been behaving himself for so long. It was good for him to lead a moral life. He just hoped when this was all over Alex would speak to him.

St. Louis was one of the country's biggest ports with over 170 steamboats lined up along the riverfront.

They'd arrived early in the morning and had taken rooms at the Planter's House Hotel. They'd all suffered during their days on the trains and were eager to relax for a while. Winn and Matt shared a room that connected to Alex's.

Alex felt as if she were in seventh heaven as she took full advantage of the lush accommodations. She enjoyed a hot bath and washed her hair, then napped on the soft comfort of the bed and its clean sheets. She hadn't realized how exhausted she was until she'd lain down. The minute her head hit the pillow, she was lost. Only the noise of knocking on the connecting door several hours later saved her from sleeping straight through into the night.

"Alex?" a muffled voice called through the door.

"I'll be right there," she answered sleepily as she got up. She'd been napping in her chemise and she quickly threw on her wrapper before opening the door. "Sorry it took me so long, I must have been more tired than I realized."

Alex looked up, expecting Matt. To her surprise, Winn was the one waiting at the door, and she felt suddenly very self-conscious about her state of near undress, suddenly completely aware of herself as a woman and of him as a man. His shoulders so broad, his waist lean. His smile . . . oh, that smile, and his eyes seemed darker somehow as if at that moment, they held the secrets of eternity. She clutched her dressing gown more closely about her. "Oh . . . Father . . . I'm sorry . . ."

Alex's state of dress caught Winn off-guard, and before he could stop himself, his gaze had raked boldly over her. Sensual awareness throbbed to life within him. She looked absolutely beautiful with her sleep-flushed cheeks and her burnished tumble of curls. Though the wrapper covered her sedately, the fabric clung sweetly to the soft curves of her breasts and hips. He wanted to strip it from her and taste her charms. Instead, Winn hauled himself up short and repeated the oft-told lie to himself that denying his baser instincts was good for him. He told himself discipline was good for his soul and built character. He also told himself that if Alex had been the woman in his bed that last night at Merryfield, he might still be there. Winn took stern control of his less-than-honorable thoughts.

"Matt and I agree that we need to go over the book one more time," he managed to speak in a calm voice that betrayed nothing of his inner turmoil.

"Of course. Just give me a minute to put on something suitable." She was stumbling over her words, though she wasn't sure why. Heaven knows they'd been together almost constantly since they left Boston. She rationalized that her thoughts were a bit muddled because she'd been so sound asleep.

Alex closed the door and quickly pulled on a gown, stockings and shoes. She ran her brush through her hair and then opened the door to let the two of them in. They brought the chairs from the other room and gathered around a small table.

"Winn and I both agree that the whole clue has something to do with the church." Matt reread the poem. "With both saints and Heaven's gate mentioned there must be a connection. But what?"

"Why don't you and I split up and make some inquiries around town? We can meet back here this afternoon and see what we've found."

"Fine. I'll start with the churches," Matt said. "Alex, do you want to go with me?"

"I'll take Alex with me," Winn said quickly, almost possessively. "We'll check out cemeteries, and convents and whatever else there might be."

"I'll see you later then." Matt left the room.

"All set?" Winn asked Alex when they were alone.

"Yes. I'm so excited. This is our first real step toward finding the crown. With any amount of luck at all, we could get what we need and be on our way to the second clue today."

"You're definitely an optimist."

"I suppose I am. And knowing Lawrence as I did, I'm sure this isn't going to be easy. His riddles are sure to mean more than just what they say on paper. There's something hidden in this that we haven't yet figured out. It's Lawrence's way. He always wanted to see the unseeable and understand the inscrutable."

"You knew Lawrence well?" Winn asked as they made their way from the hotel.

"He and my father were very close. I'm sure Papa's going to be sorry he missed this trip." She knew that was true. Especially since she knew where he was.

"You look sad all of a sudden, are you all right? Is there something troubling you?"

"I'm fine. I was just thinking of how much Papa would have enjoyed being with us."

"He'll be proud of you for holding up his end of the bargain."

"I hope so. I hope when all this is over we'll all believe we did the right thing."

"I'm sure we will. It's what Lawrence wanted."

Alex fell silent as she thought again of Philip and Robert. She suppressed a shiver as she imagined them here, somewhere close by, watching her now with Father Winn. She wished there were some way she could thwart them, but as long as her father's life was in their hands, she would have to play their game.

Winn and Alex hired a carriage and directed the driver to take them around town to see the sights. They'd been driving for over an hour when they rode past a tall, wrought-iron fence that surrounded a churchlike building.

"Wait. Driver, what is this place?"

"This is the Convent of the Sacred Heart," he explained, reining in before the open double gate that was the entrance to the grounds.

"Winn, look!" Alex gripped his arm in excitement as she stared up at the building. Carved in stone over the main entrance was the symbol of the Sacred Heart. "This must be it!"

"You could be right," Winn agreed as he surveyed the grounds, the three-story brick building that looked a bit rundown, and the graveyard located a short distance beyond the building. The place looked almost deserted except for one lone, black-clad woman making her way through the cemetery. The convent seemed to match Lawrence's clues, but if what Alex had said about the collector's love for difficult riddles proved true, there might very well be another place even more appropriate to their quest.

Winn directed the driver back to their hotel, and they returned to their rooms to await Matt. It was near dark when Matt finally came back from his own explorations of the town.

"Any luck?" Winn asked.

"No. I had no luck at all. What about you?"

"We think we found it, Matt!" Alex quickly told him about the convent.

"So, what do we do now?"

"We'll have to make an appointment to speak with the mother superior. If we're on the right track, she should be the one who's able to help us."

"There's still one thing bothering me, though," Matt said.

"What's that?"

"The line in the clue 'two hearts should join together—one in name and purpose—till all is done . . .' What does that mean?"

"I wish Lawrence were here now so he could explain it. He wouldn't have put it in there for no reason. Everything he wrote pertains to claiming the crown. He wasn't a man who wasted words or effort. Everything in the poem is relevant, one way or another," Alex said.

Winn had been dreading this moment. Since he'd first read the line in Boston, he'd been trying to figure out exactly what Lawrence had meant, and in all that time he'd come up with only one viable solution. He didn't like it, but it seemed the only way to satisfy the riddle. "Before we go to the convent to speak to the mother superior, I think we're going to have to make a few changes."

"You have an idea of what he meant?" Alex asked quickly.

"What did you have in mind?" Matt asked, frowning as he tried to imagine what was on Winn's mind.

"There seems to be only one way to satisfy the riddle. The only logical thing is for the two of you to marry."

"What?!" Alex and Matt both reacted in shock.

"Two hearts should join together—one in name . . ." Winn quoted.

"But that's ridiculous!" Matt protested.

"It may be, but there's no way I can marry Alex, Matt," Winn pointed out logically. "So, if you want to find the crown, it has to be you."

"Marriage?" Alex put in, still reeling from the logic of Winn's conclusion.

"It's the only way, unless you've got another idea. I'm more than willing to listen."

Both Matt and Alex remained silent.

"I can perform the ceremony today, and . . ." Matt and Alex exchanged looks. "Today?"

"If I marry you tonight, then I'll be able to introduce you as man and wife at the convent. *Two hearts should join together—one in name and purpose—till all is done*. . . . As soon as we find the crown, we can have the union annulled. It will be a marriage in name only, you realize." He added quickly, suddenly perturbed by the thought of Matt having Alex all to himself—as his wife. There were lines that had to be drawn here, and he was determined to draw them.

"A marriage in name only . . . and then an annulment? It sounds so complicated."

"But we want the crown, don't we?" Matt asked, warming to the idea. Alex was a lovely woman, and he might just enjoy a 'marriage' to her.

"All right," Alex agreed as she cast a glance at Matt.

"But, Father Winn, do you really think this is necessary?"

"You knew Lawrence."

"We'll do it," she capitulated without further argument. "When do you want to perform the ceremony?"

"The sooner the better," Matt urged.

"We can do it right here. All we'll need are witnesses."

"Let me check the hall." Matt opened the door just in time to see a maid coming out of a room farther down the hall.

He called to her and told her to get one of the other maids and come back to their room as soon as she could.

"They'll be here in five minutes," Matt assured Winn, before glancing over at Alex, the woman who very shortly would be his bride. "I never thought I'd be marrying on such short notice," he told her with a grin.

"I was hoping to wear my mother's bridal gown . . ." She smiled slightly. "But the crown's worth it."

Winn didn't like the way Matt was looking at Alex, and it was all he could do not to remind him again that this was a marriage *in name only*. It occurred to Winn that he didn't have the slightest idea of what he was doing and that he'd better get his uncle's bible and come up with a ceremony real quick. "I'll get my things and be right back."

Eight

Winn disappeared into the other bedroom and closed the door behind him. Tension gripped him as he put his bag on his bed and began looking for the Bible.

I know it's in here somewhere!" he told himself in exasperation as he continued to dig through his personal belongings. "I can't believe I'm going to do this! I'm about to marry a man and woman, and I'm an impostor, a fake!"

Winn grimaced as he thought about his deception, but then he reminded himself that as long as Matt and Alex held to the bargain that it was a marriage in name only, no one would be hurt by his actions—he hoped.

"Finally!" His hand closed around the good book.

"Now, for the ceremony . . ." he muttered, sitting down on one of the beds and quickly scanning the pages. He tried to remember the last wedding he'd attended and what had been said, but as he best recalled, he'd been bored by the whole thing and hadn't paid close attention. Today, he wouldn't be bored.

"For richer, for poorer, in good times and bad, forsaking all others till death do us part," Winn repeated the part of the vows he knew, but to make the ceremony sound authentic, he was sure there should be a scripture reading and probably prayers and a blessing, too. He glanced heavenward, wondering what his uncle was thinking now.

"Let's see . . . There has to be something in here about marriage . . ." He finally found the passage in Ruth and he marked it. That done, he drew a deep steadying breath. Smiling at his own image in the mirror over the washstand, he said to no one in particular, "I'm as ready as I'll ever be."

Assuming a sedate and serious manner, Winn returned to Alex's room to perform his first wedding ceremony.

Matt was standing with Alex, smiling as he gazed down at her. The two maids had joined them, and so he was deliberately playing the besotted bridegroom while they waited for Father Winn to return. Matt found the role a pleasant one for Alex was truly lovely, and he knew he could do far worse for a 'wife.' He thought it rather amusing that he, who had sworn never to marry after Valerie, was saying his vows less than a month later. And even though this was to be a marriage strictly in name only, Matt knew he would honor the vows he spoke for as long as they were legally wed. He would do nothing to cast doubt on the validity of the marriage or bring shame to Alex. It was important that they appear to be man and wife, and so he would play the dutiful husband. The crown was worth it.

"Are you nervous?" he asked Alex gently, lifting one hand to touch her cheek.

A little surprised by his intimacy, Alex glanced up at him. As her gaze met his, she could see the twinkle of amusement in his dark eyes and knew he was playing it up for the maids. Just before they'd joined them a short time before, Matt had murmured to her to act the part of his loving betrothed, so she did not protest his touch. She gave him a sweet smile as she answered, "Just a little. This is all happening so quickly, it's taking my breath away."

"Me, too," he agreed. "But some times when things are meant to be, there's just no stopping them. And we were meant to be together."

Alex was having trouble keeping her expression from reflecting her very real amusement at his declarations. "It is an important step."

"Very, but feeling as strongly as we do . . ."

"I can't deny myself any longer."

"Neither can I. I promise I'll do everything in my power to make you happy, Alex," he vowed with convincing intensity.

Winn entered the room, and, hearing Matt's declaration, he stopped just inside the door. He didn't realize Matt was saying these things for the benefit of the maids. He looked at Alex and saw her gazing adoringly up at Matt. When she reached out and rested her hand on Matt's chest in a gesture of intimacy and affection, his grip tightened on the Bible he held. He knew he had to do something, so he quickly stepped forward to gain their attention.

"Are we ready to begin?" Winn asked.

Alex had been so intent on playing the game of

loving bride that she hadn't noticed Father Winn's return. She jumped a little nervously at the sound of his voice and moved away from Matt. Alex looked over at Father Winn, and in spite of her continual denial of her attraction to him, she had to admit to herself yet again that she was drawn to him. Her feelings defied all reason. He was the unattainable man; yet had she been able to choose, she would have picked him to be her husband this day. For real. And while there was no denying she was attracted to him physically, it was his incredible kindness to others that had won her heart. She loved him, but it was a love born of respect and admiration. And she knew that it could never be more than that.

"Yes, Father. I'm ready," Alex answered, turning her attention back to her 'intended.'

"Matt?"

"Yes, Father."

"Dearly beloved, we are gathered here today to join in holy matrimony this man, Matthew McKittrick, and this woman, Alexandra Parker. If there are any present who have any objection to this joining, speak now or forever hold your peace."

The two maids looked on in romantic contentment as he read the words of the ceremony.

"Matthew McKittrick do you take this woman, Alexandra Parker, to be your lawfully wedded wife, forsaking all others, to have and to hold, in sickness and in health, for richer or poorer till death do you part?"

"I do."

"And do you, Alexandra Parker, take this man, Matthew McKittrick, to be your lawfully wedded husband from this day forward, forsaking all others, in sickness and in health until death do you part?"

"I do."

"By the power vested in me," Winn said more slowly. "I now pronounce you man and wife. What God has joined together, let no man put asunder."

The maids sighed audibly. The wedding had a fairy tale quality to it. Each maid hoped that someday, some man would be eager to marry her this way—quickly and romantically. Silly smiles lit their faces as they imagined the night to come.

"Do you have a ring?"

Matt had considered this earlier, and he took off his gold insignia ring and slipped it onto Alex's finger. He held her hand in his, staring at the ring that marked her as his wife, and he smiled as he thought of the Crown of Desire.

"Congratulations, Mr. and Mrs. McKittrick." Winn finished in relief. He'd done it!

Matt turned to Alex. He knew all eyes were upon them, and he was determined to make this as believable a wedding as possible.

"Mrs. McKittrick . . ." Matt said softly as a devilish smile curved his lips.

His unsuspecting bride looked up at him, and before Alex could say anything, Matt swept her into his arms and kissed her. When she stiffened, his lips left hers just long enough so he could whisper, "Make it look good, my darling. We have to convince our witnesses that we can't live without each other." He kissed her again, a hot exchange that was perfectly suited to a newly married couple.

Alex was completely taken aback by Matt's unexpected embrace. While she realized the truth in his urging, she felt very self-conscious about such a passionate display right there in front of Father Winn. For a marriage in name only, it seemed to her they were off to a strange start. But while she was embarrassed by his boldness, there was little she could really do without creating a scene. Putting her hands on his shoulders, Alex accepted his embrace. Her response was passive, but to the onlookers, she appeared enthralled by her husband's ardor.

Winn's jaw tightened as he watched Matt kiss Alex. He wanted to pull them apart, to remind Matt that this was a marriage *in name only*, but all he could do was stand before them and watch. Finally, in total exasperation, he closed the Bible with a thump and cleared his throat. To Winn's relief, Matt finally ended the kiss, but he still kept a possessive arm about Alex's waist.

Alex was smiling as she gazed up at Matt. She looked like a woman in love—her eyes were shining and her cheeks were flushed with high color. She was excited, but her excitement stemmed from the knowledge that they would soon be going after the crown. She would do whatever was necessary to rescue her father, and if pretending to be Mrs. Matt McKittrick was what it took, so be it.

"How wonderful . . ." one of the maids giggled after the couple had finally broken apart.

"Congratulations!" the maids told them excitedly as they crowded around.

"Thank you." They accepted their good wishes.

That done, Matt showed the maids from the room. He paused at the door, thinking over what had just transpired.

"I'll be right back," Matt announced, wanting this night to be special in at least some small way.

"Where are you going?" Alex asked.

"It's a surprise. You'll see." With that he was gone, and Alex and Winn were alone.

She glanced at him and noticed that his expression seemed strained. "Is something wrong?"

"I know this was something that we had to do, but I feel perhaps I've abused my calling by performing the ceremony." Winn suddenly wondered what would happen if Matt and Alex discovered they really did feel something for each other and decided to take their vows seriously? How would they react to finding out their marriage was a sham, a fake ceremony performed by a phony priest. He'd brought Alex along on the adventure against his better judgment, and he'd agreed to serve as her chaperone. Winn feared now that he might have done her a disservice. He could keep her safe from his own desire, but could he keep her safe from Matt? How could he protect her from her own husband if they honestly believed they were married?

"But you married us for all the right reasons."

"Did I? Greed is one of the seven deadly sins."

"We're not doing this out of greed!" she countered quickly, thinking of her father's life hanging in the balance and fearing that Winn might be backing out. "Don't you see? That's why Lawrence picked us. It was his treasure, and he chose to leave it to us. Claiming a gift is not greed. That's what the crown's curse was all about. We're not doing anything wrong by seeking the Crown of Desire. We're doing what Lawrence wanted us to do."

Matt returned at that moment with a bottle of champagne and three glasses he'd procured at the bar downstairs.

"No wedding is complete without a toast," he remarked as he set the glasses down and opened the bottle. The cork few across the room with a resounding pop and Matt poured them each a glass of the fine wine. Lifting his in salute, he looked at Alex and said, "To my wife, Alexandra. May our marriage be a long and prosperous one."

Winn and Alex drank with him, then Winn knew he should add one of his own.

"To the lovely bride," Winn began, his gaze on Alex, "and her groom. May this marriage succeed, and may our association be a fruitful one." Winn downed the rest of his champagne, and he was pleased when Matt quickly refilled his glass. Tonight, he needed a drink. The champagne tasted particularly wonderful and had he had his way and been able to revert to the Winn of old, he might have commandeered the entire bottle.

"What do we do next?" Alex asked as she sipped from her glass.

"Tomorrow morning, we'll pay the convent a visit," Matt answered.

"I can't believe how smoothly things have gone so far," she remarked. "We found the city and the convent."

"Let's hope the hard part's over and the rest will be easy," Winn said.

"We can't relax," Alex cautioned. "If we look for the simple answers, we're going to miss the most important thing. I'm sure Lawrence did not make this easy for us. There's more here than meets the eye."

"Well, all we can do is our best. Shall we start out in the morning, first thing?" Winn asked.

"I'll be ready," Matt agreed. "Let's just hope the mother superior will be able to help us."

"Shall we call it a night?" Winn suggested.

"Yes, good night, Father Winn. My wife and I are going to enjoy our honeymoon . . ." Matt teased, giving Alex a wink.

"In name only . . ." Winn repeated sternly, not at all amused by Matt's quips.

"Yes, dear husband, I'm afraid we're going to have to spend our wedding night apart," Alex told him with smiling sympathy.

"Pity," Matt said as he pressed a soft kiss to her cheek. "You're the prettiest wife I've ever had."

"How many wives have you had?" She was laughing.

"You want me to reveal all my deepest, darkest secrets in front of a priest?" he asked in mock horror.

"Good night, Matt," she said, still smiling.

"Just let me get the rest of the champagne. It's going to be a long, lonely wedding night without it," Matt mourned with good humor.

"You'll have Father Winn for company," Alex said.

"I like the good father, but somehow, on my wedding night, I thought I'd cuddle up with a warm, willing, beautiful woman—not a bottle of champagne." He held the half-full bottle up and grimaced.

Alex was laughing at his roguish ways, but Winn was not amused.

"I'm Alex's chaperone, Matt. I'll protect her, even from you."

"But I'm her husband, Father. Have some pity on me." He cast a knowing glance toward her bed. "Ah, my wedding night, and I'll be sleeping alone."

"Don't feel so bad, I'm spending my wedding night alone, too," she pointed out.

"Good night, wife," Matt said as he regretfully followed the priest from the room.

"Good night, husband," she said lightly as she closed the door behind them.

Winn and Matt settled in in their own room.

"Want another drink, Father?" Matt offered, holding the bottle out to Winn.

"Don't mind if I do," he accepted. He'd brought his glass with him and held it steady as Matt poured him another healthy dose. It had been a long time since he'd had champagne, and it was just what he needed tonight to ease the tension within him.

Winn was annoyed with himself. The moment he'd seen Matt kissing Alex and holding her so close, he'd wanted to tear them apart and blurt out the truth. It had taken all of his considerable willpower to remain silent. Winn downed the wine and asked for one more. Matt obliged as he, too, partook of another sampling.

Wearily, Winn wondered if there was a *Saint Winston*. If not, maybe he could nominate himself for canonization when this was all over and done.

Tomorrow, Winn thought, they would venture forth to the convent. He hoped they were in the right place and that it woudn't be too difficult to figure out the next clue. He hoped they could get this treasure hunt over with as quickly as possible. He'd had just about all he could stand of playing the saint. He was tired of being under scrutiny every minute of every day, of having to watch his every word and move. He wanted his old freedom back. He wanted . . .

Winn paused in his slightly hazy musings. What did he want? A vision of Alex as she'd looked wearing the silken wrapper took shape in his mind. Right now, the one thing he wanted he couldn't have. He drained his glass, got ready for bed, muttered a harsh good night to Matt, and rolled over to go to sleep.

Matt was paying little attention to Winn as he finished off the rest of the bottle. His thoughts were on his own situation. He was a married man. . . . After Valerie, he'd never thought it would happen. Matt reminded himself quickly that it hadn't really happened. Though of course, this marriage was as real as Valerie's had been. She didn't love her husband, yet she'd married him. He didn't love Alex either, but they were man and wife now. Perhaps, he mused in a champagne-induced fog, this was the way of life. Perhaps in the final scheme of things practicality meant more than love.

Though he'd never considered himself a particularly

romantic man, the idea didn't sit well with him. Shedding his clothes, he turned down the lamp and stretched out, closing his eyes. Matt's last humorous, champagne-clouded thought as he drifted off was—some wedding night!

The three arrived at the convent just after nine the next morning. They were greeted warmly by a young novice and then shown to a darkly paneled room where they were told to wait for the mother superior. The room was large and furnished with a sofa and several chairs. The walls were unadorned save for a crucifix and several portraits of saints and martyrs. It was so quiet in the convent that they found themselves speaking in hushed tones.

"What if this isn't the right place? What if she can't help us?" Alex wondered aloud as she wandered around the room studying the paintings.

"Then we'll start over and try somewhere else," Matt answered.

Winn was standing looking out the large window that offered a view of the cemetery at the back of the convent when he heard the sound of footsteps echoing in the halls, coming their way. He turned toward the door just as a tall, stately woman appeared.

Clad in her black habit and veil with a large rosary tied at her waist, the mother superior was the picture of authority. Her features were regal, her bearing dignified. Her brown eyes mirrored the warmth of her inner being.

"Welcome to Sacred Heart Convent," she greeted them, smiling in welcome as she moved forward into the room.

"Good morning, Reverend Mother," Winn returned as he want to meet her. "I'm Father Bradford, and this is Alexandra and Matthew McKittrick."

"It's a pleasure to meet you all, but tell me. What brings you here to the Sacred Heart?"

"We're here on a quest, Reverend Mother. We were hoping you could help us," Winn explained.

"A quest?" A flicker of awareness shone in her eyes, but she quickly masked it.

Matt was watching her carefully, and he noticed the slight, momentary change in her expression. He said nothing, though, for he was certain Winn could handle the mother superior far better than he. Still, the indication that she might know what they were about encouraged him.

"Yes. According to everything that we've been able to find out, our quest begins here at your convent. Lawrence Anthony gave us books with clues and we . . ."

"Lawrence Anthony?" she repeated quickly as she gave each of them a hard look, searching their faces for some sign of deception.

"Yes, Reverend Mother. Lawrence sent us to you."

"How is he?" she asked, her dark eyes glowing as she thought of the elderly gentleman who'd come to the convent a few years before. He'd been a kind and generous man. When he'd left, he'd asked her for her help and she'd agreed to follow his wishes without question.

"Lawrence passed away several months ago," Alex told her.

"I'm so sorry to hear that. He was a good man."

"We were all very fond of him."

"Come," she invited, "join me for some refreshments. We will talk more of Lawrence and this quest."

As the Reverend Mother led the way to a small, sparsely furnished dining room, she thought of Lawrence and was saddened by his death. He'd been deeply troubled when he'd first come to her, but by the time he'd left, he'd seemed more content with his life. He'd certainly been good to the convent, endowing them with a yearly stipend and also setting up a trust in which the considerable amount of the money would be paid out to them once she'd completed the task he'd set for her.

As they sat down at the table, the Reverend Mother studied each of their faces. She'd waited all this time to hear from Lawrence again, and now, in his stead, came this priest and young married couple. Lawrence's instructions to her had been clear: she was to test the hearts of those who followed him and give the book he'd left in her keeping only to those who were pure of heart. The Reverend Mother knew she could make no fast decision. She would have to wait and watch these three for a time, and see if they were worthy.

They were served tea and small cakes, and after they'd partaken of the food, the Reverend Mother was ready to hear more.

"Tell me how you came to the convent?"

"When Lawrence died, he left three books, one to

each of us. The agreement was that we were to work together, and, using the clues he'd written in the books, we'd find the treasure he'd hidden," Winn answered.

"I see." And indeed she did, for Lawrence had shown her the ancient crown that these three young people sought.

"The crown's been lost to us for thousands of years. We believe it's time to put it safely in a museum where everyone can share in its glory," Matt put in.

"Reverend Mother?" The novice who'd greeted them earlier spoke from the doorway. "I'm sorry to interrupt you, but Sister Marian is waiting for you."

"I'll be right there." She turned back to the three visitors. "Would you care to spend the night with us? We have room, and I'd enjoy having the time to spend with you."

"Thank you. We would," Alex accepted quickly.

"Good. I must go now, but I'll speak with you later. You have the freedom of the grounds. If there's anything you need, just ask one of the sisters. They'll be happy to help you."

"Thank you, Reverend Mother."

"She knows more than she's telling us," Matt said after he was sure the mother superior was out of ear-shot.

"I don't doubt it. Shall we take a look around and see what we can find?"

"While you two do that, I'll go back to the hotel and get our things," Matt offered. "We'll meet back here at noon."

Alex wandered outside while Winn headed for the

chapel. The grounds around the convent were spacious, and it was easy to see that the sisters spent a lot of time working in the yard. Alex studied the exterior of the building, hoping to find some clue to the crown, but she found nothing unusual in the architecture. With a trained eye, she studied the layout of the building and the surrounding fence, but noted nothing out of the ordinary. These possibilities exhausted, she made her way toward the cemetery to study the headstones.

It was then, as she started toward the arched gateway that led to the sacred ground, that she saw the same woman, dressed in black, they'd seen the day before. Alex watched her slowly make her way through the rows of headstones until she stopped and knelt before a grave.

For a moment, Alex wavered, undecided about what to do. Then she finally made up her mind. By talking to the old lady, she might learn something pertinent about the convent. So, she quietly made her way through the rows of graves to join her.

"Hello," Alex spoke softly, not wanting to disturb her for she looked to be deep in prayer.

The woman looked up, her expression troubled and said. "What? Do you want something?"

"I'm sorry. I didn't mean to bother you."

"You're not bothering me," she said wearily, letting her gaze drop back to the stone. She gently touched it.

"I noticed you were here yesterday. Do you come often?"

"Every day."

Alex couldn't make out the dates, but she could see that there were two names on the tombstone—Steven Mark Andrews and Jonathan Andrews. "Was Steven your husband?"

"No. Steven was my son, my beautiful son . . ." Her voice fell flat, and her shoulders slumped under the weight of her memories. "Jonathan was my husband."

It had been years ago, yet to the mother's heart it still seemed like yesterday. They'd tried everything to save him, but he'd only gotten worse and worse. That black, terrible night that he died still haunted her. There would be no forgetting her husband's desperate search for Father O'Malley. They'd been so sure the priest could save Steven, if only he'd come in time. But Father O'Malley hadn't come in time. Steven had died in her arms just before midnight. When the priest had finally arrived late the next morning, she'd no longer cared. He'd explained that he'd been with other dying children and hadn't been able to leave them, but that hadn't mattered to her or to her husband. What mattered was that he'd failed her in her hour of need. Two days later, when her Jonathan had taken ill, too, she'd traveled to the true depths of hell. She'd lost Jonathan in the same epidemic, and she had never forgiven Father O'Malley or the church. Her faith, once the wellspring of her happiness, had dried up, leaving her barren of hope and love, and bitter as she saw endless, black, empty days stretched out before her. She was alone in the world. The legacy of her loved ones' deaths was a pointless existence of unending sorrow and pain.

"I'm so sorry," Alex sympathized, breaking into her memories.

The old woman half-smiled, but it wasn't one of happiness. "You're too young. You don't know anything about being sorry."

Alex didn't know what to say next, so she simply stood quietly with her.

"You're not one of the sisters," the woman remarked when she realized the younger woman wasn't going to go away.

"No, my name's Alexandra McKittrick." She'd almost said Parker, but had caught herself in time.

"Why did you come here? Did you lose someone, too?"

"My father." Alex thought of him in prison and felt how close he was to death. "I've come here with my husband and a friend to visit the convent. It's a beautiful old building."

"It's just a building. It has no soul . . . no life."

"Would you like to talk for a while?"

"No." She stood up and turned to walk away. "Good-bye, my dear."

Her gait was slow, and it was evident that she was ridden with physical pain as well as mental anguish. She knew there was no point in talking to this young girl. There was nothing left to say that hadn't been already said. No one cared about her, and she cared about no one. It was simpler that way. You couldn't be hurt. Her days passed in a dull blur, and that was fine with her. Soon, she hoped it would end, and she would be with Steven and John.

As Alex watched her go, her heart ached for the lonely old woman. She was deeply touched by her and wondered why she was so alone. Alex decided to seek out the mother superior and ask her. Surely, she would know something about this woman who came to the cemetery every day.

Winn was in the chapel, pondering the events that had brought him to this moment and wondering how in the world he was going to deal with the situation. He was trying to remember everything he'd ever been taught about nuns and convents and sleeping arrangements there, but for the life of him, he couldn't recall much.

"All right," he began, feeling rather self-conscious to be talking out loud, but figuring he was pretty safe since there was no one around. He'd been alone in the chapel for some time, and he knelt now as he began to speak in earnest. "Look, God, I know I haven't always been as good as I could have." He paused, thinking he'd phrased that rather well. "But right now, I could really use your help."

He waited. He didn't know what he was expecting, but a crack of thunder and the voice of God telling him what to do next would have been deeply appreciated. Whatever he'd hoped for, he didn't get it. After a moment of total silence, he started up again.

"I'm not asking this for myself. You know I'm here

for all the right reasons. But I could sure use a little support from you tonight. I'm supposed to be protecting Alex. I'm supposed to be keeping her safe. If Matt and Alex get a room of their own while we're here . . .".

He stopped and waited again. This time in his mind the thought flashed—*Thou shall not bear false witness.*

He grimaced and felt the bite of his priestly collar.

"I know, I know, but I did it all for a good cause," he pleaded his case.

Silence.

"Well, God, if you've got any suggestions about how I can get out of this without anyone getting hurt, I'd appreciate hearing them."

He realized then that this had to be one of those notorious 'gray' areas. If you stayed with black and white to begin with, you didn't get into the gray area, but once you were there, things definitely became complicated. He couldn't tell the truth now, because it might ruin their search for the crown.

He sat there a little longer, hoping against hope that the mother superior didn't have a room for a married couple.

Alex went back inside and sought out the mother superior in her office. She knocked on the door and when Reverend Mother called out for her to enter, she did.

"Could I speak with you for a moment?"

"Of course, Mrs. McKittrick. Come in."

"Thank you, and please, call me Alex." She sat in

the chair before her desk. "I was just in the cemetery and I met a woman there . . . a Mrs. Andrews."

"Ah, so you've met Eleanor." Her expression saddened and there was a catch of emotion in her voice.

"You know her?"

"Yes, we know her."

"Why is she so unhappy? Why is she so alone? I know her husband and son are dead, but doesn't she have any other family?"

The Reverend Mother saw Alex's real concern, and explained, "No, I'm afraid not, and it's a very tragic story. Her only son, Steven, and her husband were stricken by cholera during the epidemic some years ago. The son was only thirteen when he died, and her husband passed away just a few days later."

"But they've been dead so long, and yet she still comes here every day."

"Love knows nothing of time."

"She's so incredibly sad and lonely. Doesn't anyone care about her?"

"We do. In the years since their deaths, I've been to her home many times, trying to bring her back to us, but she has always refused my calls. She has a servant tell me she isn't at home."

"Why does she treat you that way? What happened?"

Alex was at a loss to understand someone who would turn away from her religion just when she needed it most.

"The night Steven was dying, Eleanor sent her husband to find Father O'Malley. She was certain if Father came and prayed over Steven, the boy would live."

"Couldn't he find the priest?"

"Oh, yes, he found Father O'Malley, and therein lies the problem. Father was with another family whose children were dying. He promised Jonathan he would come as soon as he could, but by the time he arrived, it was too late. Steven was already gone."

"Oh . . . That's terrible . . ." Alex could only imagine the horror of watching your only child die and being helpless to stop it.

"It was a terrible time for the whole city. Father tried to comfort Eleanor and Jonathan, but they held him responsible. Then, when Jonathan took sick a short time later, Eleanor turned completely against the church. She insisted on funeral masses for them, but after that, she never came back. I've been praying daily for her return to us. Father O'Malley died last year, and all he wanted on his deathbed was Eleanor's forgiveness and understanding. Unfortunately, it was never to be. She wouldn't talk to me or to any of the other sisters when we went to her and asked for her help." Reverend Mother sighed. "My heart goes out to her. I understand her pain and her anger, but I will never give up hope that one day I'll be able to reach her."

"Someone has to help her."

"We wish we could, but right now she won't let us. Her heart must change if we're going to reach her."

"There must be something we can do . . ."

"God does work in mysterious ways, and maybe one day someone or something will change her and bring her back to us." Her knowing gaze rested upon Alex. She saw the goodness and the compassion within her, and she wondered if she just might be the one who could work the miracle.

"Thank you for telling me all of this, Reverend Mother," Alex said as she rose and left the room, her heart heavy with the knowledge of the old woman's suffering. She understood now the look of complete estrangement she had seen in Eleanor Andrews' eyes.

Alex wandered back out into the gardens and picked a bouquet of bright flowers. She went to the grave and laid the flowers there, where Eleanor would see them.

Alex remained in the graveyard a little longer, studying the stones. She was unaware that the mother superior was watching her from the window.

Nine

"Father Bradford, would you say grace for us?" Reverend Mother asked as they gathered for dinner that evening.

"I'd be honored, Reverend Mother," Winn answered with a smile that hid his uncertainty. He'd made it a point to avoid the good sisters as much as possible all day for fear that they would see through his disguise. Now, forced into open prayer with no avenue for escape, he hoped his performance would be convincing.

"Let us pray. Bless us, O Lord, for these thy gifts which we are about to receive from thy bounty through Christ, Our Lord. Amen," he intoned with all due respect and solemnity. He had to admit it sounded a lot better than some of the outrageous prayers he'd offered up as an undisciplined youth.

Everyone murmured a quiet, 'Amen,' and then settled in to partake of the sparse, yet tasty fare. At their easy acceptance of his blessing, Winn drew a deep, relieved breath.

When dinner was over, the nuns went off to their evening prayers. The mother superior, however, remained behind to speak to Alex, Winn, and Matt.

"I've had a room prepared for you," she told them graciously. "We have only a single room available, so, if you have no objection, I've arranged for Mrs. McKittrick to share a room with one of the sisters. I hope that won't inconvenience you."

Matt smiled charmingly at the older woman. "I'll miss having my wife by my side, but I understand. We appreciate your hospitality."

She graced him with a smile of her own. "That is what marriage is about. Having one's life companion with you, always supporting and helping you."

"Matt and I have a wonderful relationship. We understand the importance of our vows, and we try to live them every day," Alex put in sweetly, as she met the mother superior's gentle regard.

"Bless you both. It's wonderful to see a couple so happy and so in love. Don't you agree, Father Bradford?"

"Most assuredly, Reverend Mother," Winn replied. The smile he gave her was genuine; Alex was to be removed from harm's way, and through no efforts of his own. As he cast a glance heavenward, he thought that, perhaps, there really was something to this praying. He offered up an unspoken thank you.

"I bid you good night then. One of the sisters will be here in a moment to show you gentlemen to your room," she explained. "Alex, if you'll come with me?"

Alex went to Matt and kissed his cheek. She bid both of them good night before following the mother superior from the room.

Shortly after they'd gone, another sister appeared to

guide Matt and Winn to their room. It was at the other end of the building, far away from the women. The farther they walked, the bigger Winn's smile became.

After the nun left them, Matt chuckled out loud and drew a strange look from Winn.

"A little relieved, are you, Father?"

"Am I that obvious?"

"Only to me," he said with a wide grin. "What would you have done if Alex and I had been given a room to ourselves?"

"Pray," he growled, and his answer drew another chortle of amusement from Matt as they retired for the night.

The following morning, Alex was up at dawn with the sisters. A bell tolled, calling them to morning prayer. Alex dressed quickly for she wanted to join them in the chapel. As they made their way through the halls, they passed a large bank of windows that faced the cemetery and she caught a glimpse of someone already in the graveyard. Alex fell out of the line to get a better look, and there in the distance was Eleanor, dressed in black, already on her way to begin her vigil at her son's and husband's graves.

Alex's good intention to accompany the sisters to the chapel faded as she watched the old lady move slowly through the cemetery. Alex had felt such a kinship to her last night that she knew she had to speak to her again. Slipping away from the convent, she hurried out to see her.

Eleanor was kneeling before the grave speaking to her son and husband in a low, almost inaudible voice. She sensed someone coming, and she looked up as the younger woman neared.

"You put the flowers here." It was a statement of fact, not a question.

"Yes, I did."

"Thank you. They're lovely."

"They're for you. I wanted you to have them."

Eleanor stared at this pretty stranger, trying to see into her soul. She didn't understand why was she taking the time to bother with her. Eleanor's pain was so great that she'd long ago ceased to feel anything else. This simple gift, however, had touched her in a way she couldn't begin to describe.

"This is the first time in years anyone has done anything like that for me."

"I'm glad you like them." Alex touched her shoulder with a gentle hand and saw the first flicker of a different emotion in her gaze, something other than sadness. It made her smile. "I'll see you tomorrow."

Alex returned to the convent, turning back only once to wave before she disappeared inside.

Eleanor watched her go. When Alex waved, she didn't wave back, but kept watch until she was safely inside. As she moved out of sight, Eleanor felt a warm tugging at her battered heart, and the feeling frightened her. She didn't want to care about anyone. She didn't want to feel anything. The black numbness that surrounded her protected her, and she couldn't risk losing her last defense against the total devastation of reality.

Eleanor glanced up in the direction the young woman had gone, and wondered why she suddenly felt like crying.

Matt had been biding his time, searching around the convent and surrounding buildings for some hint of what they were supposed to do next. His search left him empty-handed, though, and he was growing impatient. Nothing made sense. He wanted to get on with the hunt for the crown, yet he was stymied. He was in the hall near the chapel when an elderly sister, who'd been introduced to him earlier as Sister Agnes, approached.

"Mr. McKittrick?"

"Matt, please, Sister."

"Matt." She said his name thoughtfully, thinking how wondrously young and strong he was. "Are you going to be with us long?"

"Only another day or two," he answered.

"Pity."

"Why? Did you need something?"

"No, no. I realize how busy you must be."

"If you need my help, I'll be glad to do what I can, Sister."

"Well, now that you mention it," she began, smiling up at him. "I could use the help of a strong man. Could you spare me a few minutes?"

Sister Agnes was short, barely topping five feet. Matt could only guess at her age, speculating that she was every bit of sixty. Old or not, her blue eyes were clear and intelligent, full of mirth and unquestioning love, and Matt was drawn to her. When she'd smiled at him, he'd been lost, for she had a smile that could light up an entire room. "Surely, Sister Agnes," he agreed without another thought.

As she led him down the hall in a different direction, she began to explain, "I'm working with several of the other sisters, helping a poor family that lives not too far from here. Do you have time to help us this afternoon?"

With neither Winn nor Alex anywhere in sight, he decided to do what he could for the sweet nun. "Of course, Sister Agnes. Just lead the way. I'll follow you anywhere."

"Thank you, Matthew."

He was tempted to correct her, to tell her his friends called him Matt, but somehow Matthew sounded right coming from her.

As they made their way through the streets, Matt was impressed by the number of people who called out happy greetings to the nun. She had a kind word for everyone and introduced Matt proudly as her friend. As they rounded one corner, a group of unkempt, dirty children came charging toward them.

"Sister Agnes! Sister Agnes!" they cried, surrounding her and practically fighting each other for the chance to give her a hug.

Matt stood back and looked on as she took the time to hug each child in return and ask them about their families and their activities. Just watching her touched his heart. He fought down thoughts of his own lonely childhood. When at last she was ready to move on, he returned to her side.

"They certainly love you," Matt remarked a bit bewildered by her outpouring of love and kindness.

She cast him a sidelong glance. "That's because I love them," she told him simply.

They moved on to a small house that was little more than a shack.

"This is it," she said as she paused for a moment before the abode so he could understand the poverty of the family who lived there. "Come and meet Mrs. Hawkins."

Sister Agnes drew him inside with her. "Matthew, this is Deborah Hawkins. Deborah, this is Matthew. He's come to help us."

Deborah Hawkins had been pretty once, but there was a great weariness about her now. She was heavy with child, and two other children, little more than babes themselves, were playing on the floor at her feet. For all that the family was desperately poor, the house was well-kept, and the children were neat and clean.

"Hello, Mrs. Hawkins," Matt said.

Sister Agnes led him back outside. "Her husband was killed just a little over a month ago in an accident on the riverfront. She's all alone with no family to help her. We're doing her as much as we can, but our funds are limited. The other sisters and I have been bringing food, and trying to get her house repaired before the new baby comes. A doctor friend has agreed to help her with the baby, so it's just a matter of seeing that she's as safe and comfortable as possible and making sure that she has enough so she can feed her children."

"I'll be glad to help however I can," Matt offered, touched by her generosity and caring. "What would you like me to do?"

Sister Agnes had been hoping for just such a willingness from him, and within minutes she had him painting the outside of the house with paint she'd gotten as a donation from the owner of a mercantile. Once she was certain he was working without any problems, she returned to the convent to see to some other business. It was there that she found Father Bradford, looking for Matt.

"I know just where he is. If you'll come along with me, I'll take you to him."

As they neared the Hawkins home, Winn saw Matt, his shirt open in the afternoon heat, busily painting the rundown house. Another sister was supervising his efforts. Winn fought down a grin as he approached his friend.

"I see you're busy," Winn remarked, watching Matt wield the paintbrush with reasonable skill.

"Yes, and I could use a little help here, Father," Matt said over his shoulder without missing a stroke. "Grab a brush and pitch in. There's more than enough work for two able-bodied men."

It was an offer Winn couldn't refuse. He shed his coat and collar and started to paint in his dark clothes, but Deborah Hawkins quickly came out to talk to him.

"I appreciate your help, Father, but wouldn't you

want some different clothes? I'd hate to think that you ruined your suit helping me."

"I'm afraid I don't have any work clothes with me."

"I still have some of my husband's things. You're about his size, and you're welcome to them."

The idea of being freed from the constraints of his 'priesthood,' if only for a little while, was liberating to Winn. He struggled not to sound too eager in his acceptance.

"Well, thank you. It certainly would make things easier."

A few minutes later, Winn emerged from the house wearing a pair of work pants and a threadbare but clean blue shirt. The shirt was a little small, but he didn't care. He felt like himself again.

Winn attacked the painting job with a zest that surprised even himself, for he was not really accustomed to physical labor. His rather decadent way of life at home had not included hard work or sacrifices.

The day grew warmer. Had Winn been anywhere else, he would have stripped off his shirt, but he knew he had a certain standard to uphold. Instead, he satisfied himself with just unbuttoning it. He worked alongside Matt, reaping high praise from the nuns as they did their share of the work indoors.

Alex had been hard pressed to find Matt or Father Winn all afternoon. Finally in desperation she went to the mother superior to ask if she'd seen them.

"They're helping Sister Agnes?" Alex repeated what

she'd just been told, surprised that they'd let themselves be sidetracked this way. They were here to find the crown, and every day they delayed, her father remained in prison, possibly coming closer to death.

"Yes, my dear, they are, and, according to sister, they're doing a marvelous job. Sister Agnes is a firm believer that idle hands are the devil's workshop, but she's such a charming taskmaster that no one ever seems to care. I doubt they'll be back much before dark. Knowing sister as I do, she'll keep them going as long as their strength holds up and there's enough light to work by. Shall we go see?"

They made their way to the widow's home.

"There they are," the mother superior told her pointing out the small house ahead.

Alex could see two men who were painting. One she recognized immediately as Matt, and though the other was wearing clothes she didn't recognize, she knew instinctively that he was Father Winn.

Alex couldn't look away from the sight of him, laboring in a workman's clothes, his shirt unbuttoned to the waist. She stared at him in wonder. She'd thought him handsome before, but now she knew the truth. He wasn't just handsome. He was devastating. When he turned slightly, and she was treated to a full view of his bared chest, her heart lurched in her breast. The broad, powerful expanse drew her, and she imagined running her hands over the hard, sculpted muscles and . . .

Winn, as if sensing someone was watching him, glanced in her direction. When he saw Alex standing there with the mother superior, he waved and smiled in welcome.

Alex wasn't sure what to think about her reaction to Father Winn. She knew it wasn't right to feel this way about him, but she couldn't help herself.

"How is the painting going, Father?" the mother superior asked as they joined them.

"Sister Agnes looks like an angel, but she's really a martinet," he teased.

"Sometimes looks can be deceiving," the Reverend Mother said with a smile.

"I know what you mean." Winn felt the bite of his conscience.

"We're very proud of what our dear sister accomplishes," she went on, unaware of his discomfort. "Sister Agnes is a veritable Pied Piper, and all who meet her are continually impressed by her ability to convince others to help her. It's one of her many gifts."

"Will you be done soon?" Alex asked, her gaze still on Father Winn as he turned back to his work. She did not look away until Matt put down his brush and came to give her a light, husbandly kiss. She accepted it passively, but sweetly.

"We'll be here at least another few hours."

"Then I might as well help, too."

Sister Agnes appeared in the doorway. "We could certainly use your help in here with the young ones." Alex moved off to do her bidding.

* * *

The next few days fell into a simple pattern. Each morning, Alex made it a point to seek out Eleanor, and she always brought her a fresh bouquet of flowers. The older lady began to talk more freely as she began to trust her more. She spoke of her disillusionment and the pain of what she believed to be the church's betrayal. Alex wanted to believe that she was reaching her, but she was never sure. Still, she was determined not to miss a morning visit. In the afternoons, she joined Father Winn and Matt in helping Sister Agnes with whatever challenge she could find for them that day.

Dawn of their fourth day at the convent found the sky dark and ominous. The possibility of a bad storm had kept Alex indoors, but when she saw Eleanor from the window, braving the weather to visit her son and husband, she knew she couldn't leave her out there alone.

"Good morning," Alex said, offering her the fresh-picked, fragrant bouquet. It had become a ritual she truly enjoyed.

Eleanor took the blossoms with a smile, and she hoped Alex didn't notice the way her hands were trembling. When Alex hadn't been there earlier as she usually was, she'd been afraid that she'd tired of their meetings and had left.

"It's kind of you to come here every morning."

"I enjoy our visits. I spend so much time with men, it isn't often I get to talk to women friends."

"I haven't had a friend in so long . . ." Eleanor's voice trailed off.

"Well, you have one now." Alex put a reassuring hand on her arm.

In the distance, thunder rumbled.

Alex glanced up at the black clouds. "Why don't you come inside with me? We'll be safe there and out of the weather."

Panic mirrored in Eleanor's eyes. "No . . . no, I can't go in there."

"It would just be us and the sisters. I could introduce you. They're wonderful women."

"No, I can't go inside."

Again the thunder echoed over the land, this time even more threateningly.

"You can't or you won't, Mrs. Andrews?"

"I don't know. I'll go on home now. I think I can make it back before the storm hits."

"Mrs. Andrews, please, don't go," Alex pleaded with heartfelt sincerity. "Haven't you lived in sadness long enough? It's almost as if you willed yourself to die when your son and husband did. You're a kind and gentle woman. You have so much to offer others. Please don't keep yourself locked away any longer. Come with me to the chapel. We can wait there until the storm passes."

"No, I'd better go. There's nothing here for me."

"I'm here for you."

"You're so young . . . You just don't understand. My life is over. There's no reason to pretend otherwise."

"How can you say that when you have so much worth living for? Open your heart. Think of your son. Would Steven want you to live this way?"

"Steven . . ." Tears welled up in her eyes as an image of her boy, laughing and happy, danced through her thoughts.

"Think of your son, Eleanor. Think of what he would want for you." Alex knelt beside her and took her hands in hers. "I'm going to the chapel where it's safe, where I'll be out of the rain. Come with me."

A pain tore at Eleanor's heart, but this time it was a different kind of pain. It was a longing, a deep and desperate need for warmth . . . happiness . . . closeness with another human being, with someone who cared. She'd been alone and lost for so long, though, she didn't know what to do now.

"Everything I loved is lost. Don't you see? I think I may already have died . . . inside . . ."

Alex was touched by the depth of the woman's despair. She held her hand tighter. "Come join me. We'll pray for Steven and for Jonathan."

Thinking of her son, Eleanor lifted a tormented gaze to Alex's. "He would have been just about your age . . ."

"And he would have been a fine man. With a mother like you, he couldn't have been anything else."

Eleanor's tears flowed freely. "Thank you for that," she whispered in a tear-choked voice.

Alex put her arm around the frail old woman's shoulders and hugged her close.

Eleanor accepted Alex's touch. Sobs wracked her, and she gave herself into this young woman's keeping. She trusted.

A rumble of thunder sounded and the first splattering of rain was loosed from the heavens. It was a warm, cleansing rain, and it hid the tears Alex was crying.

"Come to the chapel. You won't be alone any more." She stood and drew the old woman to her feet.

Eleanor did not resist. "I've been away so long . . . My prayers won't even be heard."

"I'll add mine to yours. Who could turn us both down?"

Taking her arm, Alex helped Eleanor from that place of death and despair. They made their way to the chapel. When Eleanor hesitated in the doorway, wary and cautious, Alex paused to let her gather her nerve again.

They entered silently. The nuns were still at prayer, so she directed Eleanor to go ahead of her into one of the back pews, and they knelt there together. Alex gave her a reassuring smile, then turned her attention to the front, leaving the older woman to her own thoughts and prayers.

After a moment of intense reflection, Alex noticed that the door opened again, and someone came in. She felt someone beside her and, strangely enough, knew it was Father Winn without looking. His warm masculine presence beside her in the pew filled her with a deep abiding sense of peace and safety. Somehow, when he was near, Alex believed everything was really going to be all right.

Alex wanted to reach out and touch him, but she didn't. Instead, she just looked over at him, and their eyes met. The depth of emotion she saw in his gaze touched her heart. He was such a fine, honest, honorable man. She wondered how he'd ever come to be so generous and good. There weren't many men like him. Her heart skipped a beat as her pulse quickened, and she forced herself to look away. He was there with her. That was what mattered.

The sisters started to rise, their morning prayers completed. They filed from the chapel in an orderly fashion, the mother superior rising last. As she passed down the aisle, she saw Alex with Eleanor and stopped before them, amazed.

"We've missed you," she told Eleanor sincerely.

"You've been away from us for too long."

"I never thought I'd come here again, but Alex helped me to see what's really important."

"Alexandra is truly special." The mother superior meant it, for Alex had performed a miracle. The woman they'd thought lost to them forever had returned.

"I understand why you feel that way." Eleanor gave Alex a warm, affectionate look.

"I can't tell you how happy I am to see you again."

"Thank you, Reverend Mother."

She reached out to touch her hand. "Would you like to talk for a while? I've missed you."

"I'd like that, very much. There's so much I need to say. So many sad things I've harbored in my heart . . ."

Winn and Alex left the pew and Reverend Mother sat down beside Eleanor. She looked up at Alex as they were leaving.

"Thank you, Alex."

Alex had tears in her eyes. "You're welcome."

"Yes, Alex, thank you," Eleanor stood and opened her arms to her.

Alex went to her and they embraced. She gave her a kiss on the cheek, then followed Winn from the chapel, leaving the two women alone.

"That was a very kind thing you did," Winn told her, his gaze warm upon her.

"I was glad I could help her. I just hope she finds some peace now. It must be awful to be so lost and alone."

"It is," he answered distantly, remembering how devastated he'd been after he'd lost his parents. He'd been lucky. His Uncle Edward had been there for him. This poor old woman had had no one.

Later that afternoon, Winn, Matt, and Alex sat together in the men's bedroom, trying to decide what they needed to do next. They'd searched everywhere possible, but had turned up nothing. Their quest for clues was at a dead end. Matt kept going over his book with the second clue, hoping to find some link there that might help them see what they were missing.

"This makes no sense at all," he complained as he read the second mysterious passage out loud.

" 'Onward, ever onward, cease not your search.

Here two shall be as one, but your fate is not that to be.

Seek here the bearer of the path, whose gift will guide you on.

Love is the key to all that thrives, its power can conquer the curse.'"

"I wonder what Lawrence was thinking of when he wrote this," Winn mused, as confused as Matt.

A knock on the door interrupted them as they were pondering the collector's mysterious words. Alex answered it to find Sister Agnes there.

"Reverend Mother would like to speak with you now. She's in her office."

"We'll be right there," Alex told her. They quickly answered her summons.

The mother superior was standing behind her desk as they entered. Her expression was serious as she studied them. She remembered Lawrence Anthony's instructions about the book he'd left in her care, and she knew the time had come to follow through on his wishes. Her gaze rested fondly upon Alex. This young woman had been an instrument of change, her kindness had wrought a beautiful miracle. She had helped to save Eleanor from a life of loneliness and suffering.

"Please, sit down," she invited. When they'd made themselves comfortable, she began, "When Lawrence Anthony came to me, he was a deeply troubled man. He told me of his sons and of their endless greed and desire for wealth. When he left the convent, he entrusted something very precious into my safe-keeping with the instruction that I was to keep it until I'd judged those coming for it worthy of the honor. Lawrence asked me to look into the hearts of those who would claim the crown. I have watched each of you and I have seen the truth of your hearts and your words mirrored in your actions. You have not tried to use the convent for your own gain. You have given to us. You did not take or demand, as some would have in their eagerness to gain the priceless relic you seek. You shared your personal treasure with us. It is for that generosity and goodness that I now give you the treasure Lawrence left in my care,"

She picked up a small, wrapped package that had been on her desk.

"I am firmly convinced that my judgment in this is right. I wish you good fortune as you continue on your quest."

She handed the book to Winn.

"Thank you, Reverend Mother."

"It is my pleasure to be giving this to you, Father Bradford. I had long hoped that the day would come when I could pass along this key to the crown, and now I've done so. Your kindness has wrought many changes here. Thanks to you, Father, Matthew, Widow Hawkins' house is now repaired, and thanks to Alexandra, Eleanor Andrews has returned to our fold. We have been blessed by your presence."

"Don't give us too much credit, Reverend Mother," Alex cautioned.

"It was Lawrence who sent us here," Matt added.

"Without his foresight, none of us would have had this chance to come together."

"I pray Lawrence is resting in peace."

"So do we."

"Our prayers will be with you as you continue your

journey, my friends. Travel safely and if you ever need anything from us, just send word."

They returned to the bedroom where Winn quickly unwrapped the package. As they'd suspected, it was another book. Winn opened it and began to read aloud,

" 'Let the waters be your guide, to the south where they merge.

From this place a saint did come, in her quest to set men free.

Life's little flowers will now grow, warmed by a gentle sun.

See the unseen, and you will find the treasure that will be yours.' "

"Father Winn, wait!" Matt grabbed his book. "Listen to this . . . 'Onward ever onward, cease not your search.' Now, read your first line again."

" 'Let the water be your guide, to the south where they merge.' "

" 'Seek here the bearer of the path, whose gift will guide you on.' "

"Here two shall be as one, but your fate is not that to be,' " Matt added his next line.

" 'From this place a saint did come, in her quest to set men free.' "

" 'Life's little flowers should now grow, warmed by a gentle sun.' "

" 'Love is the key to all that thrives, its power can conquer the curse.' "

" 'See the unseen, and you will find the treasure that will be yours.' "

Alex was smiling widely as they finished. "I knew it!"

"Knew what?"

"That Lawrence was saying more than just the obvious. Now, the 'two shall become as one' in the first clue makes more sense than ever. The books!"

"How soon do we head south?"

Matt already had the map out. "Let's see . . . There's New Orleans . . . That's it! St. Joan came from France . . . from Orleans! It has to be New Orleans!"

"This time we're traveling by steamer," Winn insisted, bound and determined never to take a train again. "I'll go down to the riverfront and check the schedules. We'll leave on the next boat."

Later, when they left the convent for the final time, the mother superior went out with them to bid them good-bye. As they departed in a hired carriage, she closed the gates to the grounds behind them. When the two wrought-iron gates were joined, what had appeared to be an abstract design on either side became two hearts entwined. The three in the carriage were so intent on the next leg of their search, they did not look back and see.

Ten

The lap of luxury—that's what traveling on the Westlake Steamship Line felt like after their endless hours on the trains. The paddlewheeler was one of the most modern boats on the river, and Alex, Winn, and Matt were reveling in its white, glittering splendor.

As they dined on their second night in the elegant salon, Alex finally relaxed and began to enjoy herself. The meal was superb as befitted the steamer's reputation. The table was set with a white linen tablecloth, the finest china and crystal, and highly polished silverware. An assortment of fine wines were offered with the roast duck and wild rice, assorted steamed vegetables, hot rolls and creamy golden butter. They ate the sumptuous meal with gusto and then enjoyed the fancy, rich-to-the-point-of-being-decadent desserts.

"Isn't gluttony one of the seven deadly sins, Father?" Matt asked as he downed the last bite of his dessert. It was a thick slice of chocolate cake, heavily covered with fudge icing and then smothered in raspberry sauce.

"Yes, and I think after tonight we probably all need to go to confession," Winn laughed, finishing off his own delicious dessert and leaning back in total, sated comfort.

"I think your idea to travel by steamer was the best one you've had yet, Father Winn," Alex told him as she, too, savored every luscious bite of her food.

"Maybe some day in the near future, travel by rail will be as smooth and fast and comfortable, but for right now, riverboats are by far more modern."

"Paddlewheelers are nice," Alex agreed, gazing around at the high-gloss white walls, crystal chandeliers, and abundance of mirrors that reflected the pristine beauty of their surroundings. "There's so much more to do and see on a steamer."

"Indeed, there is, my dear wife," Matt said with a grin. "What do you say we go to the ballroom tonight and dance? It seems strange that we've been married all this time, and we haven't had the chance to dance yet."

" 'All this time' is really just about a week, Matt," she teased.

"Then we need to dance to celebrate our one week anniversary. What do you say, Father Winn? Will you join us?"

"Since I performed the ceremony, it's only right that I have a dance with the bride," Winn answered, not about to let them go off alone. He wanted to keep an eye on Matt while he was with Alex.

They left the dining room and entered the ballroom. The dance floor was crowded with couples enjoying a waltz, and Matt immediately took Alex in his arms and swept her out to join them.

Winn moved to the side of the room to look on. His gaze was centered on Matt and Alex as they circled the floor. He watched Matt guide her through the waltz, his hand resting possessively at her waist. When he saw Alex laugh in delight at something Matt said, Winn felt jealousy blaze to life within him. He scowled.

Damn it! he snarled to himself. He wanted to be the one holding her close, dancing with her and making her laugh, not Matt!

"Good evening, Father. Are you enjoying the trip?"

Winn was dragged back from his irritated musings to find the tall, dark-haired captain of the steamboat, Jim Westlake, standing beside him. Westlake, Winn had been told, was one of the youngest captains on the river, but those who spoke of him lauded his knowledge of the Mississippi and steamboats.

"Oh, yes, Captain," he replied in an easy tone that revealed nothing of his conflicting emotions. "Your boat is beautiful. I'm convinced this is the only way to travel."

"I'm glad you think so. We're happy to have you with us. Enjoy your trip, and if there's anything you need just let us know."

The captain moved off to visit with the other passengers, and Winn turned back to watching Matt and Alex. The need to waltz with her became almost unbearable.

It puzzled Winn that he couldn't remember another time he'd wanted to dance with a woman so badly. There had always been dances and there had always been women, but this need was different. He wanted to be the only one holding her, the one making her laugh. He wanted his hand at her waist. He wanted to feel her moving in rhythm with him. He wanted to be Lord Winn Bradford for just tonight, instead of Father Bradford, saint-in-training.

Winn's frustration grew, and by the time the waltz finally came to an end, he knew what he was going to do. He was going to waltz with Alex. Nothing and no one was going to stop him.

"The next waltz is mine," he stated as Alex returned to his side on Matt's arm.

She glanced at him in surprise, and he smiled wryly at her.

"Yes, Alex, priests really do know how to dance."

The music began again, and to Winn's pleasure, it was another waltz.

"May I have the honor of this waltz, Alex?" he asked with formal precision. He gave her a slight bow as gallant as any he'd ever offered in any of the glittering ballrooms in London.

"I'd love to dance with you," she accepted, meaning every word.

Winn led her out onto the dance floor. He took her in his arms and began to move. In that moment, he was transformed. He was no longer Father Bradford. Now, he was Lord Winn Bradford and he was in his element. His hand at Alex's waist was knowing, his steps sure, his lead confident. The music spun a magical spell around them as they swayed and swirled to its fantastic rhythm.

Alex was breathless. She'd gone into Father Winn's

arms expecting a quiet, simple dance, but as he squired her about the floor, she discovered it was much more than that. He was an excellent dancer, far better than anyone she'd ever danced with before. Waltzing with him was a purely sensual experience, and she knew such an attraction was perilous. Still, all the logic in the world couldn't stop the excitement coursing through her.

Alex surreptitiously glanced up at Winn. He wasn't looking at her right then, so she had time to study him. She'd expected him to be a little uneasy dancing; instead, he'd proven himself an expert. She'd thought he might be a bit nervous; instead, he appeared relaxed and self-assured. She realized in confusion that he seemed born to this life. He fit in here—in this sophisticated ballroom with its shimmering candlelight and graceful music. Her gaze dropped to his throat and she stared at his collar in confusion. Tonight, somehow, it seemed alien to him. She lifted her gaze again, and it was just then that Winn glanced down at her.

Winn was amazed at how she instinctively moved with him and how perfectly matched they were. He looked down at her to find her watching him, her expression unreadable. Their gazes met and locked. Everything faded from his consciousness except her nearness. His hand tightened at her waist as he spun her in a dizzying circle. It was an exhilarating move, and Alex instinctively clung more tightly to him as he all but swept her away. The intimacy of the graceful maneuver transported them. They pivoted around the dance floor, their eyes only on each other, their bodies moving as one. It was heavenly.

And then the music stopped.

Winn was abruptly forced back to reality. He would have to let her go. He didn't want to. It wasn't easy for him, but he did it. Even though he really wanted to keep her with him for the rest of the night.

Alex had been caught up in the splendor of their waltz. When the music stopped, her spirits plummeted. She was amazed at how abandoned she felt when Father Winn stopped dancing and moved away from her. Dancing with Matt had been pleasant. Being in Father Winn's arms had been wonderful. Alex knew it was wrong for her to feel this way. She also knew it was a good thing she was out of his embrace. The waltz had been delightful, but she was being foolish if she let herself forget who he was or why they were there.

"Thank you," Winn said courteously as he led the way back to Matt.

"You're welcome. You're a wonderful dancer."

"You made it easy for me," he replied, his gaze warm upon her.

She was smiling as they rejoined her 'husband,' and he quickly took her back out on the floor.

Winn remained quietly on the sidelines. His expression betrayed nothing of his inner turmoil as he watched Matt and Alex enjoying themselves. The weight of his decision to assume his uncle's role was growing more and more stifling, and he was beginning to wonder just how much longer he could maintain his charade. His logical mind told him he would do it as long as was necessary. But a nagging doubt lingered as he watched Matt see Alex to her cabin that night and press a simple kiss on her cheek.

The following day as the paddlewheeler steamed ever closer to New Orleans, they sought out a quiet place on deck and started going over Lawrence's riddle, debating the secrets hidden within. Again, there was little solid evidence to go on, but Alex seemed convinced that the phrase 'life's little flowers' somehow referred to children. They could reach no consensus and knew there was no point in trying to go any further with it until they arrived in the city. Temporarily stymied, they put the riddle aside and decided to enjoy the rest of the trip with its occasional glimpses of huge plantations built along the river.

Later that evening, the three of them dined once again in the ornate dining room. As usual, the meal was superb.

"If you have no objection, I think I'll retire to the bar tonight and try my hand at a few games of chance," Matt said as he finished his dinner. "You never know what I might find out about New Orleans after a couple of drinks in the saloon."

"Good luck," Alex told him. She was feeling a little tired and planned to retire early.

"I can escort you back to the room, if you care to go now," he offered.

"That's all right. You go ahead and enjoy yourself. I'll take Alex back to her cabin when she's ready," Winn spoke up. He'd deliberately kept a distance between himself and Alex all day, but the opportunity to be alone with her for a few minutes was tempting.

Matt disappeared toward the back of the boat where the men's saloon was located. A night of gambling and a few drinks were just what he needed right now.

"Do you want to go with him?" Alex asked, not wanting Father Winn to feel that he was stuck with her. He'd been rather cool toward her all day, and she feared that maybe she'd been too obvious about her feelings when they'd danced the night before. "I'll be fine if you do."

"No, actually I prefer your company," Winn told her as he gazed at her in the soft light of the crystal chandeliers. He reveled in the thought that they were finally by themselves—for all the good it did him. "You look lovely tonight."

"Why, thank you."

His compliment caught her off-guard. She lifted her eyes to his and was immediately lost in the dark, mysterious depths of his emerald gaze. She wanted to believe that he was really thinking of her as an attractive woman, but she told herself he was just being nice. She told herself to change the subject.

"Do you think we'll have much trouble in New Orleans?" she asked.

"I wish I knew. We'll just have to do the same thing we did in St. Louis. We'll start off looking for 'something that has to do with 'life's little flowers.' The first part of the clue is simple enough. There's no doubt Lawrence was writing about the gulf, and the river, and . . ."

"Father Winn . . ." she interrupted. "Do you suppose we could annul the marriage now?"

Winn was tempted to tell her that she wasn't married at all, and that it didn't matter, but he had no idea what lay ahead of them, what Lawrence had in mind. "It's probably best to leave things as they are for now. Are you having trouble with Matt? Is there anything I can help you with?" He frowned as he considered the possibility.

"No, Father. Matt's charming and good-natured, and he's certainly been the perfect gentleman with me."

Winn gritted his teeth as he listened to her litany of Matt's good points.

"The situation is just awkward, that's all. I'll feel better once everything is back to normal," she finished, meaning it. She wanted to be back home with her father, safe and sound.

"I will, too. We've all had to give up something to make this dream come true," he agreed, resisting the urge to loosen his collar.

Winn was trying to keep their conversation casual, but Alex looked so beautiful in the candlelight that he was having difficulty concentrating. Though her gown was demure in cut and style, that very sedateness enhanced her loveliness. Its vibrant turquoise hue set off her creamy complexion and her burnished hair to perfection. She looked completely and utterly desirable.

Winn admitted openly to himself in that moment that he wanted her badly, and, having had several glasses of wine with dinner, he asked himself again just why he was pretending to be a priest. He had some vague and distant memory of wanting to please his uncle and help Lawrence, but right now, on this romantic steamer heading south, he wasn't too concerned about all that. Right now, he wanted to take Alex out on deck into the moonlight. He wanted to kiss her and hold her close. He wanted to . . .

"The Crown is worth any sacrifice," she was saying, interrupting his fantasy. "I can hardly wait to see it. I've read the tragic story of the prince and princess so many times, that it's hard for me to believe this really might finally come true."

"The history behind it is impressive," Winn said, trying to keep his mind on history and not on the way Alex had felt in his arms when they'd waltzed.

Around them the dining room was growing more and more deserted.

"Would you like to go for a walk on deck before we retire?" Winn suggested, unable to pass up the opportunity to have her to himself alone in the moonlight.

"I'd like that. It's so nice to be able to relax and enjoy this part of the trip. Most of the time, my travels with my father tend to be like our trip on the railroads."

"Well, we'll just have to do everything we can to make sure this part of the trip is as perfect as it can be for you," he told her as he rose and went to help her from her chair.

His words sent a shiver through Alex. They sounded so romantic that she could almost let herself believe them. Almost was the key word. This was Father

Winn—her chaperone. There was nothing more to it than that.

Playing the gentleman came easy to Winn, and he guided her from the room, his hand at the small of her back. She felt delicate, almost fragile to him, and he marveled at how very womanly she was. She wore an elusive scent this night, and he inhaled the heady fragrance as he led the way outside.

When they were on the moonlit deck, Winn took her arm and linked it through his. He enjoyed touching her, and for tonight, he was going to forget any thoughts of priestly vows and pretend for just a little while that he was courting her. The collar pinched its warning, but he ignored it.

"It's a nice night," she remarked as they paused at the rail to watch the scenery.

The moon hung high overhead, nearly full. It silvered the lush countryside and cast most everything into sharp contrasts of shadow and light. She glanced up at Winn as they stood so closely together and was amazed at how the starkness of the moonlight hardened his features. There was no softness in his countenance for the pale light highlighted the angles of his face and made him seem even more harshly masculine. She had a deeply primitive desire to reach up and touch his cheek. She wanted to caress that lean flesh and press her lips to the firm line of his mouth. He was the man of her dreams, and yet she knew that's all her feelings for him would ever be—a dream . . .

Alex gave herself a fierce mental shake, reminding herself just who Father Winn was and why he was there. She had to control her wayward feelings. Winn was a man of honor. He was gentle, kind, and completely honest. She'd watched him with the sisters. She'd seen what kind of a man he was. He was everything she admired and she rued the fact that they hadn't met earlier, before he'd taken the vows that stood between them. She wanted him desperately. But sadly, she accepted that it would never be.

"What are you thinking?" he asked, unexpectedly.

"Nothing. I was just enjoying the breeze and your company." She skirted the truth, not wanting to risk ruining their friendship by letting him know how she secretly felt. They were together tonight for this little while, and that was all that mattered.

Still, as much as Alex enjoyed the innocent contact of her arm linked through his, she knew she had to move away. She slipped her arm free of his hold, and she was sorry when he didn't protest her action. "What about you? What are you thinking?"

Winn couldn't tell her the truth. He couldn't tell her that he was thinking about how lovely she was and how much he wanted her. Instead, he answered, "I was thinking about my childhood and my parents."

"I'm sure you must have had wonderful parents."

"They were. My life was very simple and secure until they died."

"What happened?"

He told her the whole story of their accidental deaths.

"That must have been difficult for you, being left alone at such a young age."

"I had my Uncle Edward. He kept watch over me.

I went rather wild for a while, but he finally managed to convince me to change my ways."

"He must have been a very good influence on you. You're a fine priest."

"Oh, yes. He did influence me greatly. A lot of what he told me through the years has turned out to be true. He was a very wise man."

The thoughts of his uncle and home seemed to come from long ago in another lifetime. In these last few weeks, he'd truly changed. He'd become a completely different man. There had been a time when he wouldn't have cared a whit about sacred vows. Now, however, he understood. He thought about breaking his silence and telling Alex the truth, but Lawrence's letter, entreating his uncle's help, held him to his disguise. He had to keep up the charade. To reveal the truth now would risk the loss of the crown—and he was determined that they were going to find it.

Winn paused over that thought. He had no idea how much more traveling they would have to do before they reached their goal, and he wondered how he was going to keep his attraction to Alex hidden if they were forced into too many more intimate situations. He was supposed to be here protecting her and keeping her out of harm's way. The difficulty was, the way he was feeling about her, *he* might be what she most needed protecting from.

"I'd say you're following in your uncle's footsteps. I've never met anyone like you."

"What do you mean?"

She turned to look up at him. Her eyes were wide

and luminous, and in the moment, all of what she felt for him was revealed in her gaze. "I mean you're honest and forthright and you always do the right thing."

He almost groaned aloud, and was glad she couldn't read his thoughts.

"You make me sound like a saint," he protested, wondering what she was going to think once she learned of his deception.

"I'd say you and Sister Agnes were well on your way," she remarked.

As Alex spoke, the steamer suddenly, unexpectedly gave a violent lurch. Striking an uncharted sandbar, it swung wildly around, battling the current and the obstruction.

Caught off guard, Winn was thrown backward, away from Alex, as she was slung forcefully against the rail. The rail gave a sickening crack, sounding as if it were about to break, and Winn reacted instinctively. He threw himself toward Alex and grabbed her, yanking her away from the rail and into the safe haven of his embrace.

Suddenly, everything was quiet. The boat was still, and they were standing on the darkly shadowed deck, wrapped in each other's arms. They were shocked and mesmerized by the current of desire that flowed between them. As they stood together, gazing at each other in awestruck wonder, everything else faded away. The universe narrowed to just the two of them.

Alex was trembling, whether from her close call at the railing or Winn's compelling nearness, she wasn't sure. All she knew was that the feel of his hard body molded to hers was ecstasy. Her hands clutched at his shoulders, and she could feel the power in him. He was a man, all man, and she wanted him . . . she wanted this . . . with all her heart.

Winn stared down at Alex, the harsh rasp of his breathing revealed the sudden terror that had gripped him. He had almost lost her. She could have fallen. . . . She could have been killed . . .

His gaze went over her upturned features, making sure she was all right. He couldn't let anything happen to her. He'd tried to deny it up until this moment, but there could be no more lying to himself. She was the woman he wanted, and she was in his arms. . . . The innocence in her eyes warred with the temptation of her lips, slightly parted as if begging for union with his, and he could restrain himself no longer.

Suddenly, it didn't matter to Winn that she believed herself to be another man's wife. Winn knew the wedding had been a fake. It didn't matter that everyone thought he was a priest. Winn knew he wasn't. In that instant, there was only the two of them, alone on deck, locked in each other's arms.

Winn couldn't stop. This was what he'd waited his whole life for . . . this moment . . . Alex in his arms, looking up at him with eyes that promised eternity. He bent his head, his gaze fixed on her lips, as he anticipated tasting the sweetness of her. He whispered her name in an agonized, verbal caress as his mouth descended to hers. "Alex . . ."

Alex knew she shouldn't do this. Every fiber of her moral being cried out to her to stop and think about what she was doing. This was Father Winn about to kiss her! She was married to Matt! They had both taken vows before God. But then his mouth claimed hers, and there was no time to think. There was only time to feel. She knew she should stop him, yet as he held her close, she couldn't deny her need. She met him in that kiss.

It was heaven, that first embrace. A sweet glory of passion, new born. They were meant to be together. They were two parts of a whole that had been lost, but were now found.

Winn's mouth moved over hers, deepening the exchange. Ecstasy pulsed through them both. He brought her more fully against him, wanting to hold her as close as he could. He'd wanted her from the first moment he'd seen her in Boston, and he meant to have her. Winn's control shattered as he felt her response to him. He knew then that he had to be the one who awakened in her the fire of her desire. He wanted to be the one who taught her of love's delights.

A distant, nagging thought of self-control taunted Winn, but he mentally shoved it away. He didn't want to deny himself. He didn't like denying himself. He wanted her and he would take her. She was clinging to him as if he and he alone were her lifeline to safety, and he reveled in the knowledge that she wanted him, too.

Winn's desire-drugged mind was already planning a way to lead her off to her cabin where they could be alone, when the steamer shuddered to life again. Reversing its engines, it gave a jarring shift as the pilot tried to back it off the sandbar.

The action jolted Alex back from the paradise she'd found in Winn's arms to the pain of reality. She tore herself free of his loving embrace, her emotions in turmoil. She was filled with fear over what she'd almost done and self-loathing for having allowed it to go even this far.

"No! We can't do this . . ." Alex gasped, horrified by her own behavior. "I won't let you do this!"

Winn stared at her, seeing her passion-glazed eyes and her flushed cheeks. A groan of pure animal desire escaped him.

"Alex . . ." he growled in desperation, needing her back in his arms, needing to taste of her sweetness, and to feel her melt against him. "Think of me as a man—not a priest."

"I can't!" she agonized, She started to turn away from him, for the desire to go back into his arms was nearly overwhelming.

Winn could not let her go. He grabbed her arm as she would have fled and stopped her. "I want you, Alex."

Tears filled her eyes. "I want you, too, but we can't do this! Please . . . let me go . . ."

"But Alex . . ."

"You've taken your vows as I've taken mine. Don't you understand? In God's eyes, I'm married to Matt!" A small sob escaped her as she tore herself away from him and ran down the deck, disappearing into her stateroom.

Winn stood alone in the middle of the dark, deserted deck. He wanted to follow Alex, to smash open her door, and claim her for his own, but her tortured, tearful words held him at bay. His body was on fire with the need to be one with hers, but there would be no relief. Alex thought him an honorable man, and despite all his wishes to the contrary, she was determined he remain that way.

Winn wished right then and there that she wasn't quite so honorable herself. As soon as he thought about it, though, he knew he was wrong. Alex could never be less than honest and forthright, and those were qualities about her that he loved. She was different from any woman he'd ever known before. There was no guile in her, no cunning or deceit. She was concerned with more important things than parties, liaisons, and the other trivial things the women of his social circle dwelt on. Alex was special.

Winn could not remember another time in his life when he'd cared what a woman thought about him, but right now he cared what Alex thought. He sighed almost painfully as he wondered what she would do once she learned he'd been lying to her. She thought he was a virtuous, noble, and self-sacrificing priest. In truth, he was a rich, titled Englishman, who hadn't done an honest day's work in his life until Sister Agnes had gotten hold of him.

His hands clenched into fists at his sides. He wanted her so badly that he physically ached with the power of his need. He knew that somehow he was going to have to convince her nothing had changed between them. Yet, even as he considered it, he realized it was crazy. Everything had changed between them. Her kiss had been unlike anything he'd ever known before. She was innocent, yet passionate, and the combination was powerful enough to bring even the strongest man to his knees and make him cast his vows aside—whatever they might be.

Winn stared down the empty deck for a moment longer, and then turned away. His mood was black, his expression thunderous, and his stride determined as he started off in the direction of the men's saloon. He needed to ease his frustration, and right now a game of cards and a straight whiskey seemed the best, and only, antidote available.

"Unsettling, wasn't it, Father?" a man's voice came from behind him, drawing him up short. "It's tricky business trying to pull off something like that."

Winn tensed, believing the man behind him had witnessed his intimacy with Alex. He silently cursed his own weakness in giving in to his need for her. Drawing a deep, steadying breath, he prepared to face the man and to try to explain the situation. He turned around to find it was Captain Westlake.

"There is an explanation . . ." he began, desperately searching for the right words to protect Alex's reputation and his own.

Jim went on, completely unaware of his discomfort. "Indeed there is. That particular bend in the river deals everyone a fit. It's dangerous even in daylight, but at night, it's treacherous."

"Oh, the river . . ." Winn didn't know when he'd

ever been so relieved. He found himself grinning almost stupidly as the steamer captain explained the dangers of sandbars.

"Yes, running aground like that can cause a lot of trouble, but mostly it's upsetting for the passengers. It takes a good pilot to back her off without any damage, and it looks like our man did a fine job. I've just been checking the decks and everything seems to be in order. Did you have any problems down here?"

"The rail may be split back there," he said, indicating the place where Alex had been thrown against it.

"Thanks, Father, I'll get some repair men on it right away." Jim Westlake stopped to inspect the rail.

Winn didn't realize how the captain's unexpected appearance had worried him until he reached the entrance to the main cabin and the tension began to ease out of him. More than ready for a stiff drink and a little diversion, he headed straight to the saloon.

Eleven

A haze of smoke hung in the air, and the mood in the bar was one of easy male camaraderie. Several card games were already in progress as Winn entered, but he decided to have a drink before joining in. He ordered his whiskey straight at the bar and then positioned himself to observe the poker game Matt was playing. Matt won easily, and Winn realized he didn't have any real competition. When one of the other players folded, he decided he'd try his luck against him.

"Mind if I sit in?" Winn asked.

"Fine with me," Matt said, and the three others who remained offered no real objection.

"You gamble a lot, Father?" one of the gamblers, a man who introduced himself as Melvin, asked. The thought of a priest joining their game bothered him a little.

"I've been known to play a hand or two in my time," Winn replied easily as he got a bottle of whiskey from the bartender and settled in at the table. He was amazed at how good it felt to be in a smoke-filled room, drinking whiskey and playing cards again.

"You don't have any connections upstairs that'll give

you an advantage over us, do you?" Melvin wondered with a laugh.

"I wish I did."

It was Matt's deal, and he did so proficiently. Play began. The player leading off was a young man named Josh. He was barely twenty by Winn's estimation, and he had the look of a farm boy. It was obvious right away that he'd had very little real gambling experience, and Winn figured the others had been winning handily off of him all night.

Several hands were played. Winn won steadily. Josh lost goodly sums each time for he refused to quit, not realizing what cards had been played and when it was time to fold. As the youth's pile of money got smaller and smaller, Winn noticed that he grew more nervous and rushed in his play.

More hands were dealt. More whiskey was drunk. Betting grew spirited. Melvin dropped out of the game first, followed by Richards. It was down to just three of them—Matt, Winn and Josh.

"Well, after this hand, I think I'll go see how my lovely wife is doing," Matt said casually, inventing an excuse to leave the game.

Winn had been enjoying himself—for a little while. He'd actually managed not to think about Alex for a few minutes. The moment Matt mentioned her name, however, he remembered her protest to him on deck that he was a priest and she was married to Matt, and his mood turned foul. With narrowed eyes and serious intent, Winn concentrated on the cards as he'd never done before. Suddenly, the game meant something. He was going to beat Matt, and he was going to beat him soundly. When he did, he was going to enjoy every minute of it. With cunning and expertise, he deliberately ran the stakes up higher and higher. He didn't give a thought to Josh. He thought only about how good it was going to feel when he trounced Matt and won the hand.

"I call," Josh announced nervously as he threw the last of his money in the pot. He'd stayed with them, matching their bets until now, but with the last raise, he'd run out of funds. He didn't know what he was going to do if he lost. He'd just bet every cent he had in the world. . . . He was scared, but he hoped the fear didn't show in his eyes.

"Let's see what you've got," Matt told him.

Josh spread out two pairs—jacks and sixes.

"Three kings, ace high," Winn announced as he spread his cards before him.

Matt muttered a frustrated curse under his breath as he tossed in his hand facedown. "Beats me. You're one helluva poker player, Father Winn. I've had enough. I'm calling it a night."

Winn was smiling in satisfaction as he raked in the substantial pot. He couldn't remember the last time he'd enjoyed winning at poker so much.

"I think I'll quit, too," he added, not wanting to give Matt any chance to have time alone with Alex. "I thank you gentlemen for letting me sit in and for a very lucrative evening."

As Winn stood up, he pocketed the cash, then picked up his bottle of whiskey and handed it to Matt to take with them. "You never know when we might need that."

Josh, meanwhile, fled the saloon. The humiliation of his defeat was almost more than he could bear. He'd lost everything. He stood outside in the black night, wondering what to do next. Before he'd left home, his mother had warned him against the evils of gambling, but he hadn't understood what she'd meant until now. The thrill of the betting had robbed him of his common sense. The possibility of winning had become an unquenchable fire in his blood as he'd sat at the table with the other gamblers. He'd believed he could win . . . he'd known he could! He was embarrassed and broke now, and at a loss for what to do next with his life.

Winn emerged from the saloon with Matt to see Josh standing alone on deck, dejected and miserable. The money in Winn's pocket weighed heavily on him. He was the reason the boy had lost everything. He'd deliberately raised the stakes high to beat Matt.

Winn stared at the stricken boy for a moment. In spite of the liquor he'd consumed, there was no ignoring the chafing of the collar he wore. It nagged at his conscience, urging him to do what was right. Winn told himself he was crazy, that he'd won the money fair and square. But still, he knew what he had to do.

"Wait for me," he told Matt.

"Where are you going?" Matt couldn't imagine what he was up to.

"I just want to talk to our young friend there for a

minute," he answered, nodding in Josh's direction. "I'll be right back."

He approached the youth quietly.

"Josh?"

"Yes, Father?"

"Did you learn a valuable lesson tonight?"

Josh gave a short bark of pained laughter. "Yes, Father. I learned a real valuable lesson."

"Are you ever going to gamble again?"

"I couldn't if I wanted to. I don't have any money left," he admitted wryly.

"But if you did have money. Would you go back to the tables?"

"No, Father. I may not be the smartest man in the world, but I'm smart enough to realize I don't have what it takes to be a gambler. I won't be betting again."

"Good." Winn smiled. "Here." He handed him the entire pot he'd just won.

"Why are you doing this?" Josh's eyes widened in surprise.

"Let's just say because it's the right thing to do. Now, you promise you'll stay out of places like that?"

"Yes, sir." He looked down at the money he held and then back up at him. He was humbled by the good Father's generosity. "Thanks, Father," he said in a choked voice.

Winn clapped him on the back and moved off to rejoin Matt.

Matt had watched the whole scene, but didn't say anything about the exchange right away. He was thinking of his lovely 'bride' and wondering if she was safe in her cabin.

"Did Alex say if she was going to stay up or not?"

"I believe she was going to bed," Winn answered, hoping to divert him from looking in on Alex. He wasn't about to let Matt visit her alone, and the last thing he needed right then was to see her again.

"Let's walk by her cabin just to make sure everything's all right, and then we can go on to bed," Matt suggested.

Winn grew tense as they neared Alex's cabin door. He was afraid that he would see her, but then again, he was afraid that he wouldn't. When there was no sign of her and everything seemed quiet, he breathed a sigh of relief. They made their way to their own stateroom, and it wasn't until they were inside that Matt brought up Winn's talk with Josh.

"That was a very kind thing you did with the boy," Matt told him as they settled in. "You really are a good-hearted man, Father Winn."

Winn had had all he could stand. Matt's simple heartfelt praise was all the spark he needed to set fire to his already heated mood. First, he'd had Alex telling him what a wonderful priest he was and how she wasn't going to let him break his vows, and now Matt!

The liquor he'd consumed loosened his tongue and heightened his frustration. Winn was bound and determined to convince Matt right then and there that he wasn't the self-sacrificing, virtuous man they thought he was. "Damn it, Matt! I'm not as good as you think

I am! I wish you and Alex would stop trying to make me into a saint!"

"But Father Winn, you . . ." Matt stared at him, stunned by his tone of voice.

"Listen to me!" Winn cut him off before he could say any more. "I'm just an ordinary man. That's all."

"Father Winn, you're anything but ordinary," he complimented him again.

"Stop it!"

"Stop what?"

"Stop what? Telling you the truth about yourself? There's nothing ordinary about you." Matt had watched him with people during their travels. He'd seen him with old women and children—and with Sister Agnes.

"No, you don't understand," he ground out, fighting the overwhelming desire to blurt out the truth and be done with it. The clue had something about 'two shall be as one, but your fate is not that to be . . . ,' so maybe the need for using his uncle's identity was over as well as the need for Matt and Alex's marriage. He'd successfully avoided the Anthony brothers and he'd won both Matt's and Alex's trust. Maybe he didn't need the priestly disguise any more. Maybe he could finish the quest as himself. Telling the truth at that moment sounded like a wonderful idea to Winn.

"Understand, what, Father Winn?" Matt was puzzled by this sudden change in the priest. He could have sworn he sounded almost angry.

"That I'm not 'Father' anything, damn it!"

Matt stared at him in real confusion. "What are you talking about?"

Winn faced him. "Matt, I think maybe it's time you learned the truth."

"The truth? What truth?"

"Matt . . ." Winn waited until he was sure he had his full attention, and then he reached up and took off his clerical collar. He tossed it on his bunk. "I'm not a priest."

Alex couldn't rest. When she'd first run away from Father Winn, she'd been terrified that he would follow her. It wasn't that she was afraid of him, so much as she was afraid of herself . . . of what she was feeling. If Father Winn had come after her, she'd feared that she wouldn't be able to resist him. She'd been attracted to him before the kiss, but now that she knew the wonder of being in his arms, she wondered how she was ever going to look him in the eye again. His embrace had been her heaven and her hell. It had been a taste of paradise, and it was never going to happen again.

At first, as nervous as she was, she'd paced her room in anticipation and fear of his coming. Then, when he hadn't followed, she'd paced her room in despair, imagining a future without him. Finally, knowing there was nothing else for her to do, she'd undressed and gone to bed.

Sleep, however, had proved elusive. Every time Alex closed her eyes, she saw Father Winn as he'd been that night in the moonlight . . . starkly handsome, wonderfully male. The very essence of him had thrilled her, and his single kiss had left her weak with desire. She'd never known a kiss could evoke such strong emotions. It was as if by that simple embrace, he'd touched her very soul.

Every time Alex had started to slip into the fantasy of being in his arms again, she mentally dragged herself back to face the truth. And the truth was painful no matter how she looked at it. Her feelings for him were forbidden. She would never have his love.

As hours passed and Winn didn't come after her, Alex knew she'd won. It was a victory she wasn't sure she'd wanted, but it was hers. They would both honor their vows. They would not sully their relationship.

The thought of seeing Father Winn the next day still troubled her. She'd discovered in keeping her secret about the Anthony brothers that she did have some acting ability. But she didn't know if she'd be good enough to maintain her composure when they came face-to-face again. If he acted as if nothing had happened, then she would be able to do the same. However, there was no guarantee what she would do if he touched her again. Her heart was still so vulnerable.

Alex lay in bed in the dark, tossing and turning for what seemed like eternity. She finally concluded that she had little hope of getting any sleep and decided what she needed was a breath of fresh air. The stateroom Matt and Father Winn were sharing was on the opposite side of the steamer, so she figured she wouldn't have to worry about seeing them again tonight. She rose and dressed again, then slipped out on deck to stand at the railing in the moonlight.

* * *

"You're not a priest?" Matt repeated as he looked from Winn to the collar he'd just tossed on his bed. "What the devil are you talking about?"

"It's a long story."

"Then the wedding was a fake?" he asked in disbelief.

"Yes."

Laughter roared from Matt as he pondered all the ramifications of Winn's disguise.

"I don't know what you find so comical," Winn told him with as much dignity as he could muster considering the circumstances.

Matt was still grinning. "It's a damned good thing Alex and I didn't take our marriage vows seriously. No wonder you were so vigilant in keeping us apart."

Winn didn't even want to talk about that. He pulled one of his own white linen shirts out of his bag and started to change into it, glad to be free to be himself again. "The good news is you won't have to worry about an annulment. There was no marriage in the first place."

"Amazing. What's this all about? If you aren't Father Winn Bradford, who are you?"

"Are you sure you want to hear it?"

"I think I'd better," he answered as he sat down on his bunk.

Winn told him about his uncle's death, about receiving the letter and book from Lawrence Anthony at about the same time, and about Philip's and Robert's visit. He explained how, after their visit, he'd read Lawrence's desperate plea to his uncle and how he'd decided to follow through on the collector's wish that the three of them should go on the hunt for the crown and also make certain that his sons did not lay claim to it.

"I wanted to get out of London without either Philip or Robert finding out, so I assumed my uncle's place and left the very next morning for Boston. Lawrence's letter indicated that only my uncle could lead the search, for his faith marked him as a man to be trusted. I did what I thought best . . . what I thought I had to do at the time."

Matt stared at Winn, seeing him for the first time in an all new light as he shed his identity as a priest. Winn was an adventurer just like himself—a man on a mission, not a priest trying to save souls and right the injustices of the world. He started to laugh again as he tried to imagine himself in the same strictures.

"Difficult, was it?"

"You'll never know," he answered, thinking of the long hours on the train and the time at the convent trying his best to act knowledgeable and not give himself away.

"What about Alex?"

"What about her?" he countered sharply.

"Why do I have a feeling that Alex is a part of the problem?"

"I don't know what you're talking about."

"I'm talking about your determination to keep our marriage one 'in name only,' and I'm talking about the way you two danced in the ballroom last night."

"It was a waltz, nothing more."

Matt didn't believe a word of what Winn was saying. "Now I know why you tried so hard to leave her behind . . ."

"It hasn't been easy."

"Do you want to keep this just between us? Do you want to maintain the charade for Alex?"

"No. I'm tired of living a lie."

"What will you tell her?"

"The same thing I've told you. The truth. This shouldn't change anything about our quest. We're still going to follow the clues and find the crown. But from now on I'm going to be simply Winn Bradford on the trail of the treasure, not Father Bradford. There's been enough deception already."

"All right. That's fine with me."

"Then, as my last official act as Father Bradford, I want you to consider your marriage officially annulled."

Matt gave a rueful shake of his head as he opened the whiskey bottle and lifted it to Winn in a mock toast. "And Alex and I could have been so happy . . ."

"I'll have a drink when you're done—a toast to my vocation," he replied.

Matt got two tumblers from where they sat on the nightstand and poured them each a healthy splash.

"I still have to tell you that you did make a very good priest. Your uncle would have been pleased," Matt told him.

"I hope so," Winn said softly as he took a deep drink from his glass.

It was nearly an hour later when they finished off the last of the liquor. Matt stretched out in contentment on his bed and fell quickly asleep. Winn, however, still feeling restless, knew it would be a pointless endeavor to try to sleep just yet. He left the cabin to stroll the deserted deck alone.

Winn was lost in thought as he tried to plan what he was going to say to Alex in the morning. He would tell her the truth, and then he would deal with her disillusionment and anger. Winn knew that it would be far easier to face those emotions from her then to let her continue to believe that she had tempted him from vows.

Winn didn't deliberately set out for Alex's stateroom. He just started walking and found himself nearing her cabin. To his surprise, Alex was standing at the rail, gazing out across the river, unaware of his presence. He quietly moved closer.

"Alex . . ." he said her name in a husky whisper.

Alex had been lost in a dream of Father Winn, reliving that one precious moment when they'd been just a man and a woman with nothing to keep them apart. She gasped as she recognized the deep timbre of his voice, and she looked up quickly to find him just a few feet away from her. For a moment, Alex almost believed that she'd somehow magically conjured him up. He was dressed casually as he had been that day in Boston when she'd gone to see him at the hotel. Seeing him again this way set her pulses spinning, and, unnerved by his nearness, her thoughts reeled in confusion.

"What do you want?"

"I need to talk to you." His voice was low and smooth.

Her expression was stricken. The last thing she wanted to do was send him away from her again, but she had to.

"It would be better if we waited until morning to talk," she told him, denying herself that which she wanted more than anything.

Alone in her stateroom, she'd berated herself for being so foolish. She'd told herself that she should never have kissed him. But now as he stood before her looking more handsome and desirable than ever, an ache grew deep within her, and she knew if he asked she would deny him nothing. Tears burned in her eyes at her weakness. She was so affected by his presence that she had to force herself to look away from him.

"What I have to say to you can't wait until morning, Alex. Please," he asked softly, "invite me in."

He waited for her answer. He would not pressure her to listen to him. She remained quiet as if she were fighting some terrible war within herself over his request.

"Alex, love, I promise you, nothing will happen between us that you don't want to happen."

Lifting her starry-eyed gaze to him, she finally answered, "All right."

She turned and opened her cabin door and went in ahead of him.

Winn stepped inside, but made no move toward her. He waited while she closed the door behind them. Only then did he speak.

"Alex, there's something very important that I have to tell you."

"No, Father Winn. Wait. Let me go first. It's important that I tell you how I feel, and as frightened as I am right now, I have to say these things before you say anything more."

"But . . ." With a simple sentence he knew he could set everything straight between them, but she would not let him speak.

"Please, Father Winn. Listen . . ."

He fell silent. She waited to make sure he wasn't going to try and stop her, then she began.

"What happened on the deck between us earlier was a mistake. I'm sorry. I shouldn't have kissed you. It's just that . . ." She stumbled over her words, trying not to speak the truth, trying not to tell him that she loved him. "It's just that I care about you deeply. I know you've dedicated yourself to another way of life, and I want you to know that I would never intentionally do anything to cause you any pain or embarrassment. Matt and I, well, I know our marriage is in name only, but I did promise to be his wife, and until the marriage is annulled, I have to keep that promise. So, I want you to know that as far as I'm concerned, our kiss never happened. I want us to be friends as we have been, Father Winn. I don't ever want to jeopardize our friendship."

Winn waited, listening to her and wondering how he'd ever gotten himself into such a mess. Her pain was so obvious, her desire to do the right thing so wonderful, that he could no more have stopped himself from holding her than he could have stopped breathing. With infinite tenderness, he closed the distance between them and took her in his arms.

"No . . . Father Winn, don't . . ." Please don't!" She tried to pull away from him, but he held her close. His grip was firm but not painful in any way. After a moment, she gave up the struggle.

"I listened to you, Alex. Now, it's your turn to listen to me." He held her slightly away from him so he could see her, and he gazed down at her tear-streaked face. "Alex, you are one of the few truly honest people I've met. I care about you . . . deeply, but there's something I have to tell you. Something I should have told you long ago, but until tonight, it was impossible."

"I don't understand." She blinked in bewilderment, trying to make sense out of what he was saying.

"I came to you tonight dressed this way for a reason. You see, I'm not wearing a collar any more."

"What are you saying?" she cried, shocked by what she believed he was implying. "You can't give up your calling! Don't you realize how wrong it would be for you to forsake your vows?"

"Alex . . ." He soothed. "I've taken no vows."

She looked up at him startled. "What are you talking about?"

"Alex. I'm not the wonderful, dedicated man you think I am."

"Yes, you are. I've watched you helping people, and I saw you with the sisters at the convent."

He chuckled tenderly. "I'm a better actor than I

thought I was. The truth is, Alex, I'm not a priest. It's all been a lie—my vocation, your marriage . . ."

"What?!" This time when she tried to get away from him, he let her go. She took a step back, distancing herself from him.

"I'm not a priest, Alex. My name is Winston Bradford. My uncle, Edward Bradford, was the priest."

"I don't understand." Her eyes had widened and her expression was bewildered. "You're not a priest?"

"No, and you're not married to Matt, so there's no need for an annulment."

Twelve

"You made a fool out of me!" she challenged, her temper flaring. "You've been laughing at me all this time, while I was trusting you completely!"

"Alex," he began in a conciliatory tone, "I know what you're thinking, but believe me, if there's one thing I've never done, it's laugh at you. The more time I spent with you, the more difficult it became for me to deny what I was feeling for you." His confession was in earnest.

"Does Matt know about this?"

"I told him just before I came here, to you. He thought the whole situation was amusing, especially the fact that your marriage wasn't valid."

"He would."

"I have to tell you now, Alex, that the night I 'married' you and Matt was one of the most difficult of my life. You will never know how worried I was that the two of you might decide to take your vows more seriously than we'd intended."

Her anger was fading rapidly before the joyous realization that he really wasn't 'Father' Winn. "I wouldn't have," she said softly.

"How was I to know that? You just sat at dinner tonight and told me how much you like him and how wonderful he is. How was I to know you weren't falling in love with him? All I could do was sit helplessly by and watch."

"Why are you telling me this now, after all this time?" Alex asked, her heart beating a powerful rhythm as she waited for his answer.

Winn took a step closer and lifted a hand to caress her cheek. "After our kiss, I couldn't live with the lie any longer or with the pain I was causing you."

His touch was unbearably tender, and his words were like a balm to her savaged soul. Alex wanted to know why he'd felt the need to lie in the first place, but she would ask that later. Right now, kissing him again seemed much more important. "Winn . . ."

Winn smiled tenderly down at her as she said his name without the 'Father' in front of it. She knew the truth now, and he could no longer deny himself the wonder of her embrace. He reached for her and drew her to him, his lips capturing hers in a slow, tantalizing kiss.

Winn's mouth seared hers with the heat of his need, and Alex responded without reserve. There was nothing standing between them now, nothing to prevent them from being together. He was the man she'd always dreamed of, and he was here, with her. They clung together, wrapped in the splendor of their desire.

Alex trembled before the power of the emotion flooding through her. *He wasn't a priest. . . . He wasn't a priest. . . .* The thought sang in her heart as she savored his closeness. When at last the kiss ended, she drew just slightly away, enough so she could look up at him.

"Winn, I could never fall in love with Matt—not when I'm already in love with someone else." She gazed up at him, seeing his passion-darkened eyes and remembering how desperately she'd wanted to kiss him the night they'd danced. She smiled dreamily as she allowed herself the luxury of touching his hard, lean cheek. "I thought I could never have you. I thought . . ." There was a catch in her voice as if she were still having trouble believing something so wonderful could have happened.

"I'm no priest, Alex. I'm just a man," Winn said gently, and he held her to his heart.

His mouth descended to hers again, and he claimed her lips in a passionate exchange. Alex knew that this was what she'd waited for all her life. She lifted her arms to him and looped them about his neck as she pressed herself against him. The contact of her soft, womanly curves with his hard lean body was electric, and Winn groaned as he pulled back from her.

"Ah, Alex, I've wanted you for so long . . . needed you. . . . But I'm supposed to be protecting you. If you don't want this to go any further, tell me now, and I'll stop." He waited tensely for her reply.

She could hear the agony of his dilemma in his voice, and she smiled at him. "Tonight, I don't want or need your protection, Winn. Tonight, I just want you."

Alex's words were an invitation he couldn't refuse. Without another word, he lifted her up into his arms and carried her to the bed. The narrow stateroom bunk was a far cry from the plush surroundings he was accustomed to, but somehow none of that mattered right now. He cared nothing about the cabin or his surroundings. He cared only about Alex . . . about pleasing her.

They came together in a fiery rush. The long-denied desire they'd harbored deep within them flared into an inferno of unquenchable passion. There would be no self-denial tonight. There would be no sleepless hours of frustration or worry. They would be together. They would be one. They would love.

Winn wanted her with a blazing need, but he knew Alex was an innocent. She was nothing like the other women who'd been in his life, and he reveled in her virtue.

With utmost care, Winn helped her undress. What could have been an awkward moment became a memory of pure beauty as they shared the intimacy with soft kisses and gentle caresses. As he stripped away the last of her clothes, baring her feminine beauty to his heated regard, an incredible rush of tenderness tempered his desire. Alex was perfect. She was slender, yet still all woman. Her creamy breasts were high and firm, their dusky pink crests taut. Her legs were long and shapely, her hips round and inviting. His throat went dry as he realized that she was giving to him her most precious gift. She was offering him her very self. The knowledge both humbled and honored him.

"You're so beautiful," he told her, his voice thick with passion. Suddenly, he could just look at her no longer. He needed to feel her flesh against his, the heat of her body pressed to his own. He began to unbutton his shirt, struggling with the buttons in his impatience.

"I'm glad you think so," Alex said as she watched him take off his own shirt and cast it aside.

When he turned back to her, naked to the waist, she reached for him hungrily. Her hands eagerly sculpted the powerful muscles of his broad chest and shoulders.

Winn had never known a woman's touch could bring such delight—and such pain. His breathing grew ragged as he gladly suffered her innocent torment. He wanted to strip away the rest of his clothing and put an end to his glorious frustration, but he knew he couldn't rush her. He had to go slowly. Even so, as logical as he was, his rationalizing was a weak defense against the compelling heat of his need. It took all of his impressive self-control to contain his desire.

"I've wanted to do this ever since the day I saw you painting the widow's house," she admitted as she caressed him.

Her touch was unschooled, but the sweet innocence of her exploration made it much more exciting.

"I didn't know."

"I couldn't let you know. You were forbidden to me. I thought I would never be able to kiss you or tell you how I felt."

"And how do you feel?" he urged.

"I love you, Winn."

At her declaration, his mouth took hers in a fiery, possessive kiss that stirred both of them to mindless ecstasy. She had touched his heart as well as his soul. He moved over her, and the softness of her breasts seared his chest as they lay together. His hands began a sensual foray over her satiny limbs. Her skin was silken beneath his touch, and his hunger grew to make her his own.

He shed the rest of his clothes and then lay down beside her. He did not know the extent of her knowledge about the male body, and he was careful to try not to distress her.

"I want to see you, too," she said, surprising him. He shifted his position so she could gaze fully upon him, and he gasped in pleasure as she reached out to explore the leanness of his hip and the flat plane of his stomach with a gentle hand. When she would have touched him even more intimately, he was forced to stop her. Catching her wrist, he brought her hand to his lips and kissed it. His control had been good so far, but he couldn't guarantee he could withstand such exquisite torture without shaming himself.

"Open to me, love. Let me make you mine now," he whispered, his eyes burning into hers.

"Oh, yes, Winn . . ."

She opened to him as a budding flower opens to the sun. He came to her then, fitting himself intimately against her and breaching her innocence as he claimed her for his own.

It was a beautiful blending of male and female. Each created perfect for the other. Hardness yielding to softness, velvet conquering steel. The offered to each other without constraint the fullness of their love.

Sheathed within the virginal heat of her body, Winn

gloried in their joining. It was ecstasy to become one with her.

Never before had Winn cared about a woman's pleasure before his own. Never before had he wanted to please someone more than he wanted to please himself. It was a new experience for him, and it was a revelation. He gave of himself from his heart and his soul. He wanted to please Alex, to satisfy her in every way.

Alex surrendered to his practiced lovemaking. She was his to do with as he pleased. For so long, she'd thought she would never know the beauty of his love. His thrilling revelation, however, had set her free to explore the wonder of her feelings for him. She gave herself over to his tender tutelage, and as he began to move within her, she matched his rhythm.

They ascended to the heights of love together. Alex reached the pinnacle of pleasure with Winn. When ecstasy burst upon her, she clung to him, savoring his strength and his warmth. They crested and then drifted softly back to earth.

Winn cradled Alex to his side, her head resting on his shoulder, her hand spread out on his chest, her silken curves nestled against him. His embrace was cherishing. Never before had lovemaking been so fulfilling, and never before had he cared so deeply that it would be.

"I knew it would be this way," Alex sighed.

"What way?" He was curious. Even as innocent as she was, she'd been more responsive and passionate than any other woman he'd ever known.

"Perfect." Came her answer.

He smiled, and they lay quietly, their limbs entwined, enjoying the freedom and intimacy of being alone together. As the night aged, though, Winn knew he had to leave her.

"I have to get back to my own cabin," he muttered regretfully.

"Don't. Stay here with me until we dock in New Orleans," she invited daringly as she raised up on one elbow to look down at him. As she did, her breasts grazed his chest.

He groaned in sweet arousal. "There's nothing I'd like better than to stay in bed with you," he admitted, pulling her down for a kiss. "But, in case you've forgotten, sweet, everyone on board still thinks I'm a priest."

"I'm glad you're not." She murmured, leaning down to press a soft kiss to his lips.

"So am I."

His arms came around her again, and for a little while longer, they forgot about everything else.

It was later as they lay together, momentarily sated, that Winn noticed the first hint of dawn brightening the eastern sky. He was putting Alex in jeopardy by staying so long.

"I have to go, Alex. I can't let anyone see me coming out of your cabin at this time of the night."

"Or day," she finished, feeling decidedly wicked after having loved him so long and so wildly. It seemed quite natural to be lying with him this way, and yet she knew that only hours before she'd believed he was unattainable and lost to her forever.

"Or day," he admitted. "I promised you when we left Boston that I would protect you, and I will." Their eyes met. "Now, more than ever."

Alex, saw the fervor in the emerald depths of his gaze as he pledged to keep her safe. "Thank you."

"Alex, I promise never to let anything hurt you."

She closed her eyes against the earnestness she saw in his gaze. Winn was a good man, and she knew he would do everything in his power to help her if she needed him. She did need him, desperately, in fact. But the situation with the Anthonys was dangerous and potentially deadly. She trusted Winn completely, and she wanted to confide in him, but fear for her father's life held her back. His life was in her hands, and she had to be careful.

Their lips met again. It was a sweet and tender exchange, and it told Winn everything he need to know about her feelings for him. When it ended, he reluctantly put her from him. The thought of having her one last time was tempting, but he had already taken too many risks with her reputation as it was. He got up and started to dress.

"I wish you never had to leave me." Alex told him.

She rose up on her knees and held her arms out to him in an innately sensuous invitation that nearly drove all logical thoughts from his mind. As he gazed at her, he knew it wouldn't take much to convince him to stay in her bed until they reached port more than a day away. A fragment of some sense remained, though, and

Winn went to her just to hold her. He marvelled at how her touch could rouse him so, for her simple embrace stirred his desire to full flame again. When he'd left London, Winn had never thought he'd discover anyone like Alex on this trip. He'd come on this journey to help his uncle's friend and to seek the hidden treasure. Now, he knew the crown was important, but the treasure he'd found in Alex made the other prize pale in comparison. Her love was the most priceless treasure of all.

"I don't want to," he said softly, and she answered him with a kiss.

"Stay with me . . ."

"I can't," Winn refused, amazing himself by his self-denial. All he wanted to do was join her on the soft bed again. Being honorable did take its toll. "I have to do what's best for you."

Moving away from her, he continued to dress.

"Winn?" When he looked up at her, she asked, "You never did tell me why you disguised yourself as a priest in the first place. Did you think it was necessary to hide your identity? Or did it have something to do with Lawrence's letter?"

"Lawrence mentioned in his letter that my uncle's faith would help him in the hunt—that his priesthood would mark him as a man to trust."

"He was right. I never doubted you."

"I'm glad that I fooled you so completely. It was important I be convincing. I didn't know what we were going to be up against getting the clues, and I wanted to do everything I could to make this work."

"But why do you care so much about the crown?"

"Actually, I'd never heard of the Crown of Desire until I read his letter. There are two real reasons why I came on this search, and their names are Philip and Robert Anthony."

"Philip and Robert?" A moment before, she had almost convinced herself to tell Winn the whole truth, but now her heart was in her throat. He'd mentioned them before, but just in connection with what Lawrence had written to them in their own letters about not trusting the pair.

"They are without a doubt the two most disgusting excuses for men I've ever had the misfortune to encounter. If I accomplish nothing else in this whole ordeal, when we find the crown, at least I'll have the satisfaction of knowing I kept it away from them. I vowed to myself to make sure Philip and Robert never get their hands on it, and as far as I'm concerned, the only way they'll claim it is over my dead body."

Panic shook Alex. Winn was determined to do everything in his power to keep the crown from Philip and Robert, while she was committed to making sure that they got it as soon as possible! To hide her sudden terror and confusion, she got up and busied herself with donning a wrapper. She kept her back to Winn as she did so for she didn't want to chance him seeing the change in her, the worry, and the fear.

"What did they do to make you feel so strongly about them?" She had to know.

"They're damned ghouls! They actually came to my home during my uncle's wake. They insisted Uncle Edward had something that belonged to them, and they pressed me to return it to them that very night." His voice grew tight and his expression was full of loathing as he remembered the scene. "I've dealt with some unsavory characters in my time, but I've never met anyone as low as they are. They are worthless scum."

"What did you do?"

"I put them off for that night, but then they had the gall to show up at my uncle's funeral the very next day! I was in mourning! Uncle Edward wasn't even cold in his grave! And there they were, standing at the gravesite, demanding I give them the book. I dismissed them as harshly as I could, but what I can't believe is that they thought I'd cooperate with their kind. Honest people don't deal with their kind. I'd rather be dead than do anything to help them."

Alex swallowed nervously as she listened to his words. She'd wanted to tell him about the Anthony brothers, but now she knew it was impossible. She was in league with the devil, and she would have to handle it herself. "What did you do?"

"I told them I'd be in touch if I found anything. Then that night, I went through my uncle's personal things and found the book and letter. After I'd read Lawrence's plea to Uncle Edward to make sure his sons didn't get their hands on the crown, I made my decision to take my uncle's place in the search."

"I see," she said quietly, and she did. As sleazy as Philip and Robert were, they'd started with Winn, and when he'd proven no help in their cause, they'd decided to come after her father—and then her. She thought of her father then, still locked in the terrible jail alone and no doubt afraid for his very life. The image of his suffering stiffened her resolve to deliver the treasure to Philip and Robert as quickly as she could. A part of her ached with the knowledge that she would ultimately have to betray Winn, yet to save her father, she would do no less.

Winn continued, "By then, I was so disgusted I would have gone to any lengths to keep them from getting what they were after. I left London the morning after the wake, and I was Father Bradford as I boarded the ship sailing for Boston."

"You really believe Philip and Robert are that terrible?" She already knew the answer to her own question, but she had to keep up the pretense of innocence. She couldn't let Winn suspect any different.

"They're worse. It's no wonder Lawrence disinherited them. I'm going to feel I've won an important victory for Lawrence when we hand the Crown of Desire over to a museum."

"You are a good man, Winn," she said, turning back to him now that she'd regained her composure.

He gave her a lopsided smile. "I'm glad you think so."

"I always will," Alex promised.

Winn embraced her one last time and kissed her gently.

"I'll see you in the morning." He hated the thought of leaving her, yet he knew there was nothing else he could do.

"What are you going to do about your disguise? Everyone onboard thinks you're a priest."

"It would seem rather sudden if I gave up my calling overnight—not that your love wasn't worth it." He grimned wickedly. "Until we dock in New Orleans, I'd better maintain the charade."

"It won't be easy pretending."

"It never was for me."

Their gazes met and he kissed her good-bye.

"Good night, Alex."

With that he was gone, and she was left alone in her stateroom. In the space of a few short hours, her life had been turned upside down. That which she'd thought she'd never have had been given to her as sweetly as any gift. Yet with that precious gift had come the swift and terrible knowledge that Winn would hate her if he knew her terrible secret.

Alex considered confiding in Winn one last time, but then she remembered his words about how he felt about the Anthonys, and she quickly dismissed the idea. Winn and Matt might be able to help her outwit the Anthony brothers when they finally found the crown, but there was no way they could help her save her father. The more she learned about Philip and Robert, the more desperate, conniving, and dangerous she knew them to be. She was certain they had some kind of arrangement for word to be transmitted to London to their men at the prison. While she might defeat them here and keep the prize out of their hands, ultimately, her victory might cost her father his life. She would do whatever was necessary to save her father. Even at the cost of losing the man she loved.

Shivering at the thought of what the future held, Alex lay back down. Her soul was chilled by the ominous memory of the Anthony brothers and their very real threat that they would see her father hang for murder if she didn't cooperate.

Alex tried to push thoughts of the menacing pair from her mind. She hugged a pillow to her breast, thinking of Winn and the beauty of his lovemaking. She didn't know how much time she'd have with Winn before they found the crown, but for what little time she did have, she was going to take the happiness he was offering to her and give back to him all she could in return. Alex told herself that she would keep nothing from him—except the truth of her deception. Her father's life meant too much to her. Though she wanted to share her burden with Winn, she wouldn't. Only she could save her father.

Alex closed her eyes against the terror that had shadowed her very existence since that day the Anthonys had invaded her life back in Boston. As she sought sleep, she hung on to the desperate hope that she could keep her connection to Philip and Robert hidden from Winn. She had to. It was her only hope. She refused to even think about what might happen if he found out.

It was dark and quiet when Winn entered his cabin. He was glad to find that Matt appeared to be still asleep. He didn't want to discuss what had just happened with Alex. He wanted to savor his memories of the night just passed in peace and quiet. After undressing, he'd started to lie down, when Matt spoke.

"You were out kind of late, weren't you?"

"It's good to know you're concerned about my safety."

"Actually, I was just lying here trying to imagine what you were doing out on deck alone all night, and then it occurred to me that you probably weren't alone—that you might have been with my 'wife.' "

"Alex is not your wife."

"It's a good thing I'm not the jealous type," he chuckled. "I had a feeling for a while now there was more between the two of you than just friendship."

Winn could hear the humor in his tone, but he didn't find his observations particularly funny. "Before tonight we were just friends."

"And now?"

"She means everything to me."

"She is irresistible," Matt agreed, smiling into the darkness at the news. His instincts about people were generally good, and he was glad to discover that he'd been right about Winn and Alex. "How did she take the news about our marriage ending so abruptly?"

"Very well."

"That's too bad. I enjoyed being married to Alex. She made a wonderful bride."

"I hope to find out for myself one day."

"Oh? Just be sure you don't perform the ceremony

yourself," he chuckled, "or you might end up all alone like me."

"I'll remember your advice."

"What did Alex think about your not being a priest?"

"Let's just say once she got over the shock, it definitely changed things between us." Winn grinned to himself as he remembered her warmth and passion.

Matt was glad that they'd found happiness, but he didn't want to put their entire expedition in danger by taking any unwarranted chances. "You were discreet, weren't you? No one saw you coming out of her stateroom, did they?"

"No. I made certain there was no one around. I want to protect her reputation, not ruin it."

"Not to mention your own reputation, 'Father' Winn. You realize you'll have to keep up your charade until we dock in New Orleans the day after tomorrow, don't you?"

"Don't remind me."

Matt heard his frustration and laughed. "Good night, 'Father.' Sweet dreams."

"I really think you're enjoying this."

Matt was still laughing as he rolled over and went back to sleep, leaving Winn to his thoughts.

They rose early the next day. Matt watched Winn dress, and he smothered a chuckle as Winn donned the collar and transformed himself into a priest once more.

"I get the feeling the next day and a half are going

to seem longer to you than our entire train ride. What do you think?" Matt quipped.

"I think we should get Alex and go for breakfast," Winn answered, refusing to be baited as he pulled on his black coat. As soon as his disguise was in place, he headed for the cabin door. He was eager to see her again. If he'd had his way the night before, he would never have left her.

Alex was ready and waiting when Winn and Matt came for her. What little sleep she'd gotten had been troubled. Even so, she drew upon her meager acting abilities to keep the turmoil of her emotions hidden. She loved Winn, but could not reveal it today. She cared for him, but would have to betray him. Alex knew the time they had left onboard the steamer was going to be a challenge, and she hoped she was up to it.

The knock at her stateroom door sent her heart leaping in her breast. Alex had to stop herself from running to answer it. Forcing herself to take a deep breath, she opened the door to come face-to-face with Winn, once more dressed as Father Bradford.

"Good morning, Father," she said. Her gaze feasted on the sight of him.

"Good morning," Winn returned, and in a low, gruff voice he added, "You look lovely this morning."

"Thank you." Her eyes shone at his compliment, and she smiled an intimate smile for him and him alone. She was barely aware of Matt standing behind Winn. "Hello, Matt." She spoke to him, but did not look away from Winn.

"Yes, you do look very pretty, Alex. But I think it's time we went on in to breakfast. Don't you, Father?" he spoke up, deliberately breaking the web of sensual reverie that was being spun between the two.

Matt's words had the effect of cold water thrown on Winn. Winn jerked his thoughts away from how beautiful Alex looked in the freshness of the new day. Matt was right. It was time for breakfast . . . and maybe a cold bath.

Breakfast passed in slow-motion torment for Winn. Sitting across the table from Alex and not being able to touch her or kiss her was agony for him. Later, when there had been little to do but sit on deck and pass the hours watching the scenery, Alex's stimulating conversation had made it enjoyable. The restriction that he couldn't touch her chafed at him. As the day aged, Winn's wandering thoughts kept going back to the sweet idea of how wonderful a short afternoon rest might be. The trouble was, if he wanted to rest today, he would be resting alone or with Matt, and enjoy Matt's company though he did, Matt was not Alex. The tension within him grew as he watched other loving couples stroll by hand-in-hand, oblivious to anything or anyone but each other. That was what he wanted to do with Alex, and that was precisely what he couldn't do.

By late afternoon, his temper was short and his need desperate. Matt had excused himself to go down to the saloon for a while, and Winn kept careful watch, praying for a moment alone. When at last their part of the deck was deserted, he made his move.

"Come with me," he urged, standing up and grabbing Alex's hand.

"What are you doing? Where are we going?"

"Be quiet," he cautioned in a low voice. He dragged her a few steps away to a small, hidden alcove that housed supplies for the crew. He'd watched crewmembers go in and out of the area all afternoon, and since there was no one nearby right now, he hoped it was safe for at least a minute.

The alcove was cool and darkly shadowed. When Winn pulled Alex in with him and kissed her, she murmured her approval. His mouth swooped down to cover hers, and their embrace was frantic and heated by the danger of discovery involved. When they broke apart, Winn crushed her against his chest.

"I'm going to make up for this one of these days."

"I'm looking forward to it," she agreed, her breathing labored.

"Go on back to your cabin now. If I stay here with you a moment longer, the next crewmember to come in here may get a surprise he doesn't want."

She gave him one last look of longing and then fled their cocoon. She had only gone a few feet before someone else came down the deck. She had already disappeared into her stateroom when Winn emerged from their hiding place, looking calm and contented to head for his own cabin.

Dinner that night was delicious as usual. Winn, however, would have traded the entire, six-course meal for stale bread and water as long as he could have dined alone with Alex. Matt suggested a night of dancing, and they'd both scowled at him. Finally they decided to retire early, for the following day they would dock in New Orleans and the second part of their hunt would begin. They had to be ready. The crown was now within their reach.

Thirteen

New Orleans

The tall, slender blonde woman hurried up the walk to the mansion. The expression on her elegant features was serious, and it was obvious that she was nervous as she mounted the steps to the front door. She knocked, then stood back to wait.

A gray-haired maid in a neatly starched uniform answered her knock. "Can I help you, ma'am?"

"Yes, I'm Catherine Sutherland from St. Joan's, and I need to speak with Mr. Markham right away. It's urgent."

"Please, wait here." The servant closed the door again.

Catherine stood impatiently, her nerves stretched taut by the missive she'd just received that very morning . . . the missive she still held clutched in her hand. She glanced down at the rumpled letter, finding it hard to believe that Mr. Markham had written this to her. It couldn't be true. It just couldn't be! She heard footsteps coming back toward the door and her anticipation grew. Drawing a hopeful breath, she watched the door swing open again.

The maid faced her, her features schooled into a mask that betrayed no hint of emotion. "I'm sorry, ma'am, but Mr. Markham is not receiving this afternoon."

"Did you give him my message?" Catherine pressed.

"Yes, ma'am but he said to tell you that there was no point in wasting either your time or his. He's made his decision, and that decision is final."

"But I must speak to him. It's urgent!"

"I'm sorry, ma'am."

Catherine was frantic. She had to protect her children! "No! Wait! You don't understand . . ." She stepped forward trying to stop the maid from shutting the door.

"Good-bye, Mrs. Sutherland," the maid repeated as a burly butler came to her side.

While Catherine's willpower might very well match the butler's, pound for pound there was no contest. Ever the lady, she decided to fall back and regroup. There had to be a way out of this terrible dilemma. All she had to do now was think of it.

The door closed with a final sound. Catherine stared at it for a moment longer, then turned away. Markham's refusal to see her, coupled with the terrible news in the letter, unnerved her. According to the letter, Markham, who was the landlord for St. Joan's, had just decided to up and sell the building right out from underneath them. He was selling it without any warning, and had given her only two weeks to find another place for the thirty-five children in her care at the orphanage.

As Catherine moved down the walk toward the street, she glanced down at the single piece of paper. She didn't know how it was possible for something so small to have the power to change her life and the lives of the children in her care so dramatically in such a short time. Revulsion and contempt filled her as she thought of Markham's cowardice. How easy it was to ruin someone's life when you never had to face them.

Catherine knew she had to do something, but she had no idea what. She had no power, no vast fortune of her own to buy the building herself. Somehow, though, in the next two weeks she had to find a way to save the thirty-five children in her care, all of whom were under fourteen years old. Her steps were slow as she made her way to the hired carriage waiting for her on the street.

Milly, her assistant, was an elderly lady who'd been with the home for as long as anyone could remember. She had come along on the trip with Catherine to offer moral support and had remained in the carriage while she'd gone up to speak to Mr. Markham. She was watching her anxiously as she drew near.

"What happened? Isn't Mr. Markham home?" Milly asked as Catherine climbed back inside and gave the driver the order to take them back to St. Joan's.

"He's home all right, but he refused to see me. According to what he told the maid, he's made his decision, so there's no reason for us to meet." Catherine lifted her troubled gaze to her faithful friend. "Milly, what am I going to do? I can't let this happen. How am I going to take care of the children if St. Joan's is gone?"

"I don't know, Miss Catherine." Milly reached out and gave her hand a reassuring pat.

"I can't let the children down. They're little more than babies. I can't . . ."

The two women fell silent as they made the trip back to the orphanage. Catherine had been the director of St. Joan's Home for Children for almost ten years now. She'd come to the orphanage to work as a volunteer after her husband and infant daughter had been killed in a tragic accident. From the first day, she'd known the home was her fate. She had so much love to give and the children were desperate for it. Catherine had dedicated herself to the work, soothing the agony of her spirit by giving of herself. Soon, the love she was giving freely was being returned full measure from the children, who'd at first been a little leery of her. They'd seen other pretty ladies come and go, so they were cautious at first about trusting her. It wasn't long, however, before they sensed she was real and meant what she said to them. Once that barrier had been breached, they had come together as a family, caring for each other and trying to love each other—in good times and bad. It hadn't been easy, but Catherine had done it. Now, suddenly, if Markham had his way, it was over, and she was helpless to do anything to prevent it.

Consumed with worries, Catherine rode in silence back to St. Joan's. The building had never been in the best condition, and during the past year Markham had stopped responding to her requests for renovations or repairs. She'd made do, not wanting to anger him, but this letter now explained everything. He didn't care about the children. He never had. The opportunity had come up, and now he was selling the building. It was as cold, businesslike, and final as that.

As they reached the home and descended from the carriage, Catherine paused to stare up at the old building. True it was rundown, but it was clean inside. She'd taught the children that cleanliness was next to Godliness, and they all did their chores every day. The sounds of happy children at play penetrated her sad musings, and she wasn't sure whether to laugh or cry. A part of her rejoiced at their happiness, but the part of her that faced reality and dealt with it daily, knew their carefree days were numbered. Two weeks . . . that's all she had . . . two weeks.

Catherine went up the steps and entered the old building with Milly to find eleven-year-old Tommy Glosier waiting for her. She couldn't help but smile. Tommy had appointed himself her protector some years before, and whenever she was away, he waited vigilantly in the hall near her office for her return.

Tommy was an attractive boy, with the potential to become a very handsome man. His hair was dark and an unruly shock of it fell across his forehead giving him a rakish look even at eleven. His eyes were blue and bright with intelligence. He was a charmer, his dimpled smile having been known to disarm even the formidable Milly on occasion. Renowned for his good humor, Tommy always had a kind word for everyone. He'd been about three years old when Catherine found him wandering the streets, abandoned by whatever family he'd had. No one had ever come to claim him, and she had taken a special interest in him. They had grown very close through the years, and Catherine would have had it no other way.

"Nothing happened while you were gone, Miss Catherine," Tommy reported very seriously. "Everyone behaved themselves."

"That's good. I appreciate your keeping track of things for me."

"Mary kept the little ones busy, so I just kinda kept an eye on the rest." He was always willing to share any praise he might get.

"I'll be sure to thank her when I see her later. You did a very good job, Tommy." She patted him affectionately on the shoulder. "I'll see you a little later."

"Yes, ma'am." The boy swelled with pride at her compliment. He adored her, and would do anything for her. Miss Catherine and the other orphans at the home were the only family he'd ever known, and he was an intensely loyal person. Now that she was back, he could go join the others and play for a while.

Catherine and Milly went on into her office and closed the door. Only then did the smile she'd managed for Tommy fade.

"What do you think we should do?" Milly asked when they were alone.

"That's what I have to figure out—and fast. Get me the list of all the people who've helped us in the last two years. Maybe if I ask for donations, I can raise enough money to buy the building from Mr. Markham myself. If not . . ."

"I'll get started on it right away." Milly didn't know if it would work, but any plan was better than just giving up. There was too much at stake.

New Orleans spread out before Winn, Alex, and Matt in all its magnificence. When their steamer had docked, they hired a closed carriage to take them to the St. Charles Hotel. As soon as they climbed in and shut the door, Winn shed his collar for the last time. He wasn't sure what the driver would think when they reached the hotel and he descended from the carriage no longer dressed as a priest, but he didn't care. He just wanted to be free to be himself again.

The driver did indeed glance at him askance as he alighted from the carriage and then turned to help Alex down, but he said nothing. Winn rewarded him with a very generous tip.

They registered under their own names at the front desk, and Winn actually felt like celebrating.

"Let's go to our rooms and get settled in. Once we're cleaned up, we'll meet in my room and go over the next clue again," Matt suggested.

About an hour later, Alex appeared at the door to his room. Winn was already there, and he answered her knock. As the door opened and he stood before her in his white shirt and dark pants, she was once again surprised by the power of her reaction to him.

He was without a doubt the most magnificent specimen of a man she'd ever seen, and she took the time to stare at him in open appreciation for a moment.

"Yes, it really is me, and I'm planning to stay this way from now on," he said huskily as he took her hand and drew her quickly inside.

Only then did Alex discover he was by himself in the room.

"Where's Matt?" she asked, her pulse quickening at the thought of being alone with him.

"He went back down to the front desk for a minute, so we're actually alone—for a little while." As he said 'alone,' he closed the door behind her.

She smiled dreamily and went straight into his arms. "I was beginning to think we would never be alone again."

"Oh, no, sweet. Somehow, no matter how long it would have taken, I would have found a way," he declared, just before his mouth claimed hers.

She molded herself against him. She could feel the hardness of him against her and reveled in the knowledge that he wanted her so badly. Winn ached to pick her up and lay her upon the bed. He longed to strip away the barriers of their clothing and kiss and touch every curve of her lush body, but he didn't. There was no telling how soon Matt would be back, and he didn't want to risk any embarrassment.

Winn had already made up his mind that tonight was going to be a special night for them. Innocent that she was, he was going to court her. He'd already won her love, but now he wanted to be worthy of it. The things he'd done as rote in London, he was now going to do with joy, because this was Alex. The evening was planned already. They had just to get to it. For now, he would satisfy himself with the pleasure of her kiss and know that even more delights awaited them both as soon as darkness fell.

The sound of Matt at the door drove them apart. When Matt came in, he took one look at the two of them and grinned knowingly.

"I got it," he announced holding up a thick ledger.

"What did you get?" Alex asked, curious.

"A city register. We know we're looking for something with St. Joan or Joan in the name, and a good bet is that it has to do with children. All we have to do is figure out what. It could be a school or an orphanage. Let's see what we can find."

Matt thumbed through the directory, checking the listings carefully.

"There's nothing under Joan. Let's try St. Joan."

"Could it be another convent or maybe a church?"

"We've got to remember the last part of the clue—'Seek here the bearer of path, whose gift will guide you on, life's little flowers should now grow, warmed by a gentle sun. Love is the key to all that thrives, its power can conquer the curse. See the unseen, and you will find the treasure that will be yours.'"

"We're getting so close . . ."

"I certainly hope so."

"Here!" Matt said urgently. "This must be it . . . St. Joan's Orphanage."

"Let's go!" Winn was ready.

They stopped at the desk only long enough to return the register and get directions. Within a few minutes, they were in a carriage on their way to the orphanage that was located in one of the poorer sections of town.

"Here it is," the driver said as he drew the vehicle to a stop before a run-down building.

Alex, Winn, and Matt eyed each other questioningly. St. Joan's Home for Children was a shabby-looking two-story building. There was nothing remarkable or attractive about it. The one thing they did notice, though, was that it was neat and clean. Though the paint on the building was peeling, the walk was swept. The swarm of children of all ages and sizes who played in front on the grass looked neat and well-fed too. It was obvious that, poor though the home might be, someone there cared.

Matt descended first and started up the walk, leaving Winn to help Alex down and pay for the carriage.

Winn's hands at Alex's waist were warm and strong, and she rested her hands on his shoulders as she climbed out. After so many days of being unable to touch him openly, she savored the chance. Her eyes met his as he set her lightly down, and they shared a knowing smile.

Matt was glad that Alex and Winn were busy with each other. Being alone for a few minutes gave him the time he needed to come to grips with entering this orphanage.

He stopped on the walkway to stare up at the structure. There was something familiar to him about the building. The place looked almost sad to him, as if it were haunted by the loneliness of its mission. It was obvious that St. Joan's was low on funds and had too many children. But as the memories of his own solitary childhood threatened to overwhelm him, he noticed that there was something very different about this place from the miserable home where he'd spent his younger years. At St. Joan's, there was laughter. The children playing in the yard might be poor, but they were full of joy.

A dark-haired boy who looked to be about twelve sat on the top step. His manner was almost like that of a castle guard as he watched Matt approach. A petite, blonde-haired girl who couldn't have been more than six or seven sat beside him, playing quietly with a doll.

Matt stopped on the step just below them when the boy spoke up.

"What are you here for?"

"We need to speak to the director of the home. Could you tell me who it is?"

"Mrs. Sutherland," he answered.

"Is she here right now?"

"Yes, sir. Just go on inside. Her office is the first door on the left."

"Thanks. . . . By the way, I'm Matt McKitrick. What's your name?" Matt asked, meeting the youth's eyes and seeing the curiosity and intelligence mirrored there.

"I'm Tommy, and this is Lisa."

"It's nice to meet you Tommy. You, too, Lisa," he said looking at the little girl and thinking how angelic she looked. The innocent beauty of children was truly a sight to behold. The girl gazed up at him with clear aquamarine eyes, the color of which he'd never seen before. He returned her gaze, momentarily mesmerized, then remembered why he was there. "Thanks for the help."

"You're welcome."

Matt entered the building ahead of Winn and Alex, and the darkness of the hall immediately returned him to the days when he'd been a virtual prisoner in the institution where he'd been raised. The meals had consisted of little more than stale bread and weak gruel. Mr. Stanton, the director of the hell hole, had seemed to take pleasure in beating the children, especially the little ones who couldn't fight back. Matt had tried to help the others for a while, but at thirteen he'd still been too small to defy Stanton's authority. Instead, he'd run away the first chance he'd gotten, and he'd never looked back.

Matt fought off the feeling of abandonment that often came whenever he remembered the prison of his childhood. His parents had died when he was five, and, with no living relatives, he'd been put in the only orphanage around. Abandoned, poor, and helpless, he'd suffered the loneliness and the loss of his parents by himself. He'd made a few friends, but mostly he'd kept to himself, reading and fantasizing about mysteries, lost treasures, and the like. Matt had been enchanted by tales of the lost continent of Atlantis, and when he'd finally escaped the abusive system, he'd known what he was going to do. Somehow, some way, he was going to search for the lost places of old. Matt hadn't know if it was some part of his deep-seated need on his part to find his own past, but he wanted to search for what had been lost, so he could save it. Also, he had no real home, so the constant traveling to new and unusual places have never bothered him. As long as he was free to come and go as he pleased, he was content. Finding the lost and hidden treasures had become his one and only way of life, and even his feelings for Valerie hadn't allowed him to give it up.

"What did the boy have to say?"

Winn's words broke through Matt's memories, and Matt was glad to shake off the dark mood that threatened him. "The director is a woman named Mrs. Sutherland. Her office is in here on the left."

Matt found the door with her name on it and knocked.

"Come in."

The voice that called out to them sounded soft and cultured, and Matt wondered just what this 'Mrs. 'Sutherland' looked like. In his mind's eye, he had an image of her as sixty-five years old, gray-haired, short and stodgy with a quick, mean temper. He opened the door, expecting a matronly, demanding woman. He was expecting to get little if no cooperation from her. Then he came face-to-face with Catherine Sutherland for the first time, and he was rendered speechless.

"Yes? What is it? Can I help you?" Catherine asked, looking up from the stack of correspondence spread out before her on her desk. She and Milly had been working almost non-stop for two days now to get the letters ready for her campaign to raise the money to buy the building. Whatever needed her attention, she wanted to deal with quickly and get it over with so she could go back to the letters that would mean life-or-death for St. Joan's. She found herself looking at one of the most good-looking men she'd ever encountered, and she blinked in surprise. She'd expected Milly or Tommy or one of the children. "Yes?" she repeated when the stranger didn't speak right away.

Matt stared at the slender, blonde beauty, completely enchanted. He'd expected a battleax. He'd got an angel. Her hair was the color of moonlight. He could tell her hair was long, but she was wearing it in a bun at the nape of her neck. Suddenly, he found an unbidden fantasy intruding on his thoughts of loosening her hair from its confines and raking his fingers through the pale silken length. Her eyes were blue in color, and he was lost in their open, honest depths. Her features were delicate without seeming fragile, and her mouth was infinitely kissable. He stared at her lips, curving now in a slight, curious smile as she stared back at him.

"Yes, sir," she repeated. "Is there something I can do for you?" Catherine had no idea who this tall, good-looking stranger was, but his presence there bothered her. She suddenly feared he'd been sent by Markham, and she rose behind her desk feeling more confident standing eye-to-eye with him.

Her movement jerked him back from the realm of enchantment that had possessed him. Gathering his wits, he quickly responded. "Yes, I'm Matthew McKittrick and these are my traveling companions, Alexandra

Parker and Winn Bradford. We're friends of Lawrence Anthony." He paused, watching her expression and waiting for her response. He'd noticed the flicker of recognition immediately in the mother superior, and he wondered what this lady's reaction would be. He hoped she knew Anthony for that would give him a reason to stay. Having just seen her for the first time, he certainly didn't want to leave yet.

"Lawrence Anthony . . . ?" she repeated the name a little puzzled, and then suddenly her eyes lit up. "Of course, I remember him. He was here a few years ago. I knew his name sounded familiar."

"So Lawrence did come here?"

"Yes. Isn't he with you now?"

"No, I'm sorry. Lawrence passed away just a short time ago."

"I'm so sorry to hear that. We'll have to tell Tommy. Did you meet him on the way in?"

"Tommy? You mean the boy sitting out front?"

"Yes," Catherine smiled. "He believes he's the protector of the orphanage. He and Mr. Anthony became close friends during the short period of time he was here in New Orleans. He was a very generous man. He helped us with some of our expenses. Mr. Anthony also had quite a way with the children and befriended many of the boys and girls. Whenever he came by for a visit, he brought penny candy for everyone. Tommy's often asked me about him since he left, but we never heard from him again. I'm sure the news of his death will upset him, but it's important that he know the truth. He did care so much for the old man."

"Did Mr. Anthony say anything to you about the fact that we would be coming after him?"

"No, why?"

"No reason. Thank you for your help."

"If there's anything I can do for you, let me know," she offered.

"Do you mind if we have a look around after we talk to Tommy?"

"Not at all. Come with me. We'll find him and tell him the news together."

Catherine led the way out into the hall and moved toward the main entrance. Tommy was having a serious discussion with the little girl.

"Tommy? Could you come here for a moment?"

"Sure Miss Catherine."

"Tommy, this is . . ."

"Mr. McKittrick. I know, he told me who he was on the way in."

"Well, Mr. McKittrick is a friend of Lawrence Anthony's. Remember the elderly gentleman who visited you regularly a few years ago?"

"Yes, ma'am," he replied cautiously.

"They have some news about him that I'm afraid isn't happy. It seems your friend has passed away."

"No . . ."

"Lawrence died just a few months ago. He left instructions for us to come here to St. Joan's in search of a path to follow."

"A path? That doesn't make sense," the boy remarked.

Matt, Winn, and Alex all felt their spirits plummet at the youth's statement. They'd hoped this orphans' home was their connection. They'd hoped it would be a simple thing to get the final clue to the crown's whereabouts and be on their way. It looked like it was going to be more difficult to solve.

"Was there anything in particular that Mr. Anthony liked about the orphanage or any place around that he enjoyed a lot?"

"No. He just liked to sit and talk to us," Tommy answered. "I'm sorry he's dead. He was a nice man."

"We liked him, too," Alex spoke up. "Are you sure he didn't say anything about our coming after him?"

"No. Why?"

"I just wondered, that's all."

"I don't know a whole lot about Mr. Anthony. We just talked and stuff, and then he left, and I never saw him again."

"Thanks, Tommy," Catherine told the boy.

"Was there anything else you needed to know about St. Joan's that I can help you with?"

"I don't think so. Do you mind if we just walk around the grounds?"

"Not at all. Make yourself at home here."

"We appreciate your help."

"If you need anything at all, just let me know."

"Thanks."

Tommy watched as Matt, Winn, and Alex moved off, then turned his attention back to Lisa.

"What do you think?" Alex asked as they left the building. "Why do you suppose things seem so old and falling apart?"

"It's not what I think, it's what I know. There's no

money. Every cent Mrs. Sutherland takes in, she spends on food and care for the children. Taking care of a building is the last thing on her list of important things to do. First come her children, and she looks to have a pretty full house."

"Why do you suppose Lawrence wanted us to come here? What does 'see the unseen' mean? What are we supposed to be seeing that we're not?"

"If I knew that, we'd have the crown already."

They checked out the surroundings, but found nothing that seemed to be a clue. Finally, in disappointment and confusion, they went back to their hotel.

Fourteen

When they reached the St. Charles, Matt went to the men's saloon to relax for a while, and Winn escorted Alex upstairs to her room.

"I'll be back for you in an hour," he said as they reached their door.

"What are we going to do?" Alex asked.

"It's a surprise," he told her gently. "Tonight, you're mine."

"What about the Crown? Shouldn't we be working on the next clue?"

Winn stepped closer, creating a greater sense of intimacy between them. "Not tonight," he said, his voice deep with meaning. "Tonight, Miss Parker, Lord Bradford is coming to call."

His gaze was warm upon her, and she felt a thrill of excitement as she stared up at him.

"I'll be ready." Her voice was a whisper of anticipation.

Winn's gaze dropped to her mouth for a moment. He wanted to kiss her, to taste the sweetness of her lips again, but an elderly couple was coming down the hall, and he was forced, for propriety's sake, to control himself. The power of the need he felt for her kept surprising him. No other woman had ever affected him this way. "I'll be back in a little while." He tore himself free of her intoxicating nearness and moved off down the hall.

Alex remained where she was, watching him until he'd disappeared into his own room. Winn greeted the older couple as he passed them and Alex heard the old lady say, "What a nice young man," after he'd gone by. Alex smiled and went into her room.

Eagerness filled Alex as she thought about the evening to come. Lord Bradford was coming to call! The days of denying her feelings for him were over. They were going out publicly together, and there would be no more deception.

In the midst of her light-hearted mood, though, thoughts of the Anthonys and her own deception slipped into her mind. Guilt gnawed at her, but she pushed it away. Tonight was her night. Tonight, she was going to be with Winn, and they could laugh and smile and enjoy each other. She would worry about the rest of it later.

Alex couldn't remember ever being so excited about seeing a man. She had only an hour to get ready, so she quickly ordered a bath and started going through her limited selection of gowns. She'd never been one to care much about fashion, and tonight, she regretted it. She wanted to look her best for Winn, but the most fashionable gown she had was the demure, turquoise one she'd worn to dinner on the steamer. With a dreamy smile, she realized that she'd been wearing it the first time he'd kissed her. Alex pulled it out and smoothed it on the bed, then began to get ready for his coming.

Winn was smiling as he got ready to begin his official courtship of Alex. While it was true that he was going about everything just a little bit backward with her, somehow it didn't matter. What mattered was that she come to know him as himself. His wardrobe was scant for he'd concentrated on priestly clothing when he'd packed so quickly that night, but he had thrown in one good suit of clothes, and he took them out now.

Winn was prompt in calling for her for he didn't want to waste a moment of the time they had together. No one knew where the search would lead them next, so they had to take their moments of happiness while they could.

"Alex?" he called her name as he knocked on the door.

Alex was brushing her hair and at the sound of his call, she went still. He was there . . . at last. Giving her curls one last stroke, she put the brush aside and hurried to admit him. Her cheeks were a bit flushed with excitement as she opened the door.

"I'm ready," she announced with a smile as she looked up at him.

She hadn't thought it possible for Winn to look any more handsome than he usually did, but this first sight of him dressed as a gentleman took her breath away. His suit was dark gray. The jacket was casually cut, yet fit his broad shoulders like a dream. The waistcoat he wore was dark green and lowcut over his snowy white shirt, high collar, and dark gray bow tie. His pants were straight-cut and hugged his powerful thighs in a tantalizing embrace. He wore black, highly polished boots. Alex blinked. Any and all traces of Father Bradford were gone forever as she saw Winn now in his true light. Lord Winston Bradford, the man of her dreams.

"You look lovely," Winn told her, smitten. She was wearing the dress she'd had on the night he'd kissed her, and he couldn't resist kissing her again, right then.

"I wanted to dress up for you, but . . ." She started to apologize.

He silenced her with another kiss. "You couldn't look any prettier. Let's go to dinner, I'm starved."

Taking her arm, Winn escorted her downstairs, through the hotel's spacious domed lobby to the opulent dining room. The dining room was elegant, surpassing even the splendor on the steamer. They were given a quiet, secluded table. After they'd ordered and the waiter had poured their wine, Winn lifted his glass to Alex in a toast.

"To our quest," he said softly, his eyes holding hers across the candlelit table.

"Our quest." She matched him in that toast, her eyes never leaving his as she drank from the crystal wineglass. Guilt played around the edges of her conscience, but she ignored it.

Winn watched transfixed as she sipped the wine. Had they not been in such a public place he would have kissed her then just to taste the sweet liquid on her lips. Before he could indulge himself in too many fantasies, their first course arrived.

The meal was sumptuous, and they savored every bite.

Alex was mesmerized by the new Winn. She thought about the night they'd waltzed together, and she remembered how foreign she'd thought the collar had looked on him. She smiled to herself now as she realized how right she'd been.

"What are you smiling about?" he asked.

"I was thinking about the night we danced on the steamboat."

"What about it?" His gaze darkened as he thought of that night.

"I remember feeling that somehow the priest's collar didn't seem right on you."

"Did I do something wrong?" He frowned.

"Oh, no. You played the priest to perfection. It was just that you'd seemed so relaxed and confident when we'd waltzed . . . almost as if you'd been in your element."

He grinned at her. "I was. I didn't lie to you when I told you my uncle was a great influence on me. He was always trying to get me to change my ways, since I spent most of my time gambling or making the rounds of the social set. Coming on this search has been an adventure for me in more ways than one."

"I'm glad you did."

Their gazes met and locked in understanding. "So am I."

When they'd finished their meal, Winn led her from

the hotel. After instructing the doorman to get them an open carriage, he took her for a romantic ride through the streets of New Orleans.

The moon hung high overhead, and the stars were shining their brightest. They rode through the Vieux Carré, past Jackson Square and the Cabildo. When they passed the opera, Winn promised to take her there the next night.

"It's lovely here," she murmured, nestling close to his side.

"It is a beautiful city, but I love London even more. One day, I'll take you there."

"I'd like that. Whenever Father and I are in London, we're usually working so hard that I don't have much time to enjoy the city."

"It will be my pleasure to introduce you to the delights of my town," he said gallantly. "Tell me about your father, Alex. You've never said much about him."

"He's a wonderful man," she began slowly, the pain of knowing he was in prison hurting her desperately. "History is his life, and he raised me to feel the same way. I deeply regret that he couldn't be with us on this trip . . ." As she spoke, tears filled her eyes.

"Alex, what's wrong?" Winn saw the emotion in her eyes and wondered at it. It seemed odd that she would get teary just talking about her father. He reached out to her with a gentle hand and lifted her chin so he could see her more clearly. "You know if there's anything troubling you, you can come to me. I'll do everything in my power to help you."

"Nothing's wrong. I just regret that Papa isn't here

with us," she denied. "Finding the crown was his dream."

"Did you leave him a note in Boston? It could be he's there right now, eagerly awaiting your return with news of the crown."

"I hope so. I truly do," she managed. Lifting her gaze, she studied Winn in the moonlight. She loved him, and she wanted to believe with all her heart that one day they would see London together. But the knowledge that she would soon betray him haunted her.

Winn was unaware of her thoughts as he kissed her. His mouth sought hers in a sweetly passionate exchange that told her without words just how much he wanted her.

"Let's go back," she whispered, wanting to be in his arms again, wanting to taste of his love while she still could.

Winn gave the order, and the driver headed back to the hotel. When they arrived, Winn climbed out first and then helped Alex down, his hands at her waist. Even through her layers of clothing, she could feel the heat of his hands, and she could hardly wait to feel them on her bare flesh. She rested her hands on his shoulders and met his eyes as he lowered her to the ground.

Hers was a telling look, and Winn felt a jolt of excitement slam through his body. He was hard pressed not to sweep her up in his arms and carry her through the lobby straight to her room.

"Flower for your lady, mister?" a young boy asked

as he stood near the main entrance, holding small bouquets of fresh flowers.

"Yes, please," he said, stopping to buy one.

"Thanks . . ."

When the boy had moved away, Winn gallantly presented them to Alex. "For you . . ."

She held them close and inhaled their sweet fragrance. "They're lovely, thank you." Her eyes were glowing as she looked up at him.

"You're welcome."

Her obvious joy over his simple gift surprised and pleased Winn. In London, when he'd gifted some of the society beauties he'd dated with bouquets of the finest roses, they'd merely thanked him perfunctorily and handed them over to a waiting servant to be disposed of. Alex looked as though this small gift was the finest present she'd ever received.

Taking her arm, Winn escorted her through the lobby and back upstairs to her room. The hallway was deserted, and he was relieved. He wanted to protect her reputation and would take every precaution to keep her safe. After unlocking the door and opening it for her, he waited for her to go in. Alex stepped inside the darkened room and pulled him in after her, quickly closing the door.

"I've been waiting for this moment ever since this afternoon . . ." Winn murmured, drawing her to him.

"I've been waiting all my life," she said, linking her arms around his neck and drawing him down for a kiss.

At the touch of her lips on his, he shuddered, then

tightened his arms around her, crushing her against his chest. The desire he felt for her erupted into a flaming inferno as he held her close, their bodies touching from thigh to breast.

Alex gasped as she felt the hard heat of him. The sensation was electrifying. It thrilled her to know that he wanted her as much as she wanted him.

"Wait . . ." she whispered, pulling away a little.

"Is something wrong?" he asked, puzzled.

"No. Everything's wonderful . . . just wait here."

Alex moved away into the darkness. He heard the scratch of a match, and she lit a lamp on the night-stand.

"I wanted to be able to see you," she said simply, returning to his waiting arms.

Winn had been with many women in his time, but none of them had ever affected him as Alex did. There was something so seductively innocent about her that it rendered him nearly senseless with the need to be one with her. With slow precision, he shed his coat and hung it on the back of the chair nearby.

"Let me . . ." Alex said with an almost brazen smile as she came forward to unbutton his vest. She ran her hands over the width of his chest as she helped him take it off, and she enjoyed the feel of his hard muscles beneath his shirt.

Alex tossed the vest on the chair with his coat, then came back to loosen his tie and unbutton his shirt. He stood before her, thrilling at her touch. He remained unmoving for fear that if he did move he wouldn't be able to stop himself from throwing her on the bed and claiming her right then and there. When she'd loosened all the buttons, he shrugged out of the shirt and waited as she tossed it aside, too.

"You have the most beautiful chest . . ." she told him.

Alex didn't know if it was the wine she'd had at dinner or just her desperate hunger for Winn that drove her, but she couldn't seem to touch him enough. Her hands skimmed over his chest, tangling in the crisp mat of hair as her lips sought his chest. She heard the sharp intake of his breath as she pressed hot kisses to his neck, and she smiled. Emboldened by the knowledge that she was pleasing him, she began to trail kisses along the path her hands had forged across his chest.

Winn had remained quiet as she'd undressed him, but at the touch of her mouth on his body, he could be still no longer. With a growl of pure animal need, he picked her up and stalked to the bed. There was no patience in him as he stripped away her gown. There was only need and want and desire.

Alex shivered with delight at his bold male play, and she gave herself over to him willingly.

The barriers of their clothes removed, they celebrated their coming together with joy and delight. Their caresses were abandoned as they each sought to please the other. Any shyness that might have existed before was swept away by the wildfire of their desire.

When Winn moved to possess her, Alex surrendered eagerly and took him deep within her. They moved as one, giving and taking, seeking and finding that glorious explosion of passion that rocked them both and sent them spiraling out of control. There was ecstasy in their oneness.

They lay together, completely lost in the wonder of their need for each other. They were perfect together. Winn had never known such bliss.

Alex clung to him, lost in a dreamy haze of contentment. She'd never known love could be so sweet. She never wanted to be out of his arms. She had found her heaven, and it was with Winn.

They made love again and again through the long hours of the night. Winn didn't leave her until the threat of dawn forced him from her bed.

"What will we do today?" Alex asked as she lay watching him dress. It seemed a shame to her that he had to put his clothes back on. She loved his body and loved watching the play of his muscles as he moved.

"What I'd like to do, and what we're going to do are two different things," he told her with a rakish grin as he pulled on his pants and then his shirt.

She chuckled softly. "I know. I feel the same way, but we have to keep looking for the crown."

"It's strange . . . You know the crown has been a blessing for us, not a curse," he remarked, feeling content. For just a few moments, he'd forgotten about the Anthonys and the quest. Reality had disappeared, and it had been just the two of them.

"You're right. If we hadn't been searching for it, we never would have met," Alex pointed out.

"The more I learn about it, the more I respect it," Winn told her.

As she watched him reach for his vest, Alex knew she had to love him one more time. His back was to her as she left the bed and went to him. She encircled him with her arms as she lay her cheek against his back.

"Are you sure you want to leave me?"

"No, love. I don't want to leave you, but I have to . . ."

"Winn . . ." She said his name softly.

The feel of her breasts against his back quickly overpowered his determination to go. He turned to her and seeing the passion of her need in her eyes, he couldn't resist. His hands cupped her breasts and his mouth covered hers in a blazing exchange. The clothes he'd just donned, he discarded without a second thought, and they came together in a rushed, rapturous joining that left them both sated.

Later when Winn finally slipped from the bed, Alex was sleeping peacefully. He dragged his clothes back on, and then, before leaving took one blossom from the bouquet and lay it on the pillow next to her. Regretfully, he returned to his own solitary bed.

The following day proved an exercise in frustration. They scoured the city looking for other places that might match Lawrence's clue, but they found nothing. Everything pointed back to St. Joan's. They returned to the hotel, thwarted and puzzled.

"I think I need to go back and speak to Mrs. Sutherland again," Matt finally said.

"I had promised to take Alex to the opera tonight, but if you want us to go with you, we will."

"There's no need," he told them. "Go ahead and enjoy the city while you can. Our next stop may not be so glamorous."

"I'm going shopping for a while," Alex said, leaving the men to their discussion. "I'll be back as soon as I can."

Alex wanted to look beautiful for Winn that night, and as she left the hotel, she'd feared it might be difficult to find a suitable gown already made. To her surprise, she found the perfect dress in Madame Chenieux's shop. The gown was made of deep, forest green silk and was off-the-shoulder in style. The bodice was low-cut, but not too daringly so, and the skirts flared out fully over a wide hoop. She was thrilled to find one that fit so well.

Alex headed back to the hotel and on the way, she passed a jeweler's. She glanced in the window and stopped. There displayed on red velvet were a pair of gold cufflinks made in the shape of crowns. Without thought, she went in and purchased them for Winn.

Alex returned to the hotel, took a leisurely bath, and washed her hair. Her hair had grown out a bit, and it dried into a tumble of burnished curls that just barely reached her shoulders. She was pleased with the look for she felt very feminine tonight in her new gown. She was ready for Winn when he came to the door. She opened it quickly to his knock and was rewarded by a blinding smile when he saw her for the first time.

"I thought you looked lovely last night, but tonight . . ." Winn stared at her entranced. The dark green gown she wore was absolutely stunning. It bared her shoulders to his avid gaze, and the decolletage revealed just enough to entice. Heat pulsed through him, and he had to quickly remind himself that they were going out for the evening. "Tonight, you look even more beautiful," he finished.

"Thank you." She rose up on tiptoes to press a soft kiss to his mouth.

"Are you ready?"

"Yes, but, first, I have something for you . . ."

"You do? What?"

"A present," Alex told him with a smile. She drew him inside and closed the door, then left him standing there while she went to retrieve her gift.

Winn stared down at the small wrapped box she held out to him. "This is for me?" He lifted his gaze to hers questioningly. In London, he'd been the one who'd always given. The women had always kept one eye on his fortune and had taken from, not given to him. Her unexpected present, given so freely without cunning or conniving, touched him deeply.

"Yes. I saw them and knew they would be perfect for you. Here." She practically had to force him to take the box.

Once he had it in hand, Winn quickly unwrapped the box. "They're wonderful . . ." He stared at the crown-shaped cufflinks, thinking they were, indeed, perfect. "Thank you."

"Let me put them on for you," she insisted, taking the box again to retrieve the links.

While she did that, he removed the cufflinks he'd been wearing. Alex went to him and, as he held out first one arm then the other, she fastened the gold crown-shaped links at his wrists. He adjusted his cuffs once she'd finished.

The crowns gleamed in the lamplight.

"You're right. They are perfect. Thank you." He went to Alex. Lifting his hands to cup her face, he gave her a gentle, cherishing kiss. "They're the best present I've ever received." His words were spoken from the heart.

Alex blushed. "Oh, I'm sure you've had better gifts than mine."

"None that meant more to me, Alex."

They stood unmoving, gazing at each other for a long moment, and then, to his disappointment, Winn forced himself to move away from her.

"If we're going to the opera tonight, we'd better get going now before my willpower surrenders to my desire for you."

"I'm ready," she said, but in her heart she would not have objected if he'd suggested spending the evening in her room.

With pride, Winn linked Alex's arm through his and led her from the room for a night on the town.

Matt lingered in the men's saloon of the hotel, trying to decide what to do with his evening. He knew Winn and Alex were going out, and that left him at loose ends. He mentally reviewed everything that had happened since they'd arrived in New Orleans, and he couldn't help but come to the conclusion that young Tommy at the orphanage was keeping something from them. On impulse, Matt decided to go back to St. Joan's and seek out Mrs. Sutherland one more time. He told himself he was going because he believed the clue was there with the boy. But the truth be told, he really wanted to see Mrs. Sutherland again.

Matt took a hired carriage to the orphanage. After paying the driver, he went up the front steps only to discover that the door was locked. He knocked, but when no one came, he refused to be discouraged. Matt skirted the building, hoping to find that the light was on in her office, but it was not to be. All was dark.

Frustrated, he had just started to leave the grounds when he heard what sounded like someone crying. He followed the direction and found Catherine Sutherland in a quiet little courtyard at the rear of the building.

"Mrs. Sutherland? Is something wrong? Can I help you?" He approached her quietly, not wanting to frighten her.

"Mr. McKittrick! What are you doing here?" Catherine started at his intrusion and quickly rubbed at her eyes in agitation.

"I came back because I wanted to ask you a few more questions. I was hoping you wouldn't be busy tonight so we could talk. From the sound of things, I'm sorry I didn't get here sooner."

"No . . . no. It's nothing. What can I help you with?" she asked bravely, wanting to distract him from her emotional outburst. It wasn't like her to cry this way, but things were going so terribly in her effort to get the money to buy St. Joan's that suddenly she couldn't hold it in any longer.

"If you're crying, it's not 'nothing.'" He handed her his clean, dry handkerchief.

She wiped her eyes again. "Thanks."

He knew she was trying to avoid telling him why she was upset, but he wasn't going to let her. "'Nothing' can make you cry?"

"Sometimes, Mr. McKittrick, no matter how hard you try to do the right thing, it doesn't help. Sometimes, all the good intentions in the world still lead to failure."

"What's happened?"

"The man who owns the orphanage is selling the building. I have less than two weeks to save the home for the children!"

"Why is he selling it?"

"The only answer I can get from him is that he's tired of it and wants his money out of the building."

"That makes no sense."

"I know. I've been trying to contact him personally to plead my case, but he refuses to see me. I've started trying to raise the funds to buy the building myself, but the responses haven't been good. Most of our sponsors are strapped for money themselves right now. The way things are going, I'm afraid in a little over a week the children and I will be out on the street."

A slow burning anger ignited within him as he thought of the man who could do this to a woman and a home full of orphans. "Who's the owner?"

"Mr. Markham."

"Why don't I go talk to him tomorrow? Maybe I can get somewhere with him."

Catherine lifted luminous eyes to Matt. "Would you do that for us? I don't know if it will help, but it certainly can't hurt."

"I'll try to see him first thing in the morning. I'll come here and report to you after I do."

"If you can convince him to save St. Joan's, you'll be a miracle worker."

"Don't give me that much credit. I just don't want to see the children hurt anymore than they already are."

"Do you like children?"

"I don't know. I've never been around many. I just know what it's like to live in a home where no one wants you and where they remind you of the fact ten times a day."

"It's not like that here," she defended her own home.

"I know." He smiled at her gently. "That's why I'm going to see Markham. I'll be in touch."

She looked irresistible in the moonlight, and he suddenly felt a driving need to kiss her. Only his common sense held him back. *She was a married woman!*

"Thank you, Mr. McKittrick."

"Matt, please."

"And I'm Catherine."

"I know."

Matt touched her cheek where the trace of a silver tear still showed, then left her. He didn't trust himself to stay with her in the privacy of the garden for too long. She was too lovely a temptation.

Tommy had heard voices in the garden below his window, and he'd looked out to see Miss Catherine talking to Matt McKittrick. He couldn't hear what they were saying, but still he kept watch, fearful that something might happen to her. When McKittrick left and Miss Catherine went back inside, Tommy crept downstairs to make sure she was all right. He hid just out of sight and watched as she entered her office. It was then that he got a glimpse of her face, and he was shocked to discover that she'd been crying.

Anger grew within Tommy. He wondered what McKittrick had done to make her cry. Tomorrow, if and when the man came back, he would find out.

"What are you doing down here?" Lisa asked in a whisper as she crept up behind where he crouched in the shadows on the steps.

Her sudden appearance startled him. "I thought you were asleep." He kept his voice low so that they wouldn't get caught.

"I couldn't sleep tonight, Tommy. What's wrong? You look worried.

"Nothing's wrong," he denied, not wanting to concern her. She was still a babe, and he wanted to protect her. That was what men did—protect their own, and Lisa was the closest thing to family he would ever have.

"You sure? You know you're my bestest friend. You can tell me if something's wrong."

"There's nothing wrong. C'mon, let's get you to bed."

"Tommy . . . are you scared about something?"

He glanced over at her quickly, surprised by her comment. "No, I ain't scared of anything." As he said the words, though, he knew there were things that frightened him. He was afraid of losing Miss Catherine and of losing Lisa. They were the two people in his world who meant the most to him, and he needed them. He didn't ever want to be separated from them. "Now, it's bedtime, Lisa. Let's go . . ."

"Tell me a story first, okay?"

She looked up at him with those angelic eyes of hers, and he was lost.

Tommy sighed. "Okay. Which story do you want to hear tonight?"

"The one about the princess who's saved by her handsome prince on a big, white horse," she said excitedly, cuddling up against him and treasuring the security she felt being so close to him.

He looked down at her as she nestled there, and he knew how much he loved her. He would do anything to make her happy. Resigned to his fate, he began her favorite story yet again. "Once upon a time . . ."

It was a good ten minutes later that Tommy finished up with, "And they lived happily ever after. The end . . ."

When Lisa didn't respond, he nudged her a little. "Lisa? You awake?"

"Umm . . ." she said sleepily.

"Now, let's get you to bed. C'mon. I'll help you."

He took her hand and, standing up, he drew her to her feet, then led the way back upstairs to the girls' dormitory.

Lisa glanced up at Tommy in the shadowed darkness of the hall and saw his calm expression. He seemed at ease, and she forgot all about any worries she'd had about him. Tommy always knew what to do. He always made everything okay, and besides, he'd just told her the story where the prince and princess lived happily ever after, just like them.

"Here you go," he said quietly as they reached the girls' wing. "Get some sleep. I'll see you in the morning."

"I will. G'night, Tommy," she promised as she disappeared into the room.

Lisa went to bed and slept peacefully.

Later, Tommy lay in his bed, thinking once again about McKittrick and silently pondering how best to deal with him. He would do something for he couldn't . . . no, *he wouldn't* let anyone hurt Miss Catherine.

Fifteen

Matt was up early the following morning. He considered waking Winn to tell him what he'd learned about the orphanage the night before, but in deference to the late night his friend had had, he left him a note instead.

As he breakfasted alone in the hotel dining room, Matt's thoughts were centered on Catherine Sutherland and her band of orphans. She had haunted his thoughts since he'd left her. She was different, unlike anyone he'd ever met before. He couldn't explain exactly what it was he felt for her, for it certainly wasn't logical, but he sensed there was a certain magic about Catherine, and it was obvious that the children felt it, too.

An image of her as she'd looked last night in the garden in the moonlight floated through his thoughts as he tried to eat. She'd been vulnerable and in pain, and a fierce desire to help her had been born within him. Matt had to give himself a mental shake to force his attention away from her and back to matters at hand. But even as he tried to concentrate on his visit to St. Joan's owner this morning, a part of him wanted to learn more about Catherine. As he finished his meal, he grew determined to find out everything he could about her and her husband, too. Matt wondered why her husband wasn't working with her to help save the children's home. Certainly, if she'd been his wife, he would have been by her side helping her in her time of trouble.

His breakfast over, Matt left the hotel, hired a carriage, and was on his way to confront Mr. Markham and, hopefully, change his mind about selling the orphanage. For the first time in his life, Matt regretted not having a lot of money. If he were rich, he could buy the building himself right now and put an end to all the turmoil. As it was, he was going to have to plead her case and hope the man listened. He arrived at Markham's mansion and boldly knocked on the door.

"My name's Matthew McKittrick. I'm from Boston and I'm in town on business. I wondered if I might speak with Mr. Markham?" Matt introduced himself smoothly to the maid who'd opened the door.

"What matter did you wish to meet with him about?" she asked, cautiously eyeing the nicely dressed, handsome young man.

"I'm interested in a piece of property he has on the market. I understand the building now being used for a founding home is for sale, and I'd like to know more about it. If he has the time to see me, that is."

"One minute." The maid was courteous, but just as diligent in protecting her employer from Matt as she had been a few days earlier in keeping Catherine at bay. After a minute, she returned and politely ushered Matt inside.

"Please have a seat in the parlor, Mr. McKittrick. Mr. Markham will be with you shortly."

"Thank you."

As Matt entered the main hallway of the mansion, he was impressed by the home's opulence. The house was in the American section of New Orleans, and it was beautiful. High-ceilinged, with crystal chandeliers and silver doorknobs, the three-story structure bespoke of elegance and wealth. He could tell at a glance that Markham didn't need the money from the sale of the orphanage, and he wondered why the man was so determined to be rid of it.

The maid directed him into a spacious sitting room, and Matt made himself comfortable, sitting on an overstuffed sofa. He took the time to study the room, hoping to learn something about the man he was about to meet from its furnishings. Everything was tastefully decorated, but revealed nothing of Markham's personality. The only personal thing in the room was a large oil portrait of a beautiful, young, fair-haired mother and child hanging over the fireplace. He glanced at it once with little real interest, and then a moment later felt his gaze drawn back to it, as if he'd missed something in his first quick appraisal.

Matt studied the portrait, wondering why the woman and child seemed familiar to him. The mother was lovely—exquisite actually. Her blonde hair, wide, innocent green eyes, and shapely figure, made her the kind of woman few men could forget. He noticed the distinctive, heart-shaped gold pendant on a fine gold chain around her neck. The little girl was as pretty as her mother, with pale hair and angelic beauty. He was certain he'd never met either of them, and yet, something about them looked so familiar. He shrugged off the impression.

"Yes, Mr. McKittrick, is it? I'm Benjamin Markham. What can I do for you this morning?"

Matt rose respectfully at the sound of the man's voice. He turned to find Markham standing in the doorway observing him with a keen eye. Matt returned his regard openly, finding his host to be a slightly heavy set, distinguished-looking man of some fifty years. There was an air of imperial authority about him, and Matt could tell right away that he wasn't someone who was used to being trifled with.

"Good morning, sir." He went forward and offered him his hand.

Markham shook hands with him, then waved him back to his seat.

"Let's be comfortable while we talk business, shall we, Mr. McKittrick?"

"By all means." When they'd been seated, Matt on the sofa again, and Markham in a chair near him. Matt asked out of curiosity, "Tell me, sir, who is the woman in the portrait?"

"That portrait is of my wife, Analisa, and my only child, Belinda."

"They are lovely."

"Thank you. They were very beautiful."

"Were?"

"They're both lost to me now. My wife died years ago when Belinda was small, and my daughter died just four years ago."

"I'm sorry."

Markham quickly changed the subject; thoughts of his daughter were painful for him. "Shall we get down to business now?"

"Of course. I came to see you this morning for I heard that the property now housing St. Joan's is on the market. Is that true?"

"Yes. I've decided to sell the place. Are you interested? The price is most reasonable considering the location."

"I'm interested in the property, Mr. Markham, but not in the way you think."

"What?"

"I'm interested in convincing you not to sell. I want to convince you to keep the orphanage open," Matt said bluntly, seeing no reason to beat around the bush with the man.

"That's out of the question, and I resent your coming here under false pretenses." Anger flared in Markham's eyes as he glared at Matt.

"I did not lie. I spoke the truth. I said I was interested in the sale of the property, and I am. I'm interested in preventing it," Matt declared.

"Good day, Mr. McKittrick." Markham stood up abruptly, ending the short interview. "I don't believe we have anything more to say to one another."

"Do you realize what's going to happen to those

children when you force them out of that building in two weeks?"

"Who sent you here? That Sutherland woman? I always knew she'd be trouble one day . . ." he muttered in disgust.

"No one sent me." He defended Catherine. "When I heard what was about to happen to St. Joan's, I came of my own accord. Have you been to the orphanage lately? Have you seen what a good job Mrs. Sutherland has done with those children? They're happy and well-cared for, Mr. Markham, and that's more than what I can say for the orphans in a lot of homes."

"No, I haven't been there and I have no plans to go," Markham snapped, unwilling to listen to this stranger telling him his own business. He had a personal reason for selling the home, and he was going to see it through. He wanted nothing more to do with children—any children. He wanted the money back he'd invested in the building, and he was going to spend it on himself and try to find some happiness in what was left of his life.

"Don't you understand the terrible harm you'll be causing if you do this?"

"Don't you understand that I don't care?" Markham returned hotly. "Good day, Mr. McKittrick."

"Mr. Markham . . ." Matt stood to leave, but as he did, he met the man's gaze squarely, searching there for some reason behind his madness. "I don't understand. Tell me why you're doing this. Right now, you own a building that's being used to provide a desperately needed service. You are saving children's lives!

Yet, for some reason you're willing to throw all that away without any thought to the misery you'll cause."

"How dare you lecture me?!" Markham was seething. "You don't know anything about me! What do you know about misery? You do-gooders are all alike! You talk a good game, but where were you and all the others when my daughter needed help? Tell me that!"

"Your daughter?"

"Yes! Belinda ran off and married against my will some years ago. The man deserted her when she became pregnant. Belinda was too proud to come home. To this day, I regret the things I said to her before she ran away . . . She became seriously ill and died. I didn't find out until months afterward."

"I'm sorry." Matt looked back up at the beautiful young girl in the portrait. It pained him to know that she was dead. Young people should never die. Death was for the aged who'd had enough of their time on Earth and were on their way to better things.

"Not nearly as sorry as I am," Markham came back at him. "When I finally got word, I began looking for my granddaughter. I've been searching for the child ever since, but there's no trace of her to be found anywhere."

"Your daughter had the baby?"

"Oh, yes. A little girl." The anger drained out of the older man, and suddenly he was just sad and pathetic in his misery and loneliness. "A precious little girl . . . and that child, the last living link to my Belinda, is lost to me forever." He paused to draw a steadying breath. "If I could have found that child, I could have

"Mr. Markham, you could be helping others just like your daughter if you continued to run the home."

The mention of St. Joan's brought him back to the present, and he grew stern and formidable again.

"Good-bye, Mr. McKittrick. I'm not interested. I'm tired, very tired, and I just want to be left alone."

He walked toward the doorway to let him know that he was serious about ending the conversation. He'd already blurted out more than he'd ever wanted to reveal, and now he wanted him out of his house and out of his life. It was too painful to think about Belinda and speculating about his lost granddaughter only made him feel worse. He just wanted to forget.

"Good-bye, Mr. Markham," he said solemnly as he left the house.

Matt's mood was dark as he made his way back to St. Joan's. He would have to tell Catherine the truth about what had happened. There could be no avoiding it. He just didn't like being the bearer of bad news. As he crossed the city to the orphanage, he sought an answer to their dilemma. He knew there had to be something else he could do to help, but right now he wasn't sure what.

Matt arrived at St. Joan's far too quickly to suit him. He was met on the steps by Tommy again.

"Good morning. Is Mrs. Sutherland here?" he asked.

"What do you want to know for?" the boy challenged with manly bravado. He'd been up all night worrying about Miss Catherine, and he was determined to protect her from Matt. He wasn't going to let this man hurt her again.

Matt was stunned by the open hostility from the boy. "Is something wrong, Tommy?"

"No. Nothing's wrong. I just want to know why you have to see her again. I want to know if you're gonna talk to her today, like you did last night."

"Last night?"

"Sure, I was watching you last night, and I don't like what you did."

"Look, son, I don't know what I did to make you angry, but if you'll tell me, we can talk it out." Matt couldn't imagine what had upset the boy, but he was determined to find out.

"I saw you here last night," he said accusingly. "I saw you leave, and I saw Miss Catherine crying after you left. You said something or you did something to make her cry. I don't want her hurt. And if you're gonna make her cry again, then just go on and go right now." Tommy's chin jutted out aggressively as he moved to stand before Matt and block his way up the steps.

Matt stared down at the youth who was facing him with all the pride and daring of a man. For one brief moment, Matt wanted to laugh, but quickly reconsidered. At eleven, Tommy was more of a man than some thirty-year-olds he knew. In that moment, Matt decided to explain to him just what was going on. With this kind of courage, the boy deserved it. It was obvious how deeply he cared for Catherine.

"Tommy, I know how important you are around here,

and how much Mrs. Sutherland relies on you. I'd like to confide in you. Can I trust you to keep a secret?"

"Yes." Tommy eyed him cautiously, unsure about returning any trust in him.

"Let's go somewhere where we can talk privately, man-to-man. What I'm about to tell you has to stay just between us, all right?"

Tommy nodded and led the way to a quiet corner where no one else could hear them. Matt noticed that as he walked ahead of him, the boy's shoulders were squared and his head was held high.

"This is safe. Go ahead," Tommy told him when they were out of earshot.

"There's big trouble here at the orphanage," he said point blank.

"What kind of trouble?" His eyes narrowed as he tried to gauge the man's sincerity.

"The man who owns the building, a Mr. Markham, is planning to sell it. He wants Mrs. Sutherland to move all the children out of here within the next two weeks."

"Two weeks?" He stared at him in horror. "But this is our home!"

"I know. That's what she was crying about last night when you saw her. That's why I'm here this morning. I went to speak with Mr. Markham this morning. I was hoping I could convince him to change his mind about selling, but he refused. Right now, I've got to talk to Mrs. Sutherland, so we can try to figure out a way to save this place for you and the other children.

Do you have any ideas? Can you think of anything that might help?"

Tommy was in shock. The thought that his home here with Miss Catherine might be disrupted had never occurred to him. She was the one constant, stable thing in his life. She was his anchor, his rock, his reason for being. Surely, Miss Catherine would be able to save them. She always took care of everything. But then he remembered her tears. . . . He frowned in concentration.

"I'll think of something. I won't let her down. I'll help her."

"I knew I could count on you," Matt praised him.

Tommy shot him a tight look. "What do you care? You're leaving. This is for me and Miss Catherine to handle. We don't need you or your help."

Matt recognized the fierce honor in him. But while he respected him for his devotion, he also knew it was important that a man be able to accept help when he needed it. "In times like these, you need all the help you can get, and I want to help. I'd like you to trust me, Tommy, but even if you don't, I'm going to do everything in my power to help Mrs. Sutherland."

They stood looking at each other for a minute—one man mentally offering his hand in support, the other soon-to-be man still harboring serious doubts about his true motives and accepting his aid. Neither male gave ground.

When the boy didn't respond, Matt calmly moved past him and went on up the stairs and into the building.

As Tommy watched him go, he carried on a mental battle with himself. Deep in his heart, a part of him wanted to believe in Matt and trust him, but he'd learned early in life how dangerous it could be to trust anyone. Right now, there was only one person he put his faith in, and that was Miss Catherine. He'd made up his mind long ago to always be there when she needed him. Having lived through the horror of desertion and loneliness, he knew firsthand how devastating it was to be completely alone. He would support Miss Catherine now, and he would do everything he could to help. He just wondered how truly serious Mr. McKittrick was about staying and helping. He hoped he meant it. But he still had his doubts.

Matt went in to see Catherine. When he'd left her the night before, he'd hoped to have good news for her the next time they met. He'd wanted to make her smile. It pained him that he couldn't tell her he'd convinced Markham to change his mind. Still, as bad as his message was, he was determined that whatever terrible challenge she faced, he would face it with her.

"Good morning." Catherine had been expecting him, and she smiled in welcome as he entered her office. Once again, she was struck by how attractive he was, but when her gaze met his and she saw the seriousness of his expression, the frivolous thought was banished from her mind. She had no time to distract herself with such things. The children were all that mattered. She had to take care of the children.

"Good morning," he greeted her, glad to see her again and glad to see that she didn't look as distressed. "Are you feeling better this morning?"

"I'm not sure." Her tone was quiet as her gaze searched his face. "You tell me how I'm feeling."

"Markham refused to listen to me," he told her the truth, seeing no reason to drag out the suspense.

"Oh." It was more of a sigh of resignation, than an exclamation. "Did you manage to find out why he was doing this? And why now, after all these years?"

"I asked him, and he got angry with me for challenging him on his decision. When I pressed him for an answer, he finally told me that his daughter had died some years ago, and how when she was in need no one had offered her any help. He lost her and his granddaughter. He's very bitter. He wants nothing more to do with children."

"I didn't know about his daughter," Catherine said sadly, lifting her troubled gaze to Matt. "It must have been awful for him. Losing a child . . ."

Matt's gaze rested warmly upon her, and he saw all the goodness and gentleness in her. Every kind thing about her was real. She possessed no pretense or artifice. She was an honest, giving person, and in his opinion that made her rare and precious. "I told Markham that by helping others now, he would be making a difference for someone else. But he wanted nothing to do with it. He's been hurt so badly by his loss that all he wants to do is forget the whole world."

"I can understand that . . ." she murmured, memories of the total blackness and complete pointlessness of her own life after she'd lost her family surging back to fill her with deep, abiding pain.

Matt saw the change in her, and he couldn't stop

himself from going to her. That look of pain on her face was so poignant, that he suddenly felt compelled to hold her and comfort her. He wanted to take her in his arms. He held himself back. "You understand his loss . . ."

When Catherine glanced up at him, her own personal agony was still evident in her eyes. "Yes. I lost the two people on Earth I loved the most—my husband and my daughter. They were killed in an accident some years ago."

Matt was stunned. He'd thought she was happily married. "I'm sorry." He reached out and put a gentle, supportive hand on her arm hoping that small humane gesture could offer her solace. He was amazed at how fragile she felt to him.

Matt's touch was comforting, and Catherine almost let herself enjoy it, but reality forced her to be strong. With an almost physical effort, she focused her thoughts back on her present problem. "Shortly after they died, I came here to St. Joan's for the first time to do volunteer work. I've been here with the children ever since. And now . . ."

"You've done a wonderful job," Matt complimented her. "I just wish I could have brought you better news on Markham, but he was adamant."

"You tried. That's more than I can say for most. I guess I'll just have to find a way out of this by myself. I do appreciate your efforts, Matt."

"I'm not through yet," he vowed. "There must be something else that can be done."

"I wish I knew what."

"Would you like to go to dinner tonight? Maybe if we work together we can think of a plan." Matt was surprised to find he was a little nervous as he waited for her answer. He'd been attracted to her from the start, but had denied it because he'd thought she was married. He would never have wished tragedy or unhappiness upon her, but he couldn't deny feeling glad that she was unattached.

"I'd like that very much," she accepted, wondering why her heart was suddenly beating such a swift rhythm.

"I'll be by for you about seven." Matt turned to go, but her call to him stopped his progress.

"Matt."

"Yes?"

"Thanks."

He nodded at her, then left the room. His mood was both elated and somber. He was thrilled that Catherine had agreed to have dinner with him, but the danger of losing St. Joan's still loomed over them. He hoped he could come up with a new idea before he saw her tonight.

Matt was just starting from the building, when he saw the little girl named Lisa wandering down the hall. She had obviously been crying and she was clutching something to her as if it were a most cherished object.

"Lisa? Is there something wrong?" He went to her and hunkered down before her. The sight of her tear-ravaged face tore at his heart.

"No. I was just lookin' for Tommy," she muttered

with a loud sniff as she wiped at her eyes with the back of her hand.

"What is it? Can I help?"

"My doll broke, and I hafta find Tommy so he can fix it." She shyly showed him her one-legged doll and then pulled the missing leg from her pocket.

"I'll be glad to try to fix it for you."

"No." Her answer came quickly. "Tommy will do it. He always fixes everything for me." She stuffed the leg back in the pocket of her dress and tucked the doll protectively under her arm.

"Tommy and I are friends, too, Lisa. I'm sure he'd want me to help you if he isn't here to do it. I'm probably not as good as he is at fixing things, but I'd like to try, if you'll let me."

Lisa heard the sincerity in his voice and gazed up at him. Her eyes met his, and she stared at him as if she were looking into his very soul.

Matt met her regard fully, and he was struck again by how lovely she was.

She paused for minute, cautious, then after wrestling with the decision, she finally held the broken toy and its leg out to him. "Okay."

Matt took her proffered treasure and moved to sit on one of the benches nearby. Lisa followed him there and stood beside him watching as he worked. It took a little doing for he wasn't all that familiar with girls' toys, but he managed. His expression was nothing short of triumphant as he looked up at the patiently waiting child.

"Here. All done." Matt handed her the doll, once again all in one piece.

"Thanks," she told him with a big, bright smile.

"You're more than welcome, sweetheart." He touched her cheek affectionately, and he was glad when she did not shy away.

"Are you gonna stay here, Mr. McKittrick?"

"I'll be here as long as necessary," he replied, not wanting to lie to her.

"What's that mean?"

"It means that I plan to stay as long as Mrs. Sutherland needs me." He meant every word.

"I hope she needs you for a long time." She grinned at him.

Matt grinned back. "Have you been here for a long time?"

"Yes. I've been here since I was little."

He chuckled. "So you're a grown-up young lady now."

"Uh-huh," she agreed.

He thought of his days in the orphanage and how he'd grown up before his time. Children deserved a carefree childhood. He was glad that Catherine was here for these little ones, and he was glad that Lisa had Tommy. He envied that they had each other. He'd had no one when he was young.

"I've got to go now," Lisa announced, all now right with her world.

"Me, too."

As he stood up to leave, the front door opened and Tommy came in.

"Tommy! Look! Mr. McKittrick fixed my doll," Lisa announced as she held it up for him to see.

Tommy's expression grew suspicious as he looked from Lisa, who was known for her shyness around strangers, to Matt, and then back again. "Let me see."

"Sure." She handed him the doll. "Didn't he do a good job?"

Tommy gave a soft snort of derision as he inspected his work.

Matt understood the boy's resentment. "Lisa had been looking for you, but when she couldn't find you, I helped out as best I could. See what you think about the job I did. I'm not very good with toys. I hope I fixed it right."

Tommy scrutinized the doll carefully and made several adjustments to the repaired leg.

Matt knew exactly what the boy was doing. He knew it was important that Tommy maintain his position of hero in Lisa's eyes, and Matt would do nothing to hurt their relationship. He smiled as he watched the two together.

Lisa looked on in awe as her Tommy corrected the other man's work. In her eyes, he could do no wrong.

"There, that should do it now," the youth said as he gave it back to her.

"Thanks, Tommy." She hugged the doll to her as she gazed up at him with open adoration.

"How did I do?" Matt finally asked.

"It wasn't right, so I fixed it."

"Then it's a good thing you came in when you did."

"Yeah, it was."

"Tommy, tonight Mrs. Sutherland and I are going out to dinner. How would you like to join us?" Matt wanted to win his trust. He could think of no better way than to include him at dinner that evening. He hoped by treating him like an adult and giving credence to his opinions, he might be able to forge a relationship with him. Matt didn't know why he felt that was important, he just knew he did. There was something about the boy that reminded him of himself at the same age.

Tommy glanced up at him sharply. "Look, Mr. McKittrick, there's no reason for you to be nice to me. I know you're leaving just as soon as you get what you came here for. You don't really care about us."

Matt's initial reaction was irritation. He wasn't used to having people doubt him, but then he reminded himself that the child had been raised in the orphanage. Catherine had done a fine job, but she couldn't erase all the pain and damage that had been done when he'd been abandoned. Tommy had to live with and accept the fact that he'd been left on the streets as a toddler and that he had no family to call his own. Matt knew the feeling, and he knew the insecurity that came with it. He still dealt with it every day. It never went away, you just learned how to handle the emptiness and fear.

"Tommy, you're wrong. I do care. That's why Mrs. Sutherland and I are going out to dinner tonight. We're going to talk about what you and I discussed earlier, and I'd like you to go along and help us. Will you? I'd appreciate it."

Tommy hesitated, then relented. "All right."

"Good. I'll tell Mrs. Sutherland that you'll be joining us."

Matt headed back toward her office as Tommy and Lisa moved off down the hall. Matt stopped to watch the two children go, and he was struck by the way Lisa moved with instinctive grace and style. There was an almost regal quality about her.

In the back of his mind, something nagged at him, though he wasn't sure just what. He dismissed the feeling as he reentered Catherine's office to tell her that the boy would be going to dinner with them.

Sixteen

Winn and Alex faced Matt across the width of Alex's room at the hotel. The note he'd left for them that morning had made it sound as if he'd found the connection to their next clue, and they were eager to hear what he'd learned.

"Where have you been? Have you figured out the clue about the orphanage?" Alex asked.

"I've got a feeling it isn't as simple as we'd hoped," Winn remarked, noticing how subdued Matt was. "You don't look much like celebrating. What's wrong?"

Matt explained what had happened since he'd last spoken to them the night before.

"That's terrible. I can't believe anyone would be so cruel. To do that to innocent children!" Alex was aghast at the news of Markham's indifference.

"I know. I've done a lot of thinking since I left St. Joan's, and I've made a decision."

"What kind of decision?" Winn asked.

"I'm not leaving here until things are resolved with the orphanage. I've got to make sure they're all safe, either at St. Joan's or in a new building," he stated. "The two of you don't need me any more. We're done with my book, so you can go on without me. But Catherine and the children do need me. I can't leave them. Not now."

"But what about the crown?" Winn was completely surprised by his decision. He'd thought the treasure was the most important thing to him.

"I trust you and Alex completely. I know you'll do the right thing when you find it," he told them. "It's just that I've discovered there are times in life when people are more important than lost treasures. You see, I grew up in an orphanage, but the one I was in wasn't anything like St. Joan's. This place is special. Catherine has made it a haven for those children. I can't just turn my back and walk away from them knowing that they might be out on the street in less than two weeks."

Fear for her father's safety was haunting Alex, yet after listening to Matt, she was filled with respect and love for him. He was willing to sacrifice everything he'd worked so hard for to save the children. Without a word, she went to him and pressed a soft kiss to his cheek. "We won't turn our backs on them either, Matt. We're not going anywhere until this is resolved. When we do go after the crown, it will be as Lawrence wanted us to go—together."

Matt glanced between them both and smiled. "Thanks."

"How are you planning to save the orphanage?" Winn asked then.

"I wish I knew. If you've got any ideas, I'd certainly like to hear them. Catherine's attempted to talk to Markham, but he wouldn't see her. So she took it upon herself to try to raise the necessary funds to buy the place, but the response wasn't good. I went to see him this morning, and I tried to convince him not to sell, but he practically threw me out of the house."

Winn looked thoughtful. "Has she looked around for another place to take the children?"

"There's nothing available for the little they can afford. Things are tight at St. Joan's. There never has been a lot of money to take care of expenses, but up until now they've somehow managed to scrape by."

"What would it take to buy the place from Markham?"

"He's asking $5,000. Why?"

"Because I think I may have found a buyer for you." Back in London, Winn had appreciated his wealth for all the comforts it had provided him. He'd never known a hungry day. He'd always gotten exactly what he'd wanted when he'd wanted it. Having money was a wonderful thing. Now, for the first time, he realized he could do something good with his fortune.

"Who?" Both Alex and Matt stared at him in surprise, wondering what he was thinking.

"Me."

"Are you serious?" Matt couldn't believe Winn was making such a generous offer.

"I'm very serious."

"Do you have enough money?"

"Money's not a problem. And I agree with you, we can't let anything happen to the children. Helping St. Joan's is the right thing to do."

"Thanks, Winn." He'd had no idea Winn was so rich, and he was humbled by his generosity and kindness.

"Shall we go tell Catherine?" Alex asked cheerfully, seeing the relief in Matt's expression.

"I'd planned to take her out to dinner tonight, but this is too important to wait. Let's go tell her about your offer, and then we can all go to Markham's together."

They found Catherine still in her office, working at her desk, trying to find a way out of the maze of her dilemma. She heard the knock at the door and looked up wearily as she called out for whoever it was to come in.

"Catherine? We need to talk to you for a minute." He opened the door and stepped inside with Winn and Alex close behind.

"Matt? I didn't expect to see you until tonight. Is there something wrong?"

"No, as a matter of fact, for once, something is right."

"I don't understand." She started to stand up to greet them.

"Please stay seated. I think you'll feel better if you do."

"Why? What have you done?" Her eyes were wide and questioning.

Winn saw her confusion and concern, and he quickly spoke up. "Matt told us about the trouble you're having, and how you were trying to raise the funds to buy the building yourself."

"I don't even have enough to make a down payment yet, but I'm working on it." She refused to admit defeat.

"Well, we've got better than a down payment for you. Winn's agreed to buy the building from Markham."

Catherine stared at Winn. "You're going to buy St. Joan's?"

"Yes. It should be a simple matter," he started to explain.

"But why would you?" she asked, stunned by such generosity.

Winn paused a moment before answering. A deep feeling of warmth filled him at the thought of doing something kind for someone else. He thought of Sister Agnes at the convent and of the children at St. Joan's. But mostly he thought of his uncle. He'd been so blessed in his life. It was only right that he help others. He smiled. "Because it's the right thing to do. You need help, and I can give it to you."

Catherine got up and circled her desk to stand before Winn. She took his hand as she looked up into his eyes, and the kindness and generosity she saw there brought tears to her eyes. She saw no avarice or deceit. He was speaking from his heart. "You're a kind and wonderful man. I thank you, and the children thank you."

"You're more than welcome," Winn returned, touched by the sincerity of her words.

"Let's go see Markham," Matt encouraged. "The faster we settle this with him, the happier I'm going to be. I don't trust the man not to sell it to someone else while we're on our way over."

They climbed into a hired carriage and made the trip across town to the old man's mansion. Once again, Matt was forced to confront the guardian maid.

"We need to see Mr. Markham," Matt told her when she stood like a ferocious guard dog in the doorway, blocking their path.

The strong-willed servant stood her ground before him. "Sir, I am sure Mr. Markham doesn't want to see you again."

"And I'm just as sure that he does," Matt insisted. "Tell him that I'm back and that I have to see him right away."

"Mr. Markham is a busy man, and he cannot be bothered."

"I advise you to tell him that I have a buyer for his property. I'm sure he'll be interested."

"Mr. McKittrick, Mr. Markham told me . . ."

With sheer boldness, Matt brushed past her and moved into the foyer, calling Markham's name. "Mr. Markham! It's Matt McKittrick. I want to talk to you."

Matt heard rumblings from the back of the house, and then a door flew open near the end of the main hall.

"What the . . . ?" Markham was growling as he came out of his study looking particularly perturbed.

"I'm sorry, Mr. Markham, but he just pushed his way in here," the maid said.

It was obvious that Markham was upset over Matt's intrusion into his home. Other servants, too, were converging on the foyer, but Matt remained where he was with Winn, Alex, and Catherine standing beside him.

"What are you doing back here, McKittrick? And you?" He looked pointedly at Catherine.

"Hello, Mr. Markham," she greeted him serenely.

"I thought I told the both of you that we had nothing more to say to each other."

"Yes, I know," Matt said evenly as he faced the irate man. "But if you'll give me a minute, I think you'll appreciate our need to see you again."

"Get . . ."

Before Markham could finish ordering them from the premises, Matt cut him off.

"We've found a buyer for St. Joan's," he said bluntly. He tensed before the other man's anger, ready for trouble, but hoping there would be none.

"You have?"

"Yes, allow me to introduce you. Mr. Markham, this is Lord Winston Bradford. Lord Bradford, this is Mr. Markham." Matt made the introductions quickly. "Lord Bradford's interested in the property and is willing to come to terms tonight, if that suits you."

Markham eyed Winn, noting his manner and the cut of his clothes. He knew a gentleman when he saw one, and he nodded. "Let's go into the parlor. We can talk there more comfortably."

Markham led the way and directed them to sit down. Matt and Catherine sat together on the sofa, while Winn and Alex took the wing chairs.

"Would anyone care for refreshments?" Markham asked, his demeanor quickly improving.

"No, thank you. This is a business meeting, not a social one," Winn told him, assuming his most arrogant, grating manner. If this man was impressed by his title, he might as well use it to their benefit. As much as he hated to admit it, intimidation did work when properly used.

"Well, Lord Bradford, why are you interested in buying this particular piece of property?"

Catherine meant to pay strict attention to what the men were saying, but when she glanced up at the portrait above the fireplace, the emotions that jolted through her dulled the sounds of their discussion to a vague and distant buzz. She blinked and peered up at the picture again, not quite believing what she was seeing. It was Lisa. . . . She reached out to Matt and gripped his forearm.

"Matt . . ." she said his name softly, not taking her eyes off the portrait of the mother and child.

Matt was deep in discussion with Winn and Markham, and he glanced at her, puzzled by her interruption. "What?"

"Look . . ." She nodded toward the painting as she told him in a soft voice. "That could be Lisa up there . . ."

Matt lifted his gaze to the little girl in the picture. As he stared at her, transfixed, all the nagging thoughts that had been troubling him for the past few hours suddenly made sense. Lisa's resemblance to Belinda Markham as a child was uncanny. She had that same angelic expression, that same smile. He felt himself grow tense with hope and expectation. "Lisa . . ."

"I beg your pardon?" Markham spoke up rather sharply, a bit annoyed that Catherine had interrupted their business talk.

"Mr. Markham, that is a portrait of your wife and daughter, isn't it?" Catherine asked.

"Yes. That's my wife, Analisa, and my daughter, Belinda."

"They were lovely."

"Indeed, they were," he said.

"Mr. Markham, I think you need to come out to St. Joan's with me." She stood up. "There's someone there I want you to meet." Hope was budding in her breast. She told herself it was crazy, but the resemblance was too astonishing to ignore.

The old man sighed. "Mrs. Sutherland, I told you before I wasn't interested in the orphanage."

"It won't take much of your time. Just a few hours, and I'm sure you won't be sorry."

"There's nothing at St. Joan's I care about."

"I wouldn't be so sure of that."

"Spare me your intrigue, Mrs. Sutherland."

"This is no trick." Catherine went to the man and put a hand on his arm. She looked him in the eye as she told him steadily, "Mr. Markham, this is important . . . almost a matter of life and death. Trust me this one time."

"There's no point in it."

"Exactly," she confirmed. "If Lord Bradford is willing to buy the building, why would I want you to go back there? It's important or I wouldn't have asked."

"No . . . . I . . ." Markham started to refuse not

wanting to see any of those children. His heart ached when he saw them and thought of Belinda and his lost grandchild. He started to turn away from her.

"Come to St. Joan's with me," Catherine pleaded. "I'll introduce you to a six-year-old girl named Lisa who looks enough like your daughter to be her twin at that age."

"You're lying . . ." His battered heart rebelled at this hope she offered. His prayers of finding the child had gone unanswered so many times that he didn't know if he could bear another disappointment.

"I would never lie to you about something so important."

"But how can you expect me to believe that you have, at a home just miles from me, the very child I've been searching all over the country for for years?!"

"Don't take my word. Accompany me to the orphanage. Come see her for yourself. Only you will know for sure if she's Belinda's daughter."

Markham was terribly afraid of being hurt yet another time, but he knew even the remotest possibility was worth again risking the pain.

"Stranger things have happened," Matt added. "You have nothing to lose but a little of your time. If it turns out that she isn't your granddaughter, then we can continue with the sale of the property. But if Lisa proves to be yours . . ." He let the thought hang for a moment. "Do you dare not go?"

Markham gave in. "All right. You win. I'll go. I'll call the carriage around."

"There's no need. We have a hired conveyance outside waiting for us."

They were in the carriage and on their way toward St. Joan's, when Markham began asking questions.

"How much do you know about the child? What do you know about her past and her parents? What's her last name?"

"Lisa is six now," Catherine explained. "She came to us about four years ago. According to the woman who left her here, Lisa had no known living relatives. Her father had deserted her mother before she was born, and then when her mother died, she was left with only the neighbors. They're the ones who brought her here. They told us her family name was Brown."

Markham's expression was pained. "Everything you've just told me fits except that last name. Belinda's married name was Stanhope. Her husband deserted her and she was too much like me . . . too proud to admit she was wrong and just come home. She was left on her own. When she died, I lost not only her, but her daughter as well. Does the child know about her family?"

"I'm not sure. I hope so. I want you to have some solid proof of her parentage, something irrefutable that will convince you she really is yours."

"I hope so, too."

They fell silent, each trying to imagine what was going to happen when they reached St. Joan's.

Matt could sense Catherine's nervousness as she sat close beside him in the carriage, and he reached out and took her hand in his. A thrill went through him when she didn't resist, but grasped his hand back. He glanced at her then, and when their gazes locked, he knew she was the woman he wanted above all others, needed above all others. She was beautiful, but that wasn't why he wanted her. It was her heart and her spirit that had taken him captive. She was the woman he needed. His logical mind told him it was ridiculous to feel this way since he'd only known her for a short time, but somehow, time seemed unimportant where they were concerned. Matt felt she had always been there for him. It had just taken him until now to find her.

Catherine's spirits were soaring. When she'd looked up at Matt, and their eyes had met, she'd seen the depth of emotion in his regard, and a warm, feminine awareness had stirred deep within her. It was a sensation she hadn't experienced in years . . . not since her husband had been alive. Frightened by the intensity of her feelings, she'd quickly turned her thoughts back to St. Joan's and Lisa.

Catherine and Matt sat together in the sunlight that shone through the carriage window, both waiting for the ride to be over.

When they finally arrived back at St. Joan's, Markham climbed out of the vehicle first and stared up at the building. He was careful to hide his feelings as he saw how shabby and rundown it was, and he ignored the twinge of guilt that stung him. He told himself he'd be glad to be rid of the building.

As he started up the walk, the sound of children's laughter came to him from somewhere nearby. It grated on him. He didn't want to think about happy children. Not when his beloved Belinda was dead and her baby lost. He felt lonelier than ever as he slowly mounted the steps. His life had no purpose, no real meaning. There was no sunshine or joy, only heartbreak and solitude.

"Come with me," Matt and Catherine told him as they came to his side, the others were following slightly behind. Matt could see the slight look of distaste and skepticism on the older man's face as they entered the building.

"Where are we going?" Markham asked.

"To Mrs. Sutherland's office. We can send for the girl and have her meet us there." Matt stopped for a moment to face him. "Mr. Markham, Lisa has no idea about any of this. So, please, if she isn't your granddaughter, at least be kind. She's only six, and in spite of all her losses and hardship, she's still an innocent child."

"Contrary to what you might think of me, McKittrick, I am not a monster."

Their eyes met in complete understanding, and Matt was relieved when he saw a flicker of gentle emotion in the depths of the other man's gaze. Catherine led the rest of the way to her office.

"I'll go get Lisa, and then I'll be right back. Please make yourselves comfortable," Catherine said as Markham, Winn, and Alex entered the room.

"I'll go with you," Matt offered.

When they were alone in the hall, he asked, "Where do we start looking for her?"

"If we find Tommy, we'll find Lisa," she explained.

"She's adored him and followed him around since the first day she came here. Even as a toddler she couldn't take her eyes off him, and he took to her hero worship without complaint. I'd say it was love at first sight."

"I can understand that emotion," Matt said with heartfelt intent as he looked at Catherine.

She felt color rise to her cheeks, and she smiled at him. Together, they made their way to the yard.

"There they are." She pointed to where the two were sitting together across the yard.

"What do you think?" Matt asked Catherine watching them for a moment and mentally comparing Lisa to the portrait of Belinda at the same age.

"I don't know. It seems too good to be true. Too perfect . . ."

"Maybe every once in a while, life needs to be perfect," Matt remarked, thinking of how frustrating life generally seemed to be. "It would be nice to know that miracles really can happen." He thought of the small miracle Alex had worked at the convent and hoped something just as wonderful could happen here.

"Let's go see," Catherine said as she walked toward them.

Tommy saw Matt and Catherine approaching. "Is it time to go to dinner already?" he asked.

"No, and from the look of things, I think we're probably going to have to skip dinner tonight, Tommy," Matt told him. "Mrs. Sutherland needs to talk to Lisa for a minute."

"What about?" The boy watched over the little girl closely, and he wanted to know what they wanted.

"We've brought someone here who wants to meet you, Lisa." Catherine sat down with them. "His name is Mr. Markham, and . . ."

"Mr. Markham?" Tommy asked quickly, remembering what Matt had told him about the man earlier.

"Yes. Mr. Markham's granddaughter has been missing for four years. He's searched everywhere for her. Today, when Matt and I saw a picture of her mother, she bore a very strong resemblance to you, Lisa. We think you may be the girl."

"Me?" She was stunned.

"It's possible. Tell me, Lisa, do you have anything that belonged to your mother? A Bible or some other keepsake from your family?"

"Why?" She looked nervously from Catherine to Tommy again.

"If you do, it might prove that you and Mr. Markham are related."

"I don't know . . ."

"Show her your little purse," Tommy urged. He knew she kept a small change purse that had been her mother's safely tucked away in her pocket during the day and then slept with it under her pillow at night. She'd shown him her treasure only once, but he had not forgotten it.

"Are you sure, Tommy?" Lisa was nervous about displaying her most precious possession, and she looked to him for moral support.

"It's all right. You can trust Miss Catherine."

"I know I can trust Miss Catherine," she answered,

"but can I trust him?" She looked straight at Matt who was standing quietly beside Catherine.

Tommy considered her worry for a moment, then answered, "Miss Catherine trusts him, so I think we can too. Go ahead and show them what you've got."

Matt didn't realize until that moment that he'd been holding his breath, waiting for Tommy's pronouncement. Relief washed over him as he realized that the boy had begun to have a little faith in him.

"Okay."

Tommy scooted nearer to Lisa to offer her moral support as she drew the small embroidered purse from deep in her pocket. The purse looked old to Catherine and Matt. It was not a child's ordinary plaything.

"You can look at it, Miss Catherine, but you can't have it. It belonged to my mother, and I have to keep it safe."

Lisa opened the purse and dug into it, drawing out a handkerchief from inside. It was tied, the four corners drawn up into a knot, and it weighed heavily with the hidden treasure kept within. Her little fingers struggled with the tight knot until Tommy reached over and quickly untied it for her. He handed it back, and Lisa gave him a grateful smile.

Matt and Catherine exchanged an understanding look as they watched the pair together. They had deliberately not crowded too close to allow them the room they needed to feel safe and unpressured. They watched now as she opened the handkerchief and revealed the contents.

"This was my mother's," Lisa said softly. "It's all I have of her."

Matt stared in shocked disbelief at the necklace she held in her hand. It was a heart-shaped golden pendant exactly like the one he'd seen Analisa Markham wearing in the portrait in Markham's parlor. They had found Benjamin Markham's granddaughter.

"Shall we go down to my office now and meet Mr. Markham?" Catherine suggested. She, too, recognized the heart and couldn't wait to see grandfather and granddaughter reunited. "He's waiting there to meet you, and I'm sure he'll be interested in seeing your necklace."

"Tommy?" Lisa looked to him for advice.

"It's all right. Let's go see him." Tommy stood up and waited for her to put her treasure back in her pocket before they started inside.

Catherine went in first, opening the door to the office when they reached it.

"It's all right, Tommy and Lisa. Come on in and meet Mr. Markham. He's here with Mr. Bradford and Miss Parker. You've met them before. They're Mr. McKittrick's friends."

Tommy followed Catherine into the office first, and Lisa trailed right behind him, afraid to let him out of her reach. He saw the older man sitting in one of the chairs before the desk, and he wondered if this man was really related to Lisa. In a way, he didn't want them to be. He and Lisa were as close as any sister and brother, and he wanted to keep it that way. He'd been taking care of her for four years now, and he intended to keep it up for as long as she needed him. His expression was serious and defensive as he stepped inside the office.

Lisa took great care to stay right behind Tommy, following in his wake. Shy as she was, she was more than a little afraid to face this stranger. It was a scary thing for a six-year-old to do.

"Mr. Markham, this is Tommy Glosier. He's Lisa's best friend."

Markham rose from where he'd been sitting and put out his hand toward the sturdy, dark-haired boy. "It's nice to meet you, young man."

Tommy moved forward to shake his hand. When he did, Lisa followed on his heels, not wanting to be left standing all alone in the doorway.

Markham shook Tommy's hand and then glanced behind him. It was then, for the first time, that he saw Lisa. Markham froze. His knees suddenly weakened and would no longer support him. He sank heavily back down on his chair, his gaze never leaving the child. His heart was pounding in his chest and he blinked several times, unable to believe what he was seeing. It seemed to Markham that he'd been transported back through time to his daughter's childhood. He could have sworn this was his own beloved Belinda standing so quietly before him.

Seventeen

"Belinda . . ." Markham gasped, staring into the face of a child whose resemblance to his daughter at the same age could only be described as phenomenal. Pain shot through him as he lifted his agonized gaze to Catherine. "Dear God . . . How . . . ?"

Catherine saw Markham's reaction to his first sight of Lisa, and tears welled up in her eyes.

"Mr. Markham," she said with great dignity. "I'd like you to meet Lisa Brown. Lisa, this is the gentleman I told you about, Mr. Markham."

Tommy was watching the man who might be Lisa's grandfather closely. His first impression of him was that he looked hard and maybe even a little mean. The minute Markham saw Lisa, though, his expression faltered and his vulnerability and pain were revealed for all to see. Tommy saw it, and he knew then it was true. He was thrilled with the knowledge that she might be finding a home, but a part of him rebelled at the thought of losing her.

"Lisa, come on. It's okay," Tommy urged.

She came to his side and grabbed his arm. She kept her eyes downcast and her manner was unsure.

"Lisa, I want you to go talk to Mr. Markham," Catherine said.

"I can talk to him from here," she replied defensively, hanging onto Tommy even tighter.

Catherine gave Tommy a look that spoke volumes, and though the last thing he wanted to do was turn her over to this stranger, he knew he had to give her the chance to find her family. "Come on, we'll talk to Mr. Markham together."

Tommy took her hand firmly in his, and drew her reluctantly forward. She balked every step of the way. Matt's heart ached for the child. He knew how frightening it could be to leave the only home you'd ever known. "Lisa, honey, there's nothing to be afraid of. No one's going to hurt you in any way. Mr. Markham is here because he cares about you. Can you show him the locker?"

She glanced over at Matt and saw the reassuring look on his face. She wanted to believe him, but Tommy was the only one she really trusted. "Tommy . . ."

"Go ahead, show him the heart," Tommy told her. "He won't take it away from you. He just wants to look at it for a minute."

"She has a heart locket?" Markham breathed, his color turning ashen.

While all looked on, Lisa pulled out the little purse and again took out the handkerchief. She untied it and lifted up the heart on its chain. She looked up at the old man who was watching her so intently. His eyes were brimming over with tears, and she finally went to him.

"Here's my heart," she said timidly as she held it out to him. "It was my mother's."

In the depths of his soul, Markham had already known the answer to his quest to find his granddaughter, but now with this solid proof he knew beyond any doubt. With trembling hands, he took the necklace from her. He stared down at the golden heart he held in his palm and immediately recognized it as the one he had given to his wife Analisa on their tenth wedding anniversary and then had passed on to Belinda after Analisa died. There was no mistaking it, for he'd had it specially crafted. He was crying openly now, and he lifted his eyes to gaze at the child he'd been searching for.

"Lisa . . ." he said in a choked voice as he dropped down to one knee before her. "I want you to know that I gave this heart to your grandmother many years ago. I told her I was giving her my heart that day." He managed a watery smile as he was overcome with emotion. "Lisa, I'm your grandfather . . . your mother's father."

"You really are my grandfather?" she repeated.

"Yes, and I've come to take you home with me."

He started to reach for her, to hug her, but she darted away from him, running straight into Tommy's arms. Her eyes were wide and frightened and tears threatened.

"No!"

"Lisa . . ." Catherine was surprised.

"No, Miss Catherine! I don't want to go home with him!"

"But Lisa, I have a big house and . . ."

"I don't care . . . I want to stay here with Tommy! Miss Catherine don't make me go! Please!"

Markham had gone from the heights of ecstasy to despair in less than a minute. He'd expected to find his grandchild and take her home and have a family again.

"Lisa, I don't understand . . . I've been searching for you for years, ever since I heard your mother died. I'm sorry it's taken me so long to find you, but now that I have, I can't give you up. I love you too much."

Real terror showed now on her face as she clung to Tommy. He wrapped his arms protectively around her. He could feel her quaking against him. His throat tightened. He wanted her to stay with him. She was the only real family he had outside of Miss Catherine. But he knew she should be with her grandfather.

"Lisa, you need to go with your grandpa," he said quietly.

"No! I won't leave you!" Her hands gripped him even tighter as she looked up at him, shocked that he would even suggest such a thing. "I don't want to go. You're my family! I want to stay here with you!"

"Tommy has been like a big brother to Lisa ever since she came to us four years ago," Catherine explained to the stricken Markham, wanting him to understand what was happening.

"Then I suppose there's only one solution," the old man said as he stood up and went to the two children.

Tommy thought Mr. Markham was going to physically take Lisa away from him. He felt his eyes begin to burn, but he fought back the tears. He was a man now. He would not let anyone know how much losing Lisa was going to hurt him. She was going to have a home. She was going to be happy. That was all he'd ever wanted for her.

Everyone else was looking on fearfully, not quite sure what Markham was about to do. Matt tensed, ready to take action if he tried to drag Lisa away from Tommy. But their worries were for naught. They watched as Markham stopped before the boy, put his hand comfortingly on his shoulder, and looked him straight in the eye.

"Tommy, I know how much you mean to Lisa. You've protected her all these years, and I'm more grateful than you'll ever know. Tommy, how would you feel about me adopting you? Would you do me the honor of becoming my grandson? If Lisa loves you, I can do no less. Will you come home with Lisa and me? Will you be a part of our family?" he offered, humbling himself before the youth who could make his granddaughter smile.

Tommy had been prepared for the worst as he'd shielded Lisa in his arms for what he thought would be the last time. He'd expected his world to end. He'd gone very pale as he'd waited for Mr. Markham to speak. Now, at his words, he could only stare up at him. "Do you really mean that?"

"Yes, Tommy I do. I'd like you to officially join our family, if you'll have us."

A sweet, exploding joy erupted within him. *Mr. Markham not only wants Lisa, he wants me, too!* He stared up at him speechlessly for a moment. Then as he fought back tears, he broke into a broad smile. "Yes, sir. I'd love to have you for my grampa . . ."

"Tommy, what's this mean?" Lisa asked, still not relinquishing her hold on him.

"It means we'll get to stay together, Lisa."

"Forever?"

"Forever," he answered.

Overcome by joy, she turned to her grandfather for the first time without being afraid. "You really are my grampa?"

"I really am," he replied solemnly.

"And you're gonna be Tommy's grampa, too?"

"I am."

"Tommy! We have a grampa!" she cried in ecstasy.

"We have a grampa!"

"Lisa? Could I have a hug?" Markham needed to hold her, to know that she was real and not a figment of his imagination.

"Yes! Oh, yes!"

When he opened his arms to her, she flew into his embrace. Her small arms hugged him back as tightly as he was hugging her.

"Oh, Lisa . . ." The old man buried his face in the softness of her hair as he crushed her to him. After a moment, he lifted his gaze to Matt and Catherine. "Thank you," he whispered.

Matt, Catherine, Winn, and Alex looked on, their own eyes filling unashamedly with tears of joy.

"Shall we go home?" Markham asked when he finally could muster the strength to let her go.

"Oh, yes, Grampa. We're ready to go home with

you." Lisa gazed up at him with starry eyes. She was beaming with happiness. "Come on, Tommy. Let's go pack our things!" Lisa took Tommy's hand.

"We'll wait here for you," Catherine said as the two children started from the room. "You and Tommy go ahead."

"We'll be right back, Grampa. I promise."

"I'll be here waiting for you. I won't leave you." Markham said the words with emotion that came from the very depths of his soul.

When the children had gone, Markham looked over at Matt and Catherine. "I can't believe she's been right here in New Orleans all this time." He paused as he lifted a tormented gaze to Catherine. "Belinda must have hated me so much to deliberately give Lisa a false last name. How terribly sad and tragic that in a fit of temper, I drove my only child away from me forever . . ."

"That doesn't matter now," Catherine said gently. "You've found Lisa."

Markham's eyes were brimming with tears. "Yes, I've found her."

He smiled up at the others. He'd been alone for such a long time, and now, at last, he had Lisa . . . and Tommy. Suddenly there was hope for the future.

"By the grace of God, and thanks to Mrs. Sutherland and Mr. McKittrick, I'm being given a second chance," Markham went on. "I can't make up for the pain I caused Belinda, but I can raise her daughter in a home filled with love. I'm going to do everything in my power to make sure she's happy." He looked over at

Matt and Catherine. "I owe you two both more than I can ever repay."

"I'm glad we forced our way into your house," Matt told him with a grin.

"So am I, young man. And Lord Bradford, I want you to know that St. Joan's is no longer for sale, not for any price. Tomorrow, I'll send one of my solicitors over to see you, Mrs. Sutherland, and I want you to tell them exactly what you need to fix up the place for the children."

"Do you mean it?" Catherine couldn't believe he was saying these words to her. Her dreams were coming true. Her eyes were filled with joy and hope.

Markham went to her and took her hands in his. "Yes, I mean it. I've been a blind, lonely old fool for too many years, but that's all about to change. There is hope for the future, Mrs. Sutherland. That hope is our children. I want the children here at St. Joan's to know that."

"Thank you, Mr. Markham." Catherine couldn't help herself. She threw her arms around him and gave him a hug.

He accepted her embrace and returned it warmly. "No. Thank you. You've given me back my life, sweet lady. You've raised my granddaughter to be a lovely child. You're a wonderful woman."

"I love the children, and I only want them to be happy."

"We'll make them happy together, Mrs. Sutherland. I promise you that."

Their gazes met and held, and she knew Markham

was a man of his word. Her heart swelled near to bursting with love and happiness. St. Joan's had been saved! And Matt was the reason. Without him, none of this would have happened.

"It's all because of you, Matt," Catherine said, turning to where he stood with Winn and Alex.

"Yes, McKittrick. If you hadn't come to the house this morning, I would never have found Lisa. Thank you."

"You're more than welcome. It's just good knowing that Lisa has a family, and St. Joan's is going to stay open."

Lisa returned then with her small bag of clothing and personal things. Tommy was taking a little longer to gather his things, so while they were waiting on him, Markham and Lisa went on out to the carriage to put her bag away.

When there was just the four of them left in her office, Catherine glanced at Matt and saw that he was looking at his friends and that they seemed puzzled and troubled about something. "Matt? Is something wrong?"

He gave her a wry grin. "No, not where the orphanage is concerned."

"Then what is it?"

"Well, we came here to St. Joan's on a quest for a clue, and we still don't have it. I've looked everywhere, and I know Winn and Alex have, too. I don't know what to do next."

"You mean Lawrence Anthony hid something for you here?"

"I don't know about 'hid,' but there should have been something he left behind, something that would help us continue the search."

"You never did tell me why you came to St. Joan's, other than Lawrence Anthony sent you."

He began to explain, knowing he could trust her with the complete truth. "When Lawrence Anthony died, he left three books with clues in them that led to a hidden treasure. Winn, Alex, and I each got one of them. In order to claim the treasure, we have to use his clues and work together."

"What is the hidden treasure?"

"It's a crown from Ancient Egypt. It was looted out of one of the graves years ago, and we want to see it in a museum where it can be kept safe. That's why Lawrence picked the three of us to work together. He knew we would never want to sell it or profit from it." He quickly explained the curse and the crown's history.

"I wish there was something I could do to help you. You've saved the home, and yet I've been no help to you at all."

"We'll figure it out somehow," Winn assured her with a smile.

"We're just not sure how yet," Alex added.

"If we can find Markham's granddaughter, we can certainly find the next clue," Matt said with a confidence he didn't really feel.

"I have every faith in you." Catherine smiled up at him.

There was a soft knock at her office door, and she

called out for them to come in. Markham entered accompanied by the two children.

"We're about ready to get on our way, but Tommy had something he wanted to say to you," Markham explained.

Catherine looked at the boy and saw he was carrying an unusual cloth sack. "What is it, Tommy?"

"It's about Mr. Anthony." He glanced at Matt, his expression a little guilty.

Matt, Winn, and Alex had suspected early on that the boy knew more than he was saying, and they all now fervently hoped he was about to reveal something important.

"Do you want to talk here in front of everybody or do you want to go somewhere by ourselves?" Catherine offered.

"Here is fine. I really need to talk to Mr. McKittrick, because it's about Mr. Anthony."

"Oh?" Suddenly they were all attentive.

"I kinda fibbed before when we first met. Mr. Anthony did leave something with me when he was here. He made me promise to give it to those who came after him. But he also made me promise that I'd make sure whoever came for it was nice."

"Nice?" Matt asked.

Tommy gave him a solemn, measuring look. "Nice," he repeated firmly and with conviction. "And you are. At first, when I thought you'd made Miss Catherine cry, I didn't think so. But now I know better. So here." He'd been holding a cloth bag, and he handed it proudly to Matt. "This is for you."

As he took the sack, Matt cast an incredulous look at Winn and Alex. "Thanks, Tommy."

He opened the bag and drew out a carved wooden box. There was no lock, so he carefully opened the lid, unsure of what he might find inside. In the bottom of it, on a bed of satin, lay a single key.

"There's a key?" Matt exclaimed.

"To what?" Winn hurried to Matt's side to take a look.

"I'm not sure. There's no note, but there is something inscribed on the key itself."

"It says 'Louisiana Trust,'" Winn said reading over his shoulder.

"That's a bank in town," Catherine advised.

"This must be the key to some kind of deposit box. Let's go find it!"

"What's happening?" Tommy asked Catherine as he watched their excitement.

"You've just given us the clue we've been searching for. We have to get to that bank right away."

"Can I go with you?" Tommy asked. He had guarded the box all these months, and he was curious to see what the key opened.

"If it's all right with your new Grampa?"

"Of course," Markham agreed. "Lisa and I will go to the house and you can meet us there after you've taken care of your business."

The thought that he'd helped Matt made Tommy feel suddenly important.

"Catherine, will you come with us?" Matt invited.

"Are you sure you want me?"

He wanted to tell her the truth of his feelings, that

he wanted her in his arms and in his bed, that he wanted her beside him for the rest of his life. But he didn't. This was not the time. Later, when the time was right, he would tell her how he felt, but right now, they had to get to the bank. His gaze held hers. "Of course, I want you with me. You're a part of this, whether you know it or not."

The eager group headed straight to the bank. Matt and Winn approached the bank official. After speaking with him and showing him the key, he led them to a back room where all the locked boxes were kept.

"This one was entrusted to my care by Mr. Anthony just as you've said. He instructed me to give it to the one bearing the key." The official took the key and unlocked the box for them. There was a large, stuffed envelope within. He handed it over to Matt.

"Thanks."

His business finished with them, the bank official left them alone in the room to discover the contents of the envelope. He discreetly closed the door after him as he went back to his duties.

"Well, whatever it is, it's not the crown," Alex remarked as Matt opened the envelope.

Matt reached in and pulled out the contents. He was shocked when he discovered the entire envelope was filled with money. There was a single page note inside.

"Winn, read this while I count this money," Matt said, handing him the missive.

"Why would he leave us money?" Alex wondered aloud.

Matt frowned as he started going through the bills.

They were in large denominations and the amount was substantial.

"To whom it may concern,

The wooden box belongs to those who pursue my hidden gift. The contents of the envelope are for the boy named Tommy Glosier. He was my friend, and he helped me in many ways during my time in New Orleans. He will be a fine young man one day; and I want him to have all the advantages my sons had, but never appreciated.

Please know that there is a private trust account set up with my attorney in Mr. Glosier's name. It is to be presented to him on his twenty-first birthday. The amount included here is to provide for him until such time that he claims the inheritance.

I would have been proud to call Tommy my son, and I regret that I didn't have more time to spend with him. Thank you, Tommy, for being my friend. God speed, and be happy.

Lawrence Anthony."

Tommy was stunned, and he stood unmoving as tears ran down his cheeks. "He really was my friend," he said slowly, almost painfully.

"That he was, Tommy. Mr. Anthony left you more than a thousand dollars in cash."

"Tommy!" Catherine couldn't believe all that was happening. "This is wonderful."

Tommy was still crying, though, and she went to hold him. "Why are you crying?"

"Because Mr. Anthony's dead, Miss Catherine. I'm never going to see him again. I'm never going to be able to thank him."

Her heart ached for the boy, and she held him close as he cried for his lost friend. When they'd first told him of Anthony's death, he'd taken the news quietly for he'd thought he'd left and never given him another thought. But now, the proof that the old man had really cared for him tore at him.

Tommy was used to people coming into his life and leaving again, never to return. Mr. Anthony had just proven to him that some people meant what they said, that some people stayed faithful to their promises. The discovery that Mr. Anthony had truly cared about him coupled with Mr. Markham's actions that day had changed his life completely.

"Mr. Anthony may not be with us physically any more, but I'll bet he's watching you right now," Winn tried to brighten his mood. "And I'll bet he's very proud of you."

"Do you really think so?" the boy asked.

"I know so," Matt reinforced Winn's words. "You did the right thing with the box, Tommy. That took a lot of courage."

He beamed at their praise. It meant a lot to him. "I wanted to do a good job for Mr. Anthony."

"You did."

"Tommy, your future is secure now. Mr. Markham has decided to adopt you with Lisa, and Mr. Anthony has provided all this money for you." Catherine gave a happy, loving laugh as she cuddled him to her.

"You're going to be just fine, little one."

"I'm no little one."

"You're right. You are well on your way to being a man," she agreed, but she noticed that he made no move to leave her embrace. "A very fine man."

"It looks like everything's turned out fine except for our next clue," Winn said in frustration as he picked up the box. "I wonder what Lawrence was thinking when he left us this."

"Maybe there's something hidden in the lining," Alex suggested.

Winn pulled it out. "Nothing."

"Why don't we go back to the hotel and try to figure it out?" Alex suggested.

"Fine. I'll see Tommy and Catherine home, and then I'll meet you there."

They went their separate ways. Catherine and Matt dropped Tommy off with Markham, and they explained to him about the boy's unexpected inheritance. They left knowing the children were going to have a wonderful life and a bright future.

"We have to go now, but I'll be seeing you soon," Catherine told Lisa and Tommy as she and Matt prepared to leave the Markham home.

"You promise?"

"I promise."

"What about you, Mr. McKittrick?" Tommy pressed.

"Are you going to come and see us?"

Matt felt stricken that he had to tell the boy he was

leaving. "I'll visit you when I can, but I'll be leaving New Orleans soon, and I'm not sure when I'll be back."

The little boy's expression fell. "Oh."

"Tommy."

He looked up.

"I will be back. That much I can promise. Will you trust me and believe me?"

Their eyes met, Matt's challenging, the boy's doubting. Finally, he answered him.

"Yes, sir. I believe you."

Matt went to him and hugged him. For a minute, Tommy tried to pretend that he didn't care, but then he relaxed and hugged Matt back.

"My friends call me Matt, Tommy, and you're my friend. I'll see you and Lisa just as soon as I can."

"Bye, Matt."

Lisa, Tommy, and Markham watched from the front door as Matt and Catherine left. When they turned back and went inside the big mansion, they all knew they were facing a future that would be full of love and happiness.

Matt and Catherine climbed in the carriage they'd arranged to have wait for them, and they sat back able to relax for the first time in days.

"I can't really believe everything turned out so well," she said in a soft, almost dazed voice as she looked at Matt. Her gaze lovingly traced his handsome features and sun-streaked hair. She had known he was special when he'd come through her office door on that first morning they'd met, but she'd never dreamed he would so quickly become this important in her life. The feeling was as frightening as it was wonderful. She cared about him. She cared deeply, but she also knew that he was leaving soon and didn't know when he'd be back.

"I'm glad it did. You deserve it."

"None of it would have been possible without you. I was almost ready to give up."

"No, you weren't," he chuckled, taking her hand in his warm grip. "If there's one thing I've learned about you in the last few days, it's that you don't give up easily or without a fight."

She laughed at his observation. "You're a very good judge of character, you know that?"

"I've always thought so." He turned toward her, and they were just a breath apart. "There's another thing I've learned since I came here."

"What's that?" she whispered, gazing at him. It had been so long since she'd thought of any man romantically. Yet Matt had managed to rekindle within her all the deep emotions she'd thought had died with her husband.

"That I really do believe in love at first sight."

His words were softly spoken, yet the power of them jolted her. She was mesmerized by his very nearness, and when he bent to her and sought her lips with his, she welcomed him eagerly. His kiss was a searing brand that marked her heart as his for all time, and she savored every second of it.

When, at last, they broke apart. Her eyes were luminous and her breathing was ragged. She felt young and beautiful and desirable. It had been so long since she thought of herself that way. Her pulse was racing and her heart beat a frantic rhythm. "I think I believe in love at first sight, too."

Matt drew her to him and kissed her again. It was a kiss that spoke of desire and devotion. But he knew he had to leave her, and the realization pained him.

"I can't stay with you now, Catherine, but I will come back to you just as soon as we find the crown."

"I think I'm angry that Mr. Anthony's clues are taking you away from me, but then his clues brought you here in the first place."

"I know. If I could find a way to stay with you, I would. But this is important. With Markham taking care of St. Joan's now, you should be all right until I get back."

She drew him back down to her for one more quick, yet urgent kiss. "I've already found my treasure, Matt McKittrick. It's you. You're worth any price to me. You've come into my life, and in just these few short days, you've turned my whole world upside down. Now, you go find your treasure. I'll be waiting here when you're done."

As the carriage stopped before the orphanage, Matt framed her face with his hands and looked deep into her eyes.

"I'll come back to you as soon as I can." His lips met hers and sealed his promise. Matt knew, at last, that he'd found a home, too.

*   *   *

Several hours later, Matt sat with Winn and Alex in frustrated silence. They'd gone over every inch of the box looking for the clue and had found nothing.

" '*Love is the key to all that thrives, its power can conquer the curse.*' We know what that part of it means. But '*See the unseen, and you will find the treasure that will be yours*' doesn't make any sense at all," Alex repeated the last part of the clue.

"See the unseen . . ." Winn spoke the phrase, irritated because he wasn't seeing anything but an empty box.

"I know we've missed something, but what?" Matt asked in frustration as he stared at the box where it lay on the table before them.

"If I knew that, we wouldn't have missed it," Alex countered with a grin.

"The answer is somewhere in this box. It's supposed to guide us on. The question is, how?" Winn picked up the small chest for yet another time and opened the lid to peer inside. He'd done it several times already, and each time he'd hoped to see that elusive clue he was missing. Again, he grew frustrated.

"We know there's no hidden compartment," Matt offered.

Closing the lid, Winn turned it over in his hands looking for anything out of the ordinary, but the wood on the bottom and sides was smoothly polished. "I don't see a thing."

" 'See the unseen . . . see the unseen . . .' " Alex murmured.

"If it's invisible, how are we supposed to see it?" Matt argued.

"It doesn't say it's invisible," Winn corrected. "It says it's unseen. There's a difference."

"What could it be? The type of wood it's made of or maybe the place where it was made?" Matt wondered aloud.

"I don't know." Alex was really puzzled, and her respect for Lawrence grew. He'd certainly outdone himself this time. "Let me take another look at it."

Winn closed the lid and gave it to her. He watched as she, too, checked for hidden clues, but found nothing.

"We've got to think of something," she said, placing the box before her and running her hand over the top of it as she spoke. "Lawrence wouldn't have given us a clue that didn't make sense. 'See the unseen' has to mean something important."

Alex sighed and closed her eyes. She was tired and frustrated and worried about her father. Each day they were delayed because she couldn't solve the clue left him rotting in prison that much longer. She had to figure this out! She had to! Unconsciously, she tightened her grip on the box, and it was then that she felt it beneath her palm. All along she'd know it was there, but she hadn't paid any attention.

"Winn! Quick get me some paper and a pencil!" she directed excitedly as she set the box down and stared at the top. " 'See the unseen'! This is it!"

"What are you talking about?" Winn asked, bringing her the pencil and paper.

"Look!"

Winn and Matt crowded around the table as she put the paper over the top of the box and began to make a rubbing of the carvings on the lid. They had thought the carvings just an attractive design on a rather ordinary box. Now, as Alex traced over the design, all was revealed to them. The design was really a detailed map—their path.

"You did it!" Winn grabbed Alex up in his arms and kissed her soundly, not caring that Matt was there.

Matt grabbed up the paper and studied what she'd uncovered. "It looks like we're going to Texas," he stated firmly, recognizing the shape of the state. "Get out your book, Winn. Let's see where in Texas we're headed."

Winn released Alex and took out his book. He read the third and final clue as they studied the map.

" 'The patron saint of all that's lost, claims your
golden crown
Seek you now that tender prize, what was hidden
is now found.
Lift your eyes heavenward, and you will see a sign,
Of perfect love and happiness, God's only true
design.
Take no more than you deserve, be not led by
greed,
Follow your heart knowing that your mission will
succeed.' "

"Who's the patron saint of lost things?'" Matt asked.

"Anthony," Alex answered, a chill skittering down

her spine as she made the connection between the saint and Lawrence. "St. Anthony. It looks like our final destination is San Antonio."

Eighteen

Alex lay with her eyes closed curled against Winn's side, her head resting on his shoulder, her hand splayed on the lightly furred width of his chest. She smiled as she listened to the pounding of his heart for she knew her own was beating a matching rhythm. Being in his arms was paradise. She had never known the physical act of love could bring such bliss. She sighed in contentment.

Winn heard her sigh and tightened his arms around her as he pressed a soft kiss to her forehead. "Are you all right?"

"I'm more than all right," she purred as she opened her eyes to gaze at him with open adoration.

He drew her up for a kiss, and he reveled in the feel of her breasts crushed against him. "You don't know how hard it is for me to keep my hands off you all day," he told her as his hands traced patterns of delight over her silken flesh.

"Probably as hard as it is for me not to touch you," she admitted, boldly caressing him with the same hungry touch. "Do you suppose Matt suspects . . ."

He groaned at her arousing ploy. "Matt's a gentleman." He dismissed her worry quickly, as thoughts of anything but having her again fled his mind. His mouth claimed hers with passion's intent as he felt the heat settle hard and fast in his loins. He'd had many women, but none of them, not even the most practiced lovers could excite him as powerfully as Alex did with just a single touch. He rolled over, bringing her beneath him and sought sweet union with her. As he sheathed himself within her, he shuddered, and when she eagerly wrapped her legs around his hips to accept him even deeper inside her, he couldn't hold back. He began to move at a thrilling pace. Winn caressed her most sensitive spots with teasing, arousing expertise, wanting to please her, wanting to satisfy her in every way. Her pleasure was foremost on his mind as he plumbed the depths of her body.

Alex clung to Winn, matching his sensual rhythm, reaching for the stars of ecstasy with him. Excitement built within her, coiling ever tighter deep in the womanly heart of her. She wanted Winn. There was nowhere else she wanted to be, but in his arms. Nothing mattered right then, but loving him. Her hands were never still, sculpting the powerful muscles of his shoulders and back, skimming lower to his hips and beyond.

Her heated caresses drove Winn on, and he moved even faster, rocking against her at passion's pace and taking them both to the peak of love's perfect pleasure. Alex cried out his name as she crested that pinnacle. She held tightly to him as they drifted back to reality, their bodies still melded, their hearts beating as one. In the quietude of ecstasy's bliss, they rested.

Much later, Alex lay beside Winn watching him as he slept. The nights they'd spent together here on the ship had been the most wonderful of her life. There could be no denying her love for him.

As she gazed at him, though, reality crept, unbidden and unwelcome, into her thoughts, and she realized why her need for him was so desperate and so painful. Soon, very soon, she would lose him. The next day they would be docking in Galveston, and then, after the trip by stage to San Antonio, their search for the crown would be over.

Tears burned in her eyes at the thought of what she had to do. She knew how much Winn hated the Anthonys, and rightfully so. She hated them herself. She could just imagine how furious he was going to be when he discovered her betrayal. Alex wished there was some other way, but there was no way out.

Sadness filled her. Unable to bear being so close to him right then, she slipped from the bed and donned a light wrapper to try and ward off the chill of her heart. She moved to stare out the porthole. The night was pitch black for heavy clouds blocked all starlight and moonlight. The night was as dark as her soul felt at that moment. She turned back to look at Winn.

"I love you . . ." she whispered.

As if sensing she'd left him, Winn stirred and came awake. He reached for her immediately, and when he discovered that she was gone, he sat up to look around. By the light of the lamp they'd left burning low, he could see her standing across the room.

"Alex?" He said her name, a little confused to find her gone from his side. "Is something wrong?"

"No," she lied, returning to him, unable to deny herself these last, few precious hours with him. As bittersweet as it was, she might never again know such happiness. She paused at the side of the bed to untie her robe and let it drop from her shoulders to a silken pool at her feet.

"You're so beautiful." Winn watched her in fascination, mesmerized by her beauty. The soft lamplight cast a golden glow over her, and his gaze was hungry as he visually caressed her high, firm breasts, slim waist, and long, slender legs. "I want you so much, Alex," he told her in a voice thick with passion.

Alex saw the flame of desire in his eyes, and her breath caught in her throat. When he held his hands out to her in invitation, she put her hands in his without hesitation. She made love to him then, wildly, passionately, desperately.

It was near dawn when Winn finally left her. They parted with one last, hungry kiss at her cabin door for they knew the new day held uncertainty, and they might not be together again for some time.

It was late in the afternoon the following day when Alex stood between Winn and Matt at the rail of the ship. They watched with interest as their ship sailed through the pass known as Bolivar Roads. To their right was Bolivar Peninsula. To their left was Galveston Island itself and its deepwater port. The port was the oldest west of New Orleans, and it was crowded with ships from around the world.

It was a gorgeous day. The sun shone brightly in a cloudless sky, and the gray-green waters were calm. Sea birds gracefully soared overhead.

"We're almost there," Alex said, her emotions in turmoil. She was elated that they were closer to the crown and that once they found it her father would be freed. Yet, she knew that the moment her deceit was revealed, Winn would turn on her. Instead of seeing caring and warmth in his eyes when he looked at her, she would see mistrust mirrored there; instead of passion, disbelief. What they'd shared she feared would be lost beyond redemption, and the prospect filled her with pain.

"Just a few more days and we'll have the crown," Matt remarked, looking forward to being done with the quest. The days had dragged by since he'd left Catherine, and as much as he wanted to find the treasure, he'd discovered that he was even more eager to return to her.

"You're awfully optimistic," Winn said with a grin.

"After the trouble we had with the last clue, aren't you the least bit concerned that Lawrence might have made this one even more difficult?"

"I refuse to even consider it," Matt said staunchly.

"I just want to get back to New Orleans."

"Don't you mean Catherine?" Alex teased.

Matt gave her a wicked smile. "Let me put it this way, as fond as I am of you, I'm very glad Winn wasn't really a priest."

"So am I," she laughed, gazing up at tall, handsome Winn standing at her side.

"The way I feel about Catherine, a legal marriage between you and me could have caused some serious problems."

"She's very nice," she agreed. "I suppose if I have to lose you to someone, I'm glad it's Catherine."

Matt slipped an arm around Alex's waist and kissed her affectionately on the cheek. "We'll be finished with this quest soon. In just a few more days, we can all get on with our lives." He'd meant to please Alex with his remark. He didn't know that his words sent pain shafting through her.

Winn listened to their easy banter, and he had to agree that he was glad he'd taken no priestly vows. He wanted Alex as he'd never wanted another woman, and when the search for the crown was over, he planned to ask her to marry him. He glanced down at her then to find her gazing up at him, a shadowed, troubled look in her eyes. As quickly as he'd seen it, the look disappeared and she was smiling again. Confused, he dismissed it, telling himself he must have imagined it.

They left the ship as soon as they could and took rooms at the Tremont Hotel in town. They ate an early dinner, and then leaving Alex to settle in, Matt and Winn went to arrange the balance of their trip to San Antonio. They were pleased to find that they could cross the bay early the next morning and then catch the stage for San Antonio that next afternoon. They made all the arrangements and then started back to the hotel. On the way, Matt stopped at a saloon to have a drink, while Winn hurried on back to the hotel and Alex. He was looking forward to this one last night with her.

Alex was eagerly awaiting Winn's return. He'd promised to come to her just as soon as they found out the stage schedule. She ached to hold him once again, to be near him. She knew that once they started on the trek to San Antonio they would have little time alone.

There was a knock at her door, and it surprised Alex. She hadn't expected Winn to return for at least another half hour. Still, she was so excited that he was back, that she opened the door without thought. A gasp escaped her as she found herself face-to-face with Philip and Robert. Her heart thumped in her breast. Just being near them made her feel dirty.

"Surprised to see us, my dear?" Philip taunted as he walked past her and into her bedroom without waiting for an invitation. Robert followed him.

"What are you doing here?" she blurted out as she quickly closed the door behind them, fearing someone would see them with her. "Are you crazy, coming here like this?"

"Crazy? I don't think so. I think determined is a better word. We told you we'd be watching you and that we'd know where you were and what you were doing all the time. Did you think we'd lied?"

"No," she bit out. "It's just that Winn and Matt will be here any minute."

"Oh, Winn, is it now?" Philip laughed heartily as he deliberately sat down on her bed and tested its comfort. He slanted Robert a knowing look. "So you found out he wasn't a priest, did you?"

"You knew?! How long have you known?" She was shocked.

"From the beginning." Philip was smug.

"You knew all along and you didn't say anything?!" "Why would we?"

"For some reason, our father wanted a priest along on the quest. Who were we to interfere when it was to our benefit to let him lead the search?" Robert added.

"Besides," Philip said smoothly, "it was fun watching him."

"Fun? You're holding my father hostage, and you think this is fun . . . some kind of a game?"

"Don't worry about your father. As long as you do just what we tell you to do, he'll be all right."

"But knowing what we do about Winn Bradford, it's been more than entertaining watching him play the priest."

"Winn's not playing at anything," she countered angrily, knowing why Winn hated them and feeling her hatred for them grow even stronger. She cursed the fact that she had to deal with them. "He's very serious about finding the crown and keeping it away from you."

Philip heard the defiance in her voice, and his eyes narrowed dangerously. "Sometimes naiveté doesn't suit you, Alex," he sneered. "Don't get the idea that Bradford is some high-minded hero seeking the crown for the good of the world."

"We know him better than that," Robert put in.

"This *has* been a game to Bradford, my dear girl." Philip's voice hardened as he prepared to tell her the truth about the man. "You're just a pawn to him. He's a rich, spoiled nobleman, who's gone through life using people for his own purposes. He's using you now just like he's used all the other women in his life—you're a dalliance, someone to enjoy while he's on this hunt and then to be discarded when it's over."

"With his money and looks, Bradford has all the women he wants," Robert added. "You should have seen him in London. He's quite the roué. His reputation with the ladies, married and single, is phenomenal. The women don't seem to care that they're just a distraction for him, though. They take him any way they can get him."

"Don't be fooled into thinking you mean something to him, Alex. You're just one of many."

"He's not like that. He's changed," Winn, knowing how good and kind he could be.

"You think so? Your innocence is incredible. You obviously know little of London society. This is all a lark for him. Haven't you seen firsthand what an accomplished actor he is? Didn't you honestly believe he was a priest? He deceived you then and he's deceiving you now. I'm sure he's convinced you that he desires you more than any other woman in the world." Philip saw her eyes widen as his barb found its mark.

Robert continued for him, "Dear girl, don't make a fool of yourself like so many others have before you, and so many will after you. He's using you to find the crown, and once he claims it, you'll never see him again."

Alex was stunned. She didn't want to believe them. Winn had told her that he wanted her, yet now that she thought about it, he'd never said he'd loved her. Her mind skimmed over memories of Winn's lovemaking, and she grew agonized as she realized he'd never declared his feelings for her.

Alex didn't want to believe them, but what these two were saying made sense. Questions haunted her. Was she really only a diversion for Winn? A body to be used to slake his desires until they found the crown? The agony of doubt raked her heart with vicious claws, but she betrayed none of her pain to Philip and Robert. She would not give them that power over her.

"So why are you here? You certainly didn't come to lecture me on Winn." She deliberately changed the subject.

"Why do you think we're here, my dear?"

"We need to know where you're going next, what your destination is."

"San Antonio," she admitted tightly, and she hated herself for telling him. "They've gone to get our tickets right now."

"Good, good. Keep up the good work. We appreciate all your efforts."

"I'm sure you do, Philip. Just make sure my father is freed when you get the crown."

"Oh, he will be. Rest assured. You uphold your part of the bargain, and we will uphold ours." They taunted her.

Philip rose slowly from the bed. As he started from the room, he deliberately stopped beside Alex. Before she could elude him, he kissed her cheek. He laughed evilly when she wiped the kiss away as if it were a vile thing.

"Soon my dear, our day will come. You're doing a great job. You almost have me convinced that you don't want me, but we both know better, don't we?"

"We'll be in touch," Robert spoke up, wanting to get his brother's mind off the woman and back on the crown.

They moved to the door and took a cautious look outside before leaving the room. It wouldn't do at all to run into Bradford right then. They didn't want to ruin their perfect plan.

When they'd gone and the door was safely closed, Alex wandered miserably to the bed and sat down. She was trembling almost uncontrollably in frustration and confusion. Her hatred for Philip and Robert was a living breathing thing, but the things they'd said about Winn left her tortured. She couldn't help but wonder if what they'd said was true. She didn't want to think so, but . . .

Alex went to the washstand and washed her face, scrubbing hard at the spot where Philip had kissed her. Still shaken, she paced the room trying to control the confusing emotions that were churning within her. Deep hurt filled her at the thought that Winn was just using her. *Was Winn that good an actor?* She knew the answer.

An angry determination grew in Alex's heart. While

it was true that she would ultimately have to betray Winn, her cause was an honorable one . . . a matter of life and death; his was not. If she was to believe what Philip and Robert had told her, then she would have to gird herself against Winn. If this was just a game to him, then she would learn to play the game, too. She would become as accomplished an actress, as he was an actor. In fact, she knew she would have to be even better than he was, for she truly loved him, and now she would have to walk away from that love.

As Winn neared the hotel, he was so intent on getting back to Alex that he paid little attention to other passersby. Philip and Robert were glad, for they had just exited the hotel and crossed the street when they saw him. They congratulated themselves on their perfect timing and went off to find a way to San Antonio that would not put them in contact with the others.

When he knocked on her door, Alex nearly bolted to answer it. She had to force herself to relax.

"Who is it?" she asked, taking no chances this time.

"Winn."

With a concentrated effort, she steadied her hand and opened the door for him. He stood before her, looking more handsome than ever, yet as she gazed up at him now, there was caution in her soul. She tried to see him as Philip and Robert had described him— the consummate user, a man who took what he wanted without thought to the consequences.

"You look pale, are you all right?" he asked. He reached out to touch her cheek.

Alex did not avoid his caress for she didn't want to arouse suspicion in him. But she knew she had to steel herself against her feelings for him. She managed a wan smile. "Actually, I'm not feeling well." It was no lie. Her heart was being shattered. "If you don't mind, I'm just going to go on to bed tonight."

He moved closer, putting an intimacy in his next word. "Alone?"

She nodded. "Yes."

He grew concerned. "Do you need to see a doctor?"

"No. I just need to be alone for a while. I need to rest." Alex would have liked to believe that he really cared about her, but she knew his concern was only an act.

With infinite tenderness, Winn kissed her cheek, then took her hand in his. His gaze searched hers.

"You're sure you'll be fine?"

"Yes. I'll be all right. Just go. I need to lie down."

"I hope you feel better by morning."

"I should. What time do we have to leave?"

"Seven, so I'll come for you at six, then we can eat breakfast first."

"Good night."

"Good night."

Alex quickly closed and locked the door, then sagged weakly against it. After a moment, she undressed and made her way to bed. She threw off the top spread that Philip had been sitting on, handling it as if it had been contaminated, then curled up under just the sheet.

Alex lay quietly, but her thoughts were racing at tortured speed. Did he really want the crown out of greed? Was this just a game for him? Was she really just another body to him? Someone to be enjoyed and then forgotten?

She lay with her eyes closed, courting sleep and forgetfulness. Tears threatened again, and this time she did not fight them. She slowly began to harden her heart against Winn, but even as she did, there was no denying her love for him.

Alex stayed awake long into the night. She did not wipe off her cheek where Winn had kissed her.

Morning came too soon for Alex. It seemed she'd barely fallen asleep when dawn brightened the eastern sky. With an effort, she'd dragged herself from bed to splash water on her face. She'd been dismayed to see the dark circles under her eyes, but she knew they'd been earned for she'd tossed and turned most of the night.

"Are you feeling any better this morning?" Winn asked when he came for her. She looked exhausted, and he wondered if she'd gotten any rest.

"I'm still tired, but I do feel a little better," Alex told him, and it wasn't a lie.

"We can stay here an extra day if you want," he offered.

"No," she replied quickly. "It's important that we keep going. We can't stop now." The last thing she wanted to do was drag this out any longer. She wanted to end this as soon as she could.

"Do you want to eat breakfast? Matt went on downstairs to get us a table in the hotel dining room, but if you'd rather rest some more, I could bring you something."

"I'm fine. Let's eat," Alex replied.

They joined Matt in the dining room and ate a large breakfast. They weren't sure when they'd get the chance for a good meal again, and they took their time to savor every bite.

As she faced Winn across the table, Alex smiled and tried to act as if everything was normal. It wasn't easy. With an effort, she finally managed to control her wayward emotions and concentrate on her one and only reason for being on this trek—to save her father. Nothing else mattered. Not the crown, and certainly not Winn Bradford! While her mind logically told her that Winn wasn't important to her, her heart taunted her with the knowledge that he was her life and her love.

They crossed the bay and made it to the stageline on time. The stagecoach was crowded. Three other passengers, a heavy-set woman, a grizzled, old man and a middle-aged man who looked like a snake oil salesman, had already taken their places on the hard wooden benches inside.

Winn, Matt, and Alex shared a pained look before they'd boarded.

"Ready?" Matt asked, the memory of the steamboat's comforts still fresh in his mind.

"As I'll ever be," Alex agreed, thinking this mode

of travel ranked even below the railroads they'd taken, and that was a hard one to beat.

Winn was busy helping hand the luggage up to the driver, so Matt gave Alex a hand up into the stage.

Relieved to board ahead of Winn, Alex deliberately sat between the woman and the older man. Matt gave her a quizzical look as he settled in opposite her. She could have had the far less crowded seat where he was sitting.

"Alex, you're welcome to sit over here with Winn, if you like," he offered as Winn climbed in and dropped down into the seat next to him.

"No, that's all right. You men sit together. It's going to be a long ride, and we might as well all be as comfortable as we can."

Alex put on a happy expression and pretended to be comfortable. In truth, she was penned in by the pair and nearly overcome by the woman's powerful perfume.

The stage had barely rumbled off, when the old man started to doze. He began to lean on her and snore loudly a few minutes into the ride. Alex sensed this was going to be one of the longest trips of her life.

Winn sat across from Alex, watching her. In spite of the dust and discomfort, she still looked absolutely beautiful to him. She was an amazing woman, unlike anyone he'd ever known before. Her spunk and determination impressed him. She handled even the worst situations with ease and charm and still came out smiling. Winn knew he loved her, and as he let his thoughts dwell on her, he wished she was sitting beside him. He wanted her near to him always. He was glad the stage was traveling at top speed. They couldn't reach their destination soon enough for him.

Forced into the unwanted intimacy of traveling in such close quarters with strangers, Alex battled to keep up her brave façade. She made chit-chat with the lady on her right for hours on end, trying to distract herself from Winn's overpowering presence across from her. Sometimes, though, she couldn't stop herself from glancing up at him. When she did, he invariably was watching her, his green-eyed gaze intent and warm upon her.

They were all glad when, late in the afternoon, the stage finally stopped for fresh horses at a way station along the route. There was little time to do anything but eat the quick, sparse meal that was offered and take advantage of the convenience out back.

When they climbed back into the carriage, Winn made it a point to claim the seat next to Alex. It was all she could do not to protest or stiffen at having him so close beside her. There was no avoiding touching him with each jounce of the stiff-springed coach. The pressure of his thigh against hers rekindled memories she was trying to suppress. Where earlier, she'd suffered the other woman's cloying scent and the old man's snoring, now she had to endure Winn's potent, arousing nearness. For her own peace of mind, Alex wasn't really sure which she preferred.

Nineteen

Alex had endured many difficult journeys in her travels with her father, but the trip to San Antonio proved to be the worst ever on her nerves. The ride was rough, the weather was hot and Winn was with her constantly. His attentiveness left her more confused than ever. She tried to see through his charade, but he had perfected his thespian skills and she could find no trace of deception in his manner.

Sleeping for any length of time in the cramped stage had proven next to impossible, and the short stops at the rest stations provided little in the way of relief. By the second day, Alex was exhausted, the lack of sleep the night before they'd left having taken its weary toll on her. Braced against the side of the stage with Winn seated next to her, she hadn't meant to fall asleep. In fact, she'd been waging a battle to keep physical contact with him to a minimum, but it was hard to do when they were so crammed in together. As her eyelids grew heavier, her efforts to keep a distance between them grew weaker, and finally without conscious thought, she gave up and slept.

"Winn," Matt said his name softly just to get his attention, then nodded toward Alex.

Winn glanced down at Alex and, seeing how awkwardly she was sitting, trapped between him and the frame of the stage, he smiled tenderly. She impressed him more every day with her grit and fierce resolve, and he admired her for it. Gently easing an arm around her, Winn brought her against him, cradling her to his chest.

"Think she's tired?" Matt asked with a grin.

"Exhausted, but she's matched us mile for mile and never complained," he praised her.

"We'll be in San Antonio late tonight, then we can all get some real rest."

Winn sat quietly with Alex nestled against him, enjoying at least this much intimacy with her. The long hours of riding in such close confines with the other passengers had grated on his nerves. He longed to be alone with her. He wanted to be giving her flowers and jewels and taking her to romantic places. Instead, he was stuck here in this stagecoach with Matt and three other people he would have preferred never to have met.

Alex was dreaming. In her reverie, she was waltzing with Winn. He was sweeping her around the room in graceful, dizzying circles and she was laughing at something wonderfully witty he'd just said.

"Winn . . ." she murmured his name in her sleep and shifted positions, just a little, her hand slipping unheeded into his lap.

Winn had been having a rough enough time, keeping

his thoughts away from the wondrous nights he'd spent in Alex's arms. When she touched him so innocently yet so intimately, the carefully banked fire of his sensual need for her flared to life. His breathing was suddenly strangled, and he clenched his jaw in a desperate bid for control. It was all he could do not to reveal his raging discomfort to the others. He steeled himself, holding to his position rigidly, refusing to squirm or move in any way for fear of losing his tenuous grip on himself. He looked down at her as she cuddled close, and his gaze went over her hungrily. God, but she was lovely! He dragged his gaze away from the tumble of red-gold curls and the sweet curve of her cheek and stared pointedly out the window at the passing landscape. He wished the damned trip was over.

Alex awakened to the comforting sound of Winn's strong, steady heartbeat beneath her ear. A soft smile curved her lips as she imagined herself alone with him in some private, wonderful place. Then the stage hit a rough spot in the road, and she was jarred violently back to reality. Her eyes flew open and she found herself staring across the stage at Matt. He was watching her with an amused expression, and she suddenly realized where she was and how she was sitting.

"Oh . . . I'm sorry . . ." She was conscious of the heat of his body beneath her accidental touch and she bit back a groan of mortification.

"Don't be," Winn answered with a smile as his eyes met hers.

Across the stage, the other woman looked on with a condemning regard. She'd been watching the pair the whole ride and had become convinced that there was more between them than just friendship. What had just transpired had only confirmed her suspicions. When the girl had been sleeping, she'd watched the man named Winn put his arm around her and hold her close. And when the young woman's hand had fallen in his lap. . . . Well! She'd been beside herself trying to decide what to do. It was so . . . so . . . outrageous!

As she watched them now, seeing the girl's blush and the man's seductive smile, she just had to take out her fan and fan herself nervously. She tried to remember the last time a man as handsome as this one had looked at her that way. She couldn't. She slanted them another look, then fanned herself with even more vigor.

Alex could see the heat in Winn's regard, and she looked away, still blushing. Winn acted as if nothing unusual had occurred, shifting slightly away from her. He closed his eyes and crossed his arms over his chest, pretending to relax. Relaxed was the last thing he felt, though. Being this close to Alex and having held her while she slept, had heated his desire for her. He wanted her badly, and while he found the biddy sitting across from them a troublesome, nosy woman, right then he was glad for her disapproving looks for they kept him sane.

They arrived in San Antonio on schedule that night and practically stumbled into the hotel to get their rooms. All three of them were exhausted, and after agreeing to meet the next morning they headed upstairs.

After so many days in close contact, Winn was not about to let Alex escape without a kiss. They were alone in the hall for Matt had already sought the soft-ness of his bed, so he took her in his arms and kissed her deeply, passionately.

"I've waited days to do that," he declared, setting her from him.

Pressing her acting ability to its limits, Alex man-aged a smile. "So have I."

But even as she answered him sweetly, she was filled with confusion. She'd worked for days to steel herself against her need for him, yet his one kiss had set her pulse racing and her heart beating a wild rhythm. It pained her to know she wanted more than just his kiss.

"I'll be back for you first thing in the morning," he promised.

"I'll be ready."

Winn kissed her softly one last time, then sought the comfort of his own bed.

Alex bathed and lay down, but she didn't fall asleep right away. Thoughts of Winn coupled with worries about her father besieged her. To relieve some of the tension she was feeling, she began to review the last clue, trying to find its hidden meanings.

" 'The patron saint of all that's lost, claims your golden crown. Seek you now that tender prize, what was hidden is now found. Lift your eyes heavenward, and you will see a sign. Of perfect love and happiness, God's only true design. Take no more than you de-serve, be not led by greed. Follow your heart knowing that your mission will succeed,' " she said it out loud, dwelling on each word and phrase in the hopes of finding something.

Lawrence had sent them to San Antonio and by his own words the crown was here. It was just a matter of finding out where in San Antonio he'd hidden it. The word 'mission' jumped out at her in the last line, and with all the Spanish missions in the area, she had a feeling there was a definite connection. The next day she would look into it.

Feeling as if she had at least some control over her life at last, she rolled over and began to drift off. Her last thought as she fell asleep was of Winn, and a tear slipped from the corner of her eye.

"I've got it!" Alex announced the following morning when Winn came for her.

"Got what?" he asked, as he stared down at her, thinking how fresh and lovely she looked after a good night's rest.

"Where the crown is hidden! Let's go find Matt, and I'll tell you both at the same time."

Minutes later she was facing them both in Matt's room.

"It must be hidden in one of the missions," she told them.

"Why?"

"The last line—your mission will succeed. San Antonio is known for its missions. It's the only place to start. I couldn't find anything else in the riddle that even remotely suggests a hiding place. His mention of

'Look heavenward and God's only true design' prove its religious in some way. What more logical connection in this town than a mission?"

"It's worth a try," Matt agreed with a chuckle. "We've already done convents and orphanages."

A short time later, the clerk at the hotel's front desk gave them a list of the missions in the area along with the directions to find them. He also told them where the nearest stable was where they could rent horses for the ride. "The Espada, Concepcion, San Jose, and San Juan Capistrano Missions are all relatively close by. The Alamo was once a mission, too, and then there's Corazon Sagrado. It's almost a day's ride west of town."

"Corazon Sagrado?" Alex repeated thoughtfully. Her Spanish wasn't the best, but she knew 'corazon' meant 'heart.'

"Yes, ma'am. It means the Mission of the Sacred Heart."

"Thank you." Matt was the one who spoke as they shared a knowing look.

They returned to his room.

"Do we go to the other missions first or go straight to Corazon Sagrado?" Matt wondered.

"Lawrence wrote 'Follow your heart knowing that your mission will succeed,'" Winn stated. "I think we need to ride for Corazon Sagrado."

"It's the one," Alex said, convinced that they were on to something.

They were on their way by mid-morning. They bought suitable clothing for the ride, denim pants for the men and a split riding skirt for Alex along with Stetsons for them all. They then went to the stable to get horses. The hand at the stable assured them that they could make it to the mission by dusk and that there would be room for them to spend the night there. He also warned them about the Comanche and encouraged them to be armed on the trip. Matt strapped on his gun. He preferred not to wear it or use it, but he knew sometimes it was necessary. They returned to the store and bought Winn a gun and holster, too.

"Do you think we really need guns?" Alex asked worriedly as she watched Winn buckle on his gunbelt.

"It's best to be prepared." Matt had been in his share of dangerous places through the years, and he was no stranger to using a firearm.

Winn was accustomed to riding with an English saddle, but, expert horseman that he was, he adapted quickly. They left town, heading west on their cross-country trek. The ride was an easy one across the low, rolling hill country.

"I can't believe we're almost there." Matt's anticipation was growing with each passing mile.

"I'm glad," Alex added.

As they rode closer to their final destination, Alex knew she had to begin planning how she could get the crown away from them and deliver it to the Anthonys. It would be simple if Winn and Matt trusted her to carry it, but she doubted that would happen since she was the weakest of the three of them and the least able to defend herself should the need arise. If Winn carried the crown with him, she would have little trouble. As soon as she could maneuver a time for them to spend a night alone, she would be able to take it and slip away into the darkness. But if Matt kept it, she would definitely have difficulty. Alex wasn't sure exactly what she was going to do, but as desperate as she was to rescue her father, she knew if it became necessary, she would use Matt's gun.

The unwelcome thought occurred to her then that someone might have already stolen the crown from Lawrence's carefully chosen hiding place, just as it had been looted from the tomb where she and her father had searched years before. Thinking of her father again, she wished he were there with her, glorying in the discovery. He would have been thrilled to finally locate the crown after all these centuries of being lost.

Keeping a vision of her father centermost in her mind, Alex concentrated only on what she had to do. She would let nothing else interfere, not her feelings for Winn or her doubts about him. She imagined her father, locked in a dark, dank cell, waiting for her to save him. Unconsciously, she put her heels to her horse and quickened their already rapid pace.

As they crossed the miles toward the mission, Winn grew excited too. As soon as they found the crown and delivered it into safekeeping, he would talk to Alex about the future—their future, together. He wanted to believe that this clue would be the simplest, but he couldn't help but wonder if Lawrence had planned any last minute surprises for them.

Matt was eager to reach the mission, and he led the way at a hurried pace. The crown, the treasure he'd been searching for for years, was within reach! He could hardly wait to get to Corazon Sagrado. Once they finally had it in their possession, they could decide which museum they would donate it to, but until then, he just wanted to revel in the fact that he'd actually gotten to see it and hold it. It was a part of a civilization long gone from the face of the Earth, yet the purity of the crown's history was ageless.

The sun was low in the western sky as they topped a low-rise to see the mission spread out before them in all its majestic glory. Made of plastered limestone, the inner buildings and the thick, white walls that surrounded the compound glowed in the fading sunlight. The cross atop the church beckoned to all who were near. The fields surrounding the mission were the picture of prosperity. Lush and green, they promised a fruitful harvest at the season's end. It had the look of paradise about it. An atmosphere of peace and quietude prevailed. It seemed as if God had decided to recreate Eden and place it right there in the heart of Texas.

They slowed their pace and rode toward Corazon Sagrado with an almost reverent air. As they neared the main entrance, the church bells began to ring as if in welcome. Only a few people were about as they entered the main yard, but those who were, greeted them warmly. Other than that, little attention was paid to them as they crossed the plaza, for strangers rode in all the time.

"Where do you want to search first?" Matt asked.

"Let's start with the church itself," Winn told him,

having taken a quick look around as they'd crossed the open area.

"And if there's nothing there?" Alex wondered, trying once again to put herself in Lawrence's place.

He slanted her a wry grin. "Your guess is as good as mine."

They reined in before the church and dismounted. Together, they circled the tall and domed building, built the century before by the Spanish missionaries. It was a magnificent structure. The windows were sculpted from the heavy limestone and adorned with roses and symbols of the church. The main, wide double doors were made of oak. It was an impressive building, and they all took great appreciation in the work that had gone into its construction. They studied all the designs of the building, but could find no connection to the treasure they sought.

Their search of the exterior yielding nothing, they decided to go inside. They entered quietly, their manner hushed and respectful as befitted a place of worship. When the heavy oak doors closed silently behind them, they were immediately surrounded by a sense of heavenly peace.

The church was deserted. The only light came from the fading glow of the sunset through the small windows and the flickering of votive candles. The inside of the church was simple, but beautiful. Alcoves were carved along the thick, stone walls holding statues of various saints. Colorful paintings adorned the walls. The pews were of hardwood, and the kneelers were hard, but practical, and worn from the many faithful who'd knelt there in prayer. The altar and crucifix rose before them, reminding all who entered of the real reason for their being.

"Lift your eyes heavenward and you will see a sign, of perfect love and happiness, God's only true design," Alex repeated staring up at the crucifix.

"It's not the crucifix," Winn murmured in a reverent tone as they moved slowly forward staring up at the crucifix. He let his gaze sweep the room, searching intently for the answer they sought.

It was then that Winn saw it for the first time. He'd been looking up at the statue of Mary, when he'd gone still. Without saying a word, he reached out to grasp Alex's arm. Matt noticed how quiet Winn had gone, and he turned to look in the same direction.

Matt, Alex and Winn stared in awe at the statue of the Virgin holding the Child. It was a simple statue, not nearly as magnificent as those they'd each seen before in museums. No, what struck them speechless was the sight of the Virgin wearing the Crown of Desire. Illuminated only by the light of the candles and the last, dying glow of day, the gold gleamed softly, almost warmly, and the ruby heart shone pure red.

"My God . . ." Matt said in a hoarse voice. He had always suspected that the crown was a thing of beauty, but he'd never thought it would be this wondrous.

"Exactly," Alex agreed, her gaze riveted on the statue. They stood unmoving and enraptured as they stared at the treasured relic. Its beauty amazed them, and they were hard-pressed to believe that they were actually seeing the crown.

Tears stung Alex's eyes as a great sense of relief filled her. She'd lived in fear that they would never find the prize and that her father would suffer the terrible consequences. Yet, here it was. They had found it! Now she could save her father from the Anthonys' evil plan!

Alex glanced around to make sure there was no one else in the church. With no one about, it would be a simple matter to take the crown from the statue and go. No one would ever have to know that they were the ones who'd taken it.

"What do you want to do?" she asked, eager to be done with it so she could see her father freed.

Winn was still looking up at the crown, seeing the mother and child. He thought of what his uncle had told him of love, the perfect self-sacrificing kind of love, and he understood. He knew what the right thing was to do.

"Nothing," he answered, not looking away from the statue that represented perfect, unselfish love.

"Nothing? What do you mean?" Alex turned to him. They had come this far. She couldn't imagine what he was thinking.

Matt, too, was staring at the Madonna, and at Winn's remark, he understood. "Of course," he agreed. "It all makes sense now."

"What does?" she insisted.

"This, Alex." Winn gestured around the church. "Corazon Sagrado. The mission is an oasis in the middle of the hill country. Where else on our ride did you see such lush crops? Where else have you ever felt

Bobbi Smith

this sense of contentment? Don't you see? The crown represents perfect love and happiness. There is no greed here. There's only love."

"The curse has been conquered, Alex. The crown has blessed this place," Matt added.

Alex turned her gaze to the treasure that meant her father's life. She knew deep in her heart that they were right, yet the terror of the Anthonys' threat lingered within her soul. There was no escaping it.

They remained silent, studying the elusive treasure they'd pursued across continents. The peace of the mission surrounded them in a loving caress and filled them with reverence.

"I think we have only one choice," Winn stated, knowing what they had to do.

"I know," Matt agreed.

"What's that?" Alex asked, expecting to hear their plan for taking the crown and readying herself to take action.

"The crown should remain here," Matt said quietly.

"No!" she protested automatically, fear seizing her heart. "We came all this way to find it . . . We can't just leave it here . . ."

"Alex," Winn spoke this time. "This is the place of perfect love. Look around you. Where better to showcase its majesty and beauty? Locked in a museum, people can only come and stare at it. But here, at Corazon Sagrado, it's bringing joy and creating good works. It's blessed this place. The people are happy. The crops are bountiful. This is where the crown belongs. It should stay here."

Alex stared at him in bewilderment. She saw the earnestness in his regard and heard the quiet resolve in his voice. Her thoughts grew chaotic. She tried to concentrate on her father, but the truth about Winn was swirling around her, leaving her dizzied and confused. *Winn actually wanted to leave the crown behind? Winn didn't want to take it back?*

The realization of what a fool she'd been hit her hard. The Anthonys had lied to her about Winn and she'd believed them! She groaned inwardly as she thought of all the doubts she'd harbored about him since she'd listened to their evil ramblings.

"Alex? Is something wrong?" Winn was watching her, and he saw that same haunted expression in her eyes that he'd seen before. She looked worried, almost frightened, and he couldn't imagine what was causing it. They'd found the treasure they'd sought. She should be happy. "Surely, you aren't upset about leaving it here, are you? It will be safe. No one really knows what it is and those who do, respect it and love it enough to keep it from harm."

Suddenly, Alex wanted to tell Winn the truth. She couldn't bear the deceit she'd been a part of any more. She wanted no lies between them. She loved him and knew now that she could trust him. It had been foolish to ever doubt him. With Winn by her side helping her, she could defeat the Anthonys and save her father, too.

"Winn . . . You don't understand. There's so much I have to tell you, so much I have to explain . . ." she began.

Winn gave her a gentle smile. He felt good, better

than he had in as long as he could remember. His heart swelled with tenderness as he lifted his hand to caress her cheek. "Ah, Alex, let's just settle this about the crown and then head back. We've got the rest of our lives to talk."

"No, Winn, listen to me. You, too, Matt!" She looked frantically between the two men. "I have to tell you about my father—and about the Anthonys!" She saw Winn's expression darken at her mention of the sons, and she rushed on, needing to tell him the truth. "I know you hate them and think they're evil. Well, believe me when I say I know how evil they are, too, for I know firsthand."

"What are you talking about?" Winn gave her a puzzled look.

"Winn, I . . ."

"There's no need for you to go on, my dear," Philip's voice boomed through the quiet church as he and Robert emerged from their hiding place in the shadows in the back.

"Philip! Robert!" she gasped their names.

"Yes, Alexandra, we're here," Robert announced.

"Alex?" Winn looked from them to her and saw the guilt and shame in her eyes. His hand dropped away from her as if he couldn't bear to touch her any more.

"Thank you for doing such a fine job for us. We appreciate all your guidance. It would have been a much more difficult ordeal without you," Philip said smoothly, watching Winn's expression with interest and gloating over the fury that was etched on his stony features.

"You look a bit upset, Bradford. Didn't you know she's been working with us all along?" Robert taunted.

"It looks like your concerns about your acting ability were unfounded, Alex," Philip said with a reptilian smile. "You fooled the both of them completely. Bravo, my dear. Well done."

Alex wanted to scream at him to shut up, but she held her tongue. Her father was still at their mercy. She couldn't ruin things now, not when she was so close to saving him. Tears of helpless frustration burned in her eyes. Just moments before she'd thought to be free of them, and now . . .

"Get the crown, Robert," Philip directed, drawing a gun from his pocket and directing it straight at Winn and Matt. "I'll keep watch over McKittrick and our friend, Bradford, here, while you do."

Twenty

"Alex, why don't you come over here by me? As soon as Robert gets the crown, we'll be leaving," Philip said not looking away from the two men. "It seems you fared the trip from Galveston quite nicely."

Philip saw Winn's expression harden and his jaw tighten as Alex moved slowly to do his bidding, and he smiled.

Matt watched all that was happening, and his anger grew. "The crown stays," he declared.

"No, I don't think so, Mr. McKittrick," Philip said haughtily. "You know, we haven't been formally introduced yet, but Alex has kept us informed of all your adventures. It's nice to finally meet you face-to-face."

"I wish I could say the same," he growled, his cold-eyed regard fixed on the gun that was pointed at him. "Just slide your weapons down the pew here toward me."

Winn and Matt were enraged, but did as they were told. They watched Alex, trying to read her expression, trying to understand what was going on, but she wouldn't look at them.

"That's fine. Now, Robert, if you'll hurry with the

crown, we can get out of here before any unexpected company happens in on us."

Robert had dragged a chair to the side of the statue and finally managed to snatch the crown from the Virgin. Jumping down, he put it into a cloth bag he'd brought with him, then turned back to his brother with a big smile. "Let's go."

"Let me take care of these two, and we'll be on our way," he said evilly.

Alex heard the note of viciousness in his voice and paled. She didn't put anything past this man and she feared for Winn's and Matt's lives. "What are you going to do?"

"You don't need to concern yourself, Alexandra. There will be no bloodshed in church." He waved his gun toward the front of the church directing Winn and Matt into the small windowless room next to the altar. "I'm going to lock them in here, so we'll have a comfortable lead on them before they can start any trouble."

"You aren't going to get away with this, Anthony," Winn snarled. He looked back at Alex. He saw her pale, strained expression, and for one poignant, heart-stopping moment their gazes met. In the depths of her eyes, he saw all the pain and agonizing fear that she'd long tried to hide from him, and in that instant, he knew the truth.

"Move it, Bradford. I'd hate to have to go back on my word to Alex."

Winn moved ahead reluctantly into the room. "I'll see you pay for this."

"Would you like to place a wager on that, Lord

Bradford?" Philip sneered. "I'm afraid it's a losing one for you, though, for I already have the crown—and the woman."

"We'll be coming after you."

"When you get out of here you can try. The walls are so thick, I think they might be soundproof and the door is certainly at least six-inches thick, too. I think you two will have a nice rest this afternoon. Perhaps we'll meet again someday, perhaps not."

Fury was etched in every taut line of Winn's body, but the knowledge that there was a loaded gun pointed at his back kept him from launching himself at Philip in a savage attack. He cast Matt a sidelong glance and knew he was having the exact same thought. Anger pounded through him.

"So Alex has been in on this with you since the very beginning?"

"How else do you think we traced you here?" he asked with fake innocence. He knew Winn was angry, and he was enjoying every minute of his discomfort. It was a pleasure to torment him. The feeling of power emboldened him. "She was more than eager to lead us to the treasure, considering the share she's going to get once we leave this Godforsaken country."

"I don't believe you," Winn argued.

"It doesn't matter to me what you believe. Alex is with us. She has been since the first, and when we ride out of here in a few minutes, she'll be riding with us."

Winn's hands clenched into fists at his sides. He had never before in his life wanted to hit a man as badly as he wanted to hit this one. His frustration was nearly overwhelming for Philip was standing triumphantly in the doorway with the gun at the ready.

"Enjoy your rest, gentlemen. It's been wonderful dealing with you."

"You'll be sorry for this," Winn threatened.

"No, Bradford, I don't think so."

When he slammed the door, Winn and Matt both reacted. They threw themselves at the heavy portal, but their efforts were to no avail. They could hear the bolt slide home as Philip locked it from the outside. Disgust filled them for they knew they were trapped until someone came and let them out. They pounded on it with all their might, but there was no response.

Philip returned to where Robert waited with Alex. "Are we ready to go?"

"More than ready," Robert replied. "The sooner I get back to London the happier I'm going to be."

"What about my father?" she demanded.

"What about him?"

"When are you going to set him free?"

Philip took Alex's arm in a firm, unyielding grip. "When we reach London, so I suggest you not try to delay us in hopes that your friends will rescue you. If you want your father out of prison, you'll stay with us and do what we say until we get there. Do you understand me?"

"Take your hands off me!" she ordered, feeling sullied by that single touch.

"Oh, no, my dear Alex. I've waited a long time for this. We're going to be traveling together for quite some time. I think you had better get used to my touch." His gaze went over her in an insultingly familiar way that made her skin crawl.

"I'll never get used to your touch. All I want is my father out of jail. You've gotten what you wanted, now it's time you hold up your part of the bargain."

"Oh, really?" He gave a soft menacing laugh. "Did it ever occur to you that I hold all the winning cards in this game of ours? I have the crown, and you, Alex, have nothing."

"I have your word," she said as a tremor of terror shook her.

"Don't worry," he said in a tone he hoped calmed her fears. He couldn't risk her making a scene as they were leaving. He would keep his plans for her secret until they were well away from town. "We'll see your father a free man again."

He continued to smile as he led her from the church through a side entrance. He loved being in control this way, and now that he had the crown, nothing could stop him. Once they sold it, he would have more money than he'd ever dreamed possible.

"Let's be on our way. The faster we travel, the faster we get back to your father. Don't you agree?"

No one was around as they emerged from the church. The plaza was deserted. Philip still wasn't completely sure that he could trust Alex, even though she had the most to lose.

"Let me make myself clear," he said as he paused just outside the doorway. "If you look nervous, if you make any move or noise that lets someone know what we're about, you'll never see your father alive. Do you understand?"

"Perfectly," she answered tersely.

Philip and Robert led the way to where their horses were tied. They had no doubt that Winn and Matt would come after them just as soon as they were freed from the room, and they needed a big lead.

"Mount the black horse, Alex. We'll be riding double," Philip instructed as he moved to untie the reins.

Alex felt as if she were alone in the world as she climbed on the horse. She remained tense as Philip mounted behind her. He deliberately pressed himself against her and drew her back tightly to his chest. He felt the resistance in her and laughed softly in her ear. The hair prickled on the back of her neck at the sound.

As soon as Robert was on his horse, they rode out. They kept their pace casual as they left the mission. They did not want to draw any undue attention to their passing.

Once they were clear of the mission, they raced like the wind in a direction away from San Antonio. Alex wasn't familiar with the area, but she sensed they were going in a different direction.

"This isn't the way to San Antonio," she said, sitting stiffly before Philip in an effort to avoid physical contact with him. It was next to impossible, but she was fiercely determined.

"Why would we want to go back there? That's the first place Bradford will look," Philip chided. "We've made other plans."

"But you don't know this area. You've never been to Texas before."

"And, God willing, I'll never come back again," Philip disparaged. "It's a wasteland. I can't wait to get back to London where civilized people live."

Alex considered asking him what he thought was civilized, since he seemed lower than the lowest animal life form to her, but she refrained, not wanting to risk his anger. Her position was not a good one, and she had to make sure her father was freed.

"For once, you and I are in complete agreement," Robert said, looking forward to the pleasures of London once they returned with their pockets full and their future guaranteed.

He thought his brother's plan to skirt San Antonio and ride straight for the coast was brilliant. They needed a big headstart to get away from Bradford and McKittrick, and this was the perfect way to do it. With any luck, they'd be sailing for England before the other two figured out what they'd done.

As far as the girl was concerned, Robert didn't quite like the way Philip was treating her. He, personally, would have preferred to leave her behind, but he didn't want to argue with his brother at such a critical moment. For now, he had given in on that point.

They traveled until dark, slowing their pace only after they'd put a good distance between them and the mission.

Philip was feeling Godlike in his power. Not only had they gotten away with murder twice, but they now had the crown and the girl Bradford wanted. He smiled to himself and tightened his hold on her pulling her closer against him. He felt the steel in her as she resisted, and out of pure spite, he forced the issue, letting her know right then that she couldn't refuse him anything without paying a price.

It was almost completely dark when they finally found the small stream that the man at the stables had told them about. They made a rough camp there with a small campfire.

Alex sat as far away from the two as she could, for she was dreading what the night might bring. Philip disgusted her. He might have delusions that she found him attractive, but he made her skin crawl. She didn't know how she was going to defend herself against him all the way to England. Somehow, though, no matter what, she would find a way.

Alex thought of Winn and wished with all her heart that he was there with her. Then she remembered his look of disgust as he'd watched her in the church with Philip and Robert, and she knew he would never want to see her again. Pain stabbed at her. Even knowing that he despised her, she wanted him. She loved him. and she regretted that she hadn't had the time to tell him the truth. She hated that they had parted as they had.

"Here. Eat this," Philip called as he tossed her a hard roll.

Alex ate it quickly, then took a deep drink from the canteen he came to hand her.

"You are one pretty woman," he said in a low voice as he took the canteen back.

Alex just glared up at him, hoping her look would discourage him. To her dismay, he only smiled back down at her.

Philip returned to sit beside his brother on the other side of the campfire. "Give me the crown," he demanded. He hadn't gotten a good look at it yet, and he could hardly wait to get his hands on it.

"Here, but be careful," Robert dictated as he handed the bag over.

Philip shot him an ugly look. Robert always managed to irritate him. He took the bag and opened it, his expression avid and hungry with greed as he took out the treasure.

The Crown of Desire gleamed hot, molten gold in the firelight, and the ruby darkened to a deep blood-red.

Philip smiled at his brother. "This was worth every minute. Do you realize how rich I'm going to be?"

"We're going to be, dear brother," Robert censured.

Philip felt his agitation with him grow. "You needn't worry that I'd forget you."

"I would hope not. As soon as we get back to London, we can contact that other collector and then we'll be set for life."

Alex sat silently as she watched and listened to them talk. Philip's face looked positively satanic, cast as it was in the red glow from the flames, and the wild look in his eyes frightened her.

" 'Set for life,' I like that." Suddenly, Philip began to laugh. It was a maniacal sound that echoed eerily through the night.

"What's so funny?" Robert asked a little uncomfortable with his brother's behavior.

"What's funny is we won! Father's no doubt turning over in his grave right now." Philip turned his crazed gaze on his brother. "And I'm glad!"

"We did outsmart him, didn't we?"

"He thought he was so clever hiding the crown and writing those stupid clue books! Hah! We didn't even have to suffer through solving the old man's ridiculous riddles. We were smart enough to let someone else do it for us, and all we had to do was walk in and claim the prize in the end! Sometimes my brilliance is amazing," Philip complimented himself.

"*Our* brilliance," Robert put in.

He ignored his brother's comment. "Father was a fool and a failure! We won! I hope he can hear me! I hope he knows how much I despised him and how glad I am he's dead!" he raved.

"Your father was not a fool! He knew what he was doing trying to keep the crown from you. He was a good man . . . a kind man," Alex spoke up, unable to listen to their hateful words. "I loved him."

Philip turned to look at her as he slowly got to his feet. His eyes mirrored only rage and lust as he crossed toward her, still holding the crown. "You loved him, did you? Well, maybe it's time you loved one of his sons."

"Are you mad? What are you talking about?" Robert demanded as he watched Philip stalk Alex.

"I just want to teach Alexandra here a lesson."

"This is hardly the time or place," he criticized.

"Don't touch me," Alex said. She watched him move closer and wished she had some place to flee to for safety.

Philip struck with lightning speed, slapping her viciously. "Don't ever tell me what to do again," he said in a deadly voice. "No one tells me what to do."

Alex hadn't known what to expect from him, but she certainly hadn't been prepared for him to hit her. The force of the blow split her lip, and she cried out in pain.

"Philip! What the hell's the matter with you?" Robert jumped up and came after him.

He bristled at his brother's criticism. "Don't you push me either, Robert. I put up with the old man because I had to, but I don't have to listen to her or to you."

His words were spoken with such venom that Robert immediately backed down.

Philip watched him move off, and he felt even more invincible. His brother's carping was driving him mad. He'd suffered his tedious company for this long just for the sake of finding the crown, but now they had it. Soon, very soon, they would be done with each other, and he would never have to see him again. The prospect appealed to him. He went back to sit down by the fire again, the crown still clutched in his hand.

"If there's one thing I don't need, Robert, it's you or anyone else telling me what to do. Need I remind you that it was my careful planning that's taken us this far?"

"I could have managed without you," Robert retorted.

He gave a snort of derisive laughter. "You would never have had the nerve to break into Bradford's house like I did," he belittled. "If it were up to you, you'd still be sitting in London, without funds, living off your friends and trying to figure out where your next meal was coming from. You always were slower than most."

Robert glared at him in the firelight. "Once we're back in London, and I get my share of the crown's price, dear brother, I plan never to see you again."

"A worthy plan. Probably one of the better ones you've come up with in your miserable life."

Alex listened to the ugly exchange and grew chilled. Her cheek was throbbing and she tasted blood from her lip. This was only her first night with them. The trip to London would take weeks, and the thought frightened her.

Philip held the crown up before him and stared into the depths of the ruby, mesmerized by its size and perfect color. It was a collector's dream, and he knew they would get a very pretty price for it. All they had to do was reach Galveston and catch the first ship out before Bradford and McKittrick found them. Once they arrived in London, they would have enough money that they could disappear and never be seen again. Philip was looking forward to that luxury. His grip tightened on the crown.

Robert stared at his brother in disgust. Philip seemed almost demented as he stared at the ruby and gold prize.

Robert had wanted the crown, too, for all these years, but he was reasonable enough to know that it was only a piece of gold. They would sell it, pocket the money, and go their separate ways. They couldn't get back to England soon enough to suit him.

He cast a glance at Alex before bedding down. She had lain down now, and he was glad. The less Philip was irritated in his current mood, the better. He'd seen him in strange moods before, but never one as unpredictable as this.

Alex lay nervously wrapped in the thin blanket they'd given her. She knew she wouldn't sleep tonight, for Philip was acting too crazy. Silently, she prayed that Winn and Matt would come, but she knew in her heart that even if they did give chase, they wouldn't be coming for her. No doubt, they believed she'd been helping the Anthonys. If they came after them, it would only be to reclaim the crown.

As Alex lay in the darkness, her heart was heavy and her future looked bleak. The only bright spot she could find was that her father was going to be freed as soon as they returned.

Taking care not to be seen watching him, she studied Philip as he sat before the dancing flames holding the crown. For years, she'd wanted to find the crown for its history and her love of the legend, and now, it meant only her father's freedom to her—nothing more. She almost wished that she'd never seen or heard of it. She closed her eyes against the sight of Philip.

* * *

Winn and Matt were about to go mad. They'd been trapped in the chamber for hours and they weren't sure how much longer it would be before they would be discovered and freed. Winn was livid. His rage was nearly out of control.

"Get us out of here!!" He pounded on the door again, shouting at the top of his voice. "Can anybody out there hear me?!"

Matt was just as angry as Winn, but he stood back in the darkness, his temper controlled, his mood pensive. "You might as well give it up for a while. There's no one around, and I doubt there will be any time soon."

"I want out of here!"

"We both want out of here," he told him.

"Just as soon as someone opens this door, I'm going after them and when I find them . . ."

"What are you going to do?"

"I'm going to find out what the Anthonys did to Alex to force her to go along with their plan." He couldn't stop thinking about how she'd been trying to tell him something important when the Anthonys had unexpectedly showed up or the way she'd looked when he'd last seen her.

"What are you talking about? They probably just promised her a cut of the money, like they said," Matt said.

"No. There's got to be more to this than we know."

"How can you be so sure?"

"Because I know Alex . . . Because I love her, Matt. Didn't you see her expression?"

Matt fell silent for a moment, remembering. "What do you think they did to force her to betray us?"

"I wouldn't put anything past them. Think about it. Remember when we were in the church right before they showed up? She had just started to tell us something important about her father and the Anthonys, and then she was interrupted."

"Her father?"

"It has to have something to do with him," Winn concluded, his thoughts racing. "One day she was determined to wait for him before we made the trek, and a short time later, she was ready to go because he'd been 'delayed' in London. What do you want to wager that that 'delay' had to do with Philip and Robert?"

"I think you're on to something," Matt replied.

"I don't trust the Anthonys with her."

At the thought of the Anthonys forcing her to accompany them against her will, they both started to pound on the door again, hoping and praying for rescue.

Twenty-one

Darkness claimed the land. Darkness claimed Philip's soul, overpowering him and filling him with a deep, terrible need to take what was rightfully his and keep it for his own.

Philip had pretended to go to bed when Robert did, just to satisfy him. When he'd lain down, he'd kept the crown next to him. He had waited far too long to let it out of his sight. It was his. All the years of waiting and planning and now it was in his grasp! He owned the Crown of Desire! Philip smiled into the night, hoping his father could see him, hoping his father would be watching when he sold it to the highest bidder and lived the rest of his life in luxury the way he was supposed to live.

Philip caressed the bag holding the crown as if it were his precious lover. He could feel the smooth, perfect metal even through the cloth. *It was his, all his.* . . . The thought kept reverberating through his mind like a pagan chant to the Gods. He would share it with no one—not even his insipid brother.

Shifting his position a little, Philip lifted his hand from the crown and touched the gun he'd brought along. It was then, as he thought of all the money he would have if he was the crown's sole owner, that he made his deadly decision.

He had always hated Robert. These last weeks traveling with him had sorely tested his patience. Now, out here in the middle of nowhere with only the girl for a witness, he knew what he would do. He'd gotten away with it twice before. Surely, a third time would be just as easy. And then . . .

Philip cast a glance toward where Alex slept on the opposite side of the campfire. He'd desired her ever since he'd first met her in London. It annoyed him that she'd always acted as if she were too good for him. Tonight, he would show her just how good he was. And when he was done, he would be on his way, and he'd be alone.

The thought thrilled him. He thought himself untouchable, and he considered his plan perfect. He'd gotten rid of their father and Henry. He'd stolen the crown back. Now, all he had to do was rid himself of Robert and the girl, and he would be free, truly free! The money would be all his, and no one would be the wiser. Who even knew if their bodies would ever be discovered this far out in no-man's land? His smile broadened as he reached for his gun.

There was no way Alex could rest with Philip and Robert so near. She wanted to run away and disappear into the night, but she didn't dare. Not with her father's life at stake. She had to be strong. She had to concentrate on him and not on the way Winn had looked at her when he'd discovered her betrayal.

She'd been lying still, trying to convince the brothers that she was asleep, when she heard someone moving around the campfire. Shifting a little, she opened her eyes and peered into the darkness. There was only a low glow coming from what was left of the fire, but it still gave off enough light to see the horror that was unfolding before her.

Philip was filled with bloodlust. He'd lain restless and excited by the slow-dying fire just waiting for the right moment. When he was certain that both Robert and Alex were sound asleep, he crept from his bed, gun in hand.

Crossing to where his brother was lying, he stared down at him for a moment. He felt nothing for this sleeping man who was his closest relative. It would be a simple thing to murder him. No one would ever know, and the crown would then be only his. That was the most important thing.

With a look of almost glee, Philip took aim. He wanted Robert dead. He wanted him out of his life forever, just like his father and just like that miserable Henry. He started to fire.

"Philip! Dear God, what are you doing?" Alex cried.

The sound of Alex's scream distracted him for a fraction of a second just as he squeezed off the shot. But his aim still seemed true for his brother collapsed without a fight, a gaping wound in his chest.

Alex started to scramble to her feet, needing to get

away, needing to escape from his madness. She was frantic and desperate.

Philip turned toward her, his face reflecting the sense of pure power that filled him. He smiled, and it was a smile that sent terror to the very center of her being.

"I'm doing what I've always wanted to do," he explained casually as he walked away from his brother and went after her. "I wouldn't run if I were you. I have no intention of hurting you." In his thoughts, though, he added 'for right now.'

Alex had always considered herself a strong, self-sufficient woman, but in that moment, having witnessed a cold-blooded murder, she found herself whimpering in terror. She started to run, blindly, wildly.

Philip was upon her in an instant. He tackled her, and they fell heavily. He landed atop her. His weight was crushing, and the heat of him seared her like a burning, painful brand. She wanted to squirm out from beneath him, but he held her pinned there.

"I've wanted you since the first time I laid eyes on you," he said thickly, his hand tearing at her blouse, groping at her body.

"Get away from me!" she screamed into the deserted black night. She pushed and shoved at him, trying to dislodge him, but he would not move.

"You want this. You know you do," he chided.

"I hate you, Philip Anthony! I've hated you from the beginning! Your father was right to disinherit you! You'll pay for this!"

"You needn't worry about it, my sweet. Neither you nor my brother will be around to see it if I do."

He stood up, intending to unbutton his pants so he could take her right there in the dirt. Alex tried to scramble away, but Philip would not be denied. He grabbed her and gave her a violent shake.

"Lie still or so help me, I'll kill you right now. Just like I did all the rest!"

Alex heard the savage intensity of his voice and knew he meant every word. He was out of his mind. She'd just watched him kill his own brother and now he was going to kill her.

"You killed your own father!" she said, shocked to the depths of her being by the discovery. She shuddered visibly.

"Of course. Who else would have done it? Your father was just too trusting, but for me that was good. Now, with my brother gone to join our father in his final reward, everything is mine," Philip was saying.

Working at the buttons of his pants, he prepared to take her. He liked seeing the fear in her eyes. The knowledge that he could make her quake with terror only excited him more. He was more than ready for her. It was just a simple matter of . . .

The shot rang out, splitting the silence of the night. The bullet exploded through Philip's body, spreading bloody testimony to its power across the front of his shirt.

Alex stared up at him, unable to comprehend what had happened. Then seeing the blood, she realized what had happened. She looked past him to where

Robert was leaning up on one elbow, his own gun in hand. The weapon looked to be almost too heavy for him, and he seemed to fade from life before her very eyes.

"Alex . . ."

Philip staggered and looked back to see his brother. His expression turned to one of total shock and disbelief. He had the power! He had everything he'd ever wanted! This couldn't have happened, yet the agony ripping through his body could not be denied.

"You!" he said that one word as if it were the most vile curse, and then he collapsed, pitching forward. He was dead when he hit the ground.

Alex bit back a scream as she scurried to get away from him.

She heard Robert's weak call, and nervously skirting Philip, she hurried to him. He had fallen back, too weak to support himself any longer, and his gun lay beside him in the dirt. Blood covered his shirt in a ghoulish drenching.

"Robert . . ." She knelt beside him and took his hand, seeing the pain in his features and wanting to help, to do something, anything.

"Alex . . ." he choked.

"I'm here," she answered, leaning closer so he could see and hear her.

"Go . . . get out of here . . ." His voice was weak, but she could hear the very real panic in it.

"I won't leave you alone."

"No, no . . . It's the crown . . . the curse . . . Run!

Run while you still can!" His breathing was rasping, and blood trickled from the corner of his mouth.

"I'm not going to leave you here like this all alone," she said. Hate him though she did, she couldn't just leave him there to die by himself.

"I'm a dead man . . . just like my brother. Leave, Alex. I don't deserve any kindness from you."

"Don't try to talk. Save your strength." She grabbed the blanket that lay nearby and pressed it to the horrendous wound to try to staunch the blood flow, but it was useless.

"It's the curse . . ." he repeated. "It's real."

"It's only a legend." She tried to keep him calm, but he would have none of it.

"Don't be a fool! Look at what it's done! Look at my father . . . my brother . . . Look at me! It's a death sentence!" With his last ounce of strength, he grabbed the bag that held the crown and thrust it toward her. "Get rid of it! Don't keep it!"

Alex took it from him. "I'll take it back to the mission." His blood had stained the bag, and in the last red glow of the nearly dead fire, it made a gruesome gift.

"Good . . ." he whispered with his last breath.

"But what about my father?" she demanded. Seeing him failing before her very eyes, she had to have the answer. She had to find out how to save her father from the terrible fate they'd plotted for him.

She got no response to her desperate plea. Robert died before he could answer her, slumping back, his life finished in the useless pursuit of riches.

For a moment, Alex, sat stunned and unable to take action. The bag containing the Crown of Desire was still clutched in her hand. She began to shake uncontrollably. She might have the crown, but in complete and total frustration she realized that she still had no idea how to save her father.

Winn and Matt were not rescued until long after dark. The priest who found them was horrified by their tale, and he helped them form a posse with worshipers from the church.

The people of Corazon Sagrado were outraged by the theft. Peace, serenity, and prosperity had reigned at the mission since the crown had been brought there by the old mysterious stranger several years before. The crops had flourished. Illness had almost ceased to exist. Everyone now lived in contentment and brotherhood, going about their daily lives with love and charity in their hearts and in their actions. Now, with the crown gone, they immediately felt the void in their lives. They wanted to bring the crown back to the mission, to the Virgin. In anger and determination, six men from the mission who were familiar with the land joined them in their search.

Matt was in his element as they rode out to catch the Anthonys. He was an accomplished tracker, having trailed people in the dark before. Carrying a torch, he led the way like a fearless knight on a crusade. They were resolved to retrieve the treasure and return it to its rightful place. Their progress proved slow, but steady.

Winn was tense as he followed Matt's lead. Every fiber of his being was concentrated on following the trail. He had to find Alex. The crown was important, too, but it was Alex he loved. He realized then as they rode at a steady, but slow pace through the night-shrouded countryside that he had never actually told her that he loved her. He regretted that now, and he vowed to make it up to her the minute he saw her again.

Concern about her being alone with Philip and Robert tormented him. He knew what kind of man Philip was, and he didn't trust him, not one bit. He hoped and prayed that she remained safe until he could find her. He rode by Matt's side, tense with fear and worry.

Alex sat frozen for a time, surrounded by death and destruction. When she finally managed to look around at the carnage, icy fingers of terror traced up and down her spine. She knew she had to get out of there. She had to run as fast and as far as she could.

Somehow, Alex saddled her horse, and after tying the crown's bag over her saddle horn, she mounted and started off. It wouldn't be easy riding at night, but the memory of Philip's near assault and the killings left her frantic to get away. She needed Winn and the haven of his arms around her. She needed to feel safe and protected again.

Even as she thought it, though, Alex knew Winn hated her now. She hoped she could redeem herself by returning the crown to the church, but she wasn't sure. The only thing she was sure of was that she now believed in the curse. She had seen its power and its devastation.

The moon offered some light as she tried to head back the way they'd come. After traveling in the wilds with her father on so many treks, she had a trained eye to keep track of landmarks and distances. But tonight, she was frightened, deeply frightened, and could only pray that she was riding in the direction of Corazón Sagrado.

As Alex rode on alone and scared, she thought of Princess Análika so many centuries before, and she understood the heartbreak and agony that had caused her to put the curse on the crown. Análika had lost everything with the death of her prince. She'd had nothing left to live for. He had died for the crown, and Alex knew, as Análika had, that the crown and all its riches were nothing compared to human life and love.

Alone in the Texas night, Alex felt a kinship with the princess. She had lost Winn. Not to death, but to betrayal and deceit. Tears traced down her cheeks. She didn't bother to wipe them away.

Alex forced herself to concentrate on her father as she made her slow, painful progress back toward the mission. She would leave the crown there where it belonged and then depart as quickly as she could for London. She didn't know who the Anthonys were paying at the prison to keep her father locked up, but she was going to find out and see him freed. Alex wasn't sure how she was going to do it, she just knew she wouldn't stop until he was.

* * *

"Are you sure we're following the right trail?" Winn asked Matt after they'd been riding for hours.

"I trusted you with the clues, now it's your turn to trust me. This is one of the things I do best," he told him as he reined in and dismounted to study the ground by torchlight. "They're headed to the north and east. It looks like they're trying to circle around San Antonio and ride straight for Galveston."

"It would be easier for them to disappear in Galveston, and that's the nearest port."

They rode on again, the moon helping to guide them on their way.

Alex had been riding at a steady, measured pace along a creek she remembered from earlier that night. It was near three in the morning when she saw the first flickering light of a torch in the distance. Her heart leapt in her breast, and she spurred her horse to a run, praying with all her might that it was Winn and Matt. She dreaded confronting them after her open betrayal, but even their condemnation was better than the exile of loneliness she was existing in now.

The men heard the sound of racing hoofbeats, and they stopped where they were to peer into the darkness.

"Someone's riding this way," Matt announced, his hand moving to the rifle one of the men from the mission had loaned to him for the journey.

"Maybe it's Alex," Winn said hopefully.

"Maybe it's not," Matt cautioned.

Alex heard the murmur of their deep voices and

recognized them immediately. "Winn! Matt!" she cried out into the night.

"Alex?!" Winn shouted.

She heard Winn call her name, and a small fragment of hope sparked in her bosom. She raced toward the light. She needed Winn, wanted him, yet she was sorely afraid of what would happen when she faced him again. As she drew nearer, Alex could make out Winn and Matt in the torchlight at the front of the group.

Winn was straining to catch a first sight of Alex riding in, and when she finally reached the circle of the light, a shaft of pain tore through him. Her blouse was torn and blood-soaked, and her features were pale and tear-stained.

"Alex . . ." He said her name in a tortured groan, believing the Anthonys had hurt her and that he'd failed her by not being there to protect her. Winn all but vaulted from his horse in his rush to reach her.

Alex thought Winn was running toward her because she had the crown. Wanting to end this painful reunion as quickly as she could, she untied the bag with the crown and held it out to him. "Here . . . take the crown."

"It's not the crown I'm worried about, Alex, it's you," he told her, ignoring the proffered treasure. She was the only treasure he sought. The only treasure he needed. "Are you all right?" His voice hoarse with emotion, as his gaze swept hungrily over her.

"I'm fine . . ." she said softly, fearfully.

"But the blood . . ." He stared at her ruined blouse and puffy lip.

"The blood's theirs . . . They're dead . . . both of them . . ."

"You weren't hurt? You're sure?" Somehow he was finding it hard to believe that she had come back to him unharmed.

"I'm sure. It's a long story . . ."

"I have the rest of my life to listen." His tone was deep with meaning as he reached up and lifted her from the horse's back, lowering her slowly to the ground. He kept her body pressed close to his. He did not release her but held her tightly to him, savoring her nearness, celebrating her safety. "I love you, Alex. When I thought you were in danger . . ."

She looked up at him, her eyes shining with relief and unbelievable happiness. She touched his cheek with tender devotion. "I love you, too, Winn. Leaving with the Anthonys was the most difficult thing I've ever done. I thought you hated me . . . I thought what we had was lost forever."

"Why did you go? What were they holding over you?"

"My father," she answered quickly, including the others in her explanation. "Philip and Robert framed him for Lawrence's murder. They had him arrested and he's in jail in London now. They threatened to let him hang for the murder, unless I helped them find the crown."

Winn swore suddenly and violently. "Those bastards!"

"I know. When you were telling me about how they

came to you at your uncle's funeral and how they kept trying to force you to give them the book, I understood exactly what you were talking about. They came to me in Boston shortly after we'd met the first time. That's when they told me that if I didn't help them, they were going to let my father take the blame for Lawrence's death."

"But how could they have done that?" Matt asked as he dismounted to join them. He was as relieved as Winn that she was safe, and he felt no remorse over the Anthonys' deaths.

"Evidently my father was the last one to see Lawrence alive, and that same night they'd argued publicly."

"Alex, you should have confided in me and Matt. We would have helped you."

"I wanted to, but Philip and Robert told me if I said anything, my father would die. They were animals . . . No, they were worse than animals. Animals don't kill for enjoyment."

"What happened?" Winn pressed her, wanting to know how she'd gotten away.

"We rode for hours and then made camp. It was almost as if Philip went mad when he held the crown for the first time. They were celebrating Lawrence's death and how they'd found the crown in spite of him, and when I defended him, Philip slapped me."

Winn tensed. If the other man had still been alive, he would have throttled him, himself. He touched her lip delicately, wishing his caress could heal her pain. "I'm sorry I wasn't there to stop him."

"I was praying that you'd come for me, but I thought you hated me."

"Never," he vowed fiercely.

"They bedded down, and I thought they were going to sleep through the night. A while later, I heard something and I looked up just as Philip was about to shoot Robert."

"He killed his own brother in cold blood?" Matt asked.

"They killed each other," she finished, shivering at the memory.

Winn enfolded her in his arms. "It's all right now, love. Nothing will ever hurt you again. I'll make sure of it."

"It was horrible, Winn, and all because of their greed. They were so desperate to have the crown."

She lifted the sack holding the relic again and gave it over to Winn's safekeeping. He took it from her this time, but turned to those who'd ridden with them from Corazon Sagrado.

"The crown has been returned. Let's camp here for the rest of the night, and then we'll take it back to the mission at first light."

A hearty round of thanks followed. The men were thrilled that their priceless treasure had been saved.

"Winn, Matt," Alex said to them both, "I have to get to London as quickly as possible. I have to save my father."

"We'll go together," Winn promised. "I'm not without influence there. As soon as we take the crown back to its rightful place, we can leave for Galveston."

"Thank you." She looked up at him, her heart in her eyes. "I love you, Winn."

"I love you, too."

As everyone looked on, he kissed her. It was a gentle caress for he took care not to hurt her already sore lip. The moment was profound, transcending time and place. It was a moment of true rapture . . . of love that had survived danger and doubts to emerge stronger and more vital than ever.

In his days before Alex, Winn would not have trusted any woman. When she'd ridden off with the Anthonys, he would have dismissed her as a traitorous female. He would have walked away and never looked back. But not with Alex. He loved her. She held his heart in her hands. She had become his whole world.

Twenty-two

One of the men from the mission gave Alex the jacket he'd been wearing and she'd been grateful for his thoughtfulness. The torn blouse was a vivid reminder of what could have happened. Alex trembled in remembrance as she lay with Winn, and he held her close for the rest of the night, protecting her and keeping watch. He was never going to let her out of his sight again if he could help it.

At dawn, the group divided. While Winn, Alex, Matt and several of the men rode for Corazon Sagrado to return the crown, the rest went in search of Philip and Robert's camp.

The ride back to the mission was much easier in the daylight, and they made good time, reaching the church at mid-morning. The priest heard word of their return and rushed out to greet them.

"We've brought the crown back, Father," Winn announced as they dismounted and prepared to enter the place of worship.

The good priest was beaming with happiness over the news, but his expression faltered when he saw the blood-soaked bag. "What happened?"

"Do you know the legend of the crown's curse?"

"No," he answered, slightly bewildered by the thought.

They quickly told him of the danger that followed those who sought the Crown of Desire in greed. They knew Lawrence had placed it on the statue of Mary and the Infant for he knew that theirs was the perfect love.

"We want to return it to you and the mission, Father. This is where it belongs. Not in some museum in London, but here, where it's bringing blessings to the land and people," Matt said.

"It's treated with the reverence it deserves here at Corazon Sagrado. This is truly where it should stay," Alex agreed.

"Bless you."

Alex drew the crown from the bag and then they entered the church. She went forward, and with the others looking on she placed the crown once more on the statue of the Virgin.

The moment was one of hushed adoration. They all stood back looking on in quiet reverence. As they were standing there, suddenly the church bells began to ring out. Their joyous melody drew the people to the church, and everyone crowded around, believing a miracle had taken place. Now that the crown was back with them, all would live in peace and harmony at the mission, as was God's true design.

Winn and Alex stood together, their hands clasped, gazing up at the glorious crown on the beautiful statue. Matt, too, looked on, his heart filled with serenity and love. He had sought the Crown of Desire for as long as he could remember. In the beginning, he had hoped to place it in a museum, but now he knew that this was the right place. It was safe here. No one else would ever know of its existence. Here the crown would protect and bless those who came to worship. What better place of love and peace than in a church? Satisfied with the outcome of their quest, he walked outside into the sunshine. He was eager to get back to New Orleans. Catherine was waiting.

Winn gazed down at Alex as they lingered in the back of the mission. "Alex?" he said her name softly.

She looked up expectantly.

"Alex," he began again in a low voice for her ears only. "Will you marry me?"

Her smile was radiant and her eyes glowed with the love she felt for him. "After what Philip and Robert had told me about you, I didn't think you'd ever ask me."

He looked surprised. "What did they say?"

"When they came to see me in Galveston, they told me that you were quite the dandy in London. They mentioned that you used women for your own pleasures and then left them when you tired of them."

Winn had the grace to look embarrassed. "Before I met you, I did. Before I met you, I didn't care about anyone or anything. But now . . ." He paused to gather the courage to speak the deepest truth in his heart. "Now, I have you. I love you, Alex. I wouldn't want to live without you."

"I love you, Winn. I want to marry you, but . . .".

"But?" He tensed, hearing the hesitation in her voice.

"But first, I have to free my father. Until I know he's safe . . ."

"I understand. We can leave right away. Everything is settled here."

"Thank you." She put her hand on his arm, and he covered her hand with his own.

"There's no need to thank me. I love you. I've discovered love is the greatest obstacles, even the greatest love is the most powerful force in the world. It can conquer even the greatest obstacles, even the greatest fears. We'll save your father, Alex." His gaze locked with hers.

Alex looked deep into his eyes. She saw the strength and determination there, and she believed he would help her do it. For the first time since that fateful day in Boston when the Anthonys had shown up so unexpectedly at her home, she felt as if her future was really going to be bright.

"I love you, Winn Bradford," she whispered and then stood on tiptoe to press a soft kiss to his cheek.

Winn kept a supporting arm around her as they left the church.

Matt was waiting for them just outside. "Are we riding for San Antonio?"

"Yes, and then on to Galveston as quickly as we can. Are you going back to Boston?"

Matt smiled. "No. I'm going to New Orleans. I'm going home to Catherine."

"I understand," Winn said, glancing down at Alex. As they prepared to leave, the priest and the people emerged from the church. Alex wanted to change clothes before they rode for town, so one of the women took her to her home as the men said their good-byes.

A short time later, they rode away from the mission—and the crown. They paused on the rise to look down on Corazon Sagrado one last time. The mission shone white in the sunlight, looking heavenly in its setting. Feeling confident that all would be well there, they turned their horses toward San Antonio and toward home.

They reached town that night without incident and stayed in the same hotel they had before. They made their travel arrangements on the morning stage to Galveston and then had dinner together. They retired with the promise to meet early the next morning.

Winn and Alex went to the room they had taken for themselves. They were pleased to find the bath she'd ordered was ready and waiting for her. Winn closed and locked the door behind them. He turned to find Alex already unbuttoning her blouse.

Leaning back against the door and folding his arms across his chest, Winn watched her. A deep, hot desire sparked and burned within him as she unfastened the last button and shrugged the blouse from her shoulders.

"You are so beautiful, Alex. I love you," he said huskily as he went to her.

Alex went into his arms and rested her head on his shoulder. His embrace was her haven, the one place where she felt secure. Her life would have been perfect had it not been for her worry about her father. When Winn kissed her, though, Alex cast aside her concerns, and for just that little while, she gave herself over to the bliss of his loving.

With infinite care and tenderness, Winn helped her to undress. After shedding his own clothes, he took her hand and led her to the bed, drawing her down beside him. Sure of each other now, they came together in a passionate blending. Winn couldn't seem to touch her enough. The feel of her silken flesh beneath him was maddening. He caressed her hungrily, exploring her soft curves and tracing arousing paths over her satiny limbs.

Alex reveled in his embrace. She was as eager for Winn as he was for her. She matched him in his ardor, her hands tracing patterns of fire over his chest and stomach and then moving lower to seek the very heat of him. There was no holding back in her lovemaking. She loved him and he loved her. In that moment, nothing else mattered.

As Alex touched him so intimately, Winn groaned in pure animal pleasure. His mouth claimed hers in a demanding kiss that left them both breathless. He sought the sweetness of her throat, then trailed sensuous kisses down to her breasts.

At the touch of his lips upon her, Alex arched in wanton splendor against the hard heat of his body. She was on fire with her need for him, and she began to move restlessly, wanting to entice him to take her and make her his own.

Winn's need was as great as Alex's, and at her unspoken invitation, he moved over her. Settling between her thighs, he murmured words of love as he positioned himself and then thrust within her. Sheathed deep within the hot, tight embrace of her body, Winn knew ecstasy. He began to move as he continued to caress her.

Their passions soared and they reached for the stars. Ecstasy burst upon them as they perfected their love. In the peaceful aftermath of their union, they clung together, savoring the moment.

"It seems a shame to let that bath go to waste . . .". Winn told her as he cradled her to him.

"Um . ." she agreed sleepily.

Alex gasped as Winn rose and swept her up into his arms, but she offered no protest as he carried her to the tub and climbed in. He sat down, keeping her on his lap, unmindful of the water that overflowed. The water was still warm and they took their time bathing each other. When at last, Winn could bear it no longer, he stood, dried them off and carried her back to the bed. There they made love wildly, coming together in a rush of excitement. Later, their desire sated, they lay wrapped in each other's arms. Sleep claimed them both as together they pondered the beauty of their love.

Dawn found them on the stage with Matt, heading for the coast to set sail. Their parting at Galveston was painful.

"Will you tell Catherine that you were the best husband I ever had?" Alex asked Matt as she kissed him good-bye.

His ship was sailing first, and they'd come down to the dock to see him off.

"I'll tell her," he answered with a bittersweet grin. Next, Matt shook Winn's hand. "I think we both found treasures more valuable than anything money can buy."

"You're right." He gazed down at Alex. "Be careful on your trip."

"I will, and you take care, too." He started to board the ship, then turned back to Alex. "Oh, and Alex?" When he had her attention, he said, "When you get your father out of jail, tell him he missed a great adventure."

She smiled at his comment. "I have a feeling, Matt, that I'll be traveling back to Texas with my father one day."

"Not if I can help it," Winn spoke up. "I want you with me. We'll have to find your father another assistant to travel with."

"Good-bye . . ." Matt boarded and then waved to them from the deck. He hoped all went well for them. Under any other circumstances, he would have gone along with them to London to help, but he believed Winn could handle it. Besides, Catherine was waiting for him. There was nothing more important in his life right now than claiming her as his own.

The ship sailed, and he stayed on deck watching until he could no longer make out Winn and Alex. Ready to begin a new life, he fixed his gaze to the north and east, to New Orleans, where his love awaited him.

* * *

Catherine stood in the play yard of the orphanage, hands on her hips, supervising the workmen as they repaired some of the windows on that side of the building. She couldn't believe how much life had changed at St. Joan's since Mr. Markham had discovered that Lisa was his granddaughter. He had been a man of his word. He'd sent his workmen over as soon as she'd made her recommendations about the work that needed to be done around the place, and ever since there had been a constant round of improvements.

"Miss Catherine!"

She looked up to see Tommy and Lisa running toward her. A smile broke out across her lovely features as she opened her arms to them and hugged them both.

"Grampa let us come to play again today!" Lisa told her eagerly. Her life with her newfound grandfather was turning out to be more wonderful than she'd ever dreamed. Not only was Tommy officially her own brother now, but she had her own room, too. She was surrounded by love in the haven of her grandfather's home, and she was blossoming.

Catherine had been impressed by the old man's sensitivity. She'd feared that once the two children had left St. Joan's and gone to live with him, she'd never get to see them again. But Markham had recognized the friendships they had had at the home and had let them stay in regular touch. Now, all these weeks later, both children were well-adjusted and happy and sharing their newfound security with their friends at the orphanage.

"I'm so glad to see you. I miss you when you're away."

"We miss you, too, but Grampa is awful nice." Lisa had opened up more in the last few weeks than she ever had in all the years before. There was a shine in her eyes and the healthy glow of a loved and cherished child in her cheeks.

"What do you want to do today?" Catherine asked.

"I don't know. Just have fun, I guess."

"All right. Behave yourselves," she teased.

"Don't worry. We will," Tommy promised.

They bounded off, full of life, love, and joy. She watched them run to join their friends, and she felt a deep abiding contentment. This had all happened because of Matt.

Matt. . . . She missed him. She wondered if he'd really come back to her. Ever since he'd kissed her, she'd been caught up in a dream of having him in her arms. She knew she was being crazy. They'd only known each other for such a very short time. But then, who could explain the reasons behind feelings? Somehow, her heart knew it was right, and she believed in following her heart.

New Orleans.

Matt had been anticipating his moment of arrival in port ever since he'd sailed out of Galveston Bay. His ship docked at midday, and as soon as he disembarked, he hired a carriage to take him straight to St. Joan's.

The carriage couldn't go fast enough to please him, but he was forced to bide his time. The trek across town seemed to take longer than the entire voyage from Texas. When it finally drew to a halt in front of the orphanage, he climbed out, paid the driver, and paused to stare up at the building.

St. Joan's was already undergoing major improvements. Obviously, Markham had kept his word and the knowledge pleased Matt.

Matt drew a deep breath and started up the steps. He came face-to-face with Tommy, and he grinned broadly as he opened up his arms to the youth. Without hesitation, Tommy flung himself into his embrace.

"You did come back!" Even a little more faith in adults was restored in him as he held on tight to Matt.

"I told you I would. I came as soon as I could." He hugged him back.

"Did you find the treasure? Did my clue help?"

"Yes, we did."

"Where is it? Did you bring it with you?"

"No, it seemed that the right thing to do was to leave it right where we found it."

"Tell me all about it! Was it hard to find?"

"I'll tell you everything, but not right now. It's a long story, and I want to see Miss Catherine first."

Matt put Tommy down as he looked toward her office.

"Yeah, she's in there, and, boy, is she ever gonna be glad to see you!"

"You think so?"

"I *know so.*"

"What are you doing here?" Matt asked as he slowly made his way toward her office door.

"Lisa and me get to come over and play with the other kids. Grampa lets us come whenever we want."

"Are you both happy living with him?"

"Yeah. We're real happy."

There was a joy about Tommy that Matt had never seen before, and he was glad to know that things had turned out so well.

"I want to talk to you, but first I've got to see Catherine."

They shared a man-to-man look.

"Are you gonna marry her? You should, you know," Tommy blurted out.

"If she'll have me, I'll marry her as soon as she wants."

"Then are you gonna stay here?"

"It's up to Catherine. If that's what she wants, I'll stay."

"Good." Tommy looked particularly pleased.

"I'll see you later, after I talk to her."

"Okay, I'll go tell Lisa you're here."

Matt knocked on the office door.

"Come in."

The sweet sound of her voice was a caress to his love-starved senses. He took off his hat and entered the office.

"Matt! You're back!" Catherine hadn't known when, or even if, he would come back to her, but she'd prayed constantly that he would.

She looked more beautiful than ever to him, and Matt didn't hesitate another second. He came around the desk and swept her up into his arms. "I missed you," he vowed.

There was no denying the kiss he so desperately

needed. He kissed her passionately, telling her with his embrace just how much she meant to him.

"Catherine, I love you," he said simply.

"I love you, too, Matt. I missed you so much while you were gone. I'm so glad you're back."

Their eyes met and locked, and each saw the promise of fulfillment in the other's gaze.

"Will you marry me, Catherine?"

She kissed him with infinite tenderness. "Yes, Matt. I'll marry you."

"We can stay here, if you want. I'd like to help you with the children."

"What about your home and your life in Boston?"

"My life . . . my future is with you. This is where I belong. This is where I want to stay. You are my home, Catherine."

"And you are mine."

They came together, their lips seeking each other's in a devoted pledge of love and faithful promise that would last a lifetime.

Matt thought of Boston and the life he'd led there, and it seemed as if that all that had happened to another man in another lifetime. This was where he belonged. He'd known it since the first day he'd seen her. He was home.

Outside in the hallway, Milly, Catherine's assistant, started for the office, obviously intent on talking to her about business. Ever vigilant, Tommy intercepted her just in time.

"I don't think you want to go in there right now, Miss Milly."

"Oh?" She frowned at the boy. "Why's that, Tommy?"

"'Cause, Mr. McKittrick's back."

Milly grinned and winked at Tommy. "I see. Well, I'll just come back a little later then." A little flustered, but smiling, she found something else to do for right then. "You guard that door real good, Tommy."

"Don't worry. I will."

Milly hurried off to busy herself with other things, while Tommy stood watch over Miss Catherine. He glanced back toward the closed door and smiled. He was happy now that he had his new grandpa and Lisa, and he thought Miss Catherine and Matt should be happy, too.

Winn and Alex stood together at the rail of the ship staring out across the Atlantic. They'd been at sea for several weeks now and would be making port in Boston shortly. They planned a quick trip to her home to see if any word had come from her father. If there had been none, they would sail right away for London.

"Winn . . . I'm so afraid," Alex admitted.

He put his arm around her and drew her comfortingly to his side. "Whatever happens, love, I'll be with you."

"But what if we have to go to London and once we get there, we find out that Papa's already been executed."

Winn hastened to reassure her. "If the Anthonys had influence with the guards, then I think your father's safe. I'm sure they paid handsomely for his protection.

There was no way for the guards to know exactly when Philip and Robert were going to return, so he should be all right."

"I want to believe you. I hope you're right." She lifted her troubled gaze to him and saw the strength in his eyes. She couldn't help but smile as she remembered what the Anthony brothers had told her about him.

"Why are you smiling?"

"Because Philip and Robert told me that the minute we found the crown, you'd take it and run. They said you were a spoiled, rich, arrogant nobleman, who didn't care about anything but your own pleasures."

"There was a time when all that was true, but I've changed, Alex, and you're the reason. Before I met you, my life was pointless. I had all the money I needed and all the friends my money could buy."

"It sounds so dreadful . . . and so lonely."

"It was. I was surrounded by people, but no one I cared about and no one who cared about me. I can never go back to being the man I was before. Between Uncle Edward and you, the Winn Bradford who sailed from London at the beginning of this quest doesn't exist any more."

"I was so afraid after they told me those things about you."

"Why?"

"Because I loved you so desperately, and I was afraid you really would leave me when the search was over."

"I don't ever want you to be afraid of anything

again. Believe in me and believe in what we feel for each other."

"I do, and I'm sorry I ever doubted you." Her expression was eloquent as she looked up at him. "It was all so terribly complicated. I knew from the very beginning that I would have to betray you, and I prayed all the while that somehow you would be able to find it in your heart to forgive me when I did."

"There's nothing to forgive. You were doing what you had to do."

She sighed and leaned more heavily against him, savoring his nearness, wishing the rest of the ordeal was over and her father was already with them.

They drifted back to her cabin then and made love long into the night. They sought through the physical expression of their love for each other the peace of spirit that they couldn't find in reality.

Boston.

Tension filled Alex when, at long last, Boston Harbor came into view. She had lived night and day with the dread that she would return home to learn that something terrible had happened to her father while he was in prison. She clung to Winn's hand tightly as they disembarked and made their way to her home.

Everything looked quiet. Nothing seemed to have changed from that day all those weeks before when 'Father Bradford' had first come to call. They climbed the steps to the front porch and knocked on the door. The maid answered, and her expression, as she stared at the two of them, was nothing short of shocked. "Miss Alex! Thank goodness you're back!"

Alex's heart was in her throat, and she feared the absolute worst. "Why? What's wrong? Have you heard something about Papa?"

The question hung heavily in the air. For a moment, no one moved as they anticipated the tragic news they were sure was to follow.

"Well, Miss Alex, your papa . . ."

Suddenly, Enoch's voice sounded from the study. "Alex, my dear? Is that you?"

At the sound of his voice, she went weak-kneed and Winn quickly put an arm around her for support. "Papa?! Oh, Papa! Thank God you're here!"

She broke into a run down the hall, just as he appeared in the doorway of the study. Without saying a word she threw herself into his arms and hugged him with all her might.

"You're all right! You're really all right!" She was crying openly as she held onto him.

"Alex, I was so worried about you. All the maid could tell me was that you'd gone on a search for a crown with some friends of Lawrence's—a priest named Bradford and another man named McKittrick." Tears were burning in his eyes as well.

"Oh, Papa," she sobbed. "I thought you were going to die. I was so afraid I wouldn't be able to save you!"

"I thought I was, too, sweet."

"But how did you get out? What happened?" Alex was still crying, and she refused to let go of him. So fierce were her emotions, that she hung onto him for dear life, not wanting to be separated from him after all this time of worry and missing him and loving him.

She hadn't thought he would be there. She'd thought they would have to go to England and use all of Winn's influence to free him, and now her prayers had been answered.

"Come, come, child." He patted her on the back in a paternal fashion as he suffered her over abundance of emotion. "Let's go sit down. I think, from the looks of the both of us, that a small brandy might be in order."

"Yes, Papa." She sniffed. Then, remembering that she'd left Winn standing behind her, she quickly introduced him. "Papa, this is Winn Bradford."

"It's a pleasure." Enoch went forward and offered him his hand.

"For me, too."

"Are you related to the priest?"

Winn couldn't keep from grinning. "You could say that."

"How so?"

"Well, sir, I was the priest."

"What?" Enoch's surprise was evident in his sharp tone as he looked between the two of them.

"Papa, I can explain everything. Winn was, but he isn't."

"That certainly clarified things for me," he said drolly, still looking skeptical.

Alex realized how silly her answer had sounded, and she laughed. Keeping her arm around him, she walked with him into the study, leaving Winn to follow. "It's a long story, Papa, but I think you're going to find it very interesting."

"And what's this the maid's been babbling about the crown? I've been sitting here cooling my heels, while you've been out gallivanting around the countryside. Tell me, my dear, what's happened while I was away?"

"You first! Tell us how you got out of jail. Have you been here long?" She sat down while her father poured each of them a brandy.

As he gave them each a snifter and once they'd settled in, he started to speak. "It was terrible, Alex. The authorities came to the hotel and arrested me for Lawrence's murder. Do you believe it?!"

"Knowing Philip and Robert, yes, I believe it."

"They'll be paying now that the truth is out."

"You mean the authorities know they killed Lawrence?"

"Now they do, after the maid who knew that they were the ones who'd poisoned Lawrence finally came forward and told them what she knew."

"She did?"

"Once she realized that Philip had only been using her, she was more than happy to implicate him and his brother. If they show up in London, they'll soon be occupying my old accommodations."

"They won't be going back," Winn offered.

"What's that you say?" He glanced at Winn, his expression almost angry at the thought that the greedy duo wouldn't be paying for their heinous crimes. "They can't get away with this! I'll help hunt them down myself!"

"No, Papa. There's no need. They're dead."

A stunned silence followed her revelation. Then Enoch nodded slowly, as if satisfied that justice had been done. "I never celebrate anyone's untimely death, but perhaps this time justice has been served."

"It has," Winn said with conviction.

"Now, tell me, young man. How did you come to be involved in this? Did you know Lawrence? And what's this about your being a priest?"

Winn gave him a friendly smile as he accepted the brandy he handed him. "I knew Lawrence only in passing, but he was my uncle's best friend. My Uncle Edward was the real Father Bradford, but he passed away just after Lawrence did. I was given my uncle's things, and the book and letter from Lawrence were among them."

"So there's the connection," he remarked thoughtfully. "But the maid said a priest had come by and that Alex was traveling with him."

"Yes, sir. I took Uncle Edward's place on the search because Lawrence had said in his letter that my uncle's faith would serve him well. I thought I had to make the journey as a priest."

Enoch suddenly saw the humor in the situation as he noticed how Alex and Winn were looking at each other. "It proved a challenging role, did it?"

"You'll never know," he groaned.

Alex laughed. "He made a wonderful priest, Papa, but I'm really glad he isn't one." She gazed at Winn adoringly. "Winn has asked me to marry him, and I've accepted."

Enoch's face lit up at this news. "That's wonderful, child. Just wonderful!" He kissed her and went to shake Winn's hand again.

"Papa, there is one thing more . . . About the crown . . ."

"Yes? Did you find it? Did you bring it back?" He was eager to know, now that they'd talked through all the serious news. He was ready to think about the crown again and ready to hear how the treasure hunt had gone.

"Well . . ."

"Don't stutter or stammer. Just tell me whether you found it. That's what Lawrence and I argued about the night he died, you know. He had finally admitted to me that he'd had the crown for years—even while we were on our dig. Needless to say, I was rather perturbed about the news."

"Did you really fight?"

"It wasn't really a fight, per se. I just exploded publicly, thinking about all the time, energy, and money we'd wasted searching for it, when all the while it had been in Lawrence's private collection."

"What happened that night?"

"We went back to his house to have a drink, and he promised to tell me where the crown was the next day. I made arrangements to meet with him, but the next thing I knew I was being arrested for his murder. Philip and Robert approached me in jail and asked me for the book, but I denied having it. They told me I was going to stay there until they had the crown."

Alex shuddered as she accepted that her fears had

been real. "I'm sorry, Papa. They came to me next and blackmailed me into going after the crown with Winn and Matt and promising to turn it over to them once we'd found it."

"Matt?"

"Matt McKittrick. He was the other man Lawrence had left a clue book to. He went with us."

"He's a good man from what I understand."

"Matt's a very good man. We were married for a while," she added cooly.

"You were what?!"

Alex laughed. "It's part of our long story. Don't worry. Everything's fine now."

Enoch relaxed again and took another sip of his brandy. "This is getting more and more interesting. Why don't you start at the beginning?"

Alex told him of the Anthonys' visit to the house and of their threats.

He nodded knowingly. "They would have done it, too."

"I know. When they showed me your letters they'd intercepted, I knew there was nothing I could do but go along with them until I was sure you were safe."

"And Winn and Matt didn't know anything about it?"

"No. She carried the burden all on her own. I have to tell you, though, before they came to you, they tried to get my uncle's book from me." Winn quickly told him about his own confrontation with the greedy pair.

"It's still amazing to me that a man as good and

morally upright as Lawrence could have two such terrible offspring."

"In the letter he wrote to my uncle, he says he thought that maybe the curse of the crown had been visited on his children. Perhaps he was right."

"So, what of the crown?"

"We found it."

Enoch looked avidly interested. "You did? Where is it? Did you bring it back? I want to see it."

"You can see it, but we don't have it with us. We left it where we found it."

"Why? After all that work, why would you just up and leave it?"

"Because it's in a place of perfect love, just as the curse says it should be."

"It is?" He looked puzzled.

"Yes. It's in a mission in Texas and it's on a statue of the Virgin."

Enoch stared at them in amazement. "Lawrence took it to a church . . ." Then as understanding dawned, he said, "Of course, of course, it all makes sense. If Lawrence came to believe that the curse really did exist, then he would have turned to the church. There is no more perfect love. Certainly, I'm coming to believe that mankind isn't capable of it, try though we might."

"I think there's hope for the future, Papa," Alex said dreamily as she looked up at Winn.

"I hope you're right, child. I hope you're right."

Epilogue

London, Ten Weeks Later

Winn lay in his wide, soft bed with his bride sleeping quietly in his arms. This was their first night in London, and he was amazed at how good it felt to be back. He hadn't thought he would miss his townhouse, but with Alex by his side, it was now their home.

Alex had charmed the staff when they'd arrived that day, and they already loved her for it. He knew they were going to be happy here. He offered up silent thanks for the joy she'd brought into his life.

It was hard for him to believe that everything had turned out so perfectly, but it had. They'd received a letter from Matt and Catherine before they'd left Boston, telling them of their marriage and of Matt's decision to stay and work with Catherine at St. Joan's. Sometimes life truly was worth living.

Winn looked down at his wife and marveled at how beautiful Alex was. He loved her with all his heart and soul, and he planned to spend the rest of his life making her happy. Unable to resist the sweet temptation she made, he kissed her awake.

Alex awoke to Winn's kiss, and she responded eagerly to his advances. Though they'd been married for over six weeks, she still wanted him as desperately as she had that very first night. They came together in a blending of pure love that transcended all time. They were one, and they would love forever. He had found his heaven with her.

"Do you want children?" Winn asked later as they lay together, their limbs still entangled, their hearts still beating as one.

"I would love to give you a hundred children," she told him, rising up to press a soft kiss on his lips.

He chuckled. "One would be good for a start, but would you mind terribly if we named our first-born son Edward?"

Alex smiled down at him. "I think Edward is a wonderful name. I'd be proud to name my oldest son after your uncle. After all, he did help make you the man you are today, and I love you very much."

Winn drew her down for a passionate kiss. "I love you, Alex."

In heaven, Uncle Edward was smiling.

GREAT BOOKS, GREAT SAVINGS!

When You Visit Our Website:

www.kensingtonbooks.com

You Can Save Money Off The Retail Price

Of Any Book You Purchase!

- All Your Favorite Kensington Authors
- New Releases & Timeless Classics
- Overnight Shipping Available
- eBooks Available For Many Titles
- All Major Credit Cards Accepted

Visit Us Today To Start Saving!

www.kensingtonbooks.com

All Orders Are Subject To Availability.
Shipping and Handling Charges Apply.
Offers and Prices Subject To Change Without Notice.

More by Bestselling Author
Hannah Howell

_Highland Angel	978-1-4201-0864-4	$6.99US/$8.99CAN
_If He's Sinful	978-1-4201-0461-5	$6.99US/$8.99CAN
_Wild Conquest	978-1-4201-0464-6	$6.99US/$8.99CAN
_If He's Wicked	978-1-4201-0460-8	$6.99US/$8.49CAN
_My Lady Captor	978-0-8217-7430-4	$6.99US/$8.49CAN
_Highland Sinner	978-0-8217-8001-5	$6.99US/$8.49CAN
_Highland Captive	978-0-8217-8003-9	$6.99US/$8.49CAN
_Nature of the Beast	978-1-4201-0435-6	$6.99US/$8.49CAN
_Highland Fire	978-0-8217-7429-8	$6.99US/$8.49CAN
_Silver Flame	978-1-4201-0107-2	$6.99US/$8.49CAN
_Highland Wolf	978-0-8217-8000-8	$6.99US/$9.99CAN
_Highland Wedding	978-0-8217-8002-2	$4.99US/$6.99CAN
_Highland Destiny	978-1-4201-0259-8	$4.99US/$6.99CAN
_Only for You	978-0-8217-8151-7	$6.99US/$8.99CAN
_Highland Promise	978-1-4201-0261-1	$4.99US/$6.99CAN
_Highland Vow	978-1-4201-0260-4	$4.99US/$6.99CAN
_Highland Savage	978-0-8217-7999-6	$6.99US/$9.99CAN
_Beauty and the Beast	978-0-8217-8004-6	$4.99US/$6.99CAN
_Unconquered	978-0-8217-8088-6	$4.99US/$6.99CAN
_Highland Barbarian	978-0-8217-7998-9	$6.99US/$9.99CAN
_Highland Conqueror	978-0-8217-8148-7	$6.99US/$9.99CAN
_Conqueror's Kiss	978-0-8217-8005-3	$4.99US/$6.99CAN
_A Stockingful of Joy	978-1-4201-0018-1	$4.99US/$6.99CAN
_Highland Bride	978-0-8217-7995-8	$4.99US/$6.99CAN
_Highland Lover	978-0-8217-7759-6	$6.99US/$9.99CAN

Available Wherever Books Are Sold!

Check out our website at
http://www.kensingtonbooks.com

More from Bestselling Author
JANET DAILEY

Calder Storm	0-8217-7543-X	$7.99US/$10.99CAN
Close to You	1-4201-1714-9	$5.99US/$6.99CAN
Crazy in Love	1-4201-0303-2	$4.99US/$5.99CAN
Dance With Me	1-4201-2213-4	$5.99US/$6.99CAN
Everything	1-4201-2214-2	$5.99US/$6.99CAN
Forever	1-4201-2215-0	$5.99US/$6.99CAN
Green Calder Grass	0-8217-7222-8	$7.99US/$10.99CAN
Heiress	1-4201-0002-5	$6.99US/$7.99CAN
Lone Calder Star	0-8217-7542-1	$7.99US/$10.99CAN
Lover Man	1-4201-0666-X	$4.99US/$5.99CAN
Masquerade	1-4201-0005-X	$6.99US/$8.99CAN
Mistletoe and Molly	1-4201-0041-6	$6.99US/$9.99CAN
Rivals	1-4201-0003-3	$6.99US/$7.99CAN
Santa in a Stetson	1-4201-0664-3	$6.99US/$9.99CAN
Santa in Montana	1-4201-1474-3	$7.99US/$9.99CAN
Searching for Santa	1-4201-0306-7	$6.99US/$9.99CAN
Something More	0-8217-7544-8	$7.99US/$9.99CAN
Stealing Kisses	1-4201-0304-0	$4.99US/$5.99CAN
Tangled Vines	1-4201-0004-1	$6.99US/$8.99CAN
Texas Kiss	1-4201-0665-1	$4.99US/$5.99CAN
That Loving Feeling	1-4201-1713-0	$5.99US/$6.99CAN
To Santa With Love	1-4201-2073-5	$6.99US/$7.99CAN
When You Kiss Me	1-4201-0667-8	$4.99US/$5.99CAN
Yes, I Do	1-4201-0305-9	$4.99US/$5.99CAN

Available Wherever Books Are Sold!

Check out our website at www.kensingtonbooks.com.